toxic

ALSO BY LYDIA KANG

THE NOVEMBER GIRL

toxic

LYDIA KANG

Entangled Publishing, LLC
2614 South Timberline Road
Suite 105, PMB 159
Fort Collins, CO 80525
rights@entangledpublishing.com

Entangled Teen is an imprint of Entangled Publishing, LLC.

Visit our website at www.entangledpublishing.com.

Edited by Kate Brauning
Cover design by Clarissa Yeo
Cover images by
seecreateimages/Shutterstock
Mr.Patichat chaikaud/Shutterstock
Interior design by Toni Kerr

ISBN: 978-1-64063-424-4
Ebook ISBN: 978-1-64063-423-7

Manufactured in the United States of America

First Edition November 2018

10 9 8 7 6 5 4 3 2 1

entangled teen
an imprint of Entangled Publishing LLC

For Ben

Chapter One

HANA

Where is Mother?

Where is she?

Inside my room, my tiny bubble of a room, I pace like the tigers in their tiny iron enclosures from Earth's old menageries—what did they call them in the vids? Zoological parks? Mother is never missing at breakfast. Never. And she is always here when I wake up. I have never begun my day without her warm presence, her crinkling, smiling eyes.

Where is Mother?

To make things even more worrying, I've been asleep for too long.

It had been one entire week that I was embedded in Cyclo's matrix of the ship's walls, held down by her soothing chemicals while I slept. But normally, I sleep only for forty-eight or seventy-two hours at a time. One week is far too long.

Usually, there is breakfast on the table, perhaps some rice. Usually, there is Mother, waiting for me after a long shift in her incubation labs.

But there was no breakfast waiting for me.

No Mother, for that matter.

My stomach growls, and I press my hand against my belly, willing it to be quiet, but what I want to do is quiet my mind. My thoughts are spinning, crashing, shattering with everything that is wrong. My eyes are trained on the door, hoping that it will open and she will be here and this will all be a mistake.

Please, please be a mistake. Maybe an embryo in the lab needed desperate attention for days, and she had to leave me alone for longer than usual. My stomach grumbles again, and I wring my hands, hissing at myself.

"Silence!"

It's a familiar saying in our room. Not that anyone could hear me—the gel walls and the bony endoskeleton make it sound proof, but Mother was not born on Cyclo. She was born on Earth, where walls are made of things like trees—no, wood—and pigment—no, paint—and could readily hear conversations right through them. But maybe if I say the word again—a word that always seems to simultaneously cut and suffocate me—maybe it will bring normal back, like a prayer of wishes.

Silence.

In my thin robe, I continue to pace, my bare feet pressing against the blue gel-like matrix of the floor. It's already been over an hour since I've awoken.

"Where is she?" I demand.

No answer.

Cyclo has been taught never to answer questions not directly asked of her. Otherwise, she would answer everything. When she was a young creature, before she grew into the enormity of this three-kilometer-wide diatom in space, she would answer all the questions in her color language, and it was chaos. Crew members got headaches from the nonstop, vibrant displays. So, for their benefit, each room on the ship has a color translator to help the crew.

I don't need a translator. I understand her color language far better than the crew, and with more subtlety than the translators. I can see beyond the color spectrum that others can, thanks to Mother's genetic tinkering with my retinal cells. So Cyclo's nuances are only seen by me, not her. Other humans are like pigs trying to communicate with jellyfish; their interpretations are so primitive.

But, as a favor, Cyclo has learned to phonate air bubbles and actually speak to me, particularly when I'm lonely. I try again.

"Cyclo, where is Mother? Where is she?" My hands are now grabbing at my ponytail, clawing in agitation.

The matrix on the wall warps, involutes on itself, and a face appears. It's a woman's face, like Mother's but different. Like an ajumma, or auntie. An ajumma made of shimmering blue glass.

"Your mother is not here," Cyclo says in her vibrating, watery voice.

I stand there, not knowing what to do. Somewhere inside of me, a seed of doubt and fear grows steadily into a tree, strong as stone. Where could she be? I can't call her or communicate to her—it's strictly forbidden. After all, no one knows of my existence on the ship except for Cyclo and Mother.

Mother is the ship's reproductive engineer, in charge of making sure the crew's population on Cyclo stays steady and functional. New embryos are decided upon by the leaders of the ship, not the needs of a human who wishes to have their own child. Mother carefully tends these new crops of fetal crew members with a calm expectancy. And yet, I was not needed for the census, or for stability. I would be considered expendable. But she made me anyway, in secret. Kept me in secret. And when she couldn't be here, Cyclo cared for me.

Mother was the only person required to report census data, so she could hide me. And Cyclo, who is programmed to care for all of us, had no issue with taking care of me, too. My caloric and nutrient needs were accounted for via Mother's personal lab records, and easily hidden. There was never a reason for a random crew member to ask, "Cyclo, is there an unsanctioned, extra human aboard this ship?" So Cyclo never had to answer the question.

I stare at the membrane door. She must be busy tending to something in the labs. That has to be the reason. To search her out would be to put my very existence, and my mother, in danger. After several moments, while Cyclo pulsates a gentle, light lavender on the walls (patience, waiting), I decide.

I shall wait.

So I wait another hour. It feels like a very long time. I knit some more of a little afghan I started last week. I read some Shakespeare, *The Tempest*. I'll reread the story of Cyclo's genetic creation and birth, down to the details of which percentages of her genes have been synthesized, which were knocked out, which were enriched via cisgenesis or transgenesis. I'll read Mother's diary, filled with stories of when I was smaller and her delight over every milestone of my childhood. I eat a precooked, synthetic yam porridge that I find in our food cupboard. My mind is whirling so fast with thoughts I don't want to consider. The panic is there, simmering under my skin, but I cannot unravel over what I don't know yet. So I wait.

Mother doesn't come.

My heart is beating so fast I can barely stay standing. I have clawed my robe until it has holes in the edges.

It has been six hours now. I am absolutely forbidden to leave my room, a room that does not exist in the consciousness of any crew member except my mother, hidden as it is in the most unused part of Cyclo's body, the northeast quadrant, alpha ring.

For the last two hours, I've raised my hand countless times, poised a few inches from the door, before dropping it. Even touching the door is strictly forbidden. But I can't wait here for much longer. Where is Mother? Where could she be? I'd even read the last entry in her diary, looking to see if anything was off, but there was nothing but our last discussion on why hedgehogs are not related to sea urchins. My eyes are full of tears, and I've already cried several times out of sheer panic.

I keep my voice steady and say, "Cyclo. Please open the door."

Cyclo, not bothering to speak because the message is too urgent, blanches with white that moves in waves over the door.

Forbidden.

"Cyclo. Please open the door," I say again, this time my voice cracking. I'll only just peep my head outside, just a little look. I won't step a foot out there. I know people will be walking the hallways. But if no one is there...maybe I can make my way to her lab and see why she's delayed. I know exactly where it is. I've spent much of my life studying Cyclo's every detail—the story of her birth, the way she harvests starlight energy, the layout of the ship down to every single storage vacuole and crew member unit.

But of course, I've never seen any of it. Only my room. A day would come when Mother introduced me to the crew. The day was coming soon. We'd talked about it. And then I could say that I'm not just a parasite hidden on the ship, like a worm or a barnacle. I could tell them how much I know of Cyclo—I could be useful in any position they needed me. I would be worth keeping. Wouldn't I?

So if Cyclo could only let me out of this room, I could find Mother. Her gestational labs are located due north, in the alpha ring, only about fifteen hundred feet away, counterclockwise. Cyclo, being relatively flat and circular, was assigned the familiar Earth directional vectors of north, west, south, and east since its creators were Earth-born. And as it doesn't look like other spaceships, with an obvious way to use the traditional nautical designations—bow, stern, starboard, port side—Cyclo was mapped to feel like a huge compass within the hand of the Pleiades star cluster.

North. I need to go north.

I put my hand on the membrane. It is warm like my own skin. Cyclo acquiesces, changing her shade to a yellow with matching iridescence that shows she is worried for me, and displeased with my rule-breaking. A hole appears in the membrane, widening outward as the organic, bony edges of the door appear.

My heart is thudding so hard, I hear it in my eardrums. Cyclo can probably sense it, too—her color hasn't normalized. She can see, taste, touch all my emotions. She is worried for me. I poke my head out of the doorway quickly, looking left and right before withdrawing. I'm hyperventilating from my brashness. The hallway—which I have never seen before in my entire life—is smooth-walled and is a wavering color of blue mixed with Cyclo's worried yellow. The floor is very gently curved, with one door at each end. It is empty.

So I slow my breathing, and take a step into the hallway, feet bare, still in my thin robe. Surely, Mother is nearby. But what if I encounter a crew member? What will I say that won't get us both in serious trouble? What in the stars will I do?

Hello. I'm Hana. Have you seen Dr. Um? I need to speak with her.

Let me explain myself. I know so much about the ship. About Cyclo. I can be useful, just let me explain.

I walk quickly, maybe twenty paces. Already, my legs feel wobbly taking long strides. I am only used to walking within a room ten feet in diameter. There are rounded plastrix dots every ten feet or so. They must be the translating comms. I touch the door at the far end of the hallway, open it, pop my head through again. No one. There is another corridor. And another. Every time, I expect to introduce myself to a stranger, a real human that is not my mother. My heart rate trills with anticipation at every door, slows with disappointment and dread after each one opens.

They are all empty.

A bright purple line appears on the wall, pulsating in the direction of a leftward corridor, though I know exactly where to go. Despite my anxiousness, each new step brings a tiny thrill that makes my fingertips tingle. Here are the walls I've only studied on my vids! And the corridors on the beautiful maps of Cyclo that look like a spinning flower with smoky, ephemeral tendrils at the edges! I'm finally outside my room. I'm finally seeing Cyclo the way she's meant to be explored.

The purple flashes again for me. Strangely, the translating comm says nothing. Isn't it supposed to verbalize what Cyclo is saying? I'll have to look into why it's not. I don't remember that malfunction happening before I'd gone to sleep. I start running, feet padding along the squishy matrix, my robe flapping softly against my legs as an excruciating anguish begins to set in. The ship is vast, after all. It's a quiet quadrant, but Mother always said that it wasn't completely empty. Maybe Mother is where everyone else is.

After several more empty corridors, I enter the north

quadrant alpha. I find a room full of plastrix terminals and chairs and walls of 3D computation boards, and another curved room with a long table that's the mess hall, but devoid of food or plates. A purple line flashes to a door, and it opens into an enormous laboratory, complete with long tables, fluid-filled incubation chambers with no embryos, walls of nutrient pods, biomonitors. Everything is off, empty, blank.

Oh no. *No, no.* And now I'm crying.

Mother is not here.

On the right, there is a long window made of a clear, indestructible plastrix material embedded into Cyclo's endoskeleton.

Oh!

I have never seen outside of Cyclo before, and it is so breathtaking it nearly buckles my knees. Black and enormous and glittering with stars. I run to it, letting my hand smack against the plastrix, eyes wide and searching, tears still dripping off my chin because I am so alone, and I can't find her, and despite this breaking within me, the universe has just opened her oyster shell to me. I recognize the starshine of nearby Taygeta and Sterope, bright fists of blue light with interstellar clouds wisping around them. It's so beautiful, and Mother isn't here to share this with me. Every first of my life has been in her presence.

As I look out at the sparkling light in the velvety darkness, it's obvious what I must do, but this is foreign territory—I've never even had to process this question in my mind.

I wipe my dripping nose and eyes with my sleeve, trying to catch my breath. "Cyclo," I say.

Her voice comes from somewhere behind me on the wall. "Yes, Hana."

"Where...where is the crew of the ship?"

"The crew is not here," Cyclo answers.

Nausea fills me. I choke out words before I can possibly vomit my porridge. "Cyclo, where did the crew go?"

"The crew has evacuated onto the seven major transports of the ship. They are currently in hyperspace, and are on their way to Atlas Station IPX-400."

My knees buckle for real, and I drop to the soft floor. That station is very far away. As in, years away by hyperspace travel. And they cannot communicate with anyone while in hyperspace.

"Cyclo," I choke out. "My mother. Where is she right now? When is she coming back?"

Her colors flash in pinkish sympathy. She doesn't form a humanoid face to speak, because her colors are so much more eloquent when words are not enough, and she knows this. Ellipsoids of pink, orange, and silver pulsate with truth, sadness, and sympathy.

I read the colors with a sob.

Oh, Hana. Your mother has left the ship, forever.

Chapter Two

FENN

This trip is all about firsts.

First time away from my home planet. First interstellar travel. First spaceship job.

First time dying.

Technically, this is a list of *lasts,* too, if I'm going to be really nitpicky.

God. How did I end up here?

I'm sitting on the bridge of the *Selkirk* and glancing over the readings of our voyage so far. We should be arriving at the *Calathus* within the next hour or two. It's in sight now—a bluish-white disc in space with a wispy and irregular fringe at the edges, cut with a pattern of fenestrations. It sort of looks like a snowflake and a moon jellyfish had a wicked fight, followed by makeup sex, and then ended up birthing the *Calathus.*

"Cyclo. There it is," Portia says. "I mean *she.* She's really a beautiful crvat, isn't she?" Portia's the one actually driving the *Selkirk* right now. I don't know what crvat means. Probably "interstellar biosynthetic human habitation complex." Possibly she means "jellyfish." Learning Portia's language is not high priority at this juncture in my life. Even though I've had nine months to learn on this trip so far, I've decided that it's best to not always know what Portia is saying, particularly when we squabble over food. Which I'm always stealing because I like her Prinnia food better than the synthetics I usually eat.

What I'm damn good at, though, is driving nano-theft drones. Any drones, really. But anything ship-size is new territory. While Portia thinks I'm winding the mechanical watch in my hand (it currently doesn't need winding, but she doesn't know that), I'm secretly learning how to drive the ship. Honestly, it's habit. I pick up skills wherever I can, however I can, and by stealing if necessary. And yet, it's hard to undo that urge to survive, to make sure I come out on top, alive, ahead of the authorities nipping at my heels, a quadrant away. It's boiling inside me right now, though it's wasted energy at this point.

Portia's hair is shaved to the skull, showing off her gold Prinnia-pride tattoo—a stylized sand serpent—from her home planet. Her boot-clad legs are curled up beneath her, which seems physically impossible for someone who's seven feet tall. Those unnerving red irises flit around the readouts, checking to make sure we're not all going to die before our time, which ought to be pretty soon.

"Ah. Cyclo is magnificent," Portia murmurs.

"You mean the *Calathus*," I say. I tap my fingers on my thigh in Morse code, a soothing habit.

... -. --- --- - -.--   .--. .-. .. -. -. .. .- -..

Snooty Prinniad.

Sometimes the old ways are the best. Especially when silently insulting people. After nine months on the *Selkirk*, I've learned a lot about Portia, but she can still annoy me. I have fun teasing her. She hasn't figured out what my finger tapping really means, so she just gives me a scarlet side-eye for a moment.

"They told us we should call it by its common name." Her voice is soothing, which puts me on edge. Soothing voices, in my life, mean someone is lying to me. "You know. So we can cozy up to her, and she can feel comfortable around us."

"How comfortable can it be? It's *dying*."

"Shut up, Fenn. My God, you have the sensitivity of a laser grenade, you know that?" She bares a grin at me, with that brand of toothless smile that unnerved me as a kid. For years, I wasn't used to being around Prinniads, or non-humans on my home planet. But I got used to it once I got into the theft game. Because when you steal, everyone and everything is someone you might sell to, or steal from. I'm an equal opportunity thief.

Which answers the earlier question—why am I here?

I steal stuff. A lot of stuff. Instead of wasting time and talent in jail, I'm here. We all have our reasons, but I only know mine. My sister Callandra, through no fault of her own, has been in a medical facility for one year, since right about the time I went to jail. Most of her spinal cord was crushed when the mining dredger she was working in tumbled into a magnesium sinkhole on our home planet, Ipineq. She'll need therapy and biologic and synthetic transfer treatments her whole life. She just needs the money. And so I will die paying for it.

The captain's remote voice sounds on the wall coms. It's Doran, who's not really on the ship, but has been setting the *Selkirk's* coordinates and remotely training us for these long nine months.

"Fenn, Portia. It's time for our meeting. You're disembarking in one hour and we need to go over a few things."

"Got it." Portia puts the ship on autopilot for the landing program. I watch her movements without staring.

"Fennec," Doran barks through the intercom.

"Yes, sir." I straighten up. An old habit from prison.

"Stop trying to learn how to fly this ship. This is a one-way trip. Got it?"

"Yes, sir."

Portia stands up. She says casually, "I knew you were watching me."

"I wasn't doing any such thing." I slip the watch into my pocket and turn to the door.

Portia thrusts out a long leg, kicking my feet out from under me. In one quick movement, she slams my torso down and grips my neck hard with only two fingers—one each on the arteries of my neck, which I desperately need to keep working if I don't want to stroke out.

"Ndzia fro atzm. Ndzia!" she hisses at me with her toothless mouth. Her eyes are sparking with tiny golden flecks in the crimson. Her fingers are sharp, and her booted foot is pressed hard onto my rib cage, immobilizing me. I'm five foot ten, wiry and strong for seventeen, but Portia winded me without a problem.

"Which means?" I gasp.

"Don't cross me, or I'll kill you. I signed a contract. You signed a contract. And there's nothing in that contract that says I can't strangle you in order to fulfill my duty. My family is counting on me to do my job. And no human boy is going to take that away."

"You said all that in just four words? You guys must have the shortest books in the universe," I wheeze.

"You had nine months to learn," she says, releasing my neck, but her heavy boot is still pressed hard on my rib cage. "I learned English."

I try to push her boot off my chest, but it doesn't budge. "Isn't this a sign of affection in Prinnia? Regular near-deadly physical fights?" Portia's attacked me nearly every day, after I've teased her about something. Nine months of it, and you'd think I'd learn how to dodge her by now.

"It is," she says. "But not always. One more thing. I've heard of your work. If you fly one of your drones up my nose to steal anything—one molecule, even—I'll steal something right back. Like your liver."

"Well, that sounds fair."

Portia stops standing on me, and I try to catch my breath. She kicks me just under my right ribs, exactly where my liver is—not by coincidence, I'm sure—and I decide it's best not to say anything witty anymore.

"Let's go," she says.

We leave the cockpit and walk through the belly of the craft to the end. I rub my right side tenderly. I may not need my liver for much longer, but I sure as hell need it for now. As we wind our way from one corridor to the next, I can sense the architecture of the ship. The *Selkirk* looks a lot like a long, skinny boat, curved at the bottom like a smile and flat on top, except that it travels hull first. A Cheshire Cat grin, flying through the void.

I follow Portia at a distance. Her legs are long, and she could still land a roundhouse kick and knock my eye out. We pass through a few cargo bays only half full of supplies and reach an aft cabin with the rest of the crew awaiting us. Altogether, it's four of us.

Doran, in a hologram, stands up before the wide table before us. His hair is wiry and white, his skin the color of ashes and slightly blue. Argyrian, silver-blooded, with the muscular build to match. He looks to be in his nineties, and pretty fit for that. My grandma lived to 140, so Doran isn't so lucky, really, to be his age.

The other two crew members, I've gotten to know pretty well. One is Miki, with that ashy-blue skin like Doran, youngish with blue-green braids over her broad shoulders and a hard look in her eyes. She's a couple of years older than I am, but far larger due to her Argyrian genes. She's shorter than me but clearly stronger. Portia once threw a roundhouse kick at Miki, who promptly caught her foot and used it to scratch her armpit.

The last crew member is mostly human, a guy, with medium brown skin and dark brown hair. About my age, with an unreadable expression. Gammand. Gammand is the quietest of all of us, and we've learned his habits over the course of the trip. He likes to read, he's not very playful or jokey, and he spends a lot of time being introspective. And by that, I mean he talks to no one, ever. Outside of a few times he woke up from a nightmare screaming about the murder of his people, he's pretty harmless.

We've all been on the *Selkirk* for nine months. They gathered us all for this mission back then, knowing it would take this long to train us and to finally get to the *Calathus*. At least we didn't have to go into cryosleep. I hear the reanimation process is like being stabbed by a million needles in every part of your body. The day we boarded, we had brand new biomonitors implanted in our necks, which hurt like hell.

"All right," Doran's holograph begins. "We've less than an hour. It's been nine months of prep, and ReCOR has asked me to brief you on the status of the *Calathus* before we board."

I grimace. ReCOR is a very rich, very powerful company that makes the ships like the *Calathus*. Everything is proprietary, down to the DNA codes. And they're not happy that the *Calathus* is dying after only one hundred years. No one wants to move entire colonies; they want permanent ones, and there are only so many habitable planets in the knowable systems we all live in. If our data-gathering trip goes well, they'll understand how to make future ships live longer (read: they can charge more to republics who wish to buy them). Doran sees my grimace, and I wipe it clean before he can comment. He goes on.

"This field study requires that you hit data-gathering objectives, which are now updated here, as well as in your feeds." Doran points to a long list that's now scrolling to the right of him. "Ninety percent of the objectives must be met—"

"Wait. It was eighty percent when we signed our contract!" Portia's eyes flash with anger.

Miki shuts one eye. I think that's an Argyrian curse.

Doran's hand raises to silence us. "For which you forfeit your future in exchange for a generous death benefit bequeathed to the person or persons of your choice."

At this, we all exchange glances. After all this time together, we've gotten to know each other, but no one's spoken of their death benefit beneficiary. And no one's asked, because it's too painful. Doran better not make us tell who those people are. I'm not here to spew my life story to anyone.

Doran clears his throat. "Good news is, your objectives are now set, and will no longer change."

"Is that all ReCOR has to say?" Gammand asks in his low, calm voice. "We're ten percent more likely to fail here?"

"Now, Gammand. Remember that this is a remarkable experience, and an opportunity to benefit many in the future, including your loved ones."

I want to laugh. That's like saying, here, eat this cake! It's delicious! But it's chock full of cyanide! Be happy!

Doran goes on. "I wish I was there myself." He clearly doesn't mean this. He's just trying to make us feel special, in the non-dying kind of way. "The *Calathus* is unlike any bioship I've ever been on."

"You've been on one bioship, you've been on them all," Miki says, unimpressed.

"Not exactly. None were fully self-sustaining, or truly biocompatible with humanoids. And none were of this magnitude, and age. The biological entity that makes up the *Calathus* is unique. *Amorfovita potentia,* subspecies *cyclonica,* is the only one in existence. They engineered her well. Cyclo, as the organism itself is colloquially called, is the largest ever of its genus and is nearly a hundred years old. But it's reaching its unique Hayflick limit."

I raise my hand.

Doran rolls his eyes. "This isn't prison, and it isn't school. Just speak, Fennec."

"Call me Fenn. So, what…what are—"

Portia snorts and interrupts with a bored voice. "The Hayflick limit is the number of times that an organism's cells—"

"I know what the Hayflick limit is," I snap back. "It's cellular doomsday. After so many generations of cells dividing over and over again, they die. What I was asking before I was interrupted"—I shoot a narrow-eyed glance at Portia, who bares her gummy maw at me—"is whether the salvage option in the contract is live or not?"

"No. They've reviewed the proposal, and there is no chance this will be a junk run. ReCOR tanked that option a few days ago. The ship will not be salvageable for years," Doran tells me. "As they predicted."

Damn. I had thought that if I could collect useable material, that would mean they might collect *me,* too. There was a slim chance of this when I signed the contract, but not anymore.

Cyclo's mantle apparently had stopped photosynthesizing, which is why it's turned blue instead of its usual red color. Its tissues have been storing toxic substances all this time near its core. And while it dies, those stored toxins will be released and make the entire ship a biohazard. And then we'll become too contaminated to ever leave the ship. Which is why this is a one-way trip. I'd just hoped that they might find recycling still worth it. I guess not. I try to hide my disappointment by tapping on my leg.

.. / .- -- / ... --- / ... -.-. .-. . .-- . -.. .-.-.-

I am so screwed.

"I knew they'd trash the salvage option. We're not leaving the ship alive. Get over it already, Fenn," Portia says, completely unperturbed.

"What's the news on the toxicity of the ship?" Gammand asks.

"Cosmic radiation residues are rising linearly. Bacteria levels are normal. And the highly poisonous heavy metals and other chemicals are so far very well contained."

My mind is working. I wonder if any of them are sellable, or worth much. It's hard to sell stuff when you're dead, but who knows. I could get lucky.

But then I remember—no, Fenn. You have a contract. Doran just said no salvaging, no gathering anything that's not data. You botch that up, and Callandra won't be able to afford her treatments. So stop with the hustle. You aren't getting off this ship.

We learned along the way that the ship's internal systems were failing, but ReCOR didn't know the specifics of exactly how. Creatures like Cyclo are always in a push-pull metabolism with the human-embedded synthetics we add, including our systems. Cyclo breaks them down little by little, naturally, despite the way she was engineered. Even if the synthetics are made of plastrix, which is supposedly inert. But this is why they need humans and humanoids to do this dirty work. The systems can't record this from inside, anyway. It's all dying.

"Cyclo's crew left one week ago," Doran reports. "But we were told that system safety checks were already beginning to fail. The communication on the ship is already dead, including the translators on the wall, which helped the crew speak to the ship."

"That's fast," Portia notes.

Doran nods. "Yes, it's happening quickly.'

"Can we just wear our biohazard suits?" Miki asks. "It'll buy us more time to get that ninety percent done."

"ReCOR says no, not unless you're directly working in the central radioactive area, Miki. Our biomonitors are going to pick up how we react to the toxins as they first start to seep out. Not pleasant, but an extremely important part of the data we're gathering. It will save future lives."

"Just not ours. We're space lab rats," I say.

Doran doesn't respond to me again. He's really good at that. His hologram begins to discuss individual objectives. He speaks to Portia, who's the expert in biosynthetic symbiosis, and then to Miki, the radiation and environmental systems engineer. She's also the one who'll tell us which parts of the ship to steer clear of when they get too toxic for us. He has little to say to Gammand, whose wavy, dark brown hair is pulled back into a ball at the back of his head. Gammand is the information specialist. He's putting together the logs and diaries, coordinating all the data, finding our gaps, and leaving records in multiple copies just to be safe. They'll be on Cyclo, the *Selkirk*, and transmitted to the Cyclo's crew, who will be able to receive it in approximately a month, their first scheduled stop out of hyperspace.

It suddenly occurs to me that we're all really young. Not one of us is over twenty.

Doran finally turns to me.

"Fennec—Fenn, I mean." He pauses and studies my face. "You okay?"

"Sure thing, boss," I say in my fake subordinate voice. The one I always use with Doran.

"Any questions, then, Fenn?"

"Yeah. What's up with the age limit here? Only the good die young?"

"We needed the healthiest subjects," he says, shrugging. "Any pertinent questions, Fenn?"

"No. I fly my nano drones to gather samples. What else is there to know?"

Doran tries to smile. "Listen. You're the best driver on this side of the galaxy, and you've been trained to deal with Cyclo's particular tissues. Do some good, instead of flying up people's nostrils and stealing xerullium from their glands."

Miki looks me straight in the eye and cracks her knuckles. I guess there won't be much xerullium harvesting. It's the trace metal you didn't know you needed to live, and only exists in the amount of one kilogram per galaxy. It sells in such small quantities it would make you pucker. I'm talking picograms. Femtograms, even.

Doran taps his forehead, and all of our own holofeeds go live. Simultaneously, glowing screens pop up in front of each of our faces, a sort of half-bubble of scrolling maps of Cyclo, and biometric data.

"Your holofeed implants have been uploaded with basics of Cyclo's color language, anatomy, and schematics, so you know where you are. Since the internal communication on Cyclo is nonfunctioning, this is how we talk, and everything is on record."

Great. So I can't even be snide to Portia without it possibly ruining my contract. These days, people have holofeeds implanted in their brains, or at least in their eyes. But those are meant for internal feeds that no one can see. These forehead ones project a 3D holo outward, in front of our faces. ReCOR doesn't want us to keep info to ourselves. It's out there for Doran and the whole crew to see. I close it with a glance at a red dot in the corner, and the bubble disappears.

"Fenn, you'll fly wherever the crew asks you to. You're one of our main sources of data collection. It'll be busy, and my job will be to make sure you all stay busy. Now." Doran pushes back from the table. "A few last reminders. Our job is to observe. You're not there to save Cyclo. It's already dead, as far as ReCOR is concerned. If you interfere for any reason, your contract will be forfeit. If you die from making your own terrible choices before your job is completed—and that includes getting yourself prematurely killed—your contract will be forfeit."

He pauses and looks at us all one by one, so we hear his next words clearly. "The *Selkirk* is going to dock soon. It will have no fuel left, and once our data is uploaded, it will be set to drift until it is retrieved at a later date. Meaning, no one is leaving Cyclo. Not even your dead bodies. Let me be clear about that, in case any of you are having some very late second thoughts."

He looks hard at me, which is unnerving. Can he tell that my skin is prickling in goose bumps? That I'm sweating under my clothes? I tap the table with my fingertips.

.. -.. --- -. ·----· - .-- .- -. - - --- -... . ...-. .

I don't want to be here.

Portia shuts her holofeed off with a glance of her red eyes, and sighs. "How long do we have? That is, how much longer will the *Calathus* survive? The last update said eight weeks."

Doran pauses for a moment. "It's now about three weeks."

We all freeze. Three weeks.

Three weeks left to live.

It's a strange thing, to see the rest of your life set before you in small, measurable numbers, like three.

"Now, remember that each you have objectives that need to be met before your contract is fulfilled. When you open up your holofeeds, you'll find a progress bar for achieving your goals." I pop open my holo, and there is a huge bar now visible on the right side of my screen. It's fully red, showing 0 percent completion. Doran continues. "And if the ship's death accelerates, well, then, that means less sleep for you and more work."

Three weeks, twenty-one days, seemed like far too little. Now, at the thought that if things go wrong, there will be even less time, three weeks seems like an eternity.

And to make us feel even worse, Doran's holograph arm gestures to the table. A compartment in the center slides open, and within it, a small dais rises. Perched upon it are four small, soft packets. They each have names on them, and I grab mine and unwrap it. A square medallion hangs from a chain necklace. My name and my universal ID are on the front.

"The medallion, when pressed, has a parting hologram message from the person to whom you bequeathed your death benefit, as a reminder of why you are here, and a reminder to complete your mission," Doran says. "If you open the medallion—do not do this right now, please—you'll find a disc of cikkina poison. It is highly effective and toxic for all humanoid species. Touching it will result in a quick and painless death within a few seconds. It is there for only one purpose. On the last day of our mission, Cyclo will be completely nonfunctioning, and you will have become biohazard material yourself. You will be surviving only on the environmental systems, which will inevitably fail."

He doesn't have to say anything else. Suffocation is a hell of a way to go.

I hold my medallion, as the other crew members slowly leave the cabin and get ready to board the *Calathus*. The metal is cold and quite heavy. A platinum alloy, expensive. I don't push the button. I'm not ready to listen to what my sister has to say to me. Last I heard, she had a lot of difficulty speaking. I haven't spoken to her since before her accident.

I have this one chance to redeem myself and do something right in my life. God knows I've done all the wrong things since I can remember, including being born. This is my chance to be a hero, but I don't feel like one. I want to live, but I can't. I can't.

Like I said before, this trip is all about firsts.

For the first time in my life, I'm terrified.

But one thing is for damned sure. I'll die before I ever let anyone know the truth.

Chapter Three

HANA

She left me behind.

She abandoned me.

I have been kneeling on the floor of my mother's laboratory between empty incubators, crying, choking through hyperventilations. Through the fog of despair, my mind races around disparate things. Why? Why did everyone leave? Why did I have to be such a terrible burden that I was left behind?

Mother—wasn't I worth bringing with you?

Always, there was the idea that someday Mother would tell me that the rules by which we lived had changed. She would present me to her world with pride instead of this brand of concealment and shame that I've been woven into. Mother had even thought of pretending I was a stowaway on one of the rare supply ships. She was ready for the time that this might happen. Excited, even, to think that I could be formally accepted and adopted. Me, a girl of no nation, no people, no past.

Then, I could begin to live. Truly live.

"She told me," I hiccupped through tears. "She told me that very soon, she would tell them about me. She promised."

"Yes," Cyclo said, speaking again through the walls now that she has composed herself as well. "I remember when you spoke of it. Several times. I sensed your mother's…hesitancy… to bring up the subject."

Hesitancy.

I am so naive. If I had studied human behavior instead of Cyclo's microtubules and cell biology, maybe Mother would have thought I was ready to be introduced to the crew earlier. If I had read more on how to be an integrated social being, instead of about cheese making and the cookery of my favorite kinds of Korean namul and guk, maybe I could have read Mother's face. I studied, like a student terrified to fail, about how to do human things—concrete things. I studied Cyclo, the only home I've ever known, thinking I could convince the crew that I truly could be the one thousand and first person on board, instead of their carefully curated one thousand. But I should have studied my mother, instead. Maybe I would have understood her words better. I had become more anxious in the last few months, pushing her for a fixed day when I could finally leave my blue cage.

Oh.

It wasn't hesitancy that she had been showing. It was something else altogether.

"She was tiring of me. She was putting the answer off because this was her answer. She wanted to leave. And now she's gone," I say, voice hollow and scratchy. I sound older already. Different. "But what of the crew? Cyclo, why did they have to leave?"

Cyclo knows something else. She's been flashing patterns of magenta and ultraviolet purples in a range that only I can see. Even mother was impressed with how much I could understand because of my ability to see beyond the spectrum of light most humans detect. Cyclo is telling me more now.

They have evacuated the Calathus because conditions are no longer ideal.

I get to my feet and look around. Really look. The lights embedded in lines along the floors are still working, but Cyclo's own luminescence is slightly dull. The incubation pods where the embryos gestate are empty, of course. If they had any incubates, they are now flying away in hyperspace within new electronic and plastrix wombs, to a new home. But I stare carefully at what I haven't yet seen. I've been too busy running, panicked, through the hallways and rooms of Cyclo to notice. Her walls are always a complacent blue at rest. Usually. I squint, focusing.

There is one tiny speck of brown fixed upon the wall. It's not an emotion because it has no depth or movement like Cyclo's usual brown waves of pensiveness. I walk to the wall to examine the brown dot, the size of my pinkie fingernail, thinking it's like a freckle, like the smattering of light brown spots sprayed across the bridge of my own nose.

I touch it.

"Ahhh!" I yank my finger back. It's burning, like when I've touched the hot pot on the stove of my kitchenette. I grasp my finger, which has gone white at the tip and is throbbing.

The brown dot has enlarged from my probing, and it's glistening with wetness that drips down the membrane of Cyclo's wall, staining it brown as well. As it slips down, the brown stains turn into little ulcers and craters.

"It's acid. You burned me! What is this? What's happened?" I ask.

A small reaction. My ability to channel away my chloride metabolites has been malfunctioning.

I think. Chloride metabolites are usually coupled into harmless salts. I know Cyclo's metabolic wastes are generally stored or recycled. This is really strange. I sniff Cyclo's normal blue wall nearby. A faint sour odor.

"You're making a hydrochloric acid byproduct."

Yes.

I back away from Cyclo's wall. I know how she works. I knew she was having some metabolic issues—Mother would let me look over her shoulder at the biometric readouts of the ship every morning. She'd say I knew almost as much as the bioengineers on the crew, and I fed off her compliments by learning all I could about Cyclo. And yet, I never sensed that she was having this problem. I need to know exactly what's going on with her. Cyclo is good at taking care of me, but she can't always explain well what her processes are. Technical jargon doesn't translate well with Cyclo's methods of communication. I need to find more.

And I need answers from Mother. Which means, somehow, I have to contact her.

And if I do, I will have to ask the question.

Why did you abandon me?

Tears start coming again, and I can't stop them. They dribble down my face, my nose runs, and I'm a faucet of stickiness and saltwater. The only person who has the answers is the one person who isn't here. I find a sink in the laboratory, and the tap works. It runs clear water, and I sniff it. It seems okay, so I wash the acid off my fingertip. Normally, I would just stick my injured self right back into Cyclo, and she would remove debris, flush it, correct the pH, encourage healing. But I'm afraid to touch her again, and Cyclo is telling me in waves of golden yellow that she is sorry for hurting me.

"I just want to go home," I say. I want the solace of my room. My world, really. I miss the time when my Mother had all the answers. She was nearly ready for me to launch, as a working part of the ship. To be accepted. But I can't fight this overwhelming need to go back to when things were safe and everything was understood. And then I think of how Cyclo has an injury, something I've never seen before. Maybe Cyclo needs to be taken care of for a change.

Take care of someone or something else? I've never had to do this. I try on the concept like a new, heavy shirt I've never worn.

It feels very, very odd.

I'm not sure I like it.

I exit the lab and walk slowly around the perimeter of Cyclo. The crew and I have always lived on the outermost circle of the ship, walking on its inner edge as Cyclo rotates once per minute. In the outermost alpha ring, the gravity is strongest. The walking alone tires me out utterly, and often I just collapse into a heap on the gel floor to catch my breath and rest. I keep a keen eye out for more brown spots, which show up here and there. There are more than I would like to see.

The main bridge of the ship is on the entire other side from my room. It's where the ship's logs are. I pass by more empty mess halls—painfully clean. The crew did not leave in a hurry; they left in an orderly, organized fashion. Which means that Mother knew for some time that she would have to leave.

I take a set of carved-out ladder steps upward into the beta ring. The gravity is slightly less here, and every step feels bouncy. Here are some empty crew cabins, a hundred in this quarter section. The doors are all open. I gingerly touch their personal objects, like discarded clothes, music cubes, holo letters, and wonder what they looked like. Were they of Korean descent, as Mother designed me because that was her heritage? Was their skin cream-colored, like faded paper? Or brown, like newborn Earthen acorns? Was their hair shorn short, or curled, or braided as I have seen in the vids? Mother didn't let me memorize the personnel files; she said that was invasive.

Little did they knew they had me as a parasite on this ship the whole time.

"I missed them," I say. And I missed the opportunity to be able to talk to anyone besides myself and Mother.

Cyclo flashes a mild peach color, reminding me she is here. Of course, I have Cyclo. She flickers back to blue. She likes the idea of just her and me together. She's right; this is safety, too.

"Just us," I say. "No one to be afraid of." Or to disappoint. Because there was always that fear—that they would say to me and my mother, no. She can't be here. We have rules.

Hana is unacceptable.

But within me, there is lingering dissatisfaction. There is loneliness which makes no sense because I have always been quite alone. But I have lost what I've never had, and that is even worse. Cyclo and me, it's not quite enough this time. The next time I hibernate, Cyclo will know this. I am not looking forward to what is usually a respite, which is also a new feeling.

"The docking bays," I say aloud. "That's where I'll go."

"West alpha. One level down, twenty meters west," Cyclo says, though I already knew that.

I try to think like Mother. With logic and calmness, and without my tangential forays into Earth history and the nature of storm clouds over the Great Lakes. "Maybe the crew left some information there about how to communicate. Maybe Mother left me a note of some kind." Doubtful, but still worth a try.

Back down to the alpha ring, the docks are quite large, fifty times the size of my little room. Each seems like an enormous bite has been taken out of the edge of the ship. The six bays have ragged edges where they broke away from Cyclo on their exodus. Each is closed off to the cold reaches of space with a solid, scarred beige membrane—webbed from interconnecting adhesions, each with more tensile strength than steel.

Out a plastrix window, I can see the ragged mantle of Cyclo, like a dancer's thin tulle skirt, reaching out into space. Mother said her photosynthetic mantle was red, to best absorb the UV light from Maia, but it's not red—it's blue. Which means she isn't photosynthesizing well.

This is not good.

On my right are vid displays and control panels, but none are blinking with lights. All is quiet. Life has carved itself out and fled. Through a window, obscured by tendril growth, the stars are clear and bright against the inky backdrop of space. Three luminous ones clustered together sparkle with a particular tenacity. Somewhere in that cluster is Atlas, where Mother and the crew are headed.

One of the twinkling lights becomes brighter, as if my attention has beckoned it closer.

No, wait.

The light *is* getting closer. I lean into the window, touching the cold, clear plastrix with my fingertips. That is not a star.

I inhale sharply. "It's a ship! Cyclo, it's a ship coming to dock! Mother is coming back!"

I knew it! I knew she wouldn't leave me here; I knew it was all a mistake. Oh, and what's more—she'll introduce me to the crew. It's all over. The nightmare, short as it was, is over.

"They're coming back! They're—"

Cyclo's colors interrupt me to disagree. Flashes and colors pulse and twist in the blink of an eye because the information is coming so very fast.

No. It is not one of our ships. They are still scheduled to be in hyperspace. This is another vessel, far smaller, and they are hailing in preparation to dock and board.

My blood goes cold. "Who are they? Why have they come?"

They have not volunteered that information. But I cannot deny them entry. They have a clearance passcode, which I am not allowed to refuse.

I take several paces back. The light splits into three lights, and they shine brighter and brighter until I see the craft. Small, like a sideways parenthesis. There are windows on the bridge of the ship, but my window is too fuzzy to see what type of being resides within. It's slowing down, orienting itself to fit the nearest bay.

"Cyclo," I whisper. "Should I go? Should I hide?"

Yes, Hana. It would be safer until we know their purpose. They are still not communicating their intentions.

I head for the door to the docking bay but pause. My fear wars with my curiosity. Maybe Mother is on the ship? Maybe she left the crew to come retrieve me? Maybe not, but there will be someone coming on board in minutes. What will they look like? What language will they speak? Should I offer gifts? Should I bow the way my ancestors did with strangers? I don't know what to do. Nothing in my education prepared me for this. I am a hybrid of anticipation and worry.

Hana. Go.

I turn to exit but pause yet again. My feet are irresistibly fixed in place, and there is Cyclo flashing warning exclamations in all shades of white and yellow. There is a hard, jarring crash as the ship cracks the fine, lacy exoskeleton framework to fit itself into the dock. One of the downsides with a living bioship—damage, however reversible, is inevitable with entering and exiting ships. But that is not why I'm trembling, cowering behind the edge of the doorway, fingers gripping Cyclo so hard that I'm blanching her color away.

I've only ever known one person in my life. Mother. And since I've known her forever, I haven't really ever *met* anyone. Whoever walks off this ship will be the first real person I've ever laid eyes on. This is a moment I've been waiting for my entire life.

The ship cracks a little farther into the dock, and steam from its contact with Cyclo's tissues rises in puffs of rank-smelling clouds. Her matrix oozes forth, hardening and forming a seal around the docked ship, as she is programmed to do. Vaguely, I wonder if Cyclo is in pain, accepting this ship into her hull, but I'm too distracted to ask her. There is a knocking sound, more hissing, and metal scraping Cyclo's own bones, burning her flesh. A narrow passageway opens into the front of the bay as the door lowers.

Chunky boots appear, walking purposefully down the plank. They are attached to slim, long legs clad in regular but worn khaki work pants, with unfamiliar equipment holstered around the left thigh. Narrow hips and a baggy jacket full of pockets follow, and then I see the face.

The face of a young man—dark irises, light brown skin, and almost-black hair in a wavy but short mess. He looks around. Disappointment darkens his eyes further, until he sees me.

I gasp in surprise. He is younger than I thought at first—about my age. And he is unexpectedly handsome in a bewitching, irregular way. And suddenly, I can't breathe. He opens his mouth. He's frozen on the plank, staring at me, when he finally finds words to speak, the first words I've ever heard from a real boy.

"Who the hell are *you*?"

Chapter Four

FENN

She doesn't answer me.

It's a girl. Sixteen, maybe seventeen. She's hiding halfway behind the doorway exiting the ship's bay. The shock of seeing her competes with the shock of seeing a real, live bioship, with its flashing gold colors against the blue membranous walls everywhere. The girl has straight hair past her shoulders, black as the space between stars but with a startling white lock of hair above her forehead, which flows down in a stripe. Her eyes are brown, skin somewhat wan and sickly looking, like she's eating the wrong kind of food. She looks Asian, like the grandmother I never met on Asyx Seven. Her eyes are unblinking.

A thousand questions in my head fire at once—why is she here? Who is she? Isn't the ship supposed to be empty? But the questions collide with another weird consideration. She's really pretty. An asinine consideration, because the last thing I should care about at the end of my stubby, short life is pretty girls, but I can't help it. My face flushes with warmth as I take another step closer.

She moves back from the door, and I can see now what

she's wearing—a flimsy short robe, mid-thigh, rippling against her body. A tiny pearl pendant glimmers against the hollow of her throat. She's barefoot, too. What an unfortunate choice of clothing, considering she's on a ship in the process of crumbling around her.

She still hasn't said anything. "What are you doing here?" I ask.

Nothing. The girl just stares at me. Maybe she doesn't speak my language. Gammand has stopped behind me and joined the staring match.

"Who *is* that?" he asks me, as if I ought to know.

I haven't moved on the cargo ramp. Someone stomps behind us—Miki, probably—and the girl sways backward as she eyes the growing cluster of people. Miki moves to my side, and the girl gets a view of her ropy forearms, seeming in awe of her silvery-blue skin and wide shoulders.

"No, wait—" I start, but it's too late.

The girl turns and bolts, her black and white hair whipping behind her.

Miki shrugs. "They always run away from me."

"Who's *they*?" Gammand asks.

"Everyone," she says, and lets out the signature sigh of the physically intimidating and chronically misunderstood.

Portia exits the craft and barks, "Why are you all standing here? We have work to do."

"There's a girl," Miki says. Everything she voices sounds like a growl. "Here. On the *Calathus.*"

Portia looks about. "What girl? The ship is empty. Doran and ReCOR confirmed this."

I smirk. "My sources say they're wrong."

"Don't be a smart-ass, Fenn. Well, we'll have to report that the crew accidentally left someone behind. I suppose she might have come on another transport, too, though we were told there is no sanctioned interstellar traffic in this area," Portia says.

Gammand adds quietly, "Well, don't just stand there, Fenn. Go get her." He's already turned his attention to recording our conversation and checking readouts from his own handheld data recorder.

Portia pokes me hard the shoulder. "Go," she orders.

"Why me?"

"Because you're in the way, and because that's your job. You fetch things," Portia says. She points a long finger toward the exit door of the landing bay. "Go fetch, Fenn."

I roll my eyes. My first job here, and I'm only a glorified bird dog. But this isn't about me anymore. It's about Callandra and making things right for her. I think of her when she was three years old, with curly brown hair and a red mouth stained with brickberry juice. That was the first time she saw me, the first time her little hands reached for her big brother. Back then, I was the good guy. The sentiment didn't last. I need to bring it back.

Right now, I need to obey.

I take a first, squishy step forward onto the *Calathus's* bioskin floor. By God, this ship is really creeping me out.

"They say that the ship can see and hear everything you do." Miki grimaces. "It can even taste you."

Oh God. "Is it even safe to—"

"GO!" The entire group behind me yells.

"Fine!" I yell back.

I jog forward through the exit. There's a door on the right and a long corridor on the left. Walking on Cyclo is like running on a really freaking huge hamster wheel—it's spinning slowly and creating gravity, but you don't walk on the flat plane of the ship. You walk on the inside edge. There are periodic corridors that go up to another level, with either steps or sliding handrails. Weird.

The right-hand door nearby is disappearing as a thin membrane closes toward the center, an open oval pinching shut rapidly. I hope it doesn't grow teeth at the last minute, because I jump through the aperture just in time.

On the other side is a long, curving corridor, bright blue, with windows strangely set in the floor as well as the walls. I can see the *Selkirk* embedded awkwardly in the side of the *Calathus*, as if it were more of a crash landing than a docking. But I can also see the windows of the craft further down, just as the girl whips around a corner and into a corridor blinking bright green at the edges. But I'm close. Very close. If I don't get her, ReCOR might rescind my contract, and then I would die for nothing. I can't have that happen.

I dart forward, barreling down the hallway. There's a door I didn't realize was there, with another green, membranous aperture closing fast. I jump through it, and there she is. The girl is not a fast runner, thank the stars. She slows down to dart into a room that looks like someone's living quarters, and that's all I need. I leap forward, grab her small waist in both hands and we both crash onto the floor. The girl shrieks.

"Hey. Hey! I don't want to hurt you. I just need you to stop running. We need to know why you're here." I feel the lie filling my head, even as I say it. "We…just want to help."

The girl freezes, and her eyes go from squeezed shut to peeking at me—as if I am the brightest starlight she's ever seen, and I'm going to burn her retinas out. I can feel her breathing, fast, quick, small-animal breaths, and her eyes study me. She says nothing, but licks her dry lips and keeps staring. This is actually the first time I've been this close to a human girl, ever, and my body just realized this. My neck is suddenly sweltering, and I feel a flash of heat down to my toes. *God, calm down, Fenn. Calm down. Say something, at least.*

"Do you...do you understand me? Krkshik?" I try a different language. "Brawna? Uh, how about Parlez-vous Francais?"

"Get off me," she says in the smallest voice.

"Okay, so you speak English."

"Get off me," she repeats. After a beat, she raises her face closer to mine. She's looking at my lips and getting closer and closer. What the hell is she doing? Is she trying to kiss me?

I squeeze her waist tighter, in case this is a ploy to trick me somehow, but weirdly I'm having trouble feeling my fingertips. A strange numbness starts to creep over my hands and up my arms and legs. The girl is still looking at my lips, but now she's smiling.

"Never mind," she whispers. Suddenly, she slips right out of my hands, which have very quickly stopped working. She wriggles away from me, and next thing I know, my knees are glued inextricably to the floor. I look left and right and see that the blue matrix of the room has risen up like goo and encircled my limbs. It hasn't touched the girl at all, allowing her to scramble away from me. My body slowly melds downward, and the blood-warm floor starts to rise up against my cheek, near my mouth, coming close to my nostrils.

I yell, but there is only a tangled noise at the back of my throat. This ship, this goddamned gooey liquid thing, is trying to smother me. It's going to kill me any second. All I can see is the wall and the floor rising over my cheekbones to eat me alive, when bare feet plant themselves in my field of vision, ever-so-slightly pressing into the soft floor.

"Help!" I holler. Before I can stop myself, I cry out, "Callandra!" My sister. God, I've only just got here, and I've already failed. Callandra, I'm so sorry.

"What's Callandra?" the girl asks.

I gurgle in response. My chest is frozen in place, and I

can't take a deep breath.

The girl steps closer, and she studies the color flashes around me and through the goo encasing me. "I guess that's a complicated answer. You should know, Cyclo is not trying to kill you." Her voice is less high, more relaxed now. "She thinks you're in distress and you need to calm down." She stoops low, her hair tickling my forehead. "Were you really trying to help me? Don't lie. She'll know if you're lying."

The flashes of color come so quickly in the matrix around me, I can barely register them. A rainbow of hues, plus muted shades, too. I remember that the translators embedded in the walls of the ship aren't working, so I have no idea what this goddamn ship is saying. Most of my body is numb. Somehow, this thing has managed to transfer some sort of anesthetic into me.

"Ah," she says. Her finger touches my forehead, ever so gently. "Only partly lying. Hm. Afraid. And lonely, too, I see."

Despite my weakness, I writhe violently. Damn it. No one has a right to read my mind if I don't want it. This ship is seriously pissing me off, even though it seems to be obeying the girl like it's some sort of humongous jellied pet of hers. She seems to read the distress in my eyes as the ship itself has gone back to a placid blue color.

"Let him go, Cyclo."

At her command, I can feel the goo begin to retreat. My skin starts to prickle painfully all over as sensation returns. As soon as I can, I get to my knees, forcing air in and out of my chest. The blue matrix is still covering my lower legs. My whole body feels like needles and rubber. Finally, I can breathe normally. I don't know whether to thank her or yell at her.

"What is Callandra?" she asks again, now that I can speak.

"Not what, who."

"All right then. Who is Callandra?"

"None of your goddamned business," I growl.

"Where is my mother, Dr. Um?" she asks.

Before I can grunt that I know nothing about her parental problems, a shout issues from down the corridor. My calves are still entwined with the floor when Gammand rushes into the room.

He takes one look at the girl standing there, and me half submerged in the ship, and aims a gun straight at the girl. Where the hell did he get a weapon?

"No! Wait!" I holler, trying to hold up my hand. But it's too late. Gammand pulls the trigger, his face icy and calm, and I hear a *pfft* as something flies over my head. The walls and floor of the room flash a bright, blood-red color. At first, I think the walls are actually bleeding, but the color blanches to white. For one eternal second, the girl looks at me with an expression that chills me straight through, like somehow, I've broken a promise I never actually made. Like I just broke her heart.

And then her eyes roll up into her head, and she collapses onto the floor.

Chapter Five

HANA

Oh, my body.

It hurts all over. I've never felt pain like this before. My muscles feel battered, and my joints are like twisted, stiff paper. This is what wakes me up, the pain, not the gentle unfolding of consciousness that I usually experience, sleeping within Cyclo's matrix. Instead of oxygen being buffed into my skin with blood-warm gel around me, my body is in the open air. The angled contours of my body rest on a hard, cold, surface, and my eyelids seem glued shut. I am ravenous, thirsty, and my bladder is uncomfortably full.

I'm breathing. I'm alive. But everything feels awful. Worst of all, I am wretchedly rootless without Cyclo surrounding me. I have never, ever woken up like this, so separated from my Cyclo.

There are murmurs nearby. I keep my eyes closed, pretending to sleep.

"It should be wearing off by now. It's been almost thirty-six hours," a voice says. A young male voice. It's smooth and warm, and reminds me of the boy who tackled me, which makes my lip twitch. "Did you see that? I think she moved."

Warm fingertips encase my wrist. It's a strong hand, larger than mine. Against my will, my heart rate increases.

"How much sedative did he give her?" This voice is from a girl, but she sounds angry.

"Gammand said it was enough to drop a hundred-and-fifty-kilo male." The hand releases me gently. Inwardly, I frown.

"That's a three-fold overdose. Maybe she won't wake up. Good. Less work for us to do."

"Shut up, Miki."

Then, silence.

I try to stay still, but I'm fully awake now, and I'm itching to stretch my sore legs and shoulders. How very odd, that when I need to stay still, all my body wishes to do is the opposite. I crack open one eye, and the bright light triggers a tickle in my nose.

I sneeze violently, bolt upright, and a scorching sensation tears down my aching back. I nearly pee without wanting to. "Ooww."

"Good morning to you, too."

The boy who tackled me, and the blue girl, wider and larger than three of me, stand several feet away. Both have their arms crossed. The boy wears a reluctant, tiny smile, but the girl only scowls at me.

"Where is my mother?" I ask.

"Your mother? Who's your mother?" the boy asks. "Why didn't you evacuate with the *Calathus* crew?"

The girl moves in front of the boy and blinks purposefully. A hologram of data shows up in front of her face, like a visor-shell of glowing green information. It scrolls too fast for me to read, and it's backward for me, at that. There's some sort of red bar graph on the edge that's got only a sliver of green at the bottom. "What's your name? Your universal ID?" Her voice is deep and biting. "The Morpho recognition program does not have you registered in its database. Your DNA is unregistered, too."

So while I slept, they scanned my face and took tissues samples without my permission. Should I say that I don't exist because I'm not supposed to? I open my mouth and shut it again, unsure.

"We don't know who your mother is. I thought I heard you say her name. Doctor something?" the boy asks.

I shouldn't have asked. Won't it get her in trouble? Won't it get me in trouble? But I'm already in trouble, and there are other problems. And these problems are staring at me right now.

"Why are you here?" I ask instead.

This time, they are the ones staying silent. "Doran," the blue girl says. The reverse face of an elderly man—blue like the girl—shows up on her holo visor. "The girl is awake. I'm going to my post to start my phase two. We've already attached the last fifty scanners on the ship. Fenn will finish up the examination." She shuts off her holo visor and heads for the door.

The boy, Fenn, looks angry. "What examination, Miki? I'm no doctor. I have my work to do, too, you know. Why do I always get stuck—"

"The protocol's in your files, Fenn." She winks at him. "You studied it a month ago. Just get it done." She heads to the door. "Remember, we've known you for nine months. And it only took one month before we all figured out your bullshit." She grins. "Have fun babysitting."

Miki leaves before Fenn can say anything further.

"I am not a baby," I tell him. He ignores me, so I add, "I am sixteen years, ten months, and five days old." I think for a second. "Perhaps six days."

He ignores me and murmurs angrily with his back to me.

I go to the tiny lavatory in the room to relieve myself, and I return to find him fiddling with an oblong, rounded box, touching the keypads on it here and there. It must be taking readings of my biometrics, because he keeps tapping away. Curiously, he wears a wristwatch. A completely unnecessary item to have when time is embedded into any ship or piece of equipment anywhere.

"Is it mechanical?" I ask.

"What?"

"Your watch."

He looks up at me, surprised. He smiles quickly, before extinguishing it, as if afraid to show happiness. "Yes. It is."

"Automatic? Or manual?"

He smiles again, this time without restraint. "It's manual. I like having to wind it myself. It's not quite right—off by about a second a day. Needs a thorough cleaning. You know what a watch is?"

"Yes. I've a habit of studying old Earth culture. I like… cooking."

The boy beams. "Me, too. I mean, I wish I could cook. For real."

"And I like knitting. And writing. On paper. Mother did, too."

"I made paper once," the boy says. His eyes are alight, as if he's only just woken up for the day, though he's been technically awake all this time. "So you're an antiquist, like me. Why do you like it?"

"It's interesting," I say. "Well, and also…I am establishing myself as a person knowledgeable in a vast number of subjects."

He laughs. "You sound like you're applying for a job."

"I do really love antiquist things, but it helps if they think I'm useful."

"Who?"

"The crew of the ship. That is, when I was going to meet them." I frown. All that preparation, for nothing.

"What are you saying? That if they don't like you, they'd… get rid of you?"

I say nothing, but of course, that's the fear.

"You don't need to prove your worth to exist," he says. And the words are a small supernova in my mind. What? How could that be? How could I possibly *not* need to prove my worth on this ship, when I was never allowed to exist to begin with? He can't possibly be correct on this.

As if remembering something, he frowns. "Uh, I need to… it says you have some contusions. I need to examine them."

I'm still wearing my robe, and only that. "Oh."

He reaches for my arm and stops. "May I…is okay if I examine your skin?"

"Why not? You didn't have a problem tackling me," I comment.

He looks hurt. "I'm sorry. But you were running away, and we had no idea what…who…if you were a threat."

"I thought that when people run away, it's because they're trying *not* to attack you," I reason.

He meets my eye, but I don't back down. "I'm sorry if I hurt you. I was only following orders."

Something in his eye catches my attention. "You don't like following orders, do you?"

"No," he admits. It seems to pain him to give me the answer. "Do you?"

I think for a second. I haven't needed to resist anything. I always knew that when I met Cyclo's crew, I would be the most obedient crew member. Docility would make me likable, and that would make me worth keeping. I've had plenty of practice. All I've ever done is what Cyclo and Mother tell me. They've always had my best interests at heart.

Haven't they? If so, why did I get left behind?

"See? Not so easy to answer, is it?" He reaches for my wrist. "May I?"

I hesitate. The skin of my right forearm has a purpling color on the tender inside that extends to my wrist. My fingers feel slightly swollen, too. He watches me with large eyes lined with dark lashes. The color of his irises is different from Mother's and mine. Ours are brown with a rim of black encircling them. His is more a mix of amber and ebony, light in the centers. I decide that I would like to see his eyes better, so I extend my arm.

"All right."

He shifts closer on the hard bench that I've been lying on. With both hands, he takes my arm and carefully turns it this way and that. He lifts the data recorder and punches a few more keys. Those tiny amber flecks in his eyes are nice. In Cyclo's language, it means curiosity.

"You had some bleeding beneath the skin. It's bruising, but far more than normal. It looks like your clotting is sluggish. Your vitamin K levels are low. Iron, selenium, zinc...all low." When he releases my arm, I shift away from him and can't help but wince.

"What's the matter?"

"My back hurts," I say without thinking.

"Where?"

I untie the front of my robe and turn away, lowering the fabric so my whole back is exposed. The boy inhales sharply. His fingertips gently touch my spine between my shoulder blades, then trace down to the small of my back. I shiver.

"Your back is a map of bruises. Looks like Pangaea." He pauses. "Pangaea is—"

"I know what Pangaea is. The supercontinent on Earth during the Paleozoic era."

"Mesozoic," he corrects me.

I look over my bare shoulder to stare him down. "Cyclo, please tell us the correct era in which Pangaea existed on Earth."

To my left, the blue matrix mounds up and involutes to form a mouth. "Pangaea spanned both the late Paleozoic and early Mesozoic era. You are both right and wrong."

"It talks?" Fenn asks. His body goes tight, as if ready to run. "I didn't know it spoke. They said it just flashed colors. They said—"

"They probably say a lot of things about Cyclo," I say, a bit defensively. His hand is still on the small of my back. "Are you done?"

"Oh. Yes." The hand disappears, leaving an imprint of warmth that disappears quickly. Disappointingly fast. "You probably need some vitamin infusions to correct your deficiencies."

Deficiencies. I don't want to talk about them because they are too vast to list. But I know what he means. "I don't need vitamins. Cyclo gives me everything I need." I pull my robe back on and cinch it tightly around my waist. I stand to face him, but I'm so wobbly. My vision flashes white, then black, before returning to normal.

"Whoa." He stands to steady me, very close. "Well, apparently that's not true. You're anemic. That's why you're dizzy. Look, we know that the ship was responsible for keeping its passengers fed and healthy all the time, but the ship is probably running out of nutrients, which means you are, too, if that's how you get fed."

Running out of nutrients? Cyclo never told me such a thing. Lately, I'd been spending my spare time learning about Cyclo's birth—not the current status of her health. If I had, maybe I'd have known that the crew were going to leave.

How thoughtless of me. This is the kind of thing that would prove I'm not worthy of being a member. The thought hurts me somewhere near my stomach, a real ache, and I put my hands there.

What if my hidden requirements ended up cannibalizing everyone else's? Maybe I've been taking more than my fair share, and there was a good reason I should never have been born.

I feel terrible.

The door behind us opens. A tall Prinniad walks in, clad in a black uniform similar to the others. Her eyes are red as rubies; her legs end somewhere around my chest. Her skull shows a golden tattoo. Every humanoid I see in person is an utter surprise. I want to run my hands over her face to feel the texture of her skin, to follow the outlines of the gold tattoo. I hold my breath, waiting to hear what her voice sounds like.

She looks at the boy, smiles a little black-gummed, toothless smile, and stares at me sternly.

"Our remote group leader wants a word." Her voice is... not what I was expecting. She seems rather irritated to be in the room with me.

A visor hologram also shows up in front of her face, projected from an implant in her forehead that I now realize the boy has, too. She grasps the hologram with her fingertips, spins it around, and expands it so that I can look at the image. I've seen holograms before, but none that wanted to speak with me.

It's a hologram of an elderly gentleman, sitting who knows where—possibly systems away—behind a desk. A ReCOR logo is behind his head. I know ReCOR—they are the company that made Cyclo, and for them, I am so very grateful. He must be here to help Cyclo, then.

He has a white beard, white hair, with crinkly blue eyes

surrounded by lots of wrinkles.

"Hello! So you're finally awake." His tone is gentle, and the timbre is deep and resonant. I like it. It makes me think of photos of the Grand Canyon. "My name is Aldred Doran. I'm in charge of the *Selkirk* crew from my station of BT-78i, and I suppose I'm in charge of you, too, now." He smiles, and I immediately warm to him even though he is so far away. The blue of his eyes is just like Cyclo's happy blue. "I have some questions to ask. Please, sit." He motions to the bench, but until yesterday I have never been in a room with more than one other human, and I don't like the odds, even if he is not really here.

I lean back against the wall, touching it lightly and letting my fingertips sink into the gel. Cyclo responds, oozing forward a large bubble of matrix, and I sink into it as it supports my back and arms. A high-backed chair forms to lift me up. Flicking my eyes left and right, I see that Cyclo has made me a replica of the historic British monarchy's coronation throne, down to the lion's feet. She has done this for me in the past, and she knows how much I find it amusing, to be on a faux throne. Surrounded by her, I feel safer. I curl my legs under me, and my knees stick out like two bread buns.

Looking down at the hologram and the Prinniad and the boy, I ask timidly, "What questions did you wish to ask me?"

The Prinniad and Fenn exchange uncomfortable glances with each other.

"Let's start with your name, for one," Doran asks.

I guess there is no hiding anymore. If I am going to find out what happened with Mother, I will need help.

"'All compromise is based on give and take.' Mahatma Ghandi," I quote in not much more than a whisper. They exchange glances again. I should probably just tell them, then. "My name is Hana…" I pause here, as Cyclo flashes a silver-tinged pink iridescence around me. "…Um."

"What was that?" the boy asks, pointing at the fading pink on the wall. "What does that mean?"

"That is my middle name." Cyclo flashes it again. It is what she calls me when she is not phonating. A color she has made for me, and me alone. *It is moonbeams and orchids at dawn,* is how my mother described it. I had to look up all these pictures to understand what she said, but together, they were supposedly more extraordinary than the separate images. Finally, she found an object that described the color. Something born of an amorphous mollusk on Earth, whose innards look like mucous and shell, like ages-old rock. An oyster, it's called. And the item within, a pearl. It's the color that isn't one color. Mother gave me a silver necklace to wear with a very old pearl pendant that belonged to her great-grandmother.

I touch it now, to remind me who I am, and to soothe myself. The iridescent nacre wears off bit by bit from all my fiddling, and when I sleep, Cyclo places another layer of nacre on to keep it lustrous.

"I see. Hana…" The hologram pauses for the flash. "Hana Um. And your mother?" Doran asks.

"Dr. Yoonsil Um. But she went by Yoona, for short. She has a blue lotus tattoo on her arm," I say, showing my own forearm and swirling my fingertip to show where it was, the blue tissue of Cyclo's own matrix embedded in Mother's skin. It was beautiful. It would glow faintly all the time, a gleaming symbol of how together they parented me from the day I was one cell big.

"Why do you have no universal ID? Why is your DNA not registered?"

I go quiet. If I tell the truth, Mother will get in trouble. And I will be in trouble. But I'm already in trouble. The rules about me living my secret are too difficult to break. Instead, I point to the boy.

"What's his full name?" Cyclo flashes a tiny sliver of sparkling white to tell me I'm being rude by pointing. I put my finger down.

Doran looks at the boy, who takes his hands out of his pockets, where they've been stuffed since this inquisition began.

"Fennec."

"That is a fox," I say.

He raises his eyebrows, and the corner of his mouth twitches up in a quirky grin. I believe that means I am correct. After a long silence, the boy—Fenn—repeats the question. "Why isn't your DNA registered?"

I look away.

"Doesn't anyone know you're here?"

"No," I say, eyes still trained on the wall.

"Did you hide here on purpose?"

"No," I say again.

"I see. Curious." Doran rubs his grizzled chin. "She's unregistered. Probably born in secret on the ship. I've heard of such things. There's a steep penalty, which explains why she was hidden. And now she's been left behind so that the secret can stay a secret."

No. She wouldn't. She couldn't. "She didn't leave me behind," I tell him. "It's just a mistake. I think. I need you to contact her and let her know of my status." Cyclo flashes a faint iridescent white behind their heads again. Oh. I'm being impolite. "Please," I add.

"I understand you want to find her. But you also must understand, we have our own directives and must complete them. This is no search and rescue mission."

"Directive? What directive?"

"To document the demise of the *Calathus,* of course."

My skin prickles with goose bumps. "Demise," I repeat, tonelessly.

"Yes. You do know that this ship is dying? That the being you call Cyclo has, in fact, reached its terminal status?"

I look at Fenn, who nods. His shoulders slump as if this information causes him pain, though he is not surprised.

"No. That can't be. No," I say, but the memory of the brown dot and its acid on my fingertip flits through my mind. I grip the handrests of Cyclo's chair, but she doesn't throb back any warmth. Oh God. She knows. This is no surprise to her, either, but since I never asked... I have done nothing but immerse myself in Cyclo's past, not present, lately. "No one told me." My voice grows smaller. "Oh God. Mother never told me."

Chapter Six

FENN

Sitting high on her sapphire throne, the girl—Hana—looks utterly lost. She looks older now, and her face contorts with fleeting emotions. Confusion. Sadness. But there's one overriding emotion that, lately, I've recognized in myself: fear.

"Portia and Fenn," Doran says, "I've another meeting. Finish the inquiry and file a report. We'll discuss later."

Without so much as a goodbye, Doran disappears from Portia's visor.

"You have to tell us what you know," Portia says, her voice slightly whistling and unemotional. "We don't have communication with the parting ships."

"You can't speak to Cyclo's crew?" she asks. She squeezes the armrests of her blue throne, and it starts to shrink under her. She lands a toe and then her whole foot on the floor. She stands there, hands at her sides, looking helpless as the blob of blue chair sinks back into the floor.

"No, we can't."

"How much time does Cyclo have left to live?" she asks.

Portia answers, "We can estimate how long the ship has to live, though our estimates can be quite off. But the

Calathus has no more than a few weeks before it's completely uninhabitable. That was when we landed. We've already been here thirty-six hours."

At this, my heart starts to pound. Why doesn't it ever get any easier to hear the truth? To know my own mortal timeline? Instinctively, my hand goes to the metal pendant hanging from my neck. I still haven't watched the hologram message from Callandra. I'm still not ready.

"Our directive is very clear," I say. "This is a data-gathering mission, with huge amounts we need to collect every day, or else…" I don't want to get into our contracts, and the death benefit, and the fact that if I don't fulfill it, Callandra may not be able to afford her own life.

"I need to speak to my mother," she says.

"I don't think that's possible." Portia gives me a warning glance.

"If you don't think, then it's possible," she says.

Her words hang in the air as we try to make sense of them.

Portia sighs. "You ought to eat something. Fenn, bring her to the mess hall when she's ready. She looks malnourished for a human."

"I need to speak to my mother. I need to speak to Dr. Um," Hana says again.

My face gets hot. I don't have time for this. And that makes me angry because I would like to help her. I actually would. God, what's happened to me? I haven't time to care about anything but the mission. Even without the watch that's strapped to my wrist, I'm keenly aware of seconds ticking by, of hours I'm losing that I'll never ever get back. A smarter, more spiritual person would find some solace and profound meaning in each moment from here to the end of my life. Me, all I feel is the desperation of frantically trying to fulfill my contract. Which, by the way, I've barely started because of her.

Since she was tranquilized, all I've done is unpack the supplies into our makeshift headquarters on the ship's bridge, place a dozen data scanners around the ship for data gathering, and babysit. By now, when I pop open my holofeed, it shows I'm barely over 5 percent done. According to my requirements, I should have done at least half a dozen drone tests already. And I haven't. Three weeks, they thought we'd have. But already, we need more like six, and we don't have six weeks.

I'm no babysitter. If there's no protocol for this, well hell, there's no protocol. I think of Callandra. She's the only person that matters.

When we were little, I was the one who caught her after she fell climbing a boulder near our home. I'd fetch her from the bioluminescent caves that are everywhere on Ipineq, before the sun set and the cave scorpions got too hungry. And with every stint away from home, she'd only asked me for a small thing—a souvenir from my "travels," be it detention or military schools or a drone-thievery run. So I'd bring back tiny geodes from planet Ursulina, or a crystal that littered the ground around the juvenile detention on Ipineq's moon. It was the least I could do.

I think of her struggling to walk again, and anger boils inside. Her accident is my fault. Her life depends on me and this mission. There's no room for anyone else.

"I can't help you," I say. "I'm going to get my dinner."

I exit the room, but the web aperture doesn't close behind me. I don't know my way around the ship very well, except that it's circular. I blink twice, and the minuscule holofeed chip on my forehead turns on my holo dashboard, laid atop reality before my face. Gammand had it updated with my tasks, convo channels, and Cyclo's map. It's now live with the information streaming from the data scanners all over the ship.

If I keep going in one direction, eventually I'll find the

mess hall. Walking on the slightly squishy floor is taking me some time to get used to. The gravity here is not quite equal to Ipineq, my home planet. I come from a short-statured family, and the gravity was 1.2 times that of Earth's, which meant growing up in detention on lesser g-force planets, I ended up being the tallest person ever in the Actias family.

Every ten feet or so, an irregular window on the right shows up. Long and narrow at times, wide at others, they are embedded with a clear plastrix so I can see out to space—vast, black, glittering with stars and the Merope nebula nearby. It's beautiful. My parents would tell me, while I was away, how much my sister loved space. So much that she wants to spend her entire life flitting from one place to another. She had pilot's genes in her, just like our parents. I suppose I got them, too, though I pilot drones, not ships. My parents would tell me she was acing her tests in the junior academy. She's the smart one.

I'm the screw-up. It had started when I was ten. I'd stolen my first nano drone and had flown it into the left ear of my astrophysics teacher. I thought it was funny; it wasn't so funny when she lost hearing in that ear from the high-resonance damage I'd caused. That was when I was kicked out of Nystrade Academy, a free school, which meant my family had to pay to educate me, and that meant less money for Callandra.

Somewhere around the fifth school and third stint in juvenile detention on various planets, my parents were drained of resources. Callandra had a future thanks to scholarships, but scholarships don't take you to the most elite academies. I'd basically throttled all her hopes of being the brightest and the best. But I just couldn't say no when a new scheme popped up, each seemingly more lucrative and more of a sure thing than the last. Stealing was too alluring. And I was good at it. In school, I failed. In thievery, I was an incandescent, if intermittent, success, flickering farther and farther away from Callandra.

When Callandra was fifteen, my parents had found a great mining job for me on Ipineq, one that would ignore my police record and give me a chance. I could earn money for the family, legitimate money. I was all set to fly back for this job, loathing the idea, when I remembered my promise to Callandra to bring her back something from my travels. So I took one quick side job—stealing silver-gold electrum alloy pellets from a passing ship. One of those pellets would make a great little gift for her, and the money might help pay for her next year of school. And then our getaway ship was caught.

I didn't show up on the first day.

So Callandra did, lying about her age and promising my parents she'd study at night to finish her schooling. She was two weeks in when her mining drover fell into a magnesium crevasse.

When I heard, I was already back in prison. And all I could think of was her when she was eight years old, the first time I'd been sent away to detention. This helpless look. Her huge brown eyes said it all.

What have you done?

Why do you keep leaving? Why can't you help me?

Vaguely, it reminds me of the girl, just as I'd left her in that room by herself. *I can't help you,* I'd said. Pretty typical Fenn words. I can't help being who I am. And I'm still so angry for being me.

I stop walking and see the dazzling stars pass lazily across the windows, though I'm the one who's really spinning. Perspective is a bitch.

I sigh and turn around. It only takes me a few minutes to reach the room where I'd left her. She's still sitting there on that hard bench, looking at her feet. Well, her feet encased in blue matrix. The ship looks like it's eating her feet.

"What are you doing?" I ask.

Her head whips up. "You came back."

I smirk. "It's not like I can leave the ship."

"I can't, either." Her face is strained with pain.

"Let me get you unstuck. You need to eat something."

"I'm not stuck," she says. "It's okay, Cyclo. I'll be all right."

The blue material slowly slithers away from her calves and ankles, until it evens out as the floor beneath her, nearly solid.

"What was it doing?"

"Comforting me," she says.

I raise my left eyebrow. "By eating you?"

"Cyclo was infusing me with some dopamine. She knew I was sad. I needed a boost."

"So she dopes you up with neurotransmitters through your toes whenever you're off? You must be pretty fragile."

Something about how my words bite makes her frown. "I'm fine." She stands, still wearing that robe of hers. She needs some real clothes. "Where is the rest of the crew?"

"You probably know better than I do. They're in the south mess hall. But first, you should get dressed."

She looks down at her robe, which is stained a little from me tackling her, being the dirty space rat that I am. "All right."

She walks out the door and heads down the opposite hall. As I follow her, I notice how weirdly she walks. Her stride is short, like something is tethering her knees together. It's stiff, too. I can see the boniness of her shoulders through the thin fabric of her robe. After about five minutes, she stops walking. I'm about to ask her why we've stopped, when I realize she's panting.

"Hey. What's wrong?"

She leans against the wall, eyes closed. "I'm not...used to this much...walking," she says between deep breaths. "I need Cyclo. I need to sleep again."

"You need a steak and more exercise," I mutter.

She gives me a nasty look and pushes her white forelock back. Her voice is deeper now than before, calmer. "You're rude."

I smile. I have no idea why, but her comment is so on point, it's funny. I am rude.

"Stop laughing at me," she adds.

I put my hands up. "Who's laughing?"

She keeps walking. We pass by the docking bays, the northwest mess halls, and a bunch of empty laboratories. Soon, she takes a right turn into a windowless corridor that's pretty bare—a few doors, and fewer of the technical rooms I'd seen in the other quadrant.

"Where are we?"

"Northeast quadrant alpha," she gasps. "Here. My room." She touches the membrane door, and it shrinks away rapidly. I don't go in.

Already, I can see the ship's matrix snaking up over her ankles, and the girl is getting a fuzzy look in her eyes. "Hey. Tell it to stop that."

"But she'll help me breathe," she says.

"There's plenty of oxygen in the ship's air." I point to the readouts whizzing by on my holofeed. "We're at twenty-one percent oxygen here. Totally normal for a human. What is it with you and this ship?"

She shrugs. "All of the crew did this. We rely on Cyclo for our recalibration."

"Look. I'm really hungry." I want to say "I don't have time for this," but I'm starting to sound like a broken audio clip, so I keep my lips shut.

Hana looks at her feet, and the goo recedes again. The door membrane starts to constrict closed, and I wait. Vaguely, from behind the thin membrane, I can see her shedding the robe, her pale-skinned body walking here and there, bending and putting on clothing. It's fuzzy enough that I can't see details but clear enough to see that she's got curves on a straight figure, like one of those zero-g aerialists. My face flushes.

"Oh, shut up and shut it down," I tell my body.

The last thing I need on this trip is a distraction. And it looks like the distraction is, unfortunately, very pretty and very weird, in a way that makes me want to spend more time with her. Except that the time left I have to live is already slipping swiftly away.

Just my luck.

Chapter Seven

HANA

I can see him on the other side of the door, pacing. Once in a while, his head tilts up and attempts to see through our membrane of separation. I cannot imagine what he thinks of me.

I've always wondered what the crew thought—simple, everyday thoughts of banality. Those would be exciting for me. Do they worry about keeping their toenails trimmed? What does hunger feel like for them—it is also a knotted gnawing? Have they been to Paris in their Cyclo-supported dreams?

And now there is this boy who holds disdain for my very existence. He's so irritated by my weakness, which infuriates me. It's not my fault that I've been safely tucked in my room for my protection. My muscles are weaker from the lack of gravity equivalencies that perhaps he's had. Somehow, it makes me angry when I'm around him. It makes my pulse a little faster and my blood a little warmer.

It makes me feel a little more alive.

I've put on a pair of slim leggings and a loose tunic, and my hair is captured into a knot on the top of my head. My stomach rumbles, and I ache to go back into the walls for

Cyclo's nourishment, or at least a good steaming, milky, hot bowl of seolleongtang—mother's recipe of synthetic bone broth soup. But they want me to go eat in front of the rest of this pirate crew. Like a pig at a trough, it would seem.

I look at the trunk full of all of our precious things. Mother never would have left these behind. Not on purpose. That is, unless she left them for me as a gift. Or a message. But these thoughts only confuse me more.

Cyclo flashes a few colors for my benefit. Grassy green, mixed with iridescent yellow. She wants me to know she is concerned, and that she is here to be my place of safety.

I should be more brave. Cyclo is everywhere, no matter where I go on this ship. She is here for me. I can literally sink into her at a moment's notice if I feel unsafe. This makes me braver.

I touch the membrane of the door, and it shrinks away. The boy, Fenn, stands at attention when he sees me.

"Your hair looks like ice cream," he blurts. As soon as he says it, he hastily adds, "Never mind."

I touch the knot of hair on my head. He probably sees my white forelock is twisted against black.

"Mother gave me these colors. She said it would make me different from everyone she's ever known." I always thought that Mother wanted me to make an impression on the crew the day I was revealed. *See,* she might say. *See how lovely her hair is. See how special I made her.*

"That seems unnecessary. Everyone is already different from everyone else."

"They are?" I ask.

Fenn rolls his eyes. I believe that means that I have a lot to learn. Not much time to learn it, either, apparently—which breaks me a little. Sadness rises up like a cold hand around my throat. I would root right here and fall into the blue of the ship if I could, but this will not bring Mother back. This won't save me right now. Fenn looks at me with an inscrutable expression. He seems somewhat sickened by my sadness, and I have no idea how to process that. But then, his eyes fall to my feet.

"Where are your shoes?"

"I don't wear shoes. I cannot fathom always having something between me and Cyclo."

"Don't you sit in chairs?"

"My feet still touch the ground."

"Don't you sleep on a bed?"

"No. I sleep inside Cyclo."

Again, that look. He tries to find the words to respond to this, then shakes his head. "Let's go," he says.

We walk a full semicircle around the alpha ring, not speaking, not looking out the windows, until I notice the scent of a wheaten product, cooked plainly.

"The mess hall must be close."

"I believe so," I say.

"Don't you know?" he says, stopping his walk to stare at me again.

"Well, I have the layout of Cyclo memorized. It's about thirty feet away. But…" I pause. "I've never seen this room. I've always been confined to my own."

"Always?" His left eyebrow rises again.

"Always."

He takes a step back. "Is the first time you've even been in this hallway?" he asks, incredulous.

I look down. It's the same blue as the rest of the ship. But everything is new, and yet not new. I know there are crew rooms here, and a small engineering room ten feet back. But…

"I have never been here before."

I say the words with shame. I am a stranger in my home,

the only home I've known. What must it be like, to be a bee that has only ever lived within one prismatic hexagonal cell? Not seen the rest of the hive, nor touched the blue sky, or anything green or pink-petaled?

"Didn't you ever try to leave?"

"No," I say. The look on Fenn's face is shocking. It is flooded with pity and incredulousness. Also, disgust.

"Oh," I say slowly. "You think I'm foolish. You think I'm…" What's the word? "Ignorant. Unintelligent."

"Well…"

"Gullible. Witless. Naive—"

"That's enough," he cuts me off. "It's not my job to figure out your life story, or how you got here."

"Then why do you keep asking me questions?"

He goes silent. Down the hallway, Miki peeks her blue head out from a door.

"There you are. Come get some dinner. We were going to send Gammand after you, it's been so long."

We both walk forward. "It's only been about thirty-five minutes," I remark.

"Thirty-five less minutes of my life," Fenn says under his breath.

This is meant as some sort of smear on me, somehow, but I don't know how to unravel his meaning before we enter the mess hall. In the room, the three crew members sit around a vast oval table. Bowls and plates of food are scattered here and there. The Prinniad girl, Portia, sits before a bowlful of something that looks like grape diamonds and earthworms. Miki sits before a bowl of shapeless food that is very dark gray. She eats her food daintily, with a spoon that is far too small for her fist.

"You've met Miki and Portia. This is Gammand Sadozai."

He motions to the tall young man with the creamy brown

skin and dark hair. He looks human, for sure, except for a set of dark, shiny spots that run down either side of his neck. Oh, he's Gragorian, a humanoid that has a lot of similarities to Earth humans. There has been a lot of human and Gragorian mixing in the last century, so it's hard to tell these days who is whom. He would be handsome, but there is something about his eyes that's unsettling. He doesn't look at me.

"You're the one who shot me," I say.

Gammand raises an eyebrow to confirm this, with eyes still on his food. "Following orders."

The Prinniad steps forth. "We haven't formally met. I am Portia Ynnatryb, of Prinnia." She sits down again and smiles at me with big, black toothless gums. Her eyes are a stunning red, and I long to look at them closer. I take a step and start to reach for her face, when Portia raises a fist in response. Everyone's eyes widen a little.

I am learning that is a sign that I'm doing something not quite right, so I lower my hands.

Fenn looks relieved. Did he think there would be bloodshed of some sort, like elephant seal males having a battle? He waves at the table. "You should eat. Here, help yourself."

I sit down and regarding the mush of brown and khaki porridge before me. It smells like yeast and the telltale metallic note of vitamins and synthetic protein. I pick up a spoon and dip it in, sniffing. The metallic odor is awful. I put it down, and the spoon slops onto the porridge.

After a chew and swallow, Miki says, "Everyone has slightly different nutrient needs, but my guess is that you're *Homo sapiens*, so that should do."

"I am *Homo sapiens novum*," I say.

"Oh. You're a non-wild type," Gammand says, uninterested. He means any human or humanoid that was lab-created, or wasn't conceived "in the wild," so to speak. There are a lot of us, apparently, in the universe, and those that aren't tinkered with are "playing with fire," my mother once said. Too many mutations to leave up to chance.

"Eat," Miki says.

Something in her tone reminds me of Mother, so I immediately pick up the spoon and shovel a portion into my mouth. It's pasty and gooey and tastes cloyingly sweet. There's tangy iron and chalky calcium supplements in here, plus fat-soluble vitamins that are mixed in with the lipid globules. I force it down. I relentlessly gulp spoonful after spoonful until I realize that everyone in the room is staring at me.

"What?" I say, mouth full of porridge.

"You're very obedient," Mika says. It's not a compliment, as evidenced by the disgust on her face.

"Don't take it personally," Fenn says, smiling. "We're all lawbreakers here." He elbows Miki, and Miki elbows him back, and he nearly falls off his chair, she's so strong.

"But she said to eat," I say, pointing at Miki.

"Oh, good blurtzh," Portia says. "What are we supposed to do with this?"

"Eat it," I say. How can she not understand that?

"She means you," Fenn whispers to me.

Oh. What are they going to do with me. As in, I'm a problem. I'm in the way. Mother isn't here to speak for me, to tell me what to do. And Cyclo cares for me, but she doesn't make decisions for me. Not really. I know what I want. I want my family back, and Cyclo needs my help in a way I've never imagined. But I don't know how to fix either problem. So I stay quiet. It doesn't occur to me that they are waiting for me to speak.

"Nothing. She'll eat with us, and we'll make sure she doesn't get in the way. Beyond that, nothing," Gammand says.

Nothing. That's the answer, as they all ignore me and dig into the terrible slop they call food.

No one has told them to eat it, either. I can't understand that.

When I dreamed about the day that I could step outside my little room, I imaged vast amounts of information coming my way, tumbling in waves of faces, words, blinks, and smiles. New human interactions. New cultural customs to learn. Happy experiences to store in my memory. Learning from people, instead of a vid screen. Now that I've set myself free, I'm finding that it's true—I'm learning a lot. But I'm learning that there's a lot I don't understand.

"What research are you doing?" I ask, unable to pick up my spoon anymore. I'm already full, anyway, bowl half eaten.

Portia, Gammand, Miki, and Fenn all look at each other. Fenn shrugs.

"It's not classified," Fenn says. "We have certain requirements to achieve, or we won't...succeed." So he starts explaining, as do the rest. It's dizzying—mapping out all the areas of Cyclo, measuring levels of thousands of compounds, culturing all the known symbiotic organisms, like bacteria, on the ship...and that's only in one week. In the next two weeks, there are tests to perform, more measurements, more testing. It's dizzying. Fenn stops there.

"And then what?" I ask.

"And then, it's over," he says, hollowly. All the other crew look elsewhere.

After a long silence, Portia speaks up. "Cyclo is not estimated to survive past three weeks. Nor will we."

"No one is picking you up at the end of the mission?" I say, my voice rising.

"No." Miki points to a tiny bump on her neck. "We have biomonitors in our bodies. What happens to us, as we succumb to the environmental failures, is part of the data. It's an end-game job."

"But what about me?" I ask.

No one says a word, and no one looks at me, either.

My heart pounds, so loud I hear the blood in my ears, and my visions swims.

I cannot die here, not after I only just started to live.

I can't.

I won't.

I open my mouth to protest, then Gammand coughs awkwardly.

"Maybe it's not the right time for this," he says, "but I have some news."

Four heads swivel to stare at him.

"We don't have three weeks anymore. We have two. The data I've been collecting for the last thirty-six hours alone tells us that ReCOR's projections were too conservative. And the projections show the decline isn't linear. The *Calathus* is dying faster than we thought."

"Two weeks?" Miki says, standing. Her blue skin has paled to a light gray.

"We all just lost a week of our lives?" I say.

Gammand says nothing. He doesn't have to. His face says it all.

Chapter Eight

FENN

I would yell, but it wouldn't help me.

The contract is very clear. We signed on to deliver a certain amount of information. We were trained to gather it, trained so I could reprogram my drones for measuring chemicals instead of stealing them. It was all doable. They said we'd have plenty of time, but now I'm remembering there were no allowances for "natural disasters," as in, the ship dying faster. I remember Doran, in a hologram, telling us that it could all likely be gathered within two weeks, though we would probably have more like six, possibly longer.

Now we have exactly two. There is no more wiggle room. One less day. If we don't deliver, we will all have died for nothing, and Callandra will not receive the death benefit. The money for physical therapy. The neural implants so her spinal cord will function better.

When we all start to leave the mess hall, instead of screaming, I tap out on my leg nervously.

- .... / ... ..- -.-. -.- ... .-.-.- / - .... / ... ..- -.-. -.- ... .-.-.- / - .... / ... ..- -.-. -.- ... .-.-.-

This sucks. This sucks. This sucks.

We are all somber, standing there, when Hana says, "I can help you." Her eyes are glassy, and her voice quavers.

"What?" Miki says. She looks like she's smelled something rotten. I'm suspicious, too.

"Help how?" I ask.

"Well, I know Cyclo," she says. She wipes her tears away with a sleeve before they can fall down her cheeks, and a little kindling of anger appears, replacing the sadness. "I can try to find ways to save her."

Gammand shakes his head, and Miki's the one who says what we're all thinking. "There's no saving the ship, Hana."

She gives us all a hard look. "How do you know?"

We've had months of training for the inevitability of Cyclo's collapse. It's beyond truth for all of us now.

Miki says, "I can show you the data, Hana, but we don't have time. The numbers don't lie. The ship is rapidly dying."

Portia holds her hands up because Miki is starting to sound pissed. "Wait. Hana, how well do you know the ship?"

"I've been studying her all my life. I had little else to do besides study."

"Can you tell us about her cellular respiration cycle? The three kinds?" Portia asks. Her lip twitches. She's baiting her.

Hana narrows her eyes. "Not three, two kinds. Nitrogen based and oxygen based. But yes, I can." She pauses. "How could you possibly know that she's going to die if you don't even know how many respiration cycles she has?" Hana looks angry, as if Portia has somehow insulted Cyclo.

Portia looks impressed. "And what about her cadmium degradation—"

"Until about a year ago, it was doing fine, but I think they made a mistake by adding the carbonaceous chelator." Hana crosses her arms. "That one degrades too fast. Cyclo functions much better with the other biologic filters, the ones that run on the red algae residues."

We all stare at her blankly. This girl knows her stuff. A few months ago, I'd have no idea what she was talking about. Even now, I barely do. I'm just a miner, really. I tell my drones to fetch, and they bring stuff back.

In the ensuing silence, she says, "May I ask you a question?"

"Of course," Portia says.

"Did you bring any phosphorous binders? They help bind the calcium buildup that slows her neural networks, but we were running low last time I asked Mother. There are some things that could help. Have you considered reverse engineering her stem cells? It worked on smaller bioships. What about evaluating some of her toxins and asking—what's the company's name? ReCOR—to send in supplemental energy sources until she can regenerate?"

"We didn't…we can't…"

Miki answers for Portia. "Like we said, we're here to collect data, run a few tests, but our mission is not to save what can't be saved."

Hana looks like she's been bitten. "ReCOR has no imagination, then."

"We are expressly not allowed to interfere with Cyclo's demise. It's in our contract," I finally say. "Hana. We can't."

"Or what? You survive and Cyclo survives?" Hana says, exasperated. "Why is that bad? Why can't I try to live?"

"Because this is not about you!" Gammand roars.

We all go silent in stunned shock. Gammand never raises his voice. A blood vessel sticks out of his neck, and his eyes have gone red-rimmed. Thankfully, he doesn't have his tranquilizer gun in his thigh holster. He might shoot Hana straight between the eyes if he could.

Portia puts a hand up and turns to Gammand. "It's all right, Gammand. It's all right."

Shockingly, he turns and walks away. Of all of us, Portia has been the only person who's been able to talk to Gammand these last few months.

"Yes, Hana. You can help us," Portia says. "Look, she knows the ship better than any of us. She can help. And if it's not *us* trying to save the ship, we won't ruin our contracts." She thinks for a second. "At least, I hope not."

Miki shrugs. "In any case, we have to sleep. Living quarters are dispersed throughout the beta ring. Take your pick. We'll meet back here at oh six hundred for breakfast and get to work. Shifts will be staggered from here on out."

Despite the notion that we have a whole ship to wander around for privacy, we all stick together. After all those months on the *Selkirk*, and with the shrinking amount of time left, no one seems to want to be too alone anymore. Hana trails behind me like a shadow.

As Portia passes by us with her long legs, Hana asks in a quiet voice, "Is it true that Prinniads scream in their sleep?" She looks so impossibly sad asking the question.

Portia turns her red eyes on her. "It is true. We scream."

Gammand yawns as he walks nearby. He's cooled off considerably since a few minutes ago. "They're also known to be violent, so let that be a warning. She's not legally responsible for what she does when she's unconscious." He rubs his arm as if he'd been recently punched there.

Portia smiles her toothless smile. "Next time, a little more space is advised." She pats his sore arm, and he grunts and nods.

I think we'd all appreciate an accidental punch instead of being lonely. I like Gammand's quiet, though he's clearly hiding a rage machine behind those enormous hours of wordlessness. And Portia, as smart and snappy as she is, doles out more smiles than any of us. Despite her lack of teeth, they are appreciated. Miki? She seems alternately placid, like a grazing elephant, or silently pissed off. We've bickered plenty, but I also catch her crying when no one is looking, silently shaking when she thinks we're all sleeping, so I cut her all the slack I can.

If not for the trip to get here, I might hate them all—I've always found reasons to dislike anyone around me. I don't like spending too much time with anybody, I guess for fear I'll get attached. Look at what happened with my family. They all probably despise me for not being the perfect brother/son/pilot they always wanted, and they know me best. So nine months on the *Selkirk* with these guys was a trial at first, but they all see through my sarcasm now. We know each other well enough to know there's no time to waste on hate anymore.

After some more walking, Hana says, even quieter, "I don't scream in my sleep. But I might now."

Man. We've known for a while that we were on a death mission, but I can't imagine what it's like for Hana—coming out of her hidden room to find that she's going to die, and then even sooner than expected. Her body seems to drag as she walks along, her eyes big and empty.

I don't respond. It's been quite a day, and I'm exhausted. We just found out we have one week less to live, and it's weighing on everyone. Hana walks ahead of me, out of earshot. My holo visor buzzes on my forehead, and I blink it open. Doran appears. He's appeared on Miki's holo, too.

"I want one of you to stay with Hana," Doran says, sounding more distant than usual. He's looking strangely pixelated. "We'll need to get info on her, too, whether we like it or not. All living organisms on the ship are a source of data and must be included."

"What? That just increased our work. You know we only have two weeks now! There's nothing in our contract for that kind of change!" Miki complains.

"No, there isn't," Doran says, "but the contract is clear. All life forms. That was supposed to be only us, and any indigenous bacterial flora. But whether we like it or not, the terms are the same."

"Can we at least try to ask for a bonus?" I ask.

"Can't hurt to try, but I can't guarantee anything."

What if I could earn more for Callandra, and for my parents? That's classic Callandra, actually—going above and beyond to perform at her utmost excellence. My sister always looked for ways to improve the odds. Me, I always looked for more ways to break the rules. My conscience nudges me, and I speak up.

"I volunteer to keep an eye on the girl tonight," I say.

Doran's holographic face nods. "Fine. We'll rotate from here on out. Why don't you send a nanobot into her while she sleeps? If I had another humanoid biomonitor, I'd use it, but they only gave us four. It may be helpful to have data and samples right off the bat."

"Sure thing," I say.

"And another thing," Doran says. He opens his mouth, then his image disappears completely in a cloud of disorganized pixels.

I call to him. Miki looks at me.

"What happened?" I ask. "Why did he cut out?"

"I don't know. Maybe he had to talk to another crew."

Doran is one person on a space terminal at the center point of several ReCOR missions. A single humanoid, in charge of about four different trips. Doran is our only intermediary communication with everyone in the nearby galaxies.

"Gammand?" Miki calls. He circles back. Being the data storage guy, he's also the best at communications. She explains what happened. Gammand tries to call up Doran on his visor, but it doesn't work.

"I'll check first thing tomorrow, but Doran warned us that this might occur. Some of the radiation flares from the star clusters nearby might interfere with our communication. But our work doesn't change. Time for sleep." A curve of crew quarters comes up, and Portia takes one room, next to Miki, next to Gammand. The doors pinch closed behind them, and I run to catch up with Hana.

"Hey," I say, but she keeps walking. "Hey!" She keeps going. "Hana! Stop for a second, will you?"

She stops and turns to me, wonderingly. Her eyes are still sad and red rimmed. "Is that what you meant when you said 'Hey'?"

"Well, yeah."

"Then why didn't you just say 'stop'?"

Oh my God, this girl is going to make my brain turn to jelly. "I don't know. Look, I'm assigned to stay with you tonight."

"Why?"

"To, uh, watch you." Okay, I think I just earned the award for Most Creepy Guy in This Galaxy.

"That's unnecessary. Cyclo watches me." She adds, "I'll be fine," though she doesn't sound convincing. She looks lonely. Like I probably do, but don't want to admit.

"Doran says I must."

She nods but then stops. "Well…what if I say no?"

"Well, we signed this contract with this company called ReCOR, see, and we have to—"

"I signed no such contract."

She's right. In fact, there's nothing to prevent her from wreaking havoc on each and every part of this mission. And then what?

Then I won't be able to do my job, and ReCOR won't give my family the payout. I'll be a failure in my family's eyes, yet again. This girl, this tiny scrap of an organism, has the capability to destroy everything I've tried to make right. I start talking before I even have a plan.

"I know a story," I say.

She crinkles her eyes. "Excuse me?"

"About a girl. A girl with brown hair and golden eyes." I touch my pendant, and her eyes fall to the shining metal in my hand. "She left me a message on this, actually."

I pause there. Hana's lower lip has dropped, and she cocks her head slightly, waiting. She plays with the pearl around her neck, and her other hand goes to her eyes, wiping them where they had started watering again. I go on.

"She always smells like caramel—it's her favorite candy, and she even knows how to make it from scratch. For her twelfth birthday, her parents bought her a pair of wings."

I can even see them, in my mind's eye. Pearlescent green and blue wings, small and crumpled on Callandra's pale skin. As the biosynthetic implant began to grow a vascular system of its own, the wings began to expand and grow. I can still see them fluttering feebly, their first attempt at flying. Like most cheap biosynthetic attachments, they withered off after a few months.

Hana's eyes grow wide, and the sadness drops away. I can see for the first time that her eyes are dilating a touch, deeply black within the brown. She's thinking hard. "What happened?" she asks. "Could she fly? What does the message on your pendant say?" She steps up to me, and we're so close that I can see my reflection in her eyes. Her eyelashes are dark and straight, and I have the weird urge to reach out and touch that ice-cream hair of hers. Man, she's pretty.

Fenn, stop that, I think.

"I haven't listened to it yet. But maybe I can tell you more about her tonight. I need a place to sleep," I say.

"Only Mother sleeps in my quarters," she says, defensively.

I nod. "Sure. I don't want to cause any trouble. It'll ruin my contract. Maybe I'll tell you the rest of the story another time."

"No, wait." She puts out a hand and grabs mine. Her skin is cool and soft. "Oh." She stares at my hand, still in hers.

"What?"

"Oh. I've never held another person's hand before that wasn't my mother's." She doesn't let go, and I'm actually really glad she doesn't. "You can stay. Only this time, I guess."

"Okay."

She doesn't let go of my hand as she leads me down the corridor. She's holding my hand funny, the way that someone puts their hand over yours, instead of under.

"Here, this is how you do it," I say, moving our hands so they fit better. Internally, I'm thinking *This is absurd, don't hold her hand, don't get attached*, but it's just hands, it doesn't mean anything. But I really like this. I've never held a girl's hand before, if you don't count Callandra, but damn, I kind of sort of like this. I want to yell at myself.

Stop it, Fenn.

There are flashes of green light along the corridor floor, going left and right, showing the way to northeast alpha.

"What does that mean?" I ask.

"Oh. Cyclo is showing you the way forward, even though I already know. She's being polite."

"Hey. Can you take us through the core of this thing on the way?" I ask.

She stops and lets go, and I hide any disappointment at not having her soft hand in mine. "The gamma ring? I suppose so. I know how to get there, though I've never been myself." The floors and walls flash white streaks. She turns to frown at me. "Cyclo says it isn't safe. We'd better not."

Eventually, we'll have to go there, but I don't tell her.

Instead, she grabs my hand again, and we keep walking. This time, she says, "Can I try this? I always wanted to see what it felt like." She intertwines her fingers with mine, and I suppress a shiver. If I'm not careful, a huge grin might take over my face, so I concentrate on walking. Hana seems to have decided that I will become untethered and loose, forever lost, if she doesn't clamp on to my hand, so okay.

We travel counterclockwise within the *Calathus* for another ten minutes. The walls and floor aren't always a uniform blue, with the light streaks leading the way. I see yellow patches and brown spots oozing some corrosive liquid, leaving what looks like chemical burns on the walls. I don't turn on my holofeed to find out what the data scanners say about them, but they make me worry.

You'd think that someone who was going to die soon wouldn't worry so much, but it's not true. Every minute becomes a little more precious than the last, particularly when I have work I have to accomplish on a limited timeline. So I'm careful to not step on or touch any of the spots. I can investigate them tomorrow.

Finally, we reach her room, where she had changed before. A blue door flashes brighter blue, before disintegrating its membrane into nothingness.

"Here we are." She finally lets go of my hand. It feels rather empty now, and I hold it in my other hand, as if it's injured. Hana motions for me to enter and turns around to face me, almost like a dance partner.

I look around. It's really small. There's a tiny replica kitchenette, complete with small oven, burner top, and little shelves full of bottles of spices and cooking utensils. A pair of tongs adorns the prep top. A black lacquer chest sits against the rounded, opposite wall, inlaid with mother-of-pearl in the shape of mountains, hazy clouds, and beautiful cranes. There is no bed. One tiny ebony table sits low to the ground—I guess you're supposed to sit on the floor to eat there. There is an area where a vid screen should be, but it's shut off. That's it.

Wow. Even my jail cell was less bleak than this. I had vid screens (with limited input, of course—mostly movies heavy on the morality lessons); I had pictures of my family up (actually, that was the jail's addition, not mine—they liked to psychologically manipulate me into maximum guilt). They even let me have my watch repair station, with the sharp tools getting sucked into the wall at lights-out, or any moment my physiology sensors showed I wasn't safe to use them.

I want to look through the lacquer box. But she sees me staring at it, and she steps in front of it.

"So, you sleep—"

"In there," she says, pointing to the opposite wall. "Will you let Cyclo take you, too?"

"Excuse me?"

"To sleep. It is the only way we sleep on this ship. Surely you knew that."

I run my hand through my hair. "That's not how I sleep, and I don't plan on it. I'm here to observe you, not be the guinea pig myself."

"Pig?" Her eyebrows raise. "I'm not a—"

"It's an expression. Never mind." I reach into the pocket of my vest and take out a card. It looks like a regular plastrix card that might hold all sorts of data, but this is where my smallest drones are parked. I have a few medium-size micro and centimeter drones in my pockets, and the larger ones are still parked on the bridge with all our equipment.

I love my nanos, though. These are invisible to a human's normal vision, and electrostatically sealed to the card for safekeeping. I blink twice, and the driver program on my holofeed chip turns on. A translucent green screen pops up in a half-bubble around my face. On it, I can see one of fifty nanobots all charged and ready to deploy. Some are ready for aeronautic driving, some for aquatic, some for drilling down into solid tissue. I start mentally planning how I can drive one into her ear or nose. I could even drill one into her skin, stuck there gathering limited amounts of information. A second, if all goes well. Then I can drive one into her vascular system and park it in a capillary inside her brain.

I start by flying about ten into the nearby blue wall itself. And about ten seconds later, they all immediately register as nonfunctional on my holofeed. Damn. This ship just pinched my bots into oblivion.

Hana looks at the card with curiosity, not realizing what I just did, and not seeing the streaks of red lighting up behind her—I guess the ship might be cussing at me or something. Her eyes go from my card to the bubble of information between us, like the rest of the story is hidden in there somewhere.

"Okay. So, here's the thing. I have these nanobot drones, and I'd like to drive one to hang out in your body to record your information before you go to sleep."

"What about the story? The girl with the butterfly wings?" she asks, backing away.

I step back, giving her space. "I'll tell you later. I promise."

"Who is she?"

"Actually, she's my sister."

"And you haven't listened to her message? Why not? I would do anything to hear a message from my mother."

"Well, that's not the same thing. Never mind," I say, irritated. "But first, I have these drones—"

"No." Her fingers spread out, reaching for the wall behind her. She shakes her head no, no, no.

I thought she'd be fine with this, which is ridiculous. If

I met someone and they wanted to shove bots into me, I'd freak out, too.

"You know, it doesn't even tickle. I've done this a million times. It won't cause any harm." I'm still holding the card up in my hand, wondering if my hesitation means that I already just voided my contract. I can wheedle and lie and get these drones into any organism I've ever wanted, but I don't want to do that.

But Callandra.

Isn't she more important than what Hana wants?

"No," Hana repeats. She takes another step back to the wall, even though I've already moved backward myself. Cyclo's walls are starting to flash two colors—white, which I'm coming to realize means a warning of sorts—and green. Though, turning my head, the green is only in a place she can see, not me.

Disappointment pulls my shoulders down. No means no, and it also means I'm going to fail the promises I've made to my sister.

"Damn it," I mutter, and look down at my card, which had a bot ready to deploy. But with a flick of my eyes, I shut it down. "Damn. Okay. I won't."

Colors flash in the periphery of my vision. Something wet smacks against my right shoulder and back, hard, and I stumble forward.

"Cyclo! No!" Hana yells, her hand reaching out for me.

I look to see what's hit me, and it's a giant red wave of Cyclo's matrix that's risen up, thick like an amorphous limb, and attached to my arm and upper back. I holler, jumping forward to escape it when something hot and caustic burns my skin.

It's dissolved through my jacket, and searing pain encases my shoulder.

I roar with pain.

"Cyclo, stop it! He wasn't going to hurt me!" Hana yells and pleads, and somehow I've fallen to my knees, clawing at the thing attached to my body, trying to push it away. But you can't push away something that's amorphous and half liquid. My hand gets stuck, and the acid-burn sensation encases my hand.

I hear Hana yelling more, until she stops. The agony is so bad I can't even scream anymore. Her voice comes through the white-hot pain blotting out my thoughts. It is calm, low, commanding.

"Stop. This. NOW."

And then Cyclo's reaching arm retreats from against my body. There is still pain, but it's the pain of air touching raw nerve endings, thousands of them, like someone has plucked every nerve with a knife, over and over again.

I'm still kneeling on the floor when Hana rushes to me.

"Oh no. She's burned right through your skin. I didn't know she could do that. She must have thought you were hurting me."

"I wasn't going to," I gasp. "You said no. You said no," I repeat, over and over again, as if remembering will somehow make the pain go away. "Oh God. How am I going to do my work?" My body is shaking from the pain and shock. Tears pour from my eyes, saliva from my mouth because my body is going haywire. I look over to my right and see the raw, glistening, bloody flesh of my arm and shoulder. The skin is gone. It's been burned completely away.

"She can help. I can help. Let me…"

Hana starts tugging at the remnants of my jacket and shirt, in tatters from being eaten away by the ship. I let her. I'm in no position to refuse her help. The cool air hits my torso, and normally it might feel good, but when part of your skin's been flayed off, it doesn't much matter. When she heads for my pants, I gasp.

"What the hell are you doing?"

"We have to go inside Cyclo, to heal your skin. She'll be able to rebuild your collagen—"

"No!" I yell. "It just tried to kill me—I'm not going *inside* it!"

Hana puts her hand on my good shoulder, and her other one touches my cheek. "She was trying to help. She was. She didn't understand—I promise we can fix it. I know we can."

"This ship is falling apart. I can't go in there," I say, panting because I'm so short of breath for probably terrible reasons.

"I'll go with you. I'll be with you. She won't hurt you if I'm protecting you. It was a mistake, I promise. Look, she's so apologetic."

My eyes look left, and the color of her room is flashing in peaches and pinks. Soothing colors. If a color could mean regret, I suppose that would be it. I take another look at my shoulder—and I can't even see what's happening on my upper back but half of it is screaming in pain. The medical equipment we brought with the *Selkirk* isn't anything that can handle this severe a burn. We have no regenerative medicines because we're supposed to die here, after all. But I can't die without finishing my work.

My sister.

"Okay," I say. My entire body is shaking so hard now, and I'm shivering like I've never shivered, not when we depressurized on a smuggling trip to Vega, or when I was mining ragnium on one of its distant, three-hundred-degrees-below-zero moons. "You promise"—my teeth are chattering so hard I can barely talk—"that it's not going to kill me in there?"

"What is it they say? 'Over my dead body.' No, I will not let Cyclo harm you. We communicate even better inside her matrix. Almost instantly. It's probably why she reacted so—our verbal skills aren't as good as our chemical communication."

I'm too tired and dizzy and in pain to even respond now, aside from a weak nod. Vaguely, I notice she is shedding her clothes until she's bare and naked. It speaks to how absolutely wretched I feel that I'm not even remotely happy that a naked girl is next to me, yanking off the rest of my clothes. She pulls me, gently, toward a wall that is clear as blue ice—no curving endoskeleton marring the inside of the matrix as I've seen on other parts of the ship.

Hana goes behind me, wraps her right hand around my waist, and threads her fingers into my left hand.

"I'll be with you. You'll be all right, I promise."

Everything happens very quickly. My legs go numb, fixed in place. I look down to see the blue goo of Cyclo quickly climbing up my legs. Hana, with her arms around me and her warm body against my back, has begun to sink rapidly into the wall, as if she had fallen horizontally into a soft bed of glassy water. With me in her arms, careful so she's not touching my wounds, we start to fall into the blue, too, sending my chest into a riot of fast, furious breaths I can't control.

"Hana," I say, but when I turn my head, just over my shoulder I see that her face has already fallen beneath the surface and the blue has begun to take me as well. She closes her eyes in complete and utter surrender. The edges of blue come over her face until they reunite as liquid mercury does when it touches itself on a table—reconnecting, becoming one united mass again.

My bots and the card are lying on the floor in front of me, unlaunched.

I can feel Cyclo's matrix oozing around my upper torso and neck, and my skin has gone numb. It's covering my shoulder and the pain is already receding. Now, it's climbing around my waist—skin temperature, which is even more freaky than if it were cold. Like I'm being eaten by a blood-warm tide.

"Wait. Wait," I say, but I don't know who I'm saying it to, because Hana has been mostly pulled into the matrix behind me, and I'm halfway in, too. In a moment of panic, I reflexively slap at it where it's encased my waist.

Mistake. The goo holds on to my hand fast, stickier than anything I've ever touched. It doesn't feel like it's surrounding me—it feels like it's incorporating me. My skin tingles in an almost narcotic way. My body is being forced under a wave of Cyclo's matrix toward the wall where the girl has been sucked in. The goo is rising up to my neck now, touching my lower lip. In seconds, I won't be able to breathe. I won't be able to yell for help.

Hana's arms are still around me, and they squeeze, perhaps to comfort me, but the squeezing only makes me realize I only have a few more breaths before I can't breathe anymore.

My visor is still working, but the matrix will soon ooze over my forehead holofeed unit. Quickly, before I can even think, I flit my pupils up, right, right, blinking rapidly. On the card, a light blinks, activating a single nano drone. Using my visual-only command, I fly it straight into my open mouth—I can't scream if I tried—and down past my epiglottis, trachea, past my right mainstem bronchus. It goes left, right, left, until it finds a globular alveolus. There, it'll bore straight through the membrane between cells and settle into the flow of my bloodstream.

If this ship kills me, at least I'll die knowing this: even in death, this data will help repay the wrongs I've done.

As the blue matrix flows down my throat, fills my nostrils and ears, and blackens my already numbed consciousness, it's not my last thought, though. Only one regret plays over and over in my mind:

I never listened to the goodbye message on my pendant.

But now, it's too late even for regrets.

Chapter Nine

HANA

He struggles. So very much.

If he knew better, he would know that Cyclo is here to help. Here to make him relax, to nourish him, and bring him to a sense of equilibrium and peace.

Of course, Cyclo did attack him, and for that, Cyclo and I need to have a talk.

A serious talk.

And then—and then—I have to find a way to survive. To help Cyclo survive. To find Mother. The idea of death coming to snatch me before I'm ready makes me so utterly sad, but it also makes something glow like a fireplace ember within me.

I cannot die here. Not when I've only just hatched out of my room after seventeen years.

But first, I remind myself, Cyclo must help Fenn.

Cyclo has pulled us deep into her matrix, well beyond the wall of my room where I am usually stored during my sleep. Fenn has writhed about so much that my arms no longer encase his body. Some distance away, she is pulling him along. Fenn struggles within Cyclo's unseen grasp. Within the blue, glass-like thickness between us, he is kicking and punching. At what? Cyclo has no face that can be struck. She has no heart that can be broken. And she will keep him down for as long as is necessary to subdue him.

I want to go to him, to tell him to be calm, but I'm also terrified to touch him again. Pulling him in the matrix was one thing—he was agitated and sick, and this was the only way to get help. But now I am nervous. I have never been so shy about being so bare. And he is, too, and I'm almost afraid to set my eyes on him.

But Fenn is struggling. He doesn't understand. He needs me.

So I swallow my nervousness and tell Cyclo to draw me closer to him. My body is gently pushed forward. Technically, I don't need garments here, but I wish I had them now. Relaxation is buffed into my skin, making my anxiousness wane. My oxygen levels are being kept high and normal. A sound not unlike a gurgle transmits through the gel. I open my eyes again and blink, willing my eyes to adjust to the refractive properties of the matrix.

Fenn is closer, eyes open and frantic, limbs still struggling and flailing. The raw and flayed skin on his shoulder and arm ooze blood, pink clouds diffusing into Cyclo's matrix. They disappear in seconds, as she absorbs them. Fenn doesn't understand that Cyclo is helping. What she communicates isn't a planetary language. More a chemical trail that just... makes sense.

He sees me, and in his flailing panic he reaches forward and grasps my wrist. That's when I realize why he's struggling so—he's not getting enough oxygen from her matrix into his skin, or down into his lungs, because of his panic.

And now, Fenn is drowning.

I have to tell her what to do. She's fighting him, too, and her efforts to sedate him chemically aren't working. I can feel the sedatives seeping closer to me, making my own skin numbed here and there, because they're stirring away from the small hurricane of movement around Fenn.

You need to calm him, I say.

It's not working. He's resisting.

He needs more oxygen!

My ability to concentrate oxygen is slower than before. I can do it, but he's consuming too much oxygen in his excited state. Hana—he'll die if we can't calm him.

Next time, don't attack him, Cyclo. He meant no harm.

I read harm in his movements. Perhaps I read them wrong.

Perhaps, I think. That is troublesome, and worrisome, but not for us to unpack now.

He needs oxygen now. Right now, he must be calmed.

I let his hands find mine, and he squeezes them frantically. He struggles, eyes open and wild, and I pull myself closer so he can focus on my face. I stare at him through the glassy blue between us, trying to tell him as best as I can, without speaking.

Fenn. Stop struggling. Relax. Please.

Fenn sees me, but he shakes his head and opens his mouth. A few bubbles issue into the gel, trapped there. A cry caught in time, as a mosquito might be captured in tree sap, only to turn into a fossil, then a jewel—beauty in death.

I can't let him die. His eyes are rolled up in his head. His mouth is still silent, open.

Cyclo. Help him. Help him breathe.

Should I?

I pause. What kind of question is that? Doesn't Cyclo's entire existence revolve around the care and keeping of her crew? But then, Fenn and his group aren't *her* crew. What is her responsibility to them? To Fenn? Which is when I realize—I have no allegiance to anyone or anything but Mother and Cyclo. And now Cyclo is all I have, and soon she will no longer be. What I need is not what this blowfly cloud of a crew wants—

they have come to settle on the carcass that Cyclo is becoming, according to what they've told me.

I can make my own decision, can't I? My own demands?

Hana. This boy. What shall I do? Cyclo reminds me there are other tasks at hand. Fenn's life hangs in the balance, and for the first time, Cyclo tells me I am in charge of someone outside of myself. I think of something that Mother once told me:

Hana. Everything that Cyclo and I do for you, we do for your benefit. We both put ourselves in danger to keep you well, alive, and hidden. It is all for you. In the real world, people often do things with the hope of a future payment. Money, often. Or they hope that the person will pay them back someday—even with just a thank you, or a smile. Everything in the universe has a price, Hana, but you.

Everything has a price.

But I want to help, only to help. Not to make myself more acceptable to a wealth of strange crew members, which has been my only goal for so long.

Help him, I tell Cyclo. Do it.

I feel the buzzing tingle as she changes the chemical content around us. My own consciousness perks up with the burst of oxygen. She's pushing oxygen into his lungs, diffusing it through his alveoli, into his skin. I let go and move behind him. Fenn is searching for my hands again, and as I reach around his torso with my arms, he clasps them, winding my arms around him. His hands won't let go, still clawing to keep me close, still frantic. My right hand is flat against his rib cage, over his heart. Vaguely, I think: I have never touched another human like this. His heartbeats are erratic and weak, his skin almost feverish. I make sure not to touch his injured shoulder and arm, letting Cyclo's gel rub its healing chemicals into him.

As I cradle him, waiting for him to calm down, and reading the beats of his heart like a poem, I have a moment to think, again: I have my arms around a boy. A person. My mother's own words invade my mind, bringing with them the customs and mores that I'm always forgetting.

He is naked. I am naked. And my hands are clasping his body close to me, and his hands are holding on to mine. Though weak and shaking, he doesn't let go. If hands could speak plainly, they would say this: *please don't leave me.* And yet, in a single second, a flurry of strange longings and warm sensations flood my mind and body.

I have my arms around a boy.

Fenn suddenly starts to writhe in panic. Don't panic, I think, but he can't understand me. His legs buck and kick, and he spins around, snatching my wrists in his hands. Within the blue, he looks at me. Wonderingly. His chest convulses as he tries to breathe, but it's impossible—there is no air to push in and out. Only Cyclo, inside, outside, everywhere. My hair is in a waved, tangly mess around my eyes, and I ask, without asking, for Cyclo to control it. Cyclo pulls my locks cleanly away from my face. His mouth is an open scream. I take my hand and touch his face and try to tell him.

It's okay. It's going to be okay.

I motion to my face, to the fact that I'm not breathing and I'm all right. I make a rolling gesture with my palm to relax. And in that everlasting moment of panic, he finally registers that his breathlessness is gone. It's only the claustrophobia of having Cyclo encasing him, and of being suspended.

And then, face-to-face, now that the danger is behind us, it comes back to me in a crashing wave that I am naked in front of this boy, and those fleeting sensations of warmth within my body begin to return. My face goes hot, and my hands jerk away from his. Fenn, too, looks down and realizes that we are unclothed. His eyes go wide, and he blinks with sheer embarrassment.

Cyclo! I say. Can you…oh my God…can you increase the opacity around us?

But that is not necessary for his oxygenation—

Oh, Cyclo, just do it!

In seconds, the matrix around me dulls to a solid blue, so that we look as if we're floating in two opaque, navy-blue bags. I relax and blink slowly. Fenn, too, looks as if he could exhale in relief except that he can't exhale. He smiles a little, though, and blinks sleepily.

He will live. As he drifts off, his hand reaches out to me. I let my fingers entwine with his, and just as he pulls me a little closer, and the two blue bags of thick gel hiding our bodies bumping against each other, he mouths:

I'm sorry.

Thank you.

Fenn drifts off to unconsciousness, his hand still holding mine.

He's asleep.

Oh.

I've saved his life, haven't I?

The enormity of what I've done stays with me, buoys my bravery. I stay awake for as long as I can, thinking and thinking some more. I wonder over the warmth of his hand in mine. It hurts my temples to try to imagine how to save myself. I want to cry at the thought of dying too soon. But it won't be long before I'll make some demands. If I'm to find Mother and find out why she left me, and how to save Cyclo and myself, I shall have to act in ways I've never dreamed. I shall try to save the both of us.

But for now, we shall sleep. And as I, too, surrender to the blur of slumber, I wonder: why do they never put this in the vids, how wonderful it is to be unconscious, hands entwined with such a boy?

Sleep within Cyclo is like no other kind—on a planet, for example, or even in hypersleep on the Eless ships that run ferries across the Alcyone nebula. They say that normal human sleep is quite an endeavor. Hormones must be regulated, neurons rested during sleep cycles and REM stages, fluids re-equilibrated. So much work. Cyclo takes care of my body for me, as she did with everyone on this bioship when it was time to hibernate.

They say that normal sleep is a vacation from sensation. You don't smell, you don't taste, you don't feel. You have no concept of the passage of time. Of course, you can dream all sorts of fantastical things, but they could be nightmares where monsters consume you alive or you're stuck in prehistoric tar pits. Cyclo curates our dreams to maximize restorative sleep.

And so, I dream of Earth. Of cool lagoons with jeweled fish, and my ancestors clothed in pale-pink hanbok dresses for a visit to the temple. Mother's favorite time period was early- and mid-twentieth–century Korea, and it shows up in my dreams and habits as such. They feed me fruit-embedded yaksik, sticky and sweet. I can run through endless paths flanked by honey-scented meadows, while a glittering dragonfly diadem adorns me. Sometimes, I dream of knitting or crocheting for hours on end, creating soft sweaters with twisted cables that would fit a hippopotamus. But during this hibernation spell, the adventure has been different. Usually, I am alone in my dreams.

This time, Fenn has been with me all along.

My body stretches inside the matrix, set at an ambient temperature that is blood-warm, like my own. Though the matrix is gel-like, it doesn't feel wet. Visitors to our ship are always surprised by this, Mother tells me. Water is only wet when you're dry, but when you're underwater, wet means nothing because it's everything. But when I stretch, I feel long fingers knit into mine. I am still holding hands with Fenn. I like this; I like how he feels like an extension of myself. My thumb touches his wrist and notes his pulse—a quiet, insistent thrum of defiance.

Waking up takes a little while. It is not as simple as opening your eyes and pushing off a futon or a bedstead. This is what they used to call those things you sleep on. Bedstead. Not steadbed. I read about it once, in a real book that wasn't digital; it had a binding. Binding! As if books needed restraint because they might flee.

I try to calm myself. Sometimes, claustrophobia sets in just as you become more aware of how encased you are. I hope that Fenn doesn't panic. He is sleeping; he is calm. I reach for my pearl drop necklace and relax.

All this time, Cyclo has been nourishing us through our skin, so we haven't felt hungry or thirsty. She's pulled out our toxins, so there is no need for elimination. She's oxygenated us, so there's been no breathing. Slowly, she changes the chemistry of the matrix around our skin so that our oxygen levels drop. This makes me slightly air-hungry and readies me for my first breath. Under my fingertips, Fenn stirs. The matrix cools around my skin. I shiver, and the gel shimmies around me. And then I open my eyes.

Inside Cyclo's matrix, I see a translucent watery blue color, dotted with flecks of iridescence. The matrix is thinning, meaning that she is pushing us to the surface. I see Fenn, so very close. His face is at peace, his hair floating slightly within the gel. Stuck within the wall, I can see my room within the ship. Here is my black lacquered box of possessions, my table and chair, Mother's shelves of books, and the cobbled-together kitchenette of real wood and iron.

Our bodies are completely bare but still hidden in the opaque blue that Cyclo has fashioned for us. I am relieved, and this is a change for me. Nakedness never bothered me before. I did not always clothe myself as a child. Then, I often lived my waking hours "bare as a bear cub," as Mother would say. Cyclo didn't care, and I didn't, but when my body began changing several years ago, Mother insisted that I try to be more civilized.

"Why?" I had asked. "Cyclo doesn't need clothes."

"Cyclo is a ship, and a different creature, with different rules." At this, Cyclo had glowed bright blue in assent, or perhaps thankfulness that she didn't need to don underwear. Mother had crossed her arms (this, I have learned, is a warning sign). I still remember her that day, clad in snow-white pants, shirt, and her long black hair in a knot on her head, flecked with exclamations of silver hair.

"We don't need clothes. Cyclo keeps the temperature comfortable," I had countered. Naked, at age eleven, I was climbing Cyclo's walls, where she had made firm handholds and footholds for me. My white forelock had fallen into my face, obscuring my vision. "There are no blizzards on the ship, or sandstorms, or—"

"Hana." My mother had cut me off. "It's time you learned to be more…normal. Humans wear clothes. You've read books and seen the historical vids. The bare body is not meant to be seen when you're around other people."

"But I'm never around other people, ever." I was upside down on the ceiling by then. Cyclo was nervous for me and sucked my fists and feet into her matrix so I wouldn't fall.

"That's enough, Hana. It's the custom."

The custom. She says this often, as a way to end arguments. *Hana, you should eat with a fork or chopsticks. Let me show you. It's the custom.*

Hana, you must stop burping your words. I understand it's fun, but no one does this. It's the custom.

When I was a child, I'd say a word over and over again, and it would lose all meaning. Custom. Custom. Custom. Cuss-tom. Tum Kuss. Backward, it was more entertaining. I'd brought this up to Mother, who simply said, "Hana." And that was the end to it. I'd stopped exploring words in such ways for years. I'd stopped questioning the word "custom" because of her.

But there is no Mother here.

There is Fenn. There is no one to tell me that this boy before me, hand in mine, is an aberration I shouldn't allow in my sphere. I know, in my marrow, that Mother would not approve. And yet, here he is.

And he is waking.

Chapter Ten

FENN

I have the oddest dream. Odd, because it's so real I could truly taste and touch and smell everything, all at once.

I dream of my home planet, Ipineq, where the grass is purple and fields of orchid-like chartreuse flowers stretch to the mountaintops of the Fifth Country. The sky is a golden-orange color from the iron rising from the dunes past the Dry Lakes. Callandra is still very little, long before the accident.

She's small. Really small. At four years old, she has the body of an Earth toddler, but with the large cranium and wide open, understanding eyes of a child much older. She wears a fluttering dress of gray over her light brown skin, and her little legs are bowed from the extra gravity here, her hip joints already stressed in a bad way. Though human, her body isn't adapted to living on Ipineq. In my dream, she doesn't yet know that I'll leave soon and will grow an entire foot in one year after I flee to become a thief in training on the fastest pirate ship in the Pleiades.

All she sees is perfection in her older brother.

"Look," she says, pointing. "The trixxa gulls are migrating." Long, spindly creatures with four-foot wingspans cruise the thermals high above us.

"Mom and Dad say you want to fly, too."

Callandra shrugs. She won't look me in the eye. That's so her—not wanting to hurt my feelings. She says, "Mom and Dad say there's no money for the pilot's academy."

"I'll get you the money."

"No, Fenn." She reaches for my hand. "Stay with me, on Ipineq."

But on Ipineq, I'm a failure. It's why there was no money for Callandra—they've used it all getting me into home programs and out of a juvenile incarceration center. Home programs that, unfortunately, I'm failing out of because they are tedious and boring and I know everything already. Just not the way they want me to know it.

You must memorize the algorithm in this manner, they say.

I know a shortcut. There's a bypass formula—

You must memorize the algorithm this way, they repeat.

But that's so ridiculous, it's a waste of time, why should I—

And then my holofeed tells me, in spectacularly flashing 3D red, that I now have earned two demerits for "Belligerence and Noncompliance."

And I count the days until I can break another law and get the hell out of here. I'll pay Callandra back. I know I will.

Callandra tugs at my shirt. "Fenn. It's time."

"Time for what?" I say, distracted. Annoyed. I was always annoyed at Callandra, though she wasn't annoying. It was all me. Always me. I need to get out of here. God, I need to leave.

"It's time, Fenn. Time to wake up."

Wake up.

Wake up.

A hand clasps mine. Gently. Was it always there? It feels delicate but large, like a grown girl, but tugs insistently. Is it Callandra's hand? Did she age in my dreams? But no, this is something far more real. And I begin to feel things I was unaware of.

A liquid-solid, body-warm, surrounding me. Suspending me. I want to breathe, but when I expand my rib cage, it only fills more with the same stuff around me. It's suffocating, though I'm not short of breath. And there is something else.

A hand, soft and delicate, gently touching my shoulder. A shoulder that no longer hurts.

I open my eyes, and I see black and white hair floating just beyond my field of vision. I look down and see Hana blinking before me. She's encased up to her shoulders in a vague, gelatinous sack of solid navy blue. As am I.

And then I remember it all—being attacked by the ship, the searing pain of burned skin, and then being sucked into the wall with Hana. Having my clothes tugged off me. The horrific feeling of oxygen starvation, squeezing my gut. Holding her arms around me—and I hadn't let anyone embrace me in years. Her eyes, pleading for me to stop fighting. I'd finally calmed, and the feeling of asphyxiation disappeared. I must have fallen unconscious after that.

And miraculously, I am not dead.

I blink, which is such a weird sensation when encased in this gel. Blinking eyes and eyelashes aren't meant to meet resistance. We're deep within the matrix of the ship. I see the hard white bone-like endoskeleton about me. It's a grid of holes that look like a dead sea coral or something. We're suspended in a pocket of what feels like a hole of matrix-filled bone. Hana pulls slightly against my hand, only enough so that she can float to my side. It's a slow dance, as we're not in water. More like water in extreme slow motion. Her fingers stay threaded through mine. Somehow, I can see Hana perfectly well.

Her hair is floating, trapped in the gel around us, and it

softly sways in front of her face. I release a hand from hers and push it out of the way so I can see her face better, and my fingertips brush her cheek.

She closes her eyes at my touch.

Suddenly, I want to kiss her so very badly. I pull a tiny bit closer to her, and she opens her eyes, looks at mine, looks at my lips. She doesn't push away.

And just when we are only a fraction of an inch apart—a sudden and desperate air-hunger invades my body.

What's happening? I'd only just gotten used to the idea that inside Cyclo's matrix I don't need to breathe air, when I'm hit with an urge to do exactly that, right now.

I push away and flail my arms, but she reaches out to grasp my wrist. My wounded shoulder and upper back feel tight, but there's no pain. Hana seems to understand what I'm feeling. Her body glides ahead of me, and I'm kind of wishing she wasn't wearing that bag of navy blue so I could peek at the curve of her spine and elsewhere. The beautiful elsewhere. There's a brightness where she's leading me, between arches and inner corridors of the ship's skeleton. I start to get a knot in my chest from the lack of oxygen, and it tightens quickly.

Soon, I see her little kitchen coming into focus, and some garments that have been piled up near the wall. I recognize my work vest and pants, and my card of nanobots is lying neatly atop them. Good. Hopefully they're still working. And hopefully the bot I launched inside myself has gotten some useful readouts, too. This was a psychedelic experience I'm sure Doran can't wait to investigate.

Hana lets go of my wrist, and I'm left hanging behind her as I see her touch the membrane of the matrix, pop one hand and then the other through, before stepping lightly down. She emerges perfectly naked but quickly puts on some clothes as I draw closer. I hope she doesn't turn around and just spectate while I emerge fully bare. That would be even more embarrassment than I can handle.

She turns abruptly to face away from me. Good.

One by one, I push my hands through the membrane, and it breaks, pulling away completely from my skin. It doesn't leave so much as a residue behind. I get one foot out, and I'm gently lowered so I make contact with the ground. My face breaks the membrane, and I can feel the matrix withdraw from my ears, my nostrils, my throat, every square centimeter of my lungs. I gag and bend over, coughing. But it feels so good to be breathing air, instead of blue goo. I inhale and exhale deeply, as if for the first time. Before long, I get another foot on the ground, and the blue matrix is completely behind me. I collapse to my knees, coughing and shaking.

I snatch my discarded clothes, some still with acid stains and gaping holes from Cyclo's attack. Hana has already put her clothes back on, and she's standing facing away from me.

"I suppose it must be strange," Hana says, her voice soothing. "You'll get used to it."

I yank my pants on, and once they're up, I reach over to touch my wounded shoulder. The skin feels a little tender, but there's skin where it had been missing before. And it still doesn't hurt. Half clothed, I feel a little more human (which is maybe a funny thing to think — how much more human can you be than when you're naked?), and I throw on my shirt and jacket, missing my right sleeve where the acid burned it off.

"I'm dressed," I say, and Hana turns around. She runs up to me, and her hands hover over my bare shoulder without touching it.

"It looks so much better. Are you…how are you?" she asks. Her eyes are wide and fearful.

"It feels weird. And tight. But okay." Our eyes meet, and we both look at the floor as if we're both remembering that we were naked only moments ago. And holding hands. Awkward. And what's more awkward is that I want to hold her hand again because I miss her being close by.

"I...I am so sorry," Hana says.

"For what? For saving my life?"

"I'm sorry Cyclo did that to you. And I know you'd never wanted to go into her, but it was the only way to... You were going into shock."

"I shouldn't have pressured you about using the drone. I'm the one who should be sorry." I offer a handshake. "Truce?"

"Truce." She puts her hand into mine, but instead of shaking, she just holds it. She cups the back of my hand with the other. I like this better, actually. I take a step closer, wanting to say something, because that would be better than getting on with the business of dying.

"Hana, I—"

The walls flash colors of orange and red. Hana's head turns to the door, as if Cyclo's announced someone's arrival. The door widens, and Portia, Gammand, and Miki run inside.

"What the hell happened here?" Portia says. "We've been trying to contact you for hours. You weren't in any of the rooms. We couldn't find either of you!"

Hana and I look at each other. And we both blurt out, simultaneously, "It was my fault."

Three sets of eyebrows raise, and we explain. How I was going to put a drone in her, but Hana's worry and refusal triggered an attack from the ship, and then I was hurt and in shock and going into Cyclo was the only way to get my pain under control, and now I'm healed and here we are. I say nothing, of course, about how we were holding hands throughout most of it, partly naked, and it was maybe the most unbelievable experience—aside from the whole acid attack thing—that ever happened to me.

"Fascinating," Miki says. Her holo visor is on, and she holds out a sensor toward me. "An attack. And she healed you? So quickly? That's faster than the top-of-the-line regenerative serums would have worked. At this level of decay, I'm impressed. We'll have to see if it's depleted her abilities in other areas."

Gammand, Portia, and Miki all start chattering a parsec per second about the data trove this just caused, and how they might score more points by going above and beyond the data they're required to at this point. Gammand yanks me by the arm, asking if I've downloaded the drone data from within my body, when Hana steps forward.

To be honest, we all sort of forgot about her for a few minutes.

"I have a request."

"A what?" Portia asks.

"I need to contact my mother."

"Well, we're not allowed to—" Miki starts, but Hana's not done.

"And a second thing. I need to access the data you're gathering, so I can start working to boost Cyclo's energy stores and help her regenerate the parts of her that are failing."

Portia frowns. "This is expressly against our mission guidelines."

"Your mission?" Hana says. She looks at Portia, then Gammand, then Miki and me. The floor flashes several colors, one after another, in a psychedelic display. "Your mission is not our mission."

Before Portia can respond, before I realize what's happening, a long tendril of blue drops down from the ceiling and sucks a small scanning device from Miki's outstretched hands. Before she can even try to recover it, it's stuck to the ceiling. Her face blanches a very pale blue, almost green.

Hana and Cyclo aren't passive creatures. We can't just do

whatever we wish to them. She and this ship can sabotage our work in an instant. Mission over, incomplete. And our contracts will be obsolete. Our deaths will be for nothing. I mean, Cyclo could have killed me last night, though it was in defense of Hana. What if they felt really threatened?

"Doran," Portia says. Her holo winks on, and after a moment of no response, his pale blue face shows up, and she swings the holofeed so everyone can see it. "You've been listening."

"I have," Doran says. "All right, Hana. What are your terms?"

"I want you to help me contact my mother," Hana says.

He pauses. "Is that really what you want? You told us that she hid you, against protocol. You would be putting her in danger. She might be imprisoned for her actions. You might be eliminated."

Hana bites her lip and tugs on her hair. She paces around the room as if waiting for the ship to color in with an opinion, but it stays blue. "Well," she says, "I'm going to die anyway, won't I? And I'm going to be part of your research and in your records. My existence already reveals what she's done. Reaching out to her doesn't change that. Does it?"

She asks this as if she's really unsure, though her logic is sound. I want to tell her to stop questioning herself and just ask for what she wants, but I get the feeling she's not used to saying what's on her mind.

"You have a good point," Doran concedes.

"There's something else, too," she adds. "I want your research to investigate how to save Cyclo."

Doran's eyes bulge at little at this. "No. Absolutely not." Despite his words, I can tell he's already on unsteady ground. She's backing him into a corner.

My face glows with excitement. If Doran agrees, that

means there's a chance we could find a way for the *Calathus* to not die. I mean, our mission is to find out what the natural death process of the ship is. But if death doesn't happen, and it's not because of something we directly do—I mean, we're just gathering info, and if this girl can turn things around—well, that means that I might live after all. *And* I might still fulfill my contract at the same time. I try not to grin like a little kid. Doran tries to keep his face neutral, and soon his expression is once again inscrutable.

"I'm sorry, Hana. I have my orders. I—"

A slight cracking noise issues above Doran while he speaks. Cyclo is starting to crush the data scanner right over his head.

Miki squeals. "That's the only scanner I have! Doran!"

Doran's hologram puts up both his hands. "Wait, Hana. Please. The crew brought limited equipment, and they need it!"

"Well, I need things, too," Hana says.

I cross my arms, eyebrows raised appreciatively. This girl just got Doran (and, hell, all of us) by the balls and squeezed with a literal pair of alien pliers. I have to say, I'm damn impressed. I don't think I've ever forced anyone to do anything I wanted. I mean, I've stolen a hella lot of stuff, but no one ever agreed to be robbed.

"Very well. We will do our best to help you," Doran says.

"And the ship," Portia adds hastily, glancing with a nervous red eye, left and right.

Cyclo drops the data recorder, just in time for Miki to catch it in her hands, exhaling with relief that it's mostly intact.

Hana grins, wider than I've ever seen. "That," she says, "is most magnificent."

What a weirdo, this girl. But despite my feeling that she's so very odd, part of me also misses that moment when I woke up to find her so close to me. How can you miss someone you've barely known for twenty-four hours?

Chapter Eleven

HANA

The crew of the *Selkirk* aren't happy with me. I follow them and Fenn to the bridge that's now their central encampment. All their gear has been placed here—multiple cargo boxes full of complicated equipment.

"All right. We have a list of all our objectives for the next few days," Portia begins. "How are we doing?"

One by one, they each frown. "I'm already behind," Fenn says.

Miki nods in agreement. "Me, too."

"I am, too. How can we already be so off-schedule?" Portia asks.

Miki grimaces and points to me. "We have a wrench in the works," she says. "And no allowance for extra time."

"Stop calling me a wrench," I say. But I calm myself. There's no time to be irritated. "Look, I can help. I know I can. Why is it taking longer to do your work?"

"Well, for one thing, the ship hasn't allowed us to gather some materials," Portia says. "I've done several biopsies, but Cyclo moves her matrix around to avoid giving me live tissue."

"Well, if you knew someone wanted a piece of your body,

you'd give up a piece of hair, or a fingernail clipping. Something unnecessary. That's what she's doing."

"Can you get her to cooperate?" Portia asks.

"I can ask. Haven't you?"

The crew goes silent. Of course it never occurred to them to ask permission. They just think Cyclo is this unthinking blob. Shame on them.

"Try asking nicely. And I can tell you where to get good quality samples that won't physically irritate her as much."

Miki gives a look of approval. "What about the radioactive areas? In the core?"

"There's a circadian rhythm to how permeable those areas are. Certain times of the day will be safer than others for you to go there."

"Oh," Portia says. "That wasn't in our training info. Without a sunrise or sunset, I didn't think Cyclo would have cycles like that."

"She makes her own cycles. She's healthier that way." Oh! That might help her. If I can help her regulate her wake and sleep cycles, it could help her stress levels. If I could somehow give her a boost of hormones to help, she might last longer. It's not a fix, but it's a patch. "I could design a treatment to slow her aging. But I still want to contact my mother." And find out why she left me. "Gammand, you're the data person here, right? Can I access your—"

"I don't have time for side projects," Gammand says tonelessly.

"Well, a little chaos has been thrown our way, and we all need to make it work," Portia says.

Ugh. She means me. I'm the chaos. I think of myself as being pretty well put together, as an organism. Perhaps I have an inflated sense of biological self-esteem.

"Fine. What?" Gammand puts his tablet down. It has a colored image that looks like a rotating jellyfish with flashing lights here and there. Oh. It's Cyclo, some sort of macrobiological readout of the ship.

Portia asks him, "All of the ship's data went with the *Calathus* crew. And we can't ask them directly while they're in hyperspace. Can you see if there are any ghost or duplicate records we can look at?"

Fenn glances at them and goes to a pile of equipment. When my eyes meet his, he looks away quickly. His cheeks flush a little. Mine do, too, in response. This is so strange. He's so distracting.

Gammand frowns. "What kind of records?"

I force myself not to keep stealing glances at Fenn. "Perhaps any information about the evacuation?" I raise a finger. "Oh! What about any misconduct investigations? What if Mother was in trouble? What if she was sick? Health records, too…"

Gammand rolls his eyes. "Do you want me to look at everything?"

My eyes grow wide. "Can you?"

Gammand turns to Portia. "This is more than just a little work. I'll upload that data, and you can search it all you want." He starts walking away, then turns to glare at me. "Are you coming, or not?"

I trot quickly to catch up to him. Fenn is watching us and stands. "Where are you headed?"

"Gamma ring," Gammand says. "It's where the hard drives are kept on the ship. Luckily I have to go there anyway."

"I have to work there, too," Fenn says.

I've only ever been in the alpha ring, the largest circular hallway on the edge of Cyclo. She has three rings and a core, all connected irregularly with her open-air hallways and matrix-filled tunnels. At the thought of us all going together, I perk up. How extraordinary to have company to do things. An absolute unknown, and hence a luxury for me. I reach up and hook Gammand's arm in my left, and then Fenn's in my right.

Gammand stops walking. "What the hell are you doing?"

"Oh. I just thought…" I'd done this with Fenn yesterday, and it was okay. I find that I can't seem to stop wanting to touch humans now that I've the chance.

He throws my arm off and walks ahead of us.

My eyes water. His tone was so bitter, it makes my eyelids ache. "Was that wrong?" I ask Fenn.

"You can't just…" He runs his hand through his hair. "Look, when you talk to people, you don't touch them." His words are a tangle I don't quite understand. People in the vids I watch touch each other all the time. Holding hands and singing. Hugging and kissing. Tackling each other over an ovoid, slightly pointed brown ball on a marked green field.

"I don't understand," I say.

He sighs. "People are complicated. Those vids you probably watched—that everyone watches—they aren't real. They aren't what real life is like, just a tiny portion, and the context is different." He starts walking so we can catch up to Gammand, but his arm is still under mine. He hasn't jerked away.

"But they came from somewhere. Those were real people. That's all I had to learn from," I explain.

"Well, that's not life. Just like what we did last night—that wasn't sleep."

"Or eating, I guess?" I add.

"What, you mean we were fed while we were asleep?"

I nod. "When we sleep, Cyclo infuses us with nutrients and calories. Didn't you notice that you weren't hungry when you woke up?"

He touches his stomach with his other hand while we walk. I touched that stomach, too, with my bare hand. My own skin grows warm, and my neck prickles.

"Well, that's just not the same as eating real food. I wish I could cook you something."

"Sometimes I cook. I've read so much about it."

He smiles at me. "You're the only other person I've ever met who likes that. Most people are happy to just get the ready-made, dial-your-taste-choices MorphoMeals. They look like the real thing, but they're entirely synthetic. By the way," he asks, lowering the tone of his voice. "Do you really think you could slow down Cyclo's aging process? With hormones?"

"Cyclo's oldest ancestor, *Turritopsis nutricula,* could turn itself young and be immortal. Cyclo is so different. But maybe she can be triggered, artificially, to stop aging. I'm going to try." I stop in the hallway, and Gammand gives me a look when he realizes I'm slowing him down. I put my hands onto the wall, and the matrix encloses them. Warm, comforting. It feels like my own hands have dissolved inside her, and I can't tell where she begins, or where I end.

Cyclo, I say through my fingertips. The stress hormones that you give to the crew when we're sick—you must have them encapsulated somewhere in your matrix.

I do. They are located in each quadrant, along with the other micropackets of nutrients.

I want you to release all of them into your own matrix, immediately. The cortisol, the epinephrine, the norepinephrine, the corticotrophins. All of them.

But Hana, they are for humans.

Just do it. It might make you feel better.

Very well.

I withdraw my hands slowly from the matrix, and Gammand and Fenn look at me expectantly.

"Okay. I asked her to dump all her stores of stress hormones into herself. They'll give her a burst of energy and might slow down some of the faulty processes she has."

"You just did that? By sticking your hands in the goo?" Gammand says, surprised.

"I did."

"Okay. Well, we've had monitors on the ship for the last few days. We'll know soon if the ship shows any improvement." He starts walking again, and Fenn just stares at me.

"That's amazing," Fenn says. "Did the crew talk like that to her?"

"Not that I know of."

"Wow."

Gammand turns around. "Hey. Lovebirds."

Fenn glances sheepishly at me, and I glance back, biting my lip. And then we snap back to attention as Gammand points to a passageway above us.

"We're going up here," Gammand says. There are stairs heading into a vertical, tunnel-like hallway. It goes up to the next smaller ring, the beta ring. Gammand takes the steps into the tunnel and then looks down at us.

"Keep in mind, the g-force decreases with each inner ring. This'll feel like the Earth's moon."

When we step out onto the beta ring, I feel it immediately. I bounce when I walk, without trying. My hair fluffs around my shoulders a little. And the curve of this ring is steeper than alpha. It's a smaller radius, for sure.

And then I remember that this may be the last new experience I ever have.

Cyclo is dying, and I am dying, too. Days, hours, seconds. It may be all I have. And then it will all stop, when Cyclo dies, and we all die along with her. But not if I can help it.

And yet, I start making lists in my head of all the things I have yet to do. A desperate list, full of things like:

See a real sunset on an actual planet

Swim in a natural body of water

Kiss someone in a romantic way

Catch a flying insect

See a sky in at least three different colors
Fall in love
Climb a mountain
Have a baby
Leave Cyclo

They are lists I've always made in my mind, but it occurs to me now that I might not do most of them. They will be impossible. They will dissolve before my life has even started. I look at Fenn and Gammand, wondering if they make such lists.

After a few minutes of walking (now I notice the passageways down to the alpha ring, up to the gamma ring—Cyclo feels so much more holey here), Gammand leads us up another set of steps to the internal gamma ring.

"Woop!" I say inadvertently, when I collide with Gammand after too forceful a step. The g-force is so light I can't walk normally here, and I bounce into Fenn trying to right myself.

"Careful," he says, holding my arms. He holds them a few seconds longer than I need, I notice. I like that. Gammand's hair is very fluffy right now. He points ahead to the narrow corridor, which is rather dark, but lined with colored arrays of smaller data units covering the entire corridor walls.

"Are these…" Fenn begins.

"Data cores, stored on organic nucleic helices. Prinniad, actually. They're a little outdated, but pretty solid." Gammand starts touching his tablet here and there, and I point to which sections will receive downloads, just as I'd learned in my studies of Cyclo. Fenn, on the other hand, is taking out the card from his vest pocket. At the sight of it, I immediately tense up. He sees my reaction and shakes his head.

"Don't worry. It's not for you. I learned my lesson."

"Where are you sending it?" I point to Gammand. "Into him?"

Gammand, without turning to us, lifts his right fist and

raises only his long, middle digit. I've never seen the gesture, but it must mean "no" in his blended culture.

"Uh, nope. I'm going to fly the micro- and macrobots through Cyclo's portways and closer to the core to get some readouts. I've got a list of launches to do while I'm here."

Gammand touches his tablet a few more times and shoves it into a port a few feet away. "I'll download the most recent material. I put in a tablet, since you don't have a holofeed. You're lucky; it looks like a lot of the information hasn't been scrubbed—no point, if the ship is going to be toast anyway. When the light goes green, it's uploaded and you're ready to go."

"Thank you, Gammand. It was very kind of you to help me," I say.

Gammand meets my eyes, and I realize he has wonderfully long eyelashes. The spots along his neck are beautiful and change shape with the movement of his muscles. The belligerence behind his eyes softens a little bit, and I see that he's been holding his hand around a metal pendant this whole time. His lower lip twitches, as if he was going to smile but his mind had other plans.

"You're welcome."

He bounces past us in the dark, hooks his hands on the handles by a passageway back to the beta ring, and floats down, letting the gravity pull him there gracefully. I sit down next to the plugged-in tablet and wait, watching Fenn. He's already launched five different bots. Some are still microscopic, but a few are the size of my fist, emerging from the pockets of his vest. They look like pale-green orbs and buzz slightly. Once again, his holofeed is live, and I see his eyes zigzagging here and there, and the green holo display is awash in movement. He must be communicating with the drones.

"Oh," Fenn says. "I totally forgot I have a drone inside me. Well, might as well keep it there."

"Doesn't that bother you?" I ask.

"What?"

"Having that in you. Like it's watching everything you do."

"Isn't that what Cyclo does with you, only it's on the outside?" he says.

This quiets me. Of course, Cyclo is always watching me. How could she not? She is attuned to every exhalation I have, every frown. If I have a concern, her matrix reaches up to soothe me. But Cyclo is staying very flat underneath me. Usually, she would have comforted me by now. I put my hand down and touch the floor, and find that there are multiple spots among the blue, darker in the dim light here. They aren't the acid-producing brown color from before, but different. These are white, almost lacy at the edges, and starting to coalesce. As I stare, two small lacy white dots enlarge and touch each other, becoming one blob.

I push my hand harder against a normal part of the floor. Cyclo? Can't you hear me?

But she doesn't respond. Not a ripple, not an iota of dopamine flushed into my capillaries. How very strange.

"Hana? Are you okay?" Fenn asks.

I look up at him. "Yes. I'm fine. But Cyclo isn't watching me now. Right, Cyclo?" I ask.

The color stays its muted dark blue here. No flashes of anything. This must be what it's like to walk on a regular space vessel, or a nonsentient home on Earth. I feel very small and alone all of a sudden. I frog-shuffle a little closer to Fenn, a little too buoyant. I grab his arm and bring myself back to the floor. Thankfully he doesn't move away.

"Anything?" Fenn asks.

"No. No response."

"So I can say whatever I want, do whatever I want, and she won't eat me alive again?"

"What a strange way of putting it. But no, I don't think so."

"Interesting. I'll have to add this to the data."

As I wait, I start thinking of my list again. And I glance at Fenn. He is staring into his visor, concentrating. I look at his profile and his lips, satiny and a little dry, with a crinkle in the middle of his lower lip.

"Have you ever kissed anyone?" I ask.

Fenn abruptly chokes on nothing. After a few more coughs, he says, "What? Why do you want to know?"

"Oh, nothing. Never mind."

How ridiculous to ask. Clearly, it's not something that's to be discussed. It must not be the custom.

Fenn wipes his eyes, moist from coughing so hard. "No, really. Why did you ask?"

"You'll think this is silly. But…I have this list of things I realized I might not ever do if I can't fix Cyclo. If I…if we…die."

"Oh." He's quiet for a long time, and I wonder if he's just ignored my question and gone back to flying his drones, when suddenly he blurts out, in such a rapid and continuous waterfall of words that I can barely understand him: "I can if you want, but I get it if you think that's weird—it's just I doubt Miki or Portia or Gammand will, and I'm here right now so if you want to, it's okay, but if not, that's okay, too."

I take a breath, as Fenn keeps staring into his holo visor. He's breathing a little fast.

I think: Hana, you may never get another chance. Never.

Kiss the boy. Quickly!

So I get up, lean over, and push my face closer to him, when he puts out his hands to my shoulders.

"Wait! Not like that."

"Like how?" I ask.

"Not like you're coming in for an aerial dive-bomb. Hold up, let me put these drones on autopilot. Okay." He stands up and reaches for my hand. I stand up, too, and bounce a little before settling down on the low-g floor. He wrinkles his eyebrows at me. "You sure you want to do this?"

I nod.

"This is so strange, you know." Fenn steps closer to me. "Never thought I'd kiss a girl after we'd already seen each other naked, but okay."

I laugh. "That's not how it usually happens in books, is it?"

He shakes his head. I'm looking up at him now. He's a good six inches taller than I am. I shake out my hands. My fingers are trembling a little.

"What do I do with these?" I say, waving my hands again.

Fenn takes my hands and slips them around his waist. Without thinking, I let them slide up his back a little. He breathes a little faster, even faster than before.

"Okay." He puts his own hands on either side of my jaw, fingertips barely touching my neck, thumbs below my cheeks. "Okay," he says again. Oh. He's nervous, too.

"You don't have to do this," I say.

"I don't mind."

I nibble my lip, and he watches, before I ask, "Have you done this a lot?"

"Kissed someone when it's been requested of me because of our imminent death? No. Never."

"I mean, kiss people."

"Oh. Not really. I mean, not many."

"Well, have you—"

"Hana," he whispers. His face is really close to mine now. "I'll lose my nerve if you keep asking questions."

This time, I'm the one silently nodding. I want to ask, should I close my eyes? But I want to see him, his brown eyes as they focus on mine. Should I move my hands? Am I a terrible chore for him? But just as I start thinking of more questions, he leans closer, and my mind goes completely space-calm, airless and empty.

His pupils, dark with those tiny glints of gold, dilate as he leans in. And his eyes close, as do mine, without any effort whatsoever. They simply fall closed, as if my body has known for centuries exactly what to do.

His lips touch mine, and at first, it's just a soft pressure, sweet, and brief. He pulls back, and I'm not ready for the kiss to be over. I want it to last, I want more, and so I lean toward him, but the kiss ends anyway. And just as I part my lips to inhale my discontent, he leans in. But this time, our mouths are slightly open when we kiss again, so that I taste him, and the tip of his tongue touches mine.

My feet go tingly, and maybe we're actually in Cyclo's core because I don't feel like my feet are touching anything anymore. One of Fenn's hands slips behind my neck, pressing me closer to deepen the kiss, and his other hand encircles my waist. My hands reach up higher on his back, and I grasp his jacket as I press him closer, too.

Fenn breaks the kiss many times, as do I, so we can then reunite with mouths parted, heads tilting the other way, because this kiss must be done as thoroughly as possible, I think. But really, I just don't want to let go, I don't want to disengage, I want this to go on until I can't remember why I was even born.

Something beeps obnoxiously next to us, and Fenn and I pull away. He looks slightly intoxicated, and I must, too, because I feel like I just ingested something astonishing and incandescent and altogether strange…but in a good way. We blink sleepily at each other, and I touch my lips, wondering if what happened just really happened.

Fenn shakes his head a little, and reality appears to wake him up. He looks to the right. "Oh. Your download is done."

The tablet next to me glows blue in a tat-tat-tat of flashes, then goes green. It's done. Our arms are still around each other, but I don't let go. Fenn doesn't, either. He leans close to my cheek.

"I never would have kissed you if you hadn't asked."

"I never would have asked, if I didn't want you to." I smile.

Before I let go, I want to say thank you for giving me something so valuable that it can't possibly be measured in any way. Instead of saying a word, I just kiss him on the cheek. And he kisses mine back.

We slip our arms back to where they belong, and I'm so cold now, even lonelier than I was before. I shuffle away awkwardly, try not to fall over, and gently pull the tablet out of the wall unit. Fenn is staring straight ahead of him. Maybe he's already gone back to flying his drones, but his visor isn't on. I think that he is recovering, as am I.

I look down at the tablet, letting my body float gently to the floor with crossed legs, then grab a handhold near the wall to keep me there. There are thousands of data files here, and I can't focus well. I take a few long, deep breaths, close my eyes, and tell myself—stop thinking of Fenn. Stop it.

"I guess we'd better get back to work," he says, as if he were speaking from somewhere inside my mind. I nod, and he switches on his holo visor and goes back to driving his drones.

I stare at the tablet again. I don't even know where to begin. I open up the first one, and it's full of extremely detailed, extremely boring information on the technical readouts from the ship's log.

** **** ****

Calathus Log 0900.7B8000223.1
Census 0900.7B8
947 active duty
20 respite

5 youth cohort 1
5 youth cohort 2
5 youth cohort 3
5 youth cohort 4
5 gestational, day 241
8 medical ward step-down
0 critical
0 death
1000 total
25 cohort/pregestational

5 students in youth cohort 4 have passed training and are now active duty; ID SR889 "Sadie" has released to the environmental systems group, JP776 "Jin" has released to the biomedical group, IR103 "Ira" has released to the educational group, RX221 "Raza" has released in the core engineering group, BO744 "Betty" has released in systems communications. Graduation ceremony was held via monitor.

Environmental:
Core temperatures remain steady. Gallium counts are rising at .0008 ppm. Moisture levels are stable. Oxygen levels at .21. For full toxicity update, see...

...

My eyes take in the information greedily. Much of this is familiar—I used to also read the temperatures and moisture levels, as an Earth person might scan the atmospheric weather. I scroll through log after log, wanting to know what SR889 "Sadie" looked like, what build she had, if she loved environmental engineering or only did it to fulfill an empty spot on the ship. What did the children look like? Did the babies put their fists into their spit-filled mouths and try to bite their toes with their gummy jaws?

And yet, each daily log is very similar to the next. As the children in the youth cohorts age, they enter the next group, until they graduate. Babies are born and enter youth cohort one. Crew members die, perfectly matching, within a few months' time, the batches of embryos being added to the ship. I scan the files looking for Mother's name, but she had an ID code she went by, and I don't know that code. Looks like they only mention given names once, at graduation. I only know her as Mother, and her given name, Um Yoonsil. But somewhere I should be able to find more information about Mother. Perhaps there is a census log with the crew's rank and position. I could find her that way.

I decide to ask Fenn for help—I am no good at understanding vast quantities of data and mining them for specific things. I put my hand on Fenn's arm.

"Fenn," I say. But he's now slack-jawed and dead-eyed, staring into his drone-driving program. I don't like him like this. He doesn't respond to my touch, so I tap him harder. Still nothing. What is wrong with him? "Fenn! Fenn!" I yell.

Fenn suddenly pushes my hand away and jumps off the ground, floating for a good second before his legs meet the floor. His hand shoots out, trying to grab mine.

"We gotta go. Now!" he yells. With one hard yank, he pulls me forward, and I fly toward the corridor. My body bounces hard against the side wall, and I ricochet against the floor. I cry out from the impact. Fenn is using grips on the wall to move as quickly to me as possible.

That's when I see something in the distance, far down the curving hallway—a cloud of misty gray coming our way, choking out the normal air and barreling down, ready to suffocate us both.

"Cyclo!" I cry out. But the walls stay unchanging in color.

Even Cyclo can't save us from Cyclo right now.

Chapter Twelve

FENN

Hana's mouth is open as she watches the stifling cloud—a moving, chaotic swirl of gray and iridescent particles—barrel toward us. Why won't she move? Why won't she run?

"Hana!" I yell at her, yanking her arm even harder. It jolts her out of her shock. She starts running with me.

"Wait! The tablet!" she shrieks. She tears her arm out of my grip to run back, snatches the tablet she'd dropped in surprise, and gallops toward me.

We try to run around the gamma ring, but the lack of gravity is hindering us. Each step we bounce forward, not nearly fast enough. We are living the bad dream of running in a mire of mud, but instead of mud, it's low-g. The ship lights flicker erratically and go dark. The only light now is from the flashing hard drives on the walls. A hissing sound comes from far behind us, and it's growing louder. We bounce our parabolic jumps. Finally, there's a corridor in the floor about twenty feet away. It'll take us to the beta ring if we can only get there fast enough.

"What is it? What's happening?" Hana yells.

I can't answer her. I'm too busy looking at my holofeed,

which is reading out all sorts of terrible data I wish wasn't seeing. Oxygen levels plummeting. Nitrogen dioxide gas in critical levels, mixed with chlorine compounds and arsenic. It would kill us with one inhalation, and it would kill us painfully.

"Portia, Gammand, Miki—are you seeing what I'm seeing? Evacuate southeast gamma. I don't know how we're going to contain this."

Miki comms into my holofeed. Her face is worried instead of pissed or placid, and that is a very, very bad sign. She's running somewhere in the alpha ring. "We read you. We are evacuating our posts and heading to the bridge."

"We'll meet you there." We've reached the corridor that leads down to the beta ring, but Hana lags behind me, dragging my arm. She's so out of breath she's turning pale. She doesn't seem capable of running anymore and is doing a very fast shuffle instead. I don't think a shuffle is going to save her ass. I pivot and grab her by the waist.

"Sorry about this," I say as she looks at me with an expression of anxiety and confusion. With that, I toss her into the passageway. Gravity pulls her down, and I hear her land below with a soft thud and a squeal.

Yeah, I just threw a girl down a tunnel. Not my best day. I jump down and follow her as we keep running, looking for another tunnel in the floor that will take us to the alpha ring. Hana's only a few feet ahead of me, still shuffling slowly and breathing hard.

"Portia. Is there any way to contain it?" I yell.

She comms in. "We're not allowed to interfere with the natural deterioration of the ship, Fenn."

The windows are showing a beautiful burst of stars around Caleano, so blue and bright. Stars are ordinary enough, and not something I'd care about, but it occurs to me this may be the last star I ever see.

Suddenly, Hana throws my hand off her arm. She collapses to her knees, out of breath.

"I can't…I can't…run…anymore…" she whispers between pants.

"You have to!" I look behind us. The fog has fallen through the corridor from the gamma ring and is now spreading toward us on beta, like an inevitable wave we can't outrun. Goddammit, and I'm not allowed to do anything but run. I hate this. I hate being here. Why did I not show up that first day of work and destroy my life and Callandra's? Why did I take that last-minute job to steal electrum? Why did I not realize that maybe, just maybe, coming home empty-handed to Callandra might have been good enough?

From my feed, Miki is screaming and yelling at Doran. Her voice is filled with panic, a tone I've never heard from her. If not for the deepness of her voice, she'd sound almost like a child. "Why can't we stop it? Just shut the corridor doors? This is suicide, Doran!"

Doran's image shows up in a corner of our feeds. "We can't. We have to let it take its course, even if it kills you," he responds, calmly but with a tone of utter resignation. Spoken like a man who's not immediately at risk of dying, the bastard.

Though, it's not him, really. It's ReCOR.

Who cares. Bastards, all of them.

"We haven't even gotten any good data, yet!" Gammand joins the argument. Everyone's face is in my feed, and they're all simultaneously yelling at Doran, pleading with him. None of us is ready to die. Not a one.

"I can stop it," Hana says, between hard breaths.

I stare at her. "What did you say?"

"I said I can stop it. Your rules aren't my rules."

"What?" Oh God. We have a chance. I touch my forehead and turn off the comm completely, so none of what I say goes on record. "Do it, Hana! Talk to Cyclo! Make it stop!"

Still collapsed onto the floor, she calls out.

"Cyclo. Cyclo, please. Close off the corridors and keep the gas away."

But nothing happens.

"Maybe she can't hear you?" I say. "Is there any other way to talk to her?"

Hana nods. She plants her hands on the blue matrix beneath her and closes her eyes. The fog keeps churning forward, now about thirty feet away. Nothing is happening. "She's not responding. She's... Wait."

Hana's eyes scrunch closed, and colors—pulsating shades of yellow—start emanating from her fingers, down the hallway's floor and walls. A ridge of blue matrix starts to close along the edges of the corridor, fifteen feet away, between us and the cloud of toxic gas. Just before it hits, the matrix forms a full wall, but it's thin. Even from here, I can tell the gas is burning the matrix, dissolving it. It eats away a hole, and a puff of gray comes out.

Now it's only ten feet away. I back away, but Hana still has her hands planted on the floor. This next wave of gases hits another thin, membranous wall Cyclo's made in anticipation. But this one has had just seconds more time to form. It's just enough. The gas starts dissolving the inner layer, but this time it's held by another layer of forming matrix. There's a push and pull of layers being formed, then eaten away on the far side of the barrier. Hana and I are immobile, watching the war that Cyclo is having with her own dangerous chemical cloud.

There's a mighty groan and a cracking noise. White splinters start forming in the gel wall Cyclo is building. They keep growing and growing, until they form a lattice that becomes more opaque and solid by the second. We see them forming in the walls beyond the barrier, too, coloring the blue walls a more milky tone.

"What is Cyclo doing?" I ask, incredulous.

"The gas has mostly polar and ionic molecules. She's making a nonionic barrier from her lipids." Hana closes her eyes and stretches her fingers out even more taut. "And she's doing it up in the gamma ring, too." She opens her eyes after two long, excruciating minutes. "She's contained it. For now."

"For now?"

Hana stands. "Yes. My communication with her is off, Fenn. It takes so much energy for me to speak to her, and usually I don't even have to ask. She didn't respond to me at all in gamma, and here she can't seem to hear me. Something's not right."

"You can say that again."

"Something's not—"

"Never mind," I cut her off. "Come on. Let's meet the others and see what the damage is. My bots survived," he says, holding out his card. Around the bend, several bots of different sizes I'd previously launched arrive and land on my hand. I pocket them, and the nano landing card, too. "And they got great data. Let's go."

Hana clutches the tablet to her chest, entwines her fingers in mine, and nods. This need for her to keep holding on to me is strange, and I confess, I love it. I was never a hand-holding kind of guy, even as a kid. But let's face it, it's probably because no one ever wanted to hold my hand. Even in my own family.

And that kissing session, which was really supposed to be some sort of a mercy kiss for a girl who wanted to be kissed before she died, was not just about mercy. Some part of me drowned when we kissed, and we could have stopped after the first millisecond, but we kept going, like we were drunk on each other. I've never, ever kissed anyone like that before. And now with her hand in mine, I wonder—do I have a girlfriend?

In this last gasp of life, this is where I am?

It is some kind of fucked-up wonderful, and as long as it doesn't keep me from saving Callandra, then I'm beyond okay with it. I bring Hana's hand to my face, kiss the back of it, and she smiles at me—a sad smile.

"I think I like you, Fennec," she says. "I wish I had met you fifty years ago."

"But we're only seventeen," I say, not understanding.

"Exactly." She kisses my hand back, and in a bizarre event in synchronicity, I understand what she means. She's talking fairy tales and bending both reason and physics. God, but it would have been nice if we could have stepped outside our reality and been together.

We half jog, half walk back to the bridge on alpha. Everyone is there. Miki is nursing a scalding burn on her left leg, and Gammand is attending to it with the first aid kit, covering it with a wound healant that looks like a sheet of diaphanous spider webs. Portia is holding her head, catching her breath.

"What happened?" I ask once the door is shut.

Miki's eyes immediately go to our threaded fingers, and she smirks, but it's a genuine spark of amusement, rather than an evil smirk. I let go abruptly. Hana puts her hand to her chest as if she just got stung. Miki hobbles to a chair to sit down. "One of the central vacuoles holding liquid waste material broke open. Somehow, it depressurized and turned into poisonous vapor. It spread into the main hallways of the gamma ring."

"Well, that's telling," Portia says. "The ship's inner containment mechanisms are failing. They're supposed to have several safeguards. We knew this would happen, but I didn't expect the ship to be able to contain it."

"Yes. Look." Gammand points at a 3D projection of Cyclo floating near us. "It's built no fewer than twenty barriers.

Mostly solid, waxy material, drawn from the matrix itself. The surfaces of the affected corridors also have thickening layers of protective walls."

"The *Calathus* has given herself a bandage. Though, it took five whole minutes before she acted to do anything at all," Portia notes.

"That was me," Hana says. "I told her to seal off the damage."

Miki strides toward her. "And who told you to do that?"

Oh God. Hana, don't you dare look at me. I can't get in trouble for this, I can't. My face goes so hot it could melt the new waxy walls Cyclo just built, but Hana coolly says, "It was me, and only me. Cyclo and I talk all the time, but in the gamma ring, she couldn't communicate for some reason. She's never had to repair herself before, so I had to tell her. That's why."

"That goes directly against our mission!" Miki spits out. Miki does this—goes from peaceful to pissed in a snap. It's scared me before. "You cannot change the course of this ship's death, or I'm losing my money." She limps even closer and raises her blue fist, close enough to hit Hana. "And I refuse to breach my contract."

"I already did. I asked her to release some hormones into herself, to see if it would help." Hana shrinks her shoulders together.

"What? You may have made things worse!" Miki says.

"Now wait," Portia says. "Hana isn't part of our mission. But I believe she's trying to help. We have to work with her so we can do our jobs. Doran says we must."

"And we have no choice in this?" Miki throws her hands up in the air, and her braids bounce against her shoulders. "Are you kidding me?"

"You'd probably be dead if it weren't for me," Hana says quietly.

Miki goes quiet. Her face contorts, and pure fear flickers over her features, before settling into a despondency she rarely shows. "I don't need you," Miki says, so quiet, so sad, that I'm not sure she even said it.

"I'm calling Doran," Gammand says, and it shuts everyone up. But when he turns on his holofeed, Doran's unable to connect. Portia tries, too—nothing.

"Look. Hana is part of this ship," I say. "Hana, you can't interfere with our mission in a way that speeds up Cyclo's death or purposely sabotages our work. Right?"

"Of course, I wouldn't do that," she says. Miki is still inches from her face; Hana doesn't back down, which is impressive. And Miki relaxes when she hears her words.

"And in return, we try to find out more details on her mother, and how to possibly save the ship and get Hana off," I say, though the thought of Hana leaving me here while I live out the few days I have left makes me sick. I'm actually nauseated at the idea, though I had nine months to get used to it. Hana isn't happy with my declaration, either—she nods once, but frowns deeply.

"This is bull," Miki mutters. She's back to being crusty again. "Our job is expressly *not* to save the ship. How can you guarantee we will get our death benefits?"

"Death benefit? What is that?" Hana asks.

"We're not here voluntarily. We're getting paid. Or rather, someone gets paid once we die," I explain.

"Oh," Hana says, putting her hand to her mouth. "So there is a number, a price for a person's life. They always say in the vids that life is priceless."

"Not for ReCOR," Miki says, smirking. "And they lowballed us, but here we are."

"Quiet, everyone. Just for one millisecond." Portia stands up to her full seven feet, her head only just barely below the ceiling. "So, Fenn—you're saying that if the ship can be salvaged, it's in Hana's hands, not ours?"

"Exactly," I say. "Look, I'll go over the contracts again, but I'm pretty sure that if we don't do anything we're not supposed to, what Hana does can't affect us as long as we meet our metrics."

"Wait," Gammand says quietly. "So there's a chance we could leave this ship alive, so long as the *Selkirk* crew doesn't actively make it happen?"

"I think so. But I have to check with Doran, to be sure."

Everyone is quiet. It sounds like a good deal, which is why I'm nervous that Miki is still scowling.

"I don't buy it. I read that contract backward and forward. It says we are not to do anything to alter the natural death of this ship. By having her here"—she points rudely at Hana— "and letting her have her way, we forfeit everything!"

"Miki," Portia starts, but Miki stomps her muscled self over to her.

"No. Don't 'Miki' me like you're some benevolent boss making it all better. You're not the boss. She will ruin everything. She was never even supposed to *exist*. She might as well be dead now—it would make everything less complicated. We'd get our job done the way it's supposed to be done."

"Miki!" Portia hollers, so loud that the walls reverberate. The boom of her voice shakes us all, and Miki is silenced for a moment.

Miki says, "I'm just saying what everyone else is thinking."

I hate to admit it, but this is one of the reasons why I like Miki. She is as transparent as they come. There is no bull with her, but it also means she tells you to your face if she hates you. Hasn't happened to me yet. She's near enough that I put my hand on her thick shoulder, and Miki glances at me, slightly unsure of herself. I give her a tight-lipped look that says, I understand, but cool it.

Miki exhales. She looks at the tablet in Hana's hands. "So, what's this?"

Hana hands it over reluctantly, without even a word.

Gammand says, "Downloaded data from the hard drive. And now, it's the only data from the ship we have, since those hard drives were all chemically burned in the last fifteen minutes."

I watch Miki as she starts scrolling and searching through it. Hana looks over her shoulder as Miki taps here and there.

"What was her name?" Miki asks. "Your mother?"

"Um Yoonsil," Hana says. "But names are rarely used, and I couldn't find it in a search."

"And you don't know her universal ID? Or ship ID?"

"No." Hana looks ashamed by not knowing the basic information that every humanoid knows about each of their family members, as well as they might know their full names or birth dates. How odd that her mother never shared it with her.

"Well, that I can find." Gammand reaches over and punches in several things to the holo screen at his workstation in the corner. "Here you go. UY4021."

Miki keeps tapping and touching the tablet. Her face has a smirky expression I'm dying to slap away, then it disappears. She frowns and walks directly to Portia, handing her the tablet. Portia's red eyes study it then look at me. She doesn't look at Hana.

"What is it?" Hana wrings her hands together. "You found her? Does it say why she didn't tell anyone about me? Does she talk about me at all in the records?"

Portia finally meets Hana's eyes. She takes a deep breath, so slowly that you can barely tell she's steeling herself.

"Hana. Your mother is dead."

Chapter Thirteen

HANA

Lost.

Utterly lost.

This is the only feeling I have after Portia speaks. My mother, dead? Gone? Before, she was simply a lost part of my world, fleeing to a destination that didn't include me. But now, the warmth I've known seeing her every morning—the feeling in my heart has winked out.

Mother is gone.

Mother is dead.

And without her, I am on Cyclo, yes, and I am still a few parsecs away from the star Maia amongst the Pleiades, but none of it matters. We were a binary pair of atoms, Mother and I, rotating our energies within Cyclo. And now that she's gone—really gone—my trajectory is nowhere.

This cannot possibly be. This cannot.

Fenn comes up behind me. He looks at the information scrolling on the tablet.

"What happened to her?" he asks quietly. I'm still unable to stir a single muscle. I can't move. I am here, but I'm not.

Portia murmurs under her breath as she searches the

logs. "It was recent. Within twelve hours of the evacuation. Of course." She looks over to me, and I can barely see her now because tears have begun to pool on my lower lash line, and they'll spill soon, and I'm having trouble breathing.

"Of course? What do you mean?" Fenn asks.

Portia sighs. "That would explain why Hana didn't evacuate with the rest of the *Calathus* crew. Her mother died, and she was the only person who knew of her existence, right?"

"Well, why didn't Cyclo say anything?" Fenn's voice rises in anger.

I look up to him, and the small movement of my eyes makes the tears fall over my cheeks in two hot rivulets. "She wouldn't have said anything if no one knew to ask. Cyclo doesn't volunteer information. It's not Cyclo's fault."

As soon as the words escape me, I think of it. Fault. Faulty. Fault lines, as in the fissures that breed earthquakes and geological cataclysms. Maybe I am the faulty one. Maybe I waited too long to say something, to demand that I be made known. Maybe I could have done something to save Mother. I sway in place, unmoored. Fenn touches my arm, and his hand is cool. It jolts me out of my thoughts, out of my cataclysm.

Fenn's hand doesn't move. It feels like a tiny bridge to someone, something else. I am beyond desperate that he not move his hand away.

"Does it say what happened to her?" Fenn asks.

Portia keeps reading. She shakes her head. "I don't understand this medical terminology. But it looks like…some sort of heart arrhythmia." When I give her a quizzical look because I don't know what that means, she says, "It means her heart stopped beating normally."

"But couldn't they fix that?" I ask, as if asking could possibly change the irrevocable facts.

This time, Gammand looks at the data, and he scrolls it

back and forth. "There's only so much information here," he says. "It says she died in the morning, the very early morning, on her work shift. They found her in the lab, collapsed. But there's very little information here."

I see her in my mind, in the lab that I now know, the one I walked through the first time I stepped outside of my room. The incubators and liquid wombs here and there, empty. Maybe then, they weren't empty, and the babies waiting to be born heard her cries and could do nothing on the other side of their plastrix gestational chambers.

Early in the morning, Gammand had said. That means it was only a few hours before she was to come to my room and meet me for breakfast. Before she'd order Cyclo to awaken me. Before the evacuation, when she'd tell the rest of the crew that I, too, existed and needed to be saved. That's why I slept for almost a whole week before I finally awoke. Because mother hadn't left me behind or forgotten me. She herself had become nothing but inanimate carbon molecules.

Mother didn't intend to leave me behind.

At least there is this tiny, tender mercy.

"She was probably going to tell someone that week about me. So I could leave with her. But she couldn't. She couldn't." My voice begins to escalate and then break. "She's gone. She's gone, and I'll never see her again." I start to cry in earnest, and I cover my face because I can't stop sobbing.

Oh God, she's gone.

Hands clasp my shoulders.

"Come on, Hana. Come. Let's take you somewhere quiet." It's Fenn's voice, gentle and urgent.

Meanwhile, Cyclo hasn't tried once to soothe me by clinging to my feet and ankles, inviting me to dissolve in her watery embrace. It's not like Cyclo to be so distant when I'm in such distress.

"I need Cy—Cyclo. I should like to—to—sleep," I say, hyperventilating.

Fenn nods, but Portia steps up to us. "No. She cannot sleep within the ship's matrix any longer."

"Why?" Fenn says.

"My data says the matrix has been changing rapidly. Her ability to host humanoids isn't stable right now. You've noticed, haven't you?" Portia asks me, not unkindly. Her eyes may be a startling red, but her wire-thin eyebrows show concern, human concern. "The ship has been less communicative with you, hasn't it?"

I nod.

"I've picked up some changes in her neural patterns. Normally, Cyclo can hear, taste, touch, smell, even see. There are these beautiful photoreceptors on her surface, but they've been dying, cell by cell."

But all I have is Cyclo. "I need her," I say, not knowing how else to explain it.

"Yes, but if you went into a rest period, there is a chance you might not be able to emerge," Portia explains. "You might hit a pocket of toxins, or she might infuse the wrong combination of electrolytes. A little too much potassium and your heart would stop. Cyclo may not oxygenate you enough, and you could suffocate. There are too many possibilities that could go bad. I know we're supposed to let Cyclo run her natural course, but we cannot let you die if it's an obvious danger. I'm sorry, Hana."

"The gamma and beta southeast quadrants aren't safe right now," Gammand says. "She can sleep in one of the west quarters safely. For now."

Fenn doesn't wait for an answer from me. And I seem to no longer be able to speak. Mother is in my thoughts, consuming them and leaving only the yawning emptiness of her absence.

Fenn's hand presses gently in the center of my back as we head toward the door, and the aperture opens to accept us into the hallway. Miki is crouched near the door, counting through a box full of wafer-thin data tablets. She stands as we exit, noting the tears pouring down my face, leaving streaks on my tunic.

"Don't feel bad. She's a selfish bitch for not telling anyone you were here all this time."

It happens before I even know what I'm doing. My hand whips up and slaps Miki across the face, leaving a smear where my hand was wet from my tear drips. Miki is so strong that she hardly moves from the impact. The sting of it makes my palm go numb for a few seconds, the strike is so hard. Miki turns to me, baring her teeth like she's going to swallow me whole. I don't apologize.

"Really nice, Miki," Fenn says. "Way to go, insulting the dead. She just lost her mother, for God's sake."

"I already lost my whole family," Miki says, touching her cheek. She doesn't back away but doesn't appear willing to strike me back. "Half of them left me, like Hana's mother. And the other half? I just left *them*. We don't have time for weeping and shit. No. Fucking. Time." Her eyes are shiny with moisture, as if her own body can't bear her words.

And yet, I stare back, unblinking, and a new sensation crawls under my skin.

I have never felt this way before—the satisfaction of feeling the sting of my hand hitting flesh, the comfort of avenging my mother in even the smallest way. Miki's cruelty stings worse than anything. It's a much larger, much more cancerous feeling. It's the color red invading my bruised heart and mind, so overwhelming that it eclipses my sadness.

I feel murderous.

Chapter Fourteen

FENN

The silence in the room is caustic, ready to scald anyone who dares speak.

I didn't think that Hana had it in her to hit anyone. I didn't think her capable of anger, and it makes me realize that Hana isn't as weak as I'd thought she was. Her blood pulses red and hot, like mine. A lot like mine.

Portia lifts her chin to Hana and then to the door. She's silently telling me to separate Hana and Miki, while Gammand is lying down, eyes closed, ready to sleep. Drama is not worth losing sleep over, apparently.

I gently push Hana toward the door, and reluctantly, she pulls her glance away from Miki's own milk-curdling stare. Miki wipes her eyes when she thinks we're not watching anymore. Before I'm out the door, I make eye contact with Miki and nod at her. Just a nod, to say I get why she's mad, and I get why she's scared. Miki shakes her head at me, not wanting to even think about it. She'll be like an emotionless rock after this, for hours. She'd done this over and over on the *Selkirk*.

Once we're in the hallway, I lead Hana away, and she lets me.

"I want to go back to my room," she says, but I shake my head.

"We can't. The area is too close to parts of Cyclo that aren't safe. Maybe tomorrow we could go, after we test the areas, but not now. Not with the chance of being cut off from the rest of the crew."

"I don't care about being cut off from the crew."

"Hana."

She stops walking, forcing me to look at her.

"I don't care." Anguish transforms her face. "God, Fenn. I don't care."

She cries.

I don't know what to say. Hana's going through what I already have—saying goodbye to my family. Saying goodbye to sunrises on Ipineq, and the smell of red irises blooming at second twilight, and the taste of home-baked sweet crescents. I don't know what to say, but I know what she feels.

I slip my hand into hers and start pulling her along, and after two tugs, she shuffles morosely behind me because she's too defeated to resist. Several turns later, we find an abandoned corridor full of smaller rooms with tiny chairs and tables. These must be quarters for the children on Cyclo. Children like we once were, who Hana never met. I feel terrible, for her sake. For the people she'd never met, and the life she hasn't had.

I want to complain about everything in the few short days left in my life, but God—at least I had a real life to live, in comparison. Granted, I don't deserve to live it anymore, but still.

Once the door closes, I tell her, "We'll sleep here."

"I want to sleep in Cyclo." She won't look at me.

"You can't. You heard what Portia said. It's not safe."

She starts wringing her hands, pacing the narrow space between the walls.

I don't know what to say, so I add, "You should eat something."

"I'm not hungry." She finally crumples to the floor and wraps her arms around her knees.

I don't know what to do. I'm completely unequipped to handle mourning of any kind. Even my own. So I just sit next to her, not quite touching her, not doing anything but rubbing my nose, which has been running ever since Hana heard the news. Like my nose is crying for the both of us, somehow.

Her toes wiggle delicately and stretch a little, digging into the floor. Cyclo's matrix flits a few colors—gold and yellow—but then goes quiet. It almost seems like Cyclo's too tired to chat. But I think it's actually something else—like it doesn't know what to say to her, either. Hana ends up tucking her feet over her knees, lotus style, so there's no skin to skin contact with the floor. I guess she didn't like what she heard from Cyclo, either. We end up sitting half a foot away from each other, aching from our hard run today, stiff with discomfort and the yawning quiet within Cyclo, within space.

I doze off but awaken to hear Hana quietly singing to herself. It's a song I don't recognize, something soothing, like a lullaby.

Dal-a, dal-a, balg eun dal a, li tai bai i nol deon dal a

Her eyes are closed, and the soothing singsong actually makes me feel heavier than a lead weight on a 3g planet.

Finally, sometime after midnight, when we've both dozed off sitting against the wall, I feel a slight bump. I blink sleepily to see Hana's head has tipped over in unconsciousness and landed on my shoulder. She rouses herself to raise her head, but sleep overtakes her again in seconds and *thump*. Her temple lands on my shoulder again.

I put my arm around her, which is what I wanted to do before but was afraid to. I inch her down to the floor where her legs straighten out. She snuggles into the curve of my stomach and hips, and lets me curl my other arm over her hip. For the rest of the night, I wake up every half hour or so—the sleep of a person wholly unaccustomed to sharing bed space with a fellow creature—just to check on her. She has newly dried tracks of tears on her cheeks from when she's awoken and cried herself back to sleep.

Once, I see it happen—her eyelids flutter, her mouth turns down, fresh tears slide to her temples and spill over onto the floor. The floor receives every drop that falls and then absorbs it so fast, as if to erase its existence, like greedy desert sand.

Finally, around five o'clock in the morning, I can't sleep anymore. My arm is beyond numb from Hana using it as a pillow, and my legs are cramping. I'd sleep with her longer if I could because, honestly—I've never had the pleasure before, and I feel so much less alone.

Plus, I only have days to live. Even crampy spooning is better than being by myself. But then a voice enters my head, the voice that made me sign my contract with ReCOR, the voice that raged when I heard about Callandra's accident.

You don't deserve this life.

You don't deserve these days, no matter how few they are.

And I look at Hana's sleeping face, frowning in her slumber. I think of our kiss, and how that was a stolen bit of goodness that I didn't deserve, either.

I gently extricate my arm from under her glossy black and white hair and get up. I stretch a long stretch and leave the room.

The ship is quiet. There's always a hum in the background of machines running somewhere in the biowalls, but there's something else that sounds strange. Dripping sounds, and a random, faint hiss of gas escaping. Not soothing at all. I open my holofeed to see whether I can safely enter northeast alpha.

I can. It's time to get to work.

Callandra comes first.

I take out my card of drones and program them for the next set of data retrievals. This one will be for microorganisms. I hope Cyclo lets me send them into her matrix. I launch about two dozen, but before they hit the matrix of the wall, I ask.

"Cyclo—may I send some of my bots into you? I don't think it will hurt, and they're just looking for bacteria. They won't harm you."

I wait, and a blue color, deeper than the blue I'm used to seeing, flashes in benevolent waves.

Well. I think that's a yes.

With that, I watch as the wall puckers a dozen times while my drones enter her matrix surface. Visor on, I see them slowly traversing her matrix, some already picking up readings, and others going deeper into her endoplasm near the edge of the alpha ring. Later today, I'll send a few more in beta, and then gamma. And then I'll be back on schedule.

I leave Hana behind me and slowly make my way to her room. I want to call it her prison—that's where she was trapped her whole life, after all—but she doesn't seem to have the animosity toward it that I would have. After ten minutes of staring out the windows of the alpha ring on my walk, already bored by the sunrise of Maia over the curling mantle of the *Calathus*, I reach her room.

It's strange to be here without her. I look at her belongings—the lacquer chest, the cooking utensils laid out neatly for someone to start preparing something. The lack of beds, and the tiny shelf of books. I read the titles—*A Beginner's Guide to Needlecraft; The Autonomous Farmer; Best Short Stories of Yi Kwang-Su*—and shake my head. I was not a book reader, ever. Probably why I did so poorly in school. Every time someone told me a story was worthy and good, I acted like it was sour milk, like it might poison me somehow. I wasn't that type of kid. And look where I am now.

"Why am I here?" I ask myself, forgetting why I've come to her room.

Oh, yeah. Food. I decided that maybe Hana wouldn't eat our prepared food—perfectly healthy, but not what she likes—given the way she reacted to it yesterday. There's a tiny pot, and the cookstove seems to have some old-fashioned knobs and such. But I've never used this kind of equipment.

"What do I do?"

Colors flash around me. Cyclo is functioning here, it seems. Huh. But I don't know her color language, and the translators don't work.

"I don't understand, Cyclo. Can you…talk to me instead? Like you did before?"

There's a beat, and then a mound forms on the wall. A hole forms in the mound, like a volcano cone collapsing. A bubble of air is drawn into the cone, and the cone edges form a crude mouth.

"What is your purpose?" the disembodied lips wheeze.

"Oh. Hi, there. Uh, my purpose? I want to cook Hana something. But I don't know how to cook. I don't know where to get the water…"

"You wish to feed my Hana?"

Her Hana? Who knew a ship could get so proprietary?

"Yes. Hana," I say. "She seems like she would need some solid food. And you haven't been well. We don't know if your ability to give her nutrients is working all right."

"No, I haven't been well," Cyclo wheezes. "Well. Well. Well," she repeats. What is with her? "I should like to help you help Hana."

"Thank you. You've always taken good care of her."

"It is my directive," Cyclo says. "Dr. Um told me to care

for her, under any and all circumstances."

Her words sound oddly like a threat. Without thinking, I tap on my leg:

.-- . ... .-. -..

Weird.

"Weird," Cyclo says, interpreting my Morse code. "Am I so strange?"

I stiffen. It didn't occur to me that she'd understand. I decide to ignore this fact. "Well, Cyclo, if you show me how to get some water, we can begin."

"Allow me…" Cyclo wheezes and reverse burps, inhaling another bubble to speak. "To assist you."

Step by step, Cyclo shows me how to extract water from the matrix, pouring it into the pot from a drip off the wall. Inside a cupboard are spices and soup-based powders. Some foods are freeze-dried or in precious, never-expiring packages. Nothing here is fresh, of course. I wonder where her mother ordered it from—and how old it all is—but I try to ignore that. Soon, I have a nice little cloudy-white soup bubbling on the stove. Cyclo supplies energy through a wireless cartridge on the back of the unit. There's a tiny pot of hot, sticky white rice cooking next to the soup.

"Will you feed this to Hana?" Cyclo asks, via a different wall nearer to the stove.

"Yes. Well, she can feed herself, but I'll makes sure she has some."

"Thank you, Fennec Actias."

"You know my name?" I ask, surprised. I thought Cyclo only answered questions in a precise way. She's saying something she doesn't have to. Huh.

"I know many things. I know what your name means."

I pause.

My name. I've known that Fennec means fox, but my

surname? I thought it had a Greek or Latin origin, but all that ever comes up on a search is some sort of moth. It's very unexciting. My lineage is so mixed now that I'm not sure which great-great-grandparents it comes from. I'm a little bit Taiwanese, German, Spanish, Japanese, and Senegalese, last time I asked my parents.

"Actias is a genus of Saturniid moths," Cyclo says. "It's quite fitting."

What, that I do my best work at night? I shrug, irritated. This is nothing new. And then it occurs to me—we're really talking. Like, the way I would with another person. I wonder what it would be like to chat this way with the bacteria living in my gut. My reality shudders for a moment, and I smile at the walls. I like this ship a lot, I realize.

"I know other things. I know I am dying," Cyclo says abruptly.

Goose bumps rise on my arms. For a long time, I say nothing, until I blurt out, "I know I'm going to die, too."

"Fennec. Can you save Hana?"

I speak very slowly, choosing my words. "I...I can try."

Cyclo says nothing. Is she worried for Hana? Could she be emotionally attached to a humanoid? I'd never heard of such a thing. And then, without prompting, Cyclo asks, "Fennec. Can you save me?"

I drop the cooking spoon on the stove. There is a plaintive quality to her voice that catches me by surprise. In that split second, I understand exactly what she's feeling. Life is leaving her, parcel by parcel, just as my own days and minutes are numbered. It's the desperation of knowing your very ability to see, think, feel, cry, scream—will be winked out without so much as a fireworks send-off or a funerary procession. There will be nothing but the vastness of the space, silence, and that spark of firing neurons in this one body of mine, gone dark after one last heartbeat.

I think she feels sorry for the both of us. Does she feel pain? Is she upset, knowing what's happening? Is she sad about losing Hana, about Hana's inevitable death, too? The idea that a ship can feel that—empathy, and fear, and the horror of oblivion—it takes my breath away for a second.

"Fenn?" Hana is standing in the doorway, where a moment ago there was a membrane door. "What are you doing?"

Sleepy-eyed, she watches me with surprise. At her appearance, Cyclo's disembodied mouth melts back into the wall.

"Cyclo?" I say, but the walls stay silent. Apparently, that conversation was between me and the ship, and not for Hana's ears. I note this and save it for later, wondering what it means. Hana is still waiting for a response.

"Oh. Hey. You're awake," I say, wanting to kick myself for saying the most obvious thing ever.

"I am. But you were gone. I mi—" She clips off the end of her phrase.

Was she going to say she missed me? Something warm blossoms in my chest at the thought, though I shouldn't jump to conclusions.

"Are you…cooking?"

I smile. "I am. Luckily, I didn't blow up the ship by accident." I make a conscious decision not to tell her that Cyclo helped me.

Hana smiles. Her eyes are still sad, and it's a small smile, but it's a genuine one. She goes to the cupboard and starts taking out bowls and spoons. She helps me ladle out the food and scoop the rice, so steamy that the sweet scent makes my mouth water. In a minute or two, we're sitting at the low table and picking up our spoons.

"Wait." She turns to the lacquer box, but then says, "Never mind."

"What is it?"

"I never eat breakfast without Mother. She'd always read a page out of her diary."

"I guess you could still do that," I say, putting my spoon down.

"It doesn't feel right. She always read it. Not me. Or you, obviously."

"Would it make you feel better?" I ask.

She nods and wipes her eyes. I get up and go to the lacquer box and open it. Right on top of a bundle of colorful silk clothes, next to a collection of knitting needles, several photo albums, and old tomes, is a newer journal bound in synthetic leather. I hold it up.

"Is this it?"

"Yes!" Hana's face brightens.

"What should I read?" I ask, flipping through the pages.

"Something early. From when I was an infant."

I flip through and find a date from somewhere about fifteen or sixteen years ago. The journal is made of that special paper that's microns thin but strong as regular paper. The whole thing is as slim as my hand, but with nearly two thousand pages. I find a passage from when Hana was nine months old and start reading.

Look at how confident you are, walking at only nine months! I fear your legs will bow from being such an early walker. Today, Cyclo made an orb for you to run inside, and you'd bounce against the membranes and laugh so hard, you spit up your lunch. Your hair is long enough for two little pigtails. When you woke up today, your face was round like a planetary moon.

Dal a, dal a. My little moon!

Hana smiles at first, but it soon turns into a frown.

"I never realized that the entries are only about me. They

never say much about what Mother's life was like."

"But you talked about that, right?"

"Yes. But funny how she doesn't like to talk about her life. Only me." She shrugs. "Anyway. You must be hungry after all that cooking. Let's eat."

We pick up our spoons and dive into the soup and rice.

After a few bites and slurps, she nods appreciatively. "This is pretty great. You're a good cook."

"Well, it's all just reconstituted stuff."

She sighs. "I know. Like me."

I laugh, until I realize it's not a joke. "What do you mean?"

"I'm like this." She jabs her spoon, pointing at the soup. "I read that the way you're supposed to make this soup, to cook good seolleongtang, you need to simmer ox bones for hours and hours. I have no idea what the real thing tastes like. Just like I'm not quite the real thing. Mother engineered me, partly from her own DNA so she'd feel like we were biologically related. I have ancestral Korean DNA in me. But like most of the embryos on the ship, she pieced me together to make the best kind of Hana. I'm not really Korean. I'm the living memory of an entire culture."

I flip my holofeed on, and based on our conversation, a search for Korean culture pops up. Selecting it with a glance, I stare at the pictures. "You look Korean to me," I say.

She shakes her head. "I feel like a paper doll, trying to be real." Hana pauses over her bowl, spoon still held aloft with soup-soaked rice. Anger flits across her face.

"Your mom tried to give you a history. Wasn't perfect, but she tried. And anyway—how you're made, or who your parents are—it's part of who you are, but it doesn't define all of you."

"Doesn't it? Mother told me once she made me extra obedient for my own safety."

I stop chewing. More obedient? That could kill a person in

a second in the life I've lived, stealing and hustling my goods in the last five years. On Cyclo, hidden, I can see why.

"Obedience isn't always a good thing," I say, slowly. "Just because you're born with a gene for something, it doesn't have to be your destiny. Your existence isn't just a legacy of where your DNA came from."

"I don't know if that's true, Fenn."

Now I'm confused. Am I more than what my parents' genes gave me? I am, after all, the one who screws up all things. That is not my parents. But maybe it's my fault I didn't try hard enough. I'm trying hard now. But even if I succeed, I still don't win.

"Anyway," I ask, "don't you want to make your own decisions? For once? I mean, you have. What you said to us, threatening Doran with wrecking the research if we don't help you. That wasn't obedient."

"Oh. You're right." Hana is scraping the last dregs of the soup from her bowl with a long spoon. She doesn't seem to notice that when Cyclo was busy talking me through the cooking lesson, I slipped some high protein and vitamin micro-packets in there for her health. I know it's my imagination, but her complexion is already more blooming. It's probably just rice steaming her face, though. "Oh. I ate it all."

I smile. "Thanks to my amazing cooking skills, no doubt."

"I haven't eaten real food in a while. Mother only ever made me small portions, since Cyclo has always fed me. But now that I can't immerse myself... I guess it'll be a lot of regular food for now on."

"I'll cook it for you," I offer.

"You will?"

"Sure," I say, smiling. "I like making real things. Well," I add, since it was just reconstituted soup, "mostly real things."

We bring our bowls to wash them in the water Cyclo drips into the tiny sink, the dregs of which will be reabsorbed into the matrix and recycled. Hana's elbows bump into mine as we clean. I like it. But Hana is frowning again.

"This morning, I thought it was a dream. That mother died. That we had kissed. Neither seems real."

I whisper, "It happened. Both things." I think, *Here is where she tells me she regrets the kiss*.

"I don't have any right to be happy about one memory when I'm upset about the other." She grips the bowl in her hands and shuts her eyes.

"You do. My God, between the two of us, you should revel in any emotion that comes your way. Good and bad. That's living."

"Why not you? You said between the two of us."

"Oh." I didn't realize I'd said that, and now it's too late. "Let's just say I've made mistakes, and that I belong here."

Hana stares at me. "You deserve to die?"

I nod, unwilling to say anything out loud.

"Do you also not deserve to be happy? To have a single moment of bliss? Because they aren't the same thing."

"I don't know. I don't really want to talk about it."

"Kiss me again, Fenn," Hana says, putting her bowl down and facing me.

"Now?"

"Now." She adds, "Please. Because everywhere I turn, I see my mother, and I feel despair, and I would like to feel something for a few seconds that isn't terror."

I can't. So when I don't move, Hana slips her hands to my shoulders, rises on her tiptoes, and kisses my mouth, softly, gently, and despite myself, my hands go to her face. I close my eyes.

After a minute, she breaks the kiss and rests her head against my chest.

"There. I feel a little better. Not much, but a little."

Somehow, she knew I needed this, too, because I wouldn't give it to myself of my own free will. She doesn't ask me how

I feel, and she goes back to cleaning the dishes, and for a few more minutes, I forget that I'm not allowed to have anything resembling joy. Hana handed me a little glimpse of it, and there it was. An allowance of happiness. Something I don't deserve, but which was gifted to me anyway. She gives me one last, quick kiss. I tap against my leg before I realize what I'm doing.

.-- --- .--

Wow.

"What was that?" She looks down at my hand against my leg. She must have felt me tapping away.

"Oh. Habit of mine. I sometimes think out loud in Morse code."

"Fascinating! Teach me?"

"Well, it's just... Sure."

I show her an alphabet on my holo, and sure enough, she starts memorizing it quick as can be.

Soon, she's tapping out a message to me.

....-. . -. -.   ..   .- --   .... .- -. .-

Hi, Fenn, I am Hana.

"Nice!" I say.

Hana finishes drying the last bowl, and she says, "I guess we should get to work. I have some hormone infusions to wrangle up somewhere."

Right on time, there is a buzz from my holofeed implant, and a window opens up. Gammand's face appears, and his voice fills the quiet between us.

"Fenn, is Hana with you?"

"Yes. We just ate breakfast. What's up?"

"Come to the crew cabins on northwest beta. Immediately. Bring Hana with you. We need her."

"Why?" Hana asks.

"It's Miki. Something's happened to her. I think...I think she may be dead."

Chapter Fifteen
HANA

No, no.

The word "dead" should not, cannot, be used so soon after learning about Mother. Miki dead? I see her so very much alive in my mind's eye. I blink, and I see her. Her scowl, her sadness when no one seems to notice otherwise. Her seventeen shades of blue that probably only I can see on her beautiful skin.

She can't be dead.

We run to the northwest side of the ship. Fenn zigzags us this way and that, avoiding the areas that aren't contained and safe. Cyclo's walls are changing color. They're no longer bright, translucent blue; occasionally, we'll find a whole wall colored orange, or translucent, with a view of her bioskeleton. Sometimes there's a clear partition full of gummy knots of extruded material from the walls, steaming, it seems, from some gaseous substance emanating from her flesh.

Oh, Cyclo. Are you in pain? Does it hurt?

Last night was the first night I voluntarily slept like a normal human being, outside the confines of her matrix. And I'm shocked to say, I feel pretty well rested. My dreams this time were my own. Such very imperfect dreams, they were. No beautiful fields of lavender, no dragonfly wings or skimming the surfaces of lakes on distant planets.

There were dreams of discomfort, of loss. Of sheer happiness of seeing Mother again, helping me knit something new. Of watching blood ooze with fury from the ground where wheat grows, yellow and red admixed nonsensically. Mother, appearing on the other side of a plastrix window in space, just beyond my reach. She couldn't touch me as she drifted away. The metaphor was not lost on me.

While we're running there, Portia careens around a perpendicular corridor from beta and joins us.

"I just heard about Miki," Portia says, galloping ahead of us with her giraffe legs. We climb two sets of steps upward to the gamma ring. There are no data drives here, just strangely bumpy walls. Portia finds an opening above that must lead to the delta ring. Instead of steps, it only has hand- and footholds as the g-force here is so low. She pulls herself up and disappears, and we follow.

Ahead, we hear yelling and shouts before they go ominously quiet. There's enough gravity that we can walk, but not nearly enough. If I step too hard, my head nearly hits the ceiling. Portia and Fenn stop outside a large containment unit, holding onto the thin endoskeleton handholds on the wall. I'd only ever seen this on a map—it's where most of Cyclo's dangerous waste metabolites are housed.

Fenn reaches the door of the unit. It's enormous—at this smaller delta level, one unit goes around one quarter of the ship. It's windowless, with massive, bone-like doors that Cyclo has made of black matrix in a lattice. But the doors are all open.

We push ourselves through the narrow corridor to get in. The walls are very thick, and they look healthy. No spots, no drips of acid. I touch one wall to see if Cyclo knows I'm here, and there's no response. There are so many places she can't communicate with me. It feels like a betrayal, somehow, as if she's been keeping secrets.

The corridor opens to an enormous, curved room. There is one narrow ledge in the middle, but the floors, walls, and ceilings are otherwise studded with what look like oblong eggs, only they're no eggs that Earth humans have ever seen. They're nearly fifteen feet tall each, and maybe six feet wide. Passing by, Portia imprints her hand into one, and the entire egg undulates slightly. The contents are liquid.

"Don't do that," I say, staying her hand when she tries to touch another. "It's full of radioactive waste."

Portia snatches her hand back, holding both fists to her chest, afraid. I've never feared Cyclo in any way, but the idea that she has these pockets of toxins is a reminder that her entire being isn't kind and benign. Just as humanoids leave an ugly trail of trash behind us, so does Cyclo. We walk forward, and ahead of us there is Gammand hovering over Miki, whose lifeless body is splayed, her hands falling over either side of the walkway.

Her eyes are open, bloodshot, and her face has a brownish hue. It's terrible and strange to see when she's only ever been blue.

She's dead. I can't believe it's real. I've never in my life seen a dead person. All I've ever wished for is to meet real people, to live with them, to laugh with them. Even with Mother, there's a distance to her being gone, because I haven't witnessed it—but this is real. This is too real.

"Miki," I whisper, and then my hands go to my face. I start weeping.

Fenn immediately goes to her side and touches her wrist and neck. He looks at Gammand, who looks at Portia, and then me. His face is stricken.

"Miki," he says. And that's all he says. He's a statue for minutes, just holding her lifeless hand. Gammand and Portia, too, are quietly shocked, just staring at her. Perhaps seeing themselves, a future version of themselves.

I had no idea Fenn would be so upset. But his face reminds me of something very familiar. It's like looking into a kind of mirror. This was me when I heard about Mother. It feels like I've known for centuries that Mother died, and yet it was only yesterday. And it brings back a wave of longing so twisting, my throat aches. For Fenn, and for me.

After a long time, Fenn finally says, "I can't believe it. What happened?"

Gammand turns to give me a brutal look and yells. "Where have you been?"

"I…" His angry words hit me like a punch in the chest. "I've been with Fenn. What happened to Miki?"

"She's dead. Looks like she was strangled. Answer my question. Where the hell have you been?"

I've never been spoken to in such a tone. "I've been asleep. And then I woke up and had breakfast with Fenn."

"It's true," Fenn says. He gently lays Miki's hand on her chest before wiping his nose with his sleeve. "Why are you asking her?"

"Because I have a biomonitor in every crew member on this ship. I know where everyone's been but Hana. And no one else has been around Miki in the last few hours before she left our headquarters and came here to do some readings." He glares at me. "You were fighting with Miki last night. We all remember!"

"But I was with Fenn!" I look to him to back me up.

"For the whole time? Every minute?" Gammand says.

"Nearly."

"Nearly?" Gammand says, crossing his arms.

"Well," Fenn says finally, "I did leave to make breakfast. "But c'mon. It was barely an hour's time!"

Portia pulls herself up to her full height and she glares at me. "No one saw you right at the time Miki's biomonitor says she died." Her red eyes flash and almost pulsate with crimson. "Krshkt! Damn it. Did you kill her?" She takes a huge step forward, fist raised, and I scramble back.

Fenn thrusts his arm to hold Portia back—which he can't, but it makes her pause.

"Miki is four times her size and weight," he reasons. "It's not possible!"

I hold up my hands. "I was sleeping! I wouldn't hurt her. I wouldn't even know how!"

Gammand grimaces. "You know this ship better than anyone here. Medicines, poisons, who knows. You hated her last night." He looks down at Miki. "Maybe you hate us all, too."

I was so angry last night I almost punched her. And the way Portia and Gammand are looking at me, they remember, too. My words are worthless.

Portia kneels by Miki's prone body. She loosens the shirt near her neck. Ugly red and purple marks mar the pale skin. "They look like finger marks. Narrow ones, belonging to small hands." Her eyes look at my hands, and I flip them over. They are pink and clean. They are small, as small as those that wrung the life out of Miki.

"I swear, it wasn't me!"

"It looks like Miki got caught by surprise. Her equipment fell down here, and there," Gammand says, pointing to some areas between the storage vacuole eggs. "We'll have to retrieve it and bring Miki's body back." Gammand stands up. "I'll get a body bag." He looks at everyone. "You should know, this is all on record. Miki's own voice and video links show she was attacked from behind. We have no visual on Hana at that time."

"*It wasn't me!*" I repeat, but no one is listening.

Gammand walks us out of the containment unit, but after the third door shuts behind us, he turns abruptly and speaks to Fenn and Portia, pointedly ignoring me.

"Someone has to keep an eye on her, at all times," he says. "And we should arm ourselves and be on alert. Just in case."

"Why don't we just lock her in the *Selkirk*? If she's dangerous, it's better to keep her away from us. And then she can't interfere with our work," Portia suggests. My heart, already trilling a bit too fast, starts thudding so hard I can feel it in my neck. I can't go back to being alone and locked up. Not again, not now.

"But I didn't do it!" I say again. The way they all turn to look at me, it's like there's a filter between me and them, and the filter is all they can see. The one that says, *murderer.* "Please. If I had fought Miki, you know she would have fought me back. She's got at least two hundred pounds of Argyrian muscle I don't have. Do I look like someone who's just had a battle to the death?" I yank my sleeves up, showing the lack of bruises. I lift my tunic to show my legs—completely unmarred. "No bruises. Because all I did was wake up and eat breakfast!"

Slowly, doubt begins to soften their expressions. Gammand scratches his brown cheek, and even Portia's eyebrows twitch as she looks over me. Fenn's lips twitch, and relief warms his eyes.

"Let's see what Doran says." She calls up Doran on her holofeed, and he comes through, but it's all grainy pixels. He's actually been listening in on Gammand's feed this whole time.

"Let her stay with you, but no unsupervised moments." A bout of static interferes, followed by his face popping back. "…be on alert. You have no weapons but that tranquilizer gun, so arm yourselves in any way you can. There might be another person hiding on the ship we are unaware of. You can retrieve Miki's biomonitor and use it in Hana. That will give everyone some peace of mind."

I nod, reluctantly. If they want to tag me like a little pet, so be it.

Fenn also nods, and I sigh in relief. Fenn gives me a sharp look at my exhalation, and I try to sober up my expression.

"On to a more important question," Portia says. "Will Miki get her compensation if she's been murdered? I'd like to know."

"Me, too," Fenn says, a grim expression on his face.

When Doran doesn't reply immediately, I realize the answer isn't a good one.

"It depends. We'll run some more tests on her body later today, but if this wasn't some sort of…toxic outcome from the ship…then, no. She wouldn't be compensated. And besides, she only finished one quarter of her research objectives."

Fenn curses, and Portia claps her hands on her face. Gammand looks like he could stab Doran right in the eye if he wasn't a hologram.

"That is so fucking unfair, and you know it, Doran," Fenn hollers. "Miki is dead! This is not why she came here. This is not the death she wanted!"

Doran says, "It's in the—"

"No. Don't you dare say 'contract,' Doran," Portia says, taking her hands away from her face. "You talk to ReCOR. You tell them there is an external force at play here, and it is altering our plan."

"I'll talk to them," Doran says, but he sounds anything but convincing. "In the meantime, Miki was our radiation specialist. Everyone will have to share her work now. When Gammand goes to retrieve Miki's body, you'll need to do some data collection on her corpse."

The word "corpse" chills me, and it bothers Fenn, too. He

flicks his eyes down to his feet and nods. Portia peels off to a different sector of the ship, and Fenn walks to the outer circle. He seems to be heading for the bridge.

"Where are we going?" I ask, running to keep up.

"Come on," he says, his face still troubled. "Let's get the stuff I need, and we'll go back with Gammand and run a few tests." Along the way, he starts launching his nanobots and microbots into the air, sending them into the hallways ahead and behind us.

But he sighs incessantly. "God, Miki. I can't believe… I need to keep working. I'm behind, and now I have to take radiation readings, as well, with Miki's stuff. God, this sucks." He takes out a larger card from his jacket, with drones the size of fingernails.

I pause to face the wall. Now we're back in the alpha ring, where the floors and walls are a healthy medium blue. "Cyclo," I say. "Fenn needs to send some of his bots to check your health. Into the matrix, not the corridors. Will you let him?"

Cyclo's colors stay flatly blue around me.

"Oh. I've already done this. I asked permission before, and she was okay with it."

"She was?" I say, incredulous.

"Yes. She spoke to me in your room, you know. She… helped me cook," Fenn says.

"She did?"

"Yes. She helped me get the water, find everything." Sadness contorts his eyebrows, only for a second. It makes me wonder if they only talked about cooking.

"Cyclo isn't responding verbally," I say, frowning.

"Noted for the record," Fenn says. I realize that he's taking down data even as we've been walking. It irritates me a little — maybe I want Fenn's attention all to myself. I bite my lip. Stop it, Hana. It's not all about you.

"I wonder if she responds to this," I say.

I kneel on the floor, to maximize the contact of my skin without actually presenting my body to be taken in. I spread my palms down, fingers splayed, and try to let her read my thoughts.

Cyclo. Are you all right? They won't let me sleep inside you anymore. They say you're not safe, that you're getting sicker. Can you feel it? Do you understand what's happening? What happened to your southeast quadrant with the vacuole leak?

I am experiencing some frailty of my backup safety systems. But I have been relocating my energy sources to keep my core functions operative.

Do you know why...you're experiencing this frailty?

Certain populations of my cells are becoming senescent.

I stop here. I can't talk more. I can't bring myself to tell her, or ask her—Cyclo, do you know you're dying? How can one ask that of the person who's cared for you from when you were only one cell big? How?

I pull my hands from the floor matrix, and my imprint on Cyclo flattens out.

"Well? What did she say?"

I tell him, particularly about what she's doing to try to keep herself functioning. "We should tell the others. It may help us figure out how to help her. We're still gathering information on that hormone boost, but even if it works, it may not be enough."

"Yes. Senescence is exactly what's going on. She can't contain her toxic metabolites, her cells are dying, and the ones that aren't dead are malfunctioning." As we walk back to the bridge, he starts muttering to himself. "On Ipineq, my planet, we were able to slow the aging process. Earth humans do it, too, with stem cell transplantation. Get some nice young DNA and put it in cells that grow to replace whatever's not working—chondrocytes in the knee joint, immature brain cells after strokes."

"I wonder if Cyclo still has stem cells," I say, but Fenn shakes his head.

"Doesn't matter. We only have the equipment to record information, not do treatments or rehab for an entire two-hundred-thousand-metric-ton ship. I mean, you did that hormone release thing. That was already on the ship."

I remember Cyclo's recent exploded vacuole and us running for our lives, and I'm even more sad than before. Maybe it didn't work at all, or it was just too late.

We enter the bridge. It's messier than before, as the crew have already settled in and equipment is being used constantly. Portia is already leaving. She now has a long, thin piece of metal broken off from one of the supply containers. A short, crude spear. She says something to Gammand about doing some analyses of the borders between the contained, toxic areas of Cyclo and the normal ones. Gammand makes sure his tranquilizer gun is secure at his thigh. He sees us and hands me a bag with a strap. I take it, putting it over my shoulder.

"It's one of Miki's radiation tech packs. She had the settings all done, but I guess someone will have to do the analyses post—"

He stops before saying "post-mortem."

Fenn picks up a lumpy backpack full of what must be more drones. Gammand walks over to an equipment container and pulls out a body bag. A hover gurney has already been set up, and he gently pushes it to the door with two fingertips. He looks at me, and then Fenn.

"Don't you want some sort of weapon, Fenn?"

"No. I'm good."

"That's rather unwise." He gives Fenn a helpless look, like he's asking to be murdered. "Fine. Let's go get Miki."

He and Fenn hardly talk. At first, I think they're really unfriendly to each other, until I try to draw closer and Fenn holds a warning hand out. Gammand stares coldly at me, and when he sees Fenn's gesture, he looks relieved.

That's when I realize Fenn and Gammand know each other in a way that doesn't require words. Gammand is upset, and Fenn knows this, and also knows Gammand needs quiet and space. Especially from me.

I'm jealous of this thing they have, the crew. The banter between Portia and Fenn; how they always give Gammand the room for the silence he needs, for hours at a time; how they grieved for Miki and could see beyond her sour moments, which I could not. They are so different, but they had something to share—nine months of experiences I won't have with anyone else in the universe.

I follow them, and all the way there I keep thinking of Miki and her open eyes, the purple marks around her throat. And weirdly, I think of my hands on her throat, squeezing, squeezing, squeezing. About when one would stop squeezing, and how hard, and how to keep holding on if that person was fighting you. I don't understand why such intrusive thoughts enter my head. I've never considered the concept of hurting another human, but it makes me sick to my stomach. My days, all of them, had been spent reading about Earth history and knitting and singing and climbing the walls. Learning everything I could about Cyclo. Dreaming of milking cows, gathering warm chicken eggs, or pounding sweet rice flour to make injeolmi, my favorite sweet tteok covered in roasted soybean powder. I have never dreamt of such a thing, nor has Cyclo ever put that dream into me.

Or could she have? Could Cyclo be capable of telling my subconscious to do something like this?

"Hana. What are you doing?"

I've stopped walking, and I'm staring at my hands, making a clawing gesture, as if choking a ghost in front of me. Fenn is watching me with startled eyes.

"Oh. Nothing." I put my hands quickly behind my back.

"Well, we're here. Come on. I can't leave you out here. Doran says we have to stay together."

"Of course."

We're outside the delta containment unit. Miki's in there. Gammand has already gone ahead of us with the body bag over his shoulder and the hover gurney somewhere in front of him. Being heavier, he has less problem with the low-g here.

"We have to take some radiation measurements on her," Fenn says grimly. I nod and follow him into the cavernous containment area, already better at using the handholds to maneuver near the egg-shaped vacuoles. As we approach the bend of the corridor where Miki is, Gammand hollers. He's about twenty feet ahead of us, and his voice echoes weirdly from the bulbous walls.

Fenn and I look at each other.

"What is it?" Fenn hollers back.

"It's Miki." Gammand turns around and drops the body bag, which slowly drifts to the floor. "She's gone."

Chapter Sixteen

FENN

"Gone?" I say. "What the hell do you mean?"

"I mean she's gone, dammit! I can't understand—I mean, look," Gammand shuffles to the side of the very narrow walkway to show us, pushing the gurney aside, too. His brown eyes are wide with astonishment, and his hands are shaking. "She was right here. God, where is she? What happened to her body?"

There's an indentation where Miki's body was resting. I touch the matrix, and it's oddly warm. If someone took her, they can't have gone far. It's one thing to kill her; it's another thing to mess with her remains. My body is hot with fury. I try to run to the far end of the walkway, where there's a door. It's hard in the low-g.

"Where are you going?" Hana hollers, but I'm too busy searching to answer.

I look up and down the curved, blue hall, but no one is there. It's perfectly silent, except for that preternatural hum that is Cyclo's metabolism churning away. There are closed doors that go to Cyclo's core, full of more toxic-containing vacuoles, and passageways that go back down to the gamma ring. All along the way, I don't see any scratch marks or anything that would show that Miki was dragged away. Then again, Cyclo probably self-heals.

I turn around. Gammand is talking aloud into his holofeed, and I see him shake his head and gesticulate with agitated, jabbing motions. He turns off his holofeed and faces me.

"I just confirmed with Portia. She didn't touch the body."

"And I was with Hana this whole time, so it wasn't her." Another idea comes into my head, one that frightens me utterly. "What if we aren't the only ones on this ship? We didn't expect Hana. What if someone else is on board?"

"That can't be," Gammand says. "It can't."

"That would explain why the biomonitors showed that the murder had nothing to do with the crew."

"Hana. Can you ask Cyclo if someone took Miki's body? If Cyclo took her, maybe?"

Hana nods. When she put her hands on the floor, Gammand shakes his head.

"No. No one will know if you're making up the answers. We have to know what the ship is saying."

"Can I try to listen in?" I ask Hana. She nods.

"Remember when you were in the matrix? It helps to relax and empty your thoughts, and you can hear her with more clarity." Hana sinks her hands into the floor, and I put my hands next to hers. "Make sure they touch," she says, and I let some of my fingers overlap with hers.

I hear Hana's voice. It sounds like a dream within a dream, feminine and light and very gentle. God, this is weird, having her voice inside my head, transmitted through Cyclo and skin.

"Where is Miki? The girl that died here?" Hana asks. My own fingers and arms tingle.

The Argyrian Miki is deceased. Cyclo's words are very serene but very flat.

Hana tries again. "But where is her body?"

I do not understand the question.

"I mean, Cyclo, did someone take her body away?"

No.

Hana crinkles her eyebrows together. "Cyclo, did you move Miki's body?"

No.

"Was someone in this room before we came here?"

Yes.

"Who was it?"

I do not understand the question.

Hana and I exchange worried glances. She speaks aloud to me and Gammand. "I don't get it. She's not answering my questions, like she's missing parts of her memory."

"Let me try," I say. I close my eyes, to try to speak without speaking. I guess it's like talking to yourself in your head. Only other people are listening, too.

"Cyclo," I say silently. "Hi. It's Fennec. Can you tell us how many humanoids are on this ship?"

One thousand and one.

Hana sighs. "That's an old number. There is always a census of one thousand crew members, which includes those being gestated. Plus one, which was me. She's confused."

"We have to read data directly from her, then, instead of asking her questions. She's not reliable, the sicker she gets," I say.

Gammand snaps his fingers. "Wait. Miki's biosensor. We can track her body that way."

"You mean this?" I lean over and pick up a tiny piece of metal. I recognize it—it's the biosensor we had implanted into our necks when we first boarded the *Selkirk* so many months ago. It's a tiny little capsule, only a few millimeters long. "Whoever cut it out of her neck did a quick, clean job."

We walk back to the bridge. Hana lags behind. I keep looking back to find her gazing at the walls and the ceilings as if she's reading some message that isn't there. Finally, after the fifth time of telling her to hurry up, I ask, "What is it, Hana? What are you looking at?"

"Can't you see it?" she says. She's still staring at the walls, a medium blue—not as vibrant as before, but not the sickly pale color we'd seen elsewhere. I look around. What is she seeing? She points. "The purple waves. They're running in stripes and—oh, little swirls. I've never seen that before."

"I don't know what you're talking about." Is something wrong with her eyes? Is she delirious?

"I forgot," Hana says. "You can't see it. It's in the ultraviolet spectrum. Mother put the ability in me when she designed me. It's why I can read Cyclo's emotions better than a computer or another person can."

"And this is different?"

"Yes. It's beautiful, but it's like…she's singing, or painting, or something. How odd. I've never seen her do this before."

"Maybe it's because the damned ship just murdered Miki and is pretty proud of it," Gammand says. Everyone's thinking about it, except maybe Hana, who looks shocked at the idea.

"No! She wouldn't. Why would Miki have strangulation marks on her neck that look like human hands?"

Everyone goes silent for a while. It really doesn't make sense.

"That's pretty weird," I say. "And we have no good weapons on the ship. If a person was going to kill another person, bare hands work."

"Look. These types of ships don't kill humanoids. They never have," Hana adds.

"She's right," Gammand says. "Cyclo photosynthesizes for energy. It's like asking an oak tree to suddenly become a

carnivore and gobble up a… What did they call those burned
flying things on a stick?"

"Rotisserie chicken," I say.

"Right. That. The physiology just doesn't work that way,"
Hana says.

"Fine," Gammand says. "So the ship is vegetarian. We still
don't have an answer, though. And we have no way to scan
the ship for other hidden passengers. We have to watch our
backs. It's time to tell Doran what happened."

I comm Doran, and we explain everything, even showing
digitals from the area. It's hard not to get emotional while
explaining what happened. I clear my throat about seven
times, it aches so much. Miki is decidedly gone. We did a few
radiation readouts of the area, but there was nothing strange.

Doran sighs, which sounds like a wheeze. "We can't let
this slow our schedule. You're to continue your work today.
Since you need to stay with Hana, and she isn't doing anything,
we might as well see if she can do Miki's readings with the
equipment, so you can stay on task."

"Copy that." I thought he'd be sadder about this. Or more
scared for us. But no matter what, there's work to do, and now
the specter of the harm that's come to Miki is driving me to
work harder. "Come on, Hana. Today's the day I need to do
some in-depth matrix work with Cyclo. Let's get to it. We'll
go clockwise and start here." I point to the 3D map that my
holofeed is displaying. "It's close."

Hana points a slender finger, following the blueprint. Her
hands are beautiful and unmarred by hard work. A wall of her
black hair slips over her shoulder, and I get a waft of scent
in my direction. She smells a little like flowers, a little like a
slept-in shirt. I like it.

"How odd to see Cyclo in this way. It's like we're seeing all
her insides." To peer closer, she has to bring her cheek closer to

mine. I can feel the warmth of her skin. I try to concentrate as she speaks. "Oh. The gestational labs. That's where my mother did most of her work."

God, focus, Fenn. Do your job, I tell myself. No time for this. Not enough life left to spend time smelling girls. "Uh." I clear my throat and shake my head slightly to get my thoughts in order. "My bots can only do so much work before the matrix may make my connection harder, and I can't take the chance of losing any. Miki wanted me to send my bots to do her readings, so we can do them together."

She nods. "I can try." But something in her expression tells me she's not fully enthusiastic about the idea.

I use my holofeed to navigate the hallways to the gestational labs, and Hana asks Cyclo to show the way, so we can test if her internal spatial recognition is intact. The flashes of light keep trying to get us to go to the alpha ring on the southern quadrant. Right ring, wrong quadrant.

"She's totally off. We'll have to let Gammand know," I say.

Finally, we make it there. The gestational labs are immense. There's room after room of filtration systems, amniotic fluid synthesis machines, oxygenators, and varying sizes of the gestational chambers ranging from the size of a fist to an old-fashioned bathtub. All are empty. Completely dry, too.

"We'll start here." I take my backpack off and find several cards of bots. Using my visor, I program them quickly for the information that both Gammand and Portia had asked for—levels of radioactive tritium and chlorine-16, as well as functional levels of other elements, like oxygen, water, and byproducts that aren't getting recycled within the matrix properly. Miki's death has put me behind, but I'm going to make it drive me to work harder and be more careful. "Hana, can you tell Cyclo what I'm doing, so she doesn't kill my bots?"

"Yes." She puts her hands on the wall, then pauses. "No,

wait. I need you to do something for me, too."

"Hana, there isn't time—"

"I know," she says, cutting me off. Her expression flickers between resolve and insecurity. "That's why I need you to do this for me. I need your bots to find out if she has any healthy stem cells inside her. Anywhere."

"Why? None of this will help her, not at this point. You already tried the hormones, and look what happened. She busted open one of her toxin containers."

"That may not have anything to do with it. Maybe it saved even more vacuoles from failing. Anyway," Hana says. "I know what you're thinking. Do you give up this easily about everything?"

"What are you talking about?"

She walks up to me and slips her hand under my throat. I stiffen, ready to shove her hand away, but it's warm and soft. I freeze, not knowing how to act. She slips her fingers under the collar of my shirt and pulls out the necklace. The pendant is heavy, and when she holds it in her hand, it's a relief to feel the weight lifted.

"You still haven't listened to this, have you?"

I snatch it out of her hand and step back. "Don't. You don't know…you don't understand."

"You're right. I don't understand what it is to run away. I've been left behind. But I don't want to be content to be left behind, Fenn. You shouldn't be, either."

I sputter, and my face goes hot. But I can't respond. Because speaking out loud means talking about her, and me, and Callandra, how messed-up I am, and how I got here. I have no one to blame but myself, and I'm sick to death of being blamed for everything—even if it's my fault. But I also know what got me to think about this again.

Hana.

Hana, and her will to live.

I stare at her, and how resolute she is—how even now, her black eyebrows are lifted as if she's afraid of being struck down or reprimanded. Even after the horror of seeing Miki dead, after finding out that her mother is gone forever. She's so used to following orders, and here she is, fighting. And here I am, so willing to eat my own fate with a "thank you, and please can I have another serving of poison so I can die like a good boy."

I am sick of it all. But what makes me sicker is the idea that Callandra will pay for my sins yet again if I let my own ego get in the way—the ego that says I can survive this ship. That I dare to imagine a future with the girl in front of me.

I can't help Hana without hurting Callandra.

And while I sit on the brink of telling Hana no, she says, "I'm not asking for you to forfeit your contract, Fenn. I'm just asking…for you to give me a chance to live. Please."

Just then, my visor beeps. It glows on, and Portia's face shows up on the screen. Her crude metal spear is still in her hand.

"Is Hana with you?"

"Yes, of course," I say. I'm looking at Hana through my visor, so Portia's face and Hana's face are right next to each other.

"Well, tell her that I ran some preliminary retrievals on Cyclo's biometrics. It looks like that burst of hormones actually worked. Her deterioration in several different tissues and cell lines has slowed down. Not sure how much time she bought us. An extra day, maybe."

"What?" I say, flabbergasted. "It worked? But what about the exploding vacuole?"

"That was going to happen, no matter what. Unrelated." Portia smiles her black gums at the both of us. "Tell her thank you. And Fenn?"

"Yes?"

"Will you please get some sort of weapon on you? I trust Hana, but I don't trust that there's not another person on this ship we can't locate, who may be trying to sabotage our efforts."

"Yeah. Okay. I'll find something soon."

I turn off the comm to find Hana smiling—truly smiling, the first real one since her mother died. She raises her eyebrows at me as Portia's image winks out and I blink off my holofeed.

I exhale, long and slow, before meeting her eyes.

"Okay, Hana. Tell me what you want me to do."

Chapter Seventeen

HANA

Fenn stares at me with the strangest expression. It's something like defeat and relief mixed together.

Which is a good thing. Because I didn't know if I could stand up to him or anyone else much longer. My hands are balled in fists at my side from the excitement of learning my first efforts actually worked. I did it. But it's not enough. Fenn is willing to help, and if I have help, there is hope to save Cyclo. To save all of us.

"Okay," I say. "The first thing we need to do is find out if Cyclo has any stem cells. If she does, then maybe we can harvest them. I mean, we have gestational chambers. They're only human-sized, but if we can grow her cells in one of them, then there's hope we can repair some parts of the ship."

He turns on his holofeed and switches the settings to his drone-driving application. He starts gesticulating on the 3D display bubble in front of him before his own eyes take over. I can see there's a progress bar on the right of his feed. It's only one-third green. There's a tick mark at the middle that shows he ought to be halfway done with his work. Not good. "All right," Fenn says. "I'm at your command."

I grin back. I've read and reread about Cyclo's own birth and creation in the *Annals of Astrobiophysics*. Since Mother would happily chat away about all the intricacies of how she creates the human embryos for the ship's crew and matures them to birth, I know how to do it all, in concept. I just don't know how to work the machines. And judging from the content of her diary, she didn't document that for my benefit now. But perhaps Fenn and I can figure that out together. Right now, we just need to find stem cells.

"Okay," I say. "Stem cells are going to have very specific cellular markers on them that set them apart from other tissues. We need to program the bots to find these markers and tell us where to harvest them."

Fenn grins suddenly. "Oh. This is on Portia's list. It green-lights this as one of our collective objectives if we contribute to other crewmembers' research."

"So this won't sabotage your work?"

"No. It's good!"

Together, Fenn and I prepare to launch a dozen nanobots. Fenn sends out a cadre of a whole separate dozen set to gather info according to Doran's schedule for him—measurements of the tritium and chlorine-16, plus other compounds I'm less familiar with. But for me, we'll zone in on Cyclo's stem cells. I ask, of course, ahead of time, if Cyclo can simply point them out to us herself. But she garbles the information when she responds.

"Her communication neural network is one of the first things we have to fix. It will make everything easier," I say.

"Noted," Fenn says, but he's got that glassy stare again, which tells me he's flying his bots, concentrating mostly on navigating. "Hey, this is good news. Cyclo hasn't destroyed a single one yet. She's cooperating."

"Well, we'll see. She may not cooperate, depending on

whether her memory and understanding are okay in different parts of the ship. She doesn't have a central nervous system— it's like a sea star's. It's distributed throughout her body."

"So she may be reasonable in some parts of the ship and more erratic in others?"

"Yes."

"Can you tell by just looking at her?" Fenn asks.

"Yes." Looking around, I see a faint shimmer of the ultraviolet color that Fenn said he couldn't. "In my spectrum of vision, I've noticed some differences. She's…duller in the areas where she communicates poorly with me. Where she doesn't seem as conscious, I guess."

Fenn nods and then goes silent for a while. While he drives the drones, I tinker with Miki's equipment, reading the info from the drones driving deeper into Cyclo's matrix. So far, the readings are normal. Interestingly, some areas of Cyclo are showing a burst of normal activity after previously failing. Like Portia said, the hormones seemed to have worked for a little while.

Throughout our data gathering, I surreptitiously watch Fenn, his fingers and hands moving deftly here and there, orchestrating and conducting moves and turns that I can't see because I don't understand how to read his holofeed well. It's replete with numbers floating around intersecting lines and planes that look so foreign. It makes me a little sad, to see a beautiful creature like Cyclo distilled down to numbers and vectors and graphs. It's not the Cyclo I know.

Fenn's sleeves are rolled up so he can move his arms more freely. The muscles of his forearms are taut and beautiful. I study his face, too, carefully, without staring. His eyes are so large and brown, and his cheekbones have grown very slightly sharper since he first set foot on the ship. He's gotten thinner and looks older. Wiser.

Miki's data is still coming in at a steady clip, so I walk around the gestational lab, studying the different containers and machines. If there is a chance I can save Cyclo, I need to use these. I turn on one of the filtration machines—just to see if the energy source is still good—and the monitor lights up. I turn on one of the incubation chambers, too, a small one. This lights up, too. It looks like the levels of all the nutrients and liquids are still good. I don't ask Fenn for help here because I'm sure the *Selkirk* crew never needed to know how to gestate anything as part of their protocol.

On the wall monitor, I search for tissue culture programs. Everything is for human and humanoid, but under an obscure "other" option that I find after looking at every program, I find a drop-down menu of non-humanoid species. I clap my hands.

There. *Amorfovita potentia,* subspecies *cyclonica.*

And under the species name, a list of a thousand types of tissue and embryo programs, from larval to polyp stage and even juvenile medusas. I find a mantle tissue program and feel utter relief. Maybe if we can fix her mantle—the outer part of her body that looks like a ballerina skirt twirling around the ship, the part that produces energy from starlight—Cyclo's immune system will improve because it will have the energy to repair. It's somewhere to start.

"Whoop! I found something," Fenn says suddenly.

"What is it?" I run to his side.

"Inside some of the older endoskeleton, near the delta ring, there are some islands of cells that are still dividing. They're diffusion cells—not stem cells, but as close as we'll get to stem cells."

"Can you harvest them?"

"Already done. Next two micro drones coming back to us have your samples." He looks past me through his holofeed.

"Don't get too excited, though. They may not grow, or might die soon, or…"

"I know. Can't hurt to try, though, right?"

He nods. I wait like an expectant auntie for the drones to arrive through the matrix. After some time, I hear a slight popping sound, and two tiny drones the size of ants come buzzing toward me. Fenn lands them beautifully on my outstretched palm.

The bots actually look like tiny ants. One of the gestational chambers has a tiny tissue upload chamber, and Fenn helps release the microscopic samples into a blob of liquid, and suddenly a huge feed of numbers and data start spilling onto the screen. It's overwhelming. But what I'm reading is that the cells have been accepted. Fenn puts his drones on autopilot and calls Portia.

"Can you come to the gestational labs?" Fenn asks, on a private channel so no one, especially Doran, can hear our request.

"We have data for you!" I say, popping my face next to Fenn's.

Portia rolls her red eyes. "Lucky I'm close by. Be there in a bit."

When she arrives, her spear in hand and a shifty look around the corner, she's shocked but impressed at our enterprise.

"I'm doing this," Hana says. "Not Fenn. Please keep the data off your holofeed. I don't want anyone else to know. But I need your help. I don't know the first thing about reverse stem cell engineering, only the theory."

Reverse stem cell engineering. I'd never thought this lesson would come in handy, but I remember it from my studies a year ago. You take a cell that's already destined to be something—a nerve cell, or blood cell, and make it turn back into a cell that's more immature, and with the potential to be anything. It's like taking a space pilot and saying, hey, we're turning you back into a baby so you can start over again and become a farmer instead.

In this case, we want these cells of Cyclo to turn into mantle cells, so she can make energy again, and with the energy—make part of her systems function again.

I wait for Portia to say this is not possible, but she doesn't. Instead, she walks over to the monitor, and her fingers fly over the program so fast, I can hardly understand what she's doing. Towering over me, she's silent. After a few minutes, she steps back.

"Assuming your materials don't run out and the machines don't stop working, this will reverse engineer an embryonic stem cell from your diffusion cell, and then forward into a large culture of mantle cells capable of photosynthesis." She pivots and crosses her arms. "The only reason I'm helping you is that this took only five minutes of my life, and I honestly don't think it'll work. Too many problems can happen."

"Thank you! Oh, thank you, Portia! And please—"

"Don't tell Doran? I won't. But don't ask me to do anything like this again."

I nod, and she leaves. I watch the readouts for the next several hours, until it's time to follow Fenn's nanobots as they delve deeper into Cyclo's matrix. The information they're collecting is massive, so many readouts that a single glance of it on Fenn's visor makes me dizzy. We don't even eat until we're done, and by that time, everyone on the crew is exhausted.

Back at the bridge, everyone's ready for a meal and sleep, but Doran insists on a data review. I'm buzzing with excitement over my cell culture rebellion, but of course stay quiet, as do Fenn and Portia. Nutrient bars and drinks are handed out, but no one eats much. Portia takes a bite and forces it down, and

Gammand sniffs it and eats three at once, but he doesn't look like he's enjoying the process.

"Okay," Doran says, showing up in our holofeeds. "This is what we know so far—not that we need to know, but we can use the info to maximize our mission days here on the *Calathus*—"

Which, after a sidelong glance from Fenn, I deduce must be code-speak for our very survival.

"Possibly up to a week."

One week. The crew perks up a little. A week of extra life is nothing to sneeze at, as my mother would say, except that the idiom never made sense to me, and I never asked. Anyway.

"An extra week! That's great," Fenn says.

"No, I mean, a week total."

Wait. What?

"What did you say?" Gammand says, standing. "We have a week? We had three weeks when we landed. Then two. It's only been... We should still have eleven days left! Now only seven?" He turns to Portia. "I thought that hormone experiment extended us by a day!"

"It did," Portia says. She doesn't look shocked at all by what Doran just said. She stands to her full height and uses a portable holo projector to display a complicated graph in the center of the room.

"Everything I'm gathering involves the symbiotic relationship between humans and Cyclo, as well as the plethora of microorganisms within and on the surface of the matrix. Her microorganism biome is nonpathogenic by nature, and—"

"English," Fenn says. "Speak English, Portia. Please."

"I am. Get a translator or a dictionary or an education, I don't care." She turns to me instead and keeps going. I can see Fenn rolling his eyes next to me. "As I was saying, the bacteria that live naturally within Cyclo don't hurt her or us. But Cyclo has changed so much in only the last forty-eight hours. Many of these natural, healthy bacteria have died, and in their absence, other dangerous strains have become aggressive."

"So you're saying she's becoming a petri dish of infectious soup," Fenn says.

Portia bares her black gums at him. I tap quietly on Fenn's back.

... - --- .--.   .. -

Stop it.

He presses his lips together and settles down. Good.

"Can they affect us?" I ask. "These bacteria?"

"Possibly. You should try not to break skin when possible. We don't need new routes of infection, as we have limited first aid supplies."

"What about how Cyclo is dealing with us on board?" Gammand asks.

"So far, so good. Since no one is hibernating or sleeping within her matrix anymore, we're losing some data there—but Fenn's stay inside her matrix showed that hibernation was relatively safe at one point on the graph. Otherwise, she's accepted us like her previous crew."

"Are there any updates on what happened to Miki?" I ask.

"No," Doran says. He looks pointedly at me from Fenn's holo. "We still don't understand who did it, or why. I had Fenn run a DNA diagnostic, and at least in the areas where he's searched so far, there are no traces of Miki's DNA on the ship."

"You did?" I whisper to him. "Why didn't you tell me?"

"Doran's orders," he whispers back.

"Oh."

"What about another passenger on the ship? Someone hidden, who might have killed her?" Fenn asks Doran.

"There's so much leftover DNA scattered throughout the ship from the previous passengers that we can't verify another living life form."

Gammand stands to show us the data downloads he's been packaging into different forms—but he loses me quickly with his talk of quantum data binders and respooling DNA drives. Fenn stands and illuminates the center of the room with a structural model of Cyclo. Vast swaths of her body are color-coded. Not the Cyclo language I know, but the crew's own designations. About one quarter of her is bright red, but not all in the same places. He goes through the colors—which zones are safest for us, and which ones are too toxic. On the map, red is very bad.

"How toxic are we talking?" Portia says.

"Not compatible with organic life," Fenn says. "The info I've picked up, from drones sent through about seventy percent of the ship, shows that the toxic levels in these red zones mean we'd die within seconds. Temperatures there have plummeted to below freezing, and some of the radiation leaks are bad. But the worst is southeast delta, gamma, and a few small sections of beta. Her ability to make and store light energy in her mantle was bad before. Yesterday it got a last surge of energy input, now it's completely shot."

At this, I look out the window of the bridge and see Cyclo's filmy, ethereal mantle spreading out into space. It's a deep, dark blue, and I can barely see the edge of it as it thins out. I wish I could have seen it when it was brilliant orange and red, capturing light far into the UV spectrum from the nearby stars. Gammand coughs, and I remember to listen to him.

"The *Calathus's* energy stores are slowly depleting. She recycles waste very well, but she's running out of recyclables. So her burst vacuoles in the core are sealed for now, and Cyclo added another layer of protection in the last twelve hours. But the chemicals there are incredibly toxic. Even the hardiest organisms known in the universe couldn't survive this."

"Oh. You mean *Quintifia sporolirus,*" I say. "It can survive temperatures on both ends of the spectrum beyond any living thing, extremes of pressures and radiation levels, too." Portia nods appreciatively at my words. There is a camaraderie, I'm finding, between people who understand small units of information that perhaps no one else finds interesting. I've felt this way about Fenn. But it also makes me want to spend a whole day with Portia talking about impossibly strong, small things. I am finding that I may be one of them.

Gammand turns to all of us. "All of your holofeed units will have constantly updating info on where you can work safely. In the meantime, it's time to sleep."

"Too hungry to sleep," Portia says, groaning.

"You have your food ration," he says.

"I'm so sick of our rations," Portia says.

"I can get something different," I say. "In my room. I've a supply."

"Does it look like a lump of mud, in brick form?" Gammand asks.

"Well, no…" I say.

"Then I'm going with you." He stands up and heads for the door. "I'd prefer not to live my last days eating bricks."

"It's just reconstitutes and freeze-dried food, though. Nothing fresh," I warn.

"As if we've eaten anything fresh in the last year," Portia says. "Come on. Let's go to your little room. I'm so hungry I could trzlia grookna."

I don't know what that means, but I think perhaps I shouldn't be anywhere near her mouth when Portia is hungry.

"I'm coming, too," Fenn says. "Starving."

Gammand actually laughs. It's the first time I've ever heard him laugh out loud, and the sound is grand and bright. The corners of my mouth twitch, bewitching and asking me to smile. Portia and Fenn grin at each other. I get the feeling that these glimpses of Gammand are rare and precious, and they all seem cheered up beyond their usual selves.

I don't have a right to smile, not while so many terrible things battle to keep me lead-heavy with sadness. Mother, Cyclo, Miki. The inescapable feeling that I am losing a game that I never agreed to play.

But there is Fenn's laugh, tempting me now, right now, to find even the smallest quark of joy.

What am I waiting for?

Will I be a terrible person for feeling joy again?

Custom says I should be sad. Sad for a long time.

But I am tired, so tired of falling in neat lines, and staying inside boundaries that have been defined by everyone but myself.

I grin irreverently and laugh, too. It sounds like a bird chirping in my own ears. "Let's go."

Chapter Eighteen
FENN

I have never heard Hana laugh. And I've never seen it, either. It's an Ipineq orchid bursting its fuchsia seeds in a firework of popping luminescence. It's the first moonrise of the fall harvest.

It's me, now, a person who's never really been allowed happiness. Who am I kidding? I've never given myself permission to be happy, either.

We all follow Hana to her room. The prospect of dinner and the original brightness that came with it has already dimmed with a single statement from Portia:

"I wish Miki were here."

Gammand nods, and my smile disappears. I miss her, too. It's only been a little while since she left, and yet the heaviness of her absence shows up frequently, a blanket that swallows all of us and snuffs out any good feeling.

Instead of talking, every single crew member turns on their holofeed to review data, because the numbing effect of work is damn effective. Hana walks ahead of us and chatters quietly with the ship.

"I know, but they are hungry. They don't eat like that, Cyclo."

"Yes, but most humanoid species have some common foods

they can eat."

"Of course we'll fit in the room. You can move the wall, can't you?"

The crew and I all exchange glances as we walk.

"Have you ever needed the ship's wall translators?" Gammand asks. He points at the mounted nubs along the wall, which have been nonfunctional since we arrived.

"No," Hana says. "We had one in my room, but it was too basic."

"What do you mean?" Portia asks. Her legs are so long that she looks like she's walking super slow compared to Hana's fast-moving legs.

"Like right now. She's flashing blue, pink, and gold, with that pattern. She is asking what she should do in case you don't like the food. If you'll be warm enough, or if she should change the temperature. Oh, for you! She says that Prinniads like your environment about ten degrees warmer. Is that right?"

Portia smiles, and her red eyes sparkle, looking like star rubies. "Why yes. That's correct. I'm so used to being cold when I work with humans, but I get over it. But I've studied her language. What I see so far looks like she's saying, 'Alternate food choices offer. Warm, more. Prinniad here.'" She smiles again. "There's so much nuance when you describe her language."

The hallways flash amber and gold this time. "What do you think she said?" Hana asks.

"She said, 'Prinniad language odd.'"

"No," Hana corrects her. "She said Prinniadi is like poetry. She's saying it's beautiful, but complicated, in a nonlinear way."

"I knew I liked this ship. She's like me. Hard to understand," Portia says. "Poor thing."

I keep walking behind Hana and Portia, watching them chat together. Before long, we get to Hana's little room. But once inside, it's transformed. Cyclo has changed the walls and moved them out. We can still see some of the bony matrix receding back in disintegrating splinters to make more room. Pouffed blue blobs have marked the floor here and there. Gammand pokes one with his finger, and the blob makes itself a soft indent in the middle, with a back. Oh. They're chairs. He sits down, and his legs rise up under another blob of a footrest that lifts from the floor. He folds his hands behind his head and sighs.

"This is better than my bed at home."

Portia looks around the room, noting the few decorations still clinging to the walls—the replica rice paper calligraphy hangings; the Korean masks that look like old men and women laughing, their eyes curved in joy.

"Miki would have loved to see these," Portia says sadly. She touches one of the masks. "She was really good at painting."

"I would never have guessed," Hana says.

"Miki let us see what she wanted. But the first time she saw my eyes, it reminded her of a rare crimson paint she used to use. We spoke of her work when no one else was around."

It's silent for a second. Portia clasps her hands together, but in a way that doesn't look like she's praying or beseeching. From my time on the *Selkirk*, I know that it's a Prinniad gesture of fear. Like she's suddenly terrified of being someone that people speak of in the past tense.

Gammand walks up to her and just stands there. He's not a talker, but even I've appreciated him just being nearby. It's the closest he ever gets to a hug. I point to another mask.

"That looks like you, Gammand," I say. The mask is grimacing comically, and Portia actually laughs. Gammand tries to recreate the face, and it's hilarious.

"Miki would have loved that one, too. She'd say it was prettier than you!" Portia says. While Gammand and Portia's laughter quiets to more gentle chatter about Miki, Hana sidles up to me.

"I've never cooked for more than two people," Hana whispers to me.

"I'll help," I say, smiling. "After all, I've done this once. I can pretend to be an expert."

"What is this?" Portia towers over the tiny stove in the room. It looks like a toy next to her.

"It's for cooking," Hana says. "My mother had it brought in during a shipment around twenty years ago."

"So it works with…fire?" Portia says, examining the knobs and the back.

"It has resistive heating coils."

"How utterly primitive. Can I try?" she asks.

Interesting. I've never seen Portia this animated about anything. She's always business, business, business. Not a shred of extra energy spent on emotion of any kind.

"You can boil the water. I'll need help reconstituting the dehydrates. It's not cooking, but if you don't do it right, some of the vegetable banchan will come out very mushy."

Gammand ambles over. "There's no water containment unit here. I can go back and get some."

"Oh, Cyclo can give us ultrafiltrate right here."

"Can she?" His eyebrows go up. Hana takes him to the wall where she sets down a large, empty bowl. Water condenses on the surface of the wall and drips right into the bowl, filling it quickly. "Let me test that to make sure it's safe," he says, moving a handheld monitor over the mini waterfall. "Huh. Interesting. It's not just water. It has trace amounts of calcium, magnesium, and potassium."

"Cyclo makes it so it replicates spring water from Korea, from the nineteenth century," Hana tells him. She's already put the water on to boil, and Portia is doling out dehydrates to add. Gammand has found a collection of different-sized bowls and mismatched spoons, and is setting them on the low ebony table that Cyclo has expanded upon with blue material. It's so weird to see him actually participating.

"We're sitting on the floor?" he asks.

"It's the custom," Hana says, before she freezes. Something about her own words seems to bother her, and she shakes it off before turning back to the stove. The next hour is a flurry of boiling water, steam, mixing, seasoning, and trickles of laughter. Gammand reluctantly shares a flask of spirits that's passed around. Hana tastes it but makes a face so comical that I want to kiss it. I take a swig, but it's not my thing, these old-fashioned ways of mental alteration. I don't get thrills from mind-altering substances. Thievery is way better. The thrill of success is quite heady. It occurs to me that I haven't stolen anything recently.

Right then, Hana peeks over her shoulder to glance at me. She looks down, looks to the side. Then she sees if I'm still watching. It makes my heart run faster than the wristwatch I'm wearing, ticking gently away.

Maybe there is something I can steal, after all.

"Are we ready yet? I'm starving," Gammand gestures to the air as if trying to sweep all the food and people closer to him. I wonder how much he's been drinking. He's usually a man of very measured gestures, if any at all.

Portia and I bring the steaming bowls to the table. There are plates of small vegetables seasoned with sesame seeds, red pepper paste, and garlic, marinated dried fish, and an orangey pickled radish dish of kimchi. It's amazing what you can do when everything starts out as tiny cubes of ultra-compressed freeze-dried foods. Hana showed us how to reconstitute them using texturizers and forms, which help keep the tiny vegetable dishes from looking like piles of mush. It's not authentic, I guess, but then again—if we're engaging in a cultural tradition far removed from its origins, isn't it still valid for its own sake? I don't know the answer. I want to ask Hana, but Hana is like the food—created in time and space far from her ancient beginnings. And yet here she is, this precious thing begging to be accepted. She doesn't need anyone's permission to be what she is. She's Hana.

We all sit around the table and dig in. For a while, there is nothing but the sounds of chewing, slurping, and a few yelps of "I burned my tongue" after spoonfuls of soup. Hana is eating heartily, so different from when we first met and she seemed so frail and pale. There's a bloom in her cheeks, and they aren't nearly as carved out anymore. She hasn't been as tired when we've been working and walking the miles upon miles around the ship.

"I'm afraid the kimchi is too spicy for you," Hana says, pointing with her chopsticks.

"I'm afraid the food is going to run out too soon," Portia says. She's on her third bowl of soup and fourth bowl of rice already.

"I'm afraid of dying," Gammand says with a chuckle.

We all freeze.

Gammand doesn't chuckle about anything, and of all of us, he always seemed the one least worried about death. I've seen the fear in everyone else. When people think no one is looking, you can see it weigh down on them. A deep, pervasive sadness. No one on the ship seemed at peace with leaving this world, except Gammand, who was the same stolid, unshakable Gammand all the time. Everyone sighs in secret, except for Gammand.

So we all stare at him, spoons and chopsticks hovering above bowls, halfway to our mouths.

"I mean, who isn't afraid?"

"I'm not afraid," Portia says. She reaches with a spoon to scoop more of the bean sprout salad.

"Come on. Tell me there aren't things you wish you could still do. Could have done." Gammand leans back, slouching.

"I have regrets," Portia says. "The same as everyone here. But no, I'm not afraid to die." She isn't clasping her hands together, but I've seen her do it enough that I doubt her words. "My brother will get all my credits. He will have a better life because of me."

"Maybe it should have been you who had the better life," Gammand says.

"I've made my choices. They are mine. I don't need you to tell me what I should or shouldn't have done."

Hana glances at me, and then at Portia. "What's your brother like?" she asks.

Everyone stares at her. It's been an unspoken thing, since we all signed on, to not discuss our reasons for why we're here, or even who benefits from our death. For nine months on that ship, none of us asked that question. Hana crossed a line.

"Hana," I say, leaning close to her, "I don't think we should talk about that."

"Why not?" she says. "If I don't do something to help Cyclo, we will all die. But I know…" She blinks a few times, as if her eyes sting. "I know that I will probably die on this ship like my mother, and that in the end, you will be the only people who ever really knew me. So I should like to know you, too. Even if our memories are blitzed into oblivion, I should still like to know."

"Excellent idea!" Gammand says, and he gags for a second. God, I hope he doesn't puke all over the table. I take the opportunity to surreptitiously swipe his flask of booze and hide it under the table.

Portia mouths at me, *Thank you.*

"I'll start," Gammand says. "I'm twenty-nine years old. I'm a data packager, by trade, and worked for a mining facility. And I have no family. Everyone died on Crix while I was working remotely." He's silent for a minute. Portia looks at me. A knowing look.

And then I put it together. "Gammand, are you...related to the Shrytax family? From Crix?"

He nods.

I get it. His family didn't just die on that planet. There was some political battle over a mining contract, and an arsonist blew up a space station, hoping to make the argument completely moot. But the explosion was far larger than expected. It didn't just destroy the station. The station ended up crashing to the planet and catastrophically altered its atmosphere. Gammand helped commit accidental genocide on his own people.

"You were the arsonist?"

"Yes, I was. A damn good one, too. Too good, apparently." His eyes have a hollow look as he stares at the blue walls. "I've been helping some of my people get settled, now that they have no home. But you know how it is with interstellar goodwill missions. They only help if there's something in it for them, and Crix never signed the 90XR treaty, so it doesn't qualify for aid. What I earn on this mission helps about a hundred people get a new home."

Gammand paces around us as if we're playing some weird game of duck-duck-goose. "I have been in prison for ten years. Ten years, since I was nineteen years old, in solitary, on the surface of Jupiter, inside that red hellhole of an eye, where all I had to stare at were white walls that flashed photos of my entire family. I killed them all." He wildly flings his arms around while he circles us.

"So I had my chance to give up my life, because it was

over anyway. I was going to be executed this week, in fact. It's all very symbolic, isn't it? But in my death, I pay for a few people's freedom to start a new life somewhere else, where my murderous stink won't haunt them, and where they won't be worked to the bone anymore. So, you see," Gammand says, stopping right behind Hana. "I don't care about getting to know you. I only care about getting this godawful job done. And if you try to save this ship and ruin my chances, then my own death is really worth nothing. And I won't have that."

Chapter Nineteen

HANA

Gammand walks unsteadily to the door, where Cyclo quickly opens the membrane.

"Thank you for the meal. It was"—he burps loudly—"delicious."

The door pinches shut behind him.

"I guess he really likes our cooking," I say, eyebrows raised.

Fenn rolls his eyes at the door. "Hana. He's drunk off his ass."

I ponder this a moment, what it means to be off one's ass. Does it mean he fell off a chair? Does it mean his buttocks fell off? Because they didn't. I really should have studied the idiom dictionary Mother found for me. Too late now.

"Wow. Even on my home world, that was rude," Portia says.

"Oh. I'm sorry I asked," I say. "I shouldn't have said that." Like everyone else, I've stopped eating.

"No, don't be sorry." Portia reaches over a ridiculously long arm and pats my hand. Her red eyes find mine. "It's such a human thing to do, what you did. More human, even. So many people tread so delicately around emotions, it's like they're afraid they even exist. It makes for terribly bland conversation. But that pure emotion? It's one of the reasons why I don't completely loathe *Homo sapiens.*"

"*Homo sapiens novum,*" I say, smiling.

Portia pulls her hand back and returns to nibbling on the spinach salad. "My brother has both Prinniad and human parents. He doesn't live on Prinnia with our family. His father took him to Forxis, and he now has two little ones himself. But life there is so hard. They've all gotten blood infections, repeatedly, and it nearly killed my niece. Their immune systems aren't doing well there. My gift to them is the money it will take to buy full Prinniad citizenship. Then they can go back home. No more infections. No more suffering."

"No one can buy that. The elimination of suffering," Fenn says. His face has gone cloudy with thoughts.

"But that must be very expensive," I say. I don't quite understand the concept of what costs what, but I'm beginning to understand that what the *Selkirk* crew's families are receiving in exchange for their lives is an enormous amount of money. Enough to change many lives in a substantial way. I read that Prinniads take almost no new inhabitants from other planets. They make it prohibitively difficult. And expensive.

"I've had a good life," Portia says. "A good ten revolutions around our star. That's about twenty-two Earth years. I've fallen in love, I've learned many things. And it's time for me to share. In my death will bloom opportunity for a whole family. I cannot be sad." She smiles. For the first time, her toothless smile doesn't look strange to me at all. Happiness has a common thread in all of us, and that beauty has so much clarity right now.

"Weren't you in the penitentiary where Gammand was?" Fenn asks.

Portia laughs. "I didn't say I haven't made my share of mistakes!" She leans in close to Hana. "You're looking at the person responsible for launching the parasites on Sentress. It destroyed a whole crop of crikio blooms and made the competing company very rich. They paid me well, but I got caught."

Somewhere, far away, there is a faint thump and a yell. Portia rolls her scarlet eyes. Fenn looks at his holofeed and shakes his head. "Gammand is completely wasted. Someone needs to get him into a safe quarter to sleep it off. We don't have alcohol reversal agents on board. And we should watch him. You know."

Just in case, is what Fenn wanted to say. In case someone tries to hurt him, like they hurt Miki.

"I'll get him," Portia says. "In fact, we should all go to sleep." She looks half asleep already from eating all that rice. As I recall, Prinniads don't process carbohydrates well—they ferment in their digestive systems, so Portia is probably a bit affected as well.

Everyone stands to leave. Fenn, too, wipes his hands and prepares to leave.

"Shouldn't we clean up?" I say.

"What's the point?"

Hmm. True. But the truth is, I want to hold back from making this night end. It might be the last time I have anything this close to normal, and normal is so new to me. I'm loath to let it out of my grasp. What's worse is that simmering close, terrifyingly close, is the anguish of knowing that I have no family in this world, and that my world is shortly going to implode. It's a terrible reality I cannot undo, I can't unravel and restart, I can't scrub away. And anything that helps me forget is worth clinging to.

Fenn is standing by the doorway, watching Portia catch

up to Gammand. He looks at them almost longingly. Inside the room, it's so quiet.

"It's too quiet," Fenn says, as if he can read my mind. His eyes are still on the empty hallway, as if it holds so much more promise than I do.

What he doesn't say, and I am thinking: we're alone.

What I don't want to admit: I'm so very lonely.

I say nothing, feeling the yawning emptiness, despite Fenn being close by. But he seems elsewhere already, departed with his crew down the hallway, thinking a memory I don't share with him.

"We should go to sleep," I say. This is the one good thing about not being trusted by the crew. Fenn stays with me always, like a shadow, and I find it a relief. After seventeen years of being alone in my room, I am not at all willing to go back to solitude. It's a dirty word now.

He turns toward the room. "I guess so. God, it's so quiet. I hate the quiet sometimes."

"I could ask Cyclo to put on a newsreel. Or an old movie."

"How about some music?"

"Okay," I say. But the array of music available on Cyclo's archives is dizzying. "I never know what to listen to. Mother has me listen to music from the eighteenth and nineteenth Earth centuries."

"I like the late twentieth-century stuff. Cyclo, play some Big Star."

Cyclo finds the music immediately. It's very simple, just guitar, vocals, and a distant drum set. It is pleasant. I like it better than instrumental-only music—the violins always sound like they're crying.

I ask Cyclo to make some bed-like forms out of her matrix, and she complies. She puts them very far apart, almost against the opposite long walls, which makes me pout a little. I like to sleep when Fenn is closer. Fenn looks at the bed and shakes his head.

"You sure it's safe? We shouldn't touch Cyclo…"

"We can put some clothing down so you don't touch her directly," I say. But Fenn shakes his head again.

"I can't sleep yet, anyway. I keep thinking of Miki."

"Yes. And Miki reminds me of other things." As in, the end of everything. Of creatures in my life lost, without my permission, while my mind is in the bitter forgetfulness of sleep. But I don't want to say it out loud, and apparently, neither does Fenn. "Maybe you should do something else," I say. "Maybe wind your watch."

He turns to me, his eyes seeing me as if I'd been gone a week. "My watch. Oh." He glances at the timepiece on his wrist. "It needs a good cleaning, actually. I don't have the tools for it."

As if later, he could. As if he's going to outlive Cyclo and me and this entire decaying mess that is our circumstance right now.

"Why do you like watches? They're so imperfect." I peer closer, and he holds it gingerly out toward me, not quite ready to hand it over for a closer look.

Fenn smiles. "Because once upon a time, this was all they had to know how much time passed. Not just the sun passing overhead, or the moon rising, to pass the day. They needed to know precisely how quickly or slowly things happened. They wanted to measure it. I mean, can you imagine what you would do if you had nothing but metal and tools and the raw ingredients to craft something that could do so much, be so beautiful?"

"I do." I go to the lacquer box by the wall, where Cyclo moved it to make room for our dinner party. From inside, I pull out a set of wooden knitting needles. Nestled nearby is a square of knitted wool, about one foot by one foot. It's a beautiful piece of work, knit with cables and seed stitches in a lovely pattern that looks like ripples of water. The wool is soft and pale green. Below are several keepsakes belonging to generations of the Um family, but I don't unearth those.

"You made this?" He touches the different stitches, pressing his fingertips here and there to explore the texture.

I nod.

"What is this made of?"

"Wool. It's the hair that comes off an Earth sheep, a kind of animal."

"How the hell did you get wool way out here? And these?" He picks up the knitting needles and examines them, too. The oil and constant use by my hands have burnished them with a silken smoothness. They are the color of ripe Nebraska wheat fields. Or so a picture once told me.

"Where did you get these?"

"They belonged to my great, great, grandmother. The wool came from a small garment that she knit. But when I wanted to learn how, I ended up unraveling the sweater. Isn't it funny that it's called a sweater? It's supposed to keep you warm, so you sweat, maybe? It's such a funny word. But in England, they called it a jumper, but it doesn't make you jump—"

Here, Cyclo flashes a gentle lavender to tell me I'm running my mouth again.

"Anyway," I say, "I unraveled it back into yarn. But that wasn't enough. I wanted really to know exactly how to do it from the beginning. So I brushed and picked at all of it until it wasn't yarn anymore, just a mass of fiber. And then I hand-spun it back into yarn. And Cyclo helped me extract some cobalt, and I dyed it blue. And I looked up some books in the archives, and I knit my first tiny blanket."

Fenn looks over the square of fabric and raises his eyebrow.

"How many times did you…undo this and repeat the process?"

"A lot." I'm embarrassed by the number. A hundred and three, to be exact. A hundred and three times I dyed the wool, I spun the wool, I knit the wool, I made tiny, infant-size cardigans, and booties, and little blankets, and tiny satchels. Things that I could never use, never did use, but made for the sheer joy of making something. From scratch, is what they used to call it. Though, what scratching has to do with anything, I don't know.

"Do you know," Fenn says quietly, "how many times I took this watch apart and put it back together?" He steps closer to me, still holding the timepiece in one hand, still holding my little blanket in the other.

"A lot?" I whisper.

"Yes. Funny how, with everything available to us, we still want to learn how to do things the old ways."

I shrug and smile. "This is what antiquists do."

"Yeah. A funny word for people who find joy in the beauty of the old ways. Like singing. And dancing."

"I don't know how to dance," I say. For some reason, my cheeks are hot. I'd ask Cyclo to measure my temperature to see if I have a fever, but I'm too embarrassed to ask.

"I do. I can show you. Any good antiquist needs to know," he says, winking. A new song comes on. "I like this one. It's called 'The Ballad of El Goodo.'" A guitar begins, with a melody and chords that sound like starshine.

"I see why they're called 'Big Star.'"

"I've no idea why they're called that. I just like the music," Fenn says. The music is everywhere, and it's so sad, and so hopeful, and so aching. Before I can even think, Fenn has moved even closer and captured my waist in his left arm and clasped my right hand in his.

"I'm not going to fall," I say.

"This is dancing," Fenn tells me. "Don't you know what dancing is?"

"Yes. No. I've seen it on the vids…" My face goes hot again. "This is very strange. Usually I've watched people dancing alone."

"Put your other hand here," he says, and settles my left hand on his right shoulder.

"Is this right?" I whisper.

"Pretty much, yeah."

We sway for a while, the music everywhere, Fenn's scent everywhere. It reminds me of the time Cyclo tried to synthesize Earth scents to keep me entertained. She manufactured the saltiness of a Caribbean beach, a mountain just after a blizzard, and a Pacific Northwest forest in spring. It is the last one of these that Fenn smells of, of green things wanting so desperately to live. How fitting.

I put my cheek on his chest. "Can I rest my head here?"

"Yes," he says, but his voice sounds oddly strained. He leans his own cheek against the top of my head because he's so very tall, and we continue to sway. For this lightning-quick second of my life, there is nothing but Fenn, nothing but warmth and primeval forests and his hands keeping me from spinning into my frantic thoughts. So it's utterly illogical that I find the need to ask him a question.

"Fenn? Why were you the only person who didn't say why you're here on this mission?"

Against my head, I can tell he is frowning. "Because my story is forgettable."

"I'm forgettable, too."

"No, you're not. But I am."

He pulls away from me, and I see his face in full. His brown eyes are full of knowing, his arms hanging limply at his side.

He's giving up. I don't know what that feels like. I see him and myself on this decaying ship and think, *We are such a terrible, beautiful mess*. I do something completely strange and alien to me, and incredibly foolish, because I can't stand the idea of Fennec no longer dancing.

I can't stand the idea of Fennec no longer being.

I can't stand the idea of Fennec no longer being with me.

I reach forward, slip my hands up to clasp his face, and pull him toward me in a kiss.

Chapter Twenty

FENN

have music in my ears, and a beautiful girl before me, and she's kissing me.

She's kissing me.

I hardly know what to do, what happened, how I got here. Whether Cyclo has stopped rotating, if I've flown off into space, if I'm dreaming.

What I do know is that her lips are soft, and trembling slightly, and if I don't unfreeze and react in some way she's going to run away forever, and that will be a tragedy to end all tragedies. And just when I think, *Yes, I'd better start kissing her back*, she breaks the contact between us, eyelids fluttering, inhaling because she's been holding her breath. Her hands fall from my face and hang limply at her sides.

The music is sweet and aching, and it makes everything incandescently astonishing.

Her eyes find mine, and she frowns. I must still look a little surprised and shocked. I'm still frozen, and now she's recoiling, as if her kiss was a crime or a mistake, whichever is worse, and God, Fenn, do something. *Do something.*

Live, for God's sake.

If Hana's taught me anything, it's this.

Live, while there is life.

Hana sways away from me and bolts for the door. I wake up just in time and take two huge steps toward her to grab her wrist.

"I'm sorry, I'm sorry," she says, and before one more apology leaves her mouth, I spin her around and crush her in my arms, our mutual gravities finding each other with inevitability.

My hands clasp her back and waist against me, and I find her mouth with my own and kiss her like there will never, ever be another kiss for the rest of time. Her lips part, and we taste each other. Her hands thread into my hair, and my arms tighten on her so firmly I nearly lift her off the floor.

Vaguely, in the side of my vision, there are flashing colors. Hana breaks the kiss, allowing me the opportunity to nuzzle her silken neck. Her hands find the hem of my shirt, and one hand slides up the center of my back, pressing me ever closer.

"Cyclo," she murmurs in my hair.

"Mmm?"

Hana laughs softly. "Cyclo is telling us to stop."

I stop kissing her neck to look sideways. The lights flashing around us are a zigzagging array of what must mean distress—yellow, iridescence, and silver.

"So this is what the ship looks like when her truant daughter is caught kissing a bad boy."

Hana laughs, and at this, two long blobs start emerging from the walls, reaching toward us as if to stop us. Hana pulls me toward her, and the door is starting to pucker closed, too.

"And this is what it looks like when the truant daughter is tired of being safe. Let's go!" she whispers, and pulls me through before it can shut over my leaping feet. Hana runs down the hallway, laughing, lights still flashing in the walls.

"Where are we going?" I say. She's pretty quick, which is

such a nice change from when she could barely keep up. Now I've got to keep up with her.

"Somewhere Cyclo can't watch us. Isn't there a section of the third ring where Cyclo isn't responsive to voice commands at all?"

"Yes. This way." I turn on my holofeed and head for the sections that Gammand had marked as inert, yet safe.

We run, hand in hand, like little children on the first day of solstice break. If there were eclipses and supernovas outside of the ship, begging for our attention, we wouldn't pause a second. I pull Hana into my arms every few minutes for another kiss, and she laughs after we break each kiss, as if some new, gorgeous secret has been revealed, as if there might not be another kiss for the rest of our short lives. Knowing this is true makes each one sadder and more lucent than the last.

We finally find a small control room in the south beta, only a mere hundred feet away from the whole sectioned-off area infused with the exploded contents of Cyclo's vacuole. In the distance, we can see the spiky white, waxy wall keeping death at bay. Hana pulls me into the room, and it's got a center console used for holo work, but now the console is a blank, round dais. I lift her onto it, and she wraps her legs around my waist as she pulls my face to hers.

My body rises against hers, and all I want is the oblivion that Hana provides, right now, only now. She lifts my shirt off, and after exploring my back and chest with her hands, she pulls her own tunic off and melds herself against me, nuzzling my neck.

I push her away for a second. "Hana," I say. "Do you even know what you're doing?"

"I've read the archives," she whispers, nibbling my ear, which sends ringlets of electricity down my neck and torso. "All of them."

"But—"

"Fenn. I may not know my English idioms well, but I'm very well educated about certain things. I've just not…practiced in real life. Not yet."

"But what if—we make a—I mean, God, it's not like it matters—"

I stare at her belly as I stutter. It's ridiculous that I'm worried about her getting pregnant. As if we had time and lives for such a luxurious biological event. But if we did, God, I don't even think my mind could handle such an idea right now.

Hana smiles sadly. "I'm sterile, Fenn. Mother told me this a long time ago. I can't have babies. None of the bioengineered can."

I don't know whether to be relieved or to cry. Luckily, we don't have to worry about all those infections from last century, which were eradicated before we were born. I look back at the door, which is still open. "But what if someone—"

"Everyone is asleep. Fenn. I don't care. Nothing matters. Just you, just me. Just now. Kiss me, Fenn."

I shut up and let her pull me closer. Somewhere outside of Cyclo, stars are colliding, black holes are collapsing, and galaxies are being born. People are dying, and people are opening their eyes for the first time in their lives. But right now, Hana is the only thing in my universe.

Chapter Twenty-One

HANA

Human behavior is so very odd.

I should know; I am one of them. But I was created with the precision of an interplanetary missile. Crafted and sewn together like a tailored stuffed plaything built to suit one person—Mother, and what she thought I should be. I am so very unnatural.

But right now, in the tangle of Fenn's arms, under the delicious pressure of his lips, I can hardly process what I'm feeling and thinking, except to say, *Oh Hana. How very human you have become.*

Fenn and I can hardly bear to part with each other for a few hours. We are a cliché, we are inevitable, we are wonderful and strange and sad.

We are.

Somewhere in the aftermath of those hours, we doze in each other's arms, not even content to withdraw into unconsciousness without each other. My eyelids flutter to stillness, and in my sleep, I dream of Fenn leaving, of Fenn falling into space outside of Cyclo. In a panic, I wake up, only to find myself resting my head on his bicep, my body curled against him. It's a shock, to have dreams that bring worry and mayhem. They are nothing like the dreams that Cyclo gave me, where there was never an inkling of bad feeling—only beauty and discovery. But I'm finding that even the worry in dreams means that something in my heart has changed to make me feel in such a way. To worry, to want. And I like it. There is something extremely dissatisfying about perfection.

Fenn does the same, walking for brief moments of lucidness to touch me, bring me closer. He nuzzles against my neck, and I wonder at some point if Mother engineered my genes to enjoy nuzzling.

Finally, we awaken slowly at the same time, but it's not the sweetness of Maia's starlight rising through the window that rouses us.

It's a shout.

It's close by. Because Cyclo is not consciously present here in this part of the ship, and thus the door has stayed open all this time, the voice is very apparent. It's a deep voice, yelling with distress that rises as it gets closer.

It sounds like Portia. Fenn and I lift our heads from the dais we've been sleeping on and see a blur of a tall Prinniad whoosh past our door.

"What is she running after?" I say.

"I don't know, but we better see what the hell is going on." Fenn pulls on his clothes, and I do the same, but I'm dissatisfied by the end to our night together, how abrupt and bitter reality is. As I head for the door, Fenn catches my hand. He kisses it, the way a man kisses a lady in a storybook from centuries ago, and I love that such a simple gesture is older than anything we've ever known. He's certainly no prince, and I'm no princess, but it pleases me just the same.

"For last night," he says, shyly.

I want to smile because last night was lovely and anything

but perfect, but for me, it was everything. I kiss him gently on the lips.

"For ever," I say. "Even if we don't have forever."

It's a clumsy way to say what I feel—that there are infinite spaces in every moment we have. Ones that last for the ages.

He smiles, then squeezes my hand. "Let's go."

We run down the hallways, and Fenn's holofeed blinks on, and a voice shouts at him. It's Portia.

"Something is wrong in the south beta ring. Really wrong. It's not like the other vacuole breach—this has to do with the hull." She hesitates. "Part of the ring has evacuated into space, and Cyclo hasn't done anything to fix it. Built-in plastrix barriers are still holding for now. But they're not terribly thick, and they can't possibly hold for long. Meet me and Gammand in northwest alpha. It seems to be the most stable right now."

"Got it." Fenn looks at me, but I'm keeping up.

"And there's something else." She pauses, and I realize she's breathing pretty hard. "Someone attacked Gammand last night."

"WHAT?" Fenn yells. "Who?"

"I don't know. He couldn't turn on his visor. The attack came from behind, but his inherited Gragorian nervous system has an electrical defense mechanism—it shocks attackers. Someone grabbed his neck. Hard. And his body reacted and survived."

"Who was it? Did he see?" Fenn asks.

"No." She looks at me hard. "Let me see your hands, Hana."

I raise them so she can see them in Fenn's holofeed. "Portia, it wasn't me."

Portia narrows her eyes, looking hard at my palms. "No. It couldn't have been you. You'd have burn marks on your hands. Unless they were healed since then."

"I've been with her this whole time," Fenn says.

"Awake? Or asleep?"

Something in between, I can't say aloud, but it's the truth. Fenn blushes, and says, "Asleep, I guess."

"Then you don't know it wasn't her." She stares at me. "I want you away from Fenn. I'll keep an eye on you. I can't imagine a human can take down someone Gammand's size in hand-to-hand combat, but if I can watch you, then I will."

"It wasn't me," I say. "You have to believe me. I wouldn't hurt him, Portia!"

"Well, if it wasn't you, then someone on this ship is trying to hurt us. I can't get the monitors to do a count of living organisms. If someone is hiding on this ship, we can't know who it is."

"It can't be me or Portia," Fenn says. "What about someone from the crew of the *Calathus*. Someone who stayed behind."

"Why would anyone stay behind? Unless they had something to protect...oh."

As soon as I say it, my stomach twists. Mother? On board, and hurting people? No. Mother is dead.

"Well, are you sure she never told anyone about you? It's possible someone else knew. Someone who wanted you to be here with them and the *Selkirk* crew ruined the party," Fenn says.

"I wouldn't know," I say. It's all so much to consider.

"Let's not jump to conclusions. Not yet." Portia sighs and shakes her head. "Also, there's more bad news."

Ugh, as if I can handle more bad news.

"The loss of the quadrant ring just decreased Cyclo's life-span by at least two days. That part of her nervous system was responsible for recycling oxygen residues."

"You've got to be fucking kidding me!" Fenn shouts.

"Come on. We need to find Gammand and redistribute our work again."

Fenn abruptly stops running.

"I can't take this. Losing more days. More work. I can't do this," Fenn says, hyperventilating, his hand resting on his knees as he leans over.

"You have to. We have to," I say. "Let's find out what happened. We have to figure out how to protect ourselves." I sound so confident, I hardly recognize my own voice. But with every bit of bad news pushing at me, this new instinct in me is to shove back. Hard.

Fenn shuts his eyes for a second as if trying to reboot. "Dammit. Okay. Let's go."

We take a passageway down to the alpha ring and keep running, with me in front of us so Portia can keep an eye on me from Fenn's holofeed. They have to believe I'm not responsible for these attacks. I was in Fenn's arms all night long! It can't be.

I orient myself as we keep going forward, remembering the hallways we are in. I walked by them sometime in that first day I'd left my room, but didn't really understand what they were. The side section of the wall has scooped-out, fractured areas, fifteen feet across. Jagged edges have been repaired by Cyclo, but the fragments that show where the evacuation pods broke off are still visible. There had been a large ship, the *Hummingbird*, that was scheduled to pick up the crew, but in their haste to leave, they used the escape pods. Like Doran said, this was no quiet, organized exodus. It was panic.

"When was the crew originally scheduled to evacuate?" I ask.

Portia checks her own holofeed for a moment. "The crew evacuated a full three weeks before they were scheduled to depart. It's why they took the escape pods, not the *Hummingbird*."

We round a corner, and by the last few empty pod bays, we

see Gammand standing there, chest heaving in breathlessness. He must have just gotten there before us.

"God, Gammand! It's good to see you, man," Fenn says between gasps. "You scared me." We quickly come to his side, but he gives me a lethal grimace.

"Get her away from me," he says.

I hang back, my hands up to show I mean no harm.

Gammand looks at Portia's image. "I was only fifty feet from that section when part of the alpha ring just blew up and broke off," he says. His eyes are large and frightened.

"Has anyone spoken to Doran?" Fenn asks.

"We can't get through to him. It's so maddening. As soon as Portia told him about the explosion, he cut out. Like he's making it harder on us to get this work done. I thought he was a good guy, but damn it. They're all the same. All of them."

We reconvene at the bridge, but our group feels hopelessly small. Fenn and I can't stay too close—Portia is watching me carefully. Portia and Gammand look through our equipment, trying to figure out how the smaller experiments they were supposed to launch today can also handle getting all the info that ReCOR wants. Everyone's expression is closed and stony.

All the while, Portia and Gammand glance behind them, around corners before they walk. As if there's a ghost onboard, trying to stalk them. And they look at me, too, once in a while, as if some hidden part of me might leap up and tear out their throats.

I don't say this aloud, but what if I really have hurt people in my sleep? Mother gave me UV spectrum vision. She tried to weave history and culture into me by making me look like her Korean ancestors. But it makes me wonder. Am I only as important as the pieces that Mother mixed into me? If maybe, just maybe, there never has been a Hana. My name means "one," like the Korean word for the number, but my history isn't nearly as clear or simple. Maybe all I ever have been is pieces of a whole. And maybe I'm not even aware of the fact that Mother made part of me a killer. A killer so gifted that she keeps secrets even from me.

"I have an idea," I say. "Miki's biomonitor. We still have it. I think I should wear it."

Fenn raises a hand. "Hana, you don't have to—"

"I want to."

Gammand rummages around and picks up Miki's biomonitor. The one that's broken. "I can make this work as a tracker, but only that. It won't have anything on her biometrics. I'll get it cleaned up and reregister the device for her."

Portia nods, as does Fenn. I'm not thrilled to have this thing in me, but if it gets us some answers, I'm willing. To find the truth.

"After this, we'll stay grouped," Portia says. "Hana, you'll stay with me. Fenn and Gammand will stay together."

At this announcement, Fenn's shoulders drop. It means we can no longer be together, alone. Gammand notices; he points to Fenn.

"This trip isn't about living out your last hopes for romance, Fennec. Deal with it."

"Shut up. That has nothing to do with anything. Hana isn't the killer. I know it."

"And you have evidence how?"

He doesn't. I know he doesn't. He looks at me helplessly, but we can't even speak of us as a unit until we figure out what is going on with the attacks.

"Very well. Right now, we keep Hana on a short leash and use Miki's old biomonitor as a tracking device." Portia retrieves something that looks like a small tube and inserts a tiny metal capsule. She reaches out for my shoulder, and I let her, but my hand is clenched in a fist. "It'll hurt, but only for a moment. And it's sterilizing right now."

Fenn gives me a worried look. My fingers tap on my thigh.

--- -.-   .. --   --- -.-

Ok. It's ok.

Portia presses the metal tube against the side of my neck. "Here goes."

I feel a slight tingle, but it's not bad. And then it feels like a painful pinch, as if someone just snipped an inch of skin with a pair of scissors.

"Ow!"

"There may be some lingering soreness," she warns.

Lingering. That's what we're doing, aren't we? Just lingering. But I don't want to do that. I want to fight. I want to fight for Cyclo, want her to be the Cyclo I know. I want to find out what happened to Mother. Why everyone left Cyclo so much faster than they had planned.

Gammand, glassy-eyed, is reading the orange and white holofeed in front of his face. He nods. "Reading Hana's output okay. It's not perfect, but it'll do."

"Thank you. And now, we keep going on with our research. Our hours are going to increase to cover Miki's work, and the areas near the new blowout. And I'm updating your progress readouts to accommodate the work." Portia glances at the progress bar on her holo. It goes from 60 percent completed, down to 45, with the addition of Miki's work. "We need to know what happened there. We're going on four hours of sleep, max. I'll have supplements added to your rations to support your extra hours. And Hana stays within eyesight, even with her tracker. No matter what."

But what about my tissue cultures? How am I going to check on them and see if they're growing properly? I open my mouth to say something, anything, but if I do, it'll be more of a lost cause than if I'm quiet. Gammand and Portia will say it's a waste of precious time, and they might even destroy them. They'll say it's futile.

But it's not futile to me. It's the only possible way we have to fix Cyclo, and to keep her from being destroyed. Our only chance of saving ourselves.

But I don't say this out loud because everyone but Fenn stopped listening to me a long, long time ago.

Chapter Twenty-Two

FENN

Hana leaves the room and heads down the corridor in the opposite direction, with Portia walking warily behind her, two feet taller, as if she's a prisoner on the way to the asteroid mines. It takes all my power not to stare and watch them go. Not to worry that maybe, just maybe, the back of her black and white-striped hair is the last image I'll have of her forever. Just before she turns the corner, she steals a glance back at me. She says nothing—she's too far away to for me to hear her—but puts her hand on her chest, above her heart.

And then she's gone.

"Come, Fenn. Let's go." Gammand grabs a huge pack full of equipment and hands me a similar one. It's ridiculously heavy, but Gammand doesn't make so much as a grunt as he heaves it onto his bent back. I can see why he's chosen this job. He's not a complainer. Not even about his impending death. My father was the same. Of all the beliefs he's held, that one was the firmest—do what you must, and do it without complaint. I wasn't a complainer, not exactly; I made my gripes loud in other ways. I was a breaker and a stealer, not exactly a parent's dream come true.

Callandra was the same. She didn't complain, ever. Even when I didn't act the way family should act, she didn't complain; she just picked up the slack and then suffered for it. I touch my pendant, wondering when I'll have the guts to listen to it. I can almost hear her voice, more mature in words than the thin, childishness of her tone that, even now, I can hear clearly.

It isn't about what you want, Fenn. It's about what you can do.

"Fenn?" Gammand's staring at me with a steely eye.

"Yes? Sorry, what was that?"

"We'll head to the outer rim of the southern quadrant. It's transforming right now, and we'll get the best data there."

"Transforming?" I ask, not really caring, but I have to say something.

"Yes. Cyclo's changes, from being sentient to somehow less upwardly conscious, are happening in waves. From the data I've put together, it looks like there's a pattern in Cyclo's degeneration. First, it's happening in segments, not in the ship as a whole. Second, we notice those segments lose their ability to communicate with us."

"It's not just that, though," I say. "Not just communication. Cyclo is very emotive, have you noticed? She expresses her emotions in colors, especially with Hana. Those behaviors disappear in those areas. Like she's living but not really—alive, you know? Not thinking or feeling."

Gammand is walking really fast, and I can't tell if he hears me. But he starts shaking his head. "This ship is not emotive. It wasn't created that way."

"No. You're wrong. I've seen it disagree with Hana, and flash colors when it's not happy with her."

"It's programmed to offer options to the crew, Fenn. That's not the same thing as emotion."

"I'm telling you—"

Gammand stops walking, so abruptly that I almost crash into him. He faces me. "Tell me you have data to support this. Not just your feelings, what you see, what you hear. I should know. Our human senses are terribly inadequate in data gathering. Which is why we need these." He points at the nanobot cards sticking out of my pocket. "Not you. Not your faulty sixth sense." He starts walking again. "Anyway, *Amorfovita potentia* don't possess the anatomical substrate for emotions, like your fancy limbic system does. There's a reason why the *Calathus* resembles plankton or coral more than a primate. The engineers didn't want to deal with that level of unpredictability."

Internally, I'm fuming at his lecture. My fingers tap Morse against my thigh, since saying it out loud would be a mistake.

-.-- --- ..- .-.-.-   .- .-. . .-.-.-   .-- .-. --- -. --. .-.-.-

You. Are. Wrong.

Just barely in my peripheral vision, I see a flash of silver. I look right, just as the silver streak disappears under the blue iridescence of Cyclo's surface. Huh. I wonder if she heard that, if she was annoyed that Gammand basically said she was a thoughtless computer and nothing else.

After a few more minutes, we arrive at our destination. The sides of the passageway are honeycombed with storage areas. The walls are their usual blue, but something is different—every now and then, there's a stabbing streak of white. Just a blip here and there, but noticeable. I can't remember what that means. I wish Hana were here to help me.

"Cyclo, what does your white color mean?" I ask. But she doesn't speak to me with her artificial mouth made out of the wall. Maybe she's not healthy enough to handle it. I know that she's supposed to taste, smell, see. I wonder if she's gotten too sick to notice that my hands are all sweaty from being riled up with worry over these attacks.

I start investigating the storage areas. Some are too small

to step into—maybe Cyclo helped move things in and out. Others are long and narrow rooms with enough headspace to walk into. I step into one filled with different-sized crates. Most are empty—perhaps the crew took them along—but some still have packages of calorie-dense carbohydrate blends, huge packages of electrolytes, canisters of material recyclers. I look to see if there are any dehydrated Earth pizzas in there, but no luck.

"The storerooms of most ships usually have a lot more stuff," I say, poking here and there for any goodies that would be worth taking back to the bridge.

"Cyclo was built to deliver nutrients via hibernation cycles. She harvested light energy from Maia efficiently and made her own sugars and proteins, which were fed to the crew. So real food was only for crew morale and vitamin supplementation."

"And now she can't photosynthesize. Things are falling apart in pieces."

I wonder what that would be like. If we didn't just get old gradually, but one by one our limbs just dropped off, until there was nothing but a poorly functioning head, until that winked out, too. I shiver at the thought. Because I know how I'm going to go—like a book closing violently, a clapping end to Fennec Actias. I just don't know exactly how that book is going to get shut. Poison? Radiation? Ejected into space and frozen while my blood boils in my brain and heart? Who knows.

I busy myself with readying my nanobots. Anything to not think of *that*.

"Your bots need to be programmed for radiation measurements, in addition to neural-electrical activity."

"Already done. I've taken Miki's program and added it to my own, so everything goes slower, but I've got it."

Gammand is already muttering to himself, walking down the hallways and reading measurements into his holofeed.

"Hey. You going to be okay?" I ask. He seems more irritated than usual.

"Fine," he says, before adding, "thanks, Fenn."

I've got ten bots ready to go, but as usual, most need to fly directly into the matrix. Only two are going to take measurements in the various honeycombed hallways and storage areas.

I head to the entrance of the storage area, out of eyeshot and hearing from where Gammand is working. The walls aren't just blue with those occasional streaks of white, but here are some permanent streaks of beige. I remember—those are areas that mark where her tissues are getting scarred. There is an area dripping with that brown acid and a toxic-looking gray gas rising from where it's burning into her blue flesh. Before I launch the first one into the Cyclo's wall, nearest to the entrance of the storage area, I whisper.

"Hey. It's me, Fenn. I have to do some more studies. Is it okay if I fly my little guys into you again? Just doing measurements. Please?"

I put my hand on the floor. It flashes briefly in medium blue, and a quick bright green. Good. Knowing that Cyclo can squash the life out of my bots, it's become a habit of mine to ask permission. Not that I ever did with any being before I met Cyclo, but hey. It's never too late to stop being an official biological pirate, right?

I set my holofeed and fly the first bot into the matrix. There is a brief flash of white against the blue as the bot makes contact and penetrates her matrix, and then it's flying through her walls, and the data comes rolling down my feed in droves. Hopefully on Gammand's tablet, too. One by one, I fly each bot into different areas of the hallways. At the end, before my last launch, he finds me.

"This is interesting. Look. Calcium and phosphorous levels

are bottoming out. I need you to reprogram that last bot to stay within the membrane surface, not go deep into the matrix."

"Sure." I use my eye movements and fingertips to alter the commands, then watch as my feed readies the program. As soon as I'm ready to launch, I put my hand on the floor. Cyclo will need to know this one will be more irritating, since her membrane surface is riddled with sensory nerves. She'd be more likely to destroy this one if I don't ask.

"Cyclo," I say, "I'm sending in a new bot, but this one is different. Is it okay—"

"What the hell are you doing?" Gammand asks me. He's stopped studying his tablet and is staring at me with irritation and disgust.

"I'm…well, I'm asking permission to fly this into her membrane surface. It's going to be more physically uncomfortable."

"Who cares. Just fly it in."

"But she nearly destroyed my first fleet because I didn't ask permission."

"She doesn't care, Fenn. You're not going to hurt her goddamn feelings. Fly them in."

I stare at him. I think of what he said, how my senses are so imperfect in collecting information around me—like déjà vu, neural hiccups that feel like paranormal activity—and yet, my senses have told me that Cyclo does care. She cares about Hana. She certainly doesn't want me kissing her, that's for sure. But I can't explain this to Gammand because all I have is my own experience. Which is worth shit because it's not data he cares about.

"But—"

"Doran," Gammand barks. "I need to override Fennec Actias, permission request seven four omega delta five."

Doran's face appears on my holofeed. "What is it now, Fenn? Just do the work. Gammand has enough on his plate.

I'll give him directive over your drones, but only for an hour."

And just like that, my feed tells me that I'm no longer in command of my bots, and that Gammand has already launched my last bot off the card in my outstretched hand.

"Doran, Gammand, don't. I'm telling you, she'll be angry."

"Quiet. You're on your way to making sure that ReCOR nullifies your contract. And if you don't bring in the data, then I can't package it up, and it screws with my own contract."

"That's not fair, Gammand, and you know it." I seethe. "I'm just trying to do my work!"

"Using your faulty, human *sentiment*?" Gammand booms. Doran has disappeared from my holo, and my feed tells me that the bot has landed and is now immersing itself into the membrane between two very sensitive layers of epidermis. White lines emanate from the landing area, like rays in a star pattern. Which is when I realize—white is the color showing Cyclo is in pain. Oh no.

I hold up my hand. "Just let me talk to her—"

It happens so fast, I don't even realize what it is. A hard sting across my jaw, so hard that it turns my head a few inches. Gammand's hand is still held aloft from the slap. Inwardly, my heart goes cold and hard. Gammand and I always got along. On the *Selkirk*, we joked rarely, but mostly spent a lot of time together in silence. He liked that I didn't pester him with questions, and I liked that Gammand never judged me as a criminal. But right now? Any friendly feelings I ever had for Gammand just turned to ash.

"You'll do as you're told, Fenn, or so help me, I'll kill you. I'm going to fulfill my contract, and your feelings for this ship or that girl aren't going to ruin this."

A terrible realization chills me even more. "Wait. Miki— did you—"

"Kill her?" Gammand straightens up, and his eyes unfocus

for a second, as if looking right through me. "Don't be absurd. Of course not. And I'll thank you for stopping this conversation right now. Back to work."

I open my mouth to resist, to ask another question, anything to figure out what the hell Gammand isn't telling me. He turns away from me, but this time, when he pivots back, I see his fist raised to right-hook me into submission. He has a lot of muscle and quickness. I was wrong to think he was some quiet, morose guy. Ducking his blow, I lose my balance and stagger back.

Gammand raises his fist again, but this time there's a tranquilizer gun in it. The same one he used on Hana on the first day we were here. I back away as a shadow looms behind him.

"What are you doing?" I yell.

"Again, saying the wrong thing. You have been messing up ever since you came here. I thought you were a risk, that you were just going to steal stuff and leave our crew, contract or no contract. And you've been worse than my worst nightmare. You're slacking on your work and mooning over a girl whose very existence is threatening our contracts."

I raise my hands, but Gammand doesn't back down. That's when I realize he's not holding a tranquilizer gun in his hand— it's a downer. The kind of gun that's used to render criminals into a paralytic, resistance-less pile of human. Dialed up high enough, you stop breathing.

I thought there were no deadly weapons allowed by the *Selkirk* crew.

I was wrong. Did Doran give him the power to take out the crew if necessary?

My feed is still running, but I don't have an open channel to speak to anyone. With my eyes, I indicate on my holofeed to open up a one-way channel.

"Stop that," Gammand says, and he fires. The laser shot

goes whizzing past my head, and I turn around, plant a foot, and run for it.

A scream rises behind me. I stop running and turn my head to see Gammand, eyes wide with terror, his uplifted hand with the neural gun poised but motionless in a long extension of Cyclo's wall. Cyclo has reached out with her matrix and embedded Gammand's weaponed arm and torso.

"Gammand!" I scream.

Gammand is screaming, too, but he can't move because Cyclo has him nearly immobile. Only his one free arm is moving, frantically beating about his head and torso, trying to pummel Cyclo's matrix into letting him go. His pendant, along with the suicide medicine, is embedded in matrix enclosing his torso. Even if Gammand wanted to painlessly end his life right now, he couldn't.

Every punch Gammand lands seems to hit me, too, and my insides feel like they're being plunged into acid. My heart and brain are wailing the same thing, the noise of despair issuing from my mouth.

"Stop! Leave him alone!" I yell, but the ship seems so massively strong in overtaking Gammand, my voice seems too small to stop anything. Cyclo's colors are a riot of deep crimson mixed with silver and white—anger, distress, and pain.

A high, thin scream—a girl's scream—sounds from far away. "Cyclo! Stop!"

It's Hana, far down the hallway, where she and Portia have come running to help. I don't know whether to feel relieved or horrified that they're here. Run, I want to say, but I've suddenly lost my voice, as if my body knows the truth before I do—there's no point. Hana and Portia are gaping as Gammand's yells of protest turn into one long, excruciating howl.

We all stare as Cyclo rends his body in half, and our world changes to crimson.

Chapter Twenty-Three

HANA

The scream dies inside my throat as everything happens slower than time can possibly allow.

Gammand's body, split in half, is there for all to see for an instant. It is the color that shocks, beyond the actual tearing of a life—intestines a surprising shiny pink color, magenta liver glistening, broken vertebrae so very white. Impossibly white.

"Run!" Fenn cries, as he grabs my arm and pulls me down the hallway.

But I can't. My Cyclo. How could she do such a thing? As Fenn tries to drag me away, I watch because I cannot bear not to—my Cyclo, engulfing his body, immediately tearing him to pieces, extensions of her rising from the floor and wall to take in pieces and bits of flesh. The blood sprayed over the floor and wall is absorbed quickly, leaving only her scarred blue membrane. Through the translucent matrix, I can see Gammand's face, mouth still open in that last scream, eyes rolled into his sockets. His head is soon parted from his body, and layer by layer, Cyclo dissolves skin, then muscle, then bone.

It happens very quickly.

Gammand is utterly consumed.

I cannot move. My heart has stopped beating; my eyes won't blink. There is screaming, right in my ear, something about running away, we must run away, when Fenn sweeps me up in his arms. He gallops as fast as he can from the southern quadrant, along with Portia. I am stiff and cannot move. Fenn's arms hold me with painful tightness so that I cannot possibly escape, but he doesn't realize that there is no escape.

My Cyclo.

My Cyclo has killed Gammand.

She is a murderer.

My head is a buzz of terror and the wordless keening of a broken heart, the kind that happens when worlds fall apart. The same sound I heard in my heart when I woke up and found Mother gone. The day I found out that Mother was dead.

There is nothing in my ears but the sounds of despair.

At some point, I hear my name. *Hana, Hana, Hana. Hana, talk to us.*

I am still in Fenn's arms, and slowly my ears seem to start working again, no longer feeling like they are stuffed with cotton wool.

"She's in shock. Hana?"

"Never mind her. We need to figure out where to survive here." It's Portia's voice. Strong and steady, still working like a perfectly well-functioning, emotionless AI, except she's not AI. "Where will we be safest from her?"

"The gamma or delta ring," Fenn says. "It's the most dangerous, and closest to the vacuoles, but most of the walls have been blocked from the toxins. That is where the ship is no longer able to communicate well. Sensory organs are shut down, so it's inert—from a consciousness point of view."

"Yeah, we so much as accidentally poke the walls with our fingers, we'll be burned by radiation or acid in seconds," Portia says. I don't hear Fenn's voice, but I can hear him breathing hard and fast. He is running at a clip to keep up with Portia. "Good God, Fenn! What happened back there?"

He doesn't answer, just waves his hand onward. I can't speak yet, I just can't, but I also won't be carried when I feel well enough to walk. I wriggle in his arms, and Fenn pauses to let me down. My feet find their rhythm, and I run alongside Fenn, who's afraid to look at me. So I grab his hand, and despite our connection making running more awkward, he grasps it as hard as I do his.

Fenn tries repeatedly to call upon Doran. Again and again, he's not reachable.

"Another star flare messing up our communication," Portia says. "But as soon as he can, the first thing he'll see is the feeds. He'll know immediately."

Finally, we round the bend and face a long hallway sloping upward. Each side is covered in the white, waxy secretion that Cyclo made to keep the walls impenetrable to the water-based poisonous liquids from one of Cyclo's burst vacuoles.

"Through here," Portia says, looking at her feed. "Cyclo has no sensory capacity down in the second vacuole storage area. The radiation levels are elevated but won't incapacitate us."

"What about food? Equipment?" Fenn says.

"We have enough supplies and tech with us for now. We need a safe place while we figure things out."

While we figure out how not to let Cyclo kill us, too.

Even though it's the truth, I can't bear it.

"Let's go," Fenn says grimly, and we go forward and ascend.

This area is dark. Fenn and Portia turn something on their holofeeds, the light garishly illuminating their faces. The walls are studded with gruesome-looking blisters filled with various liquids of different colors, some nearly at the breaking point.

"Don't touch anything. Avoid stepping on anything that looks like it's about to explode."

"Best advice ever," Fenn says.

There are corridors left and right as we continue, but many are blocked off, either by beige-colored scar tissue, or thick, waxy plugs that almost glow in the darkness. Finally, Portia takes us up one last set of handholds and steps, and my stomach seems to bounce against my chest as the g-force lessens. Portia leads us into a small, circular room. Blisters pockmark the walls, but they are thicker blisters, less apt to explode or ooze, and the floor is mostly flat and normal looking. Like the rest of the ship in this area, the walls are a dead, beige color interspersed with a midnight blue.

"Cyclo cannot hear us here, nor can she sense us," Portia says.

"So we're in her blind spot," Fenn says, and Portia nods.

I, too, can feel there is no sentient Cyclo here. We might as well be living on a knocked-out tooth or fallen hair from a human, it feels so unlike Cyclo's usual vital self.

Portia sits down and passes around a flask of filtered water. We all take a few minutes to catch our breath and bring ourselves to working order. The time to be frantic is past. At least for now.

"Fenn," I say. "Tell us what happened. Every detail."

So he does. About how they'd worked for a while, until Gammand confronted him about asking Cyclo for permission to fly the last nanobot.

"You asked permission?" Portia asks. "Why?"

Fenn sighs at her questioning. Likely he went through this before with Gammand, though not as civilly.

"Because Cyclo feels," I tell her. "Because she didn't like the nanobots the first time. Fenn was trying to be considerate."

"It could have been me," Fenn says. "I might have been the one killed. When we first got here, I wasn't very…respectful of this ship."

Portia nods, acknowledging this truth. "But when he treated Cyclo as a machine, and less like a creature with a soul…"

"But she never kills people," I say. "She would never."

"How do you know, though?" Fenn asks. "I mean, you've been in seclusion all this time."

"I don't know, I guess. But I know she has never been jealous or angry. Never vindictive. Never."

"But that was then. Things are different now. She's changing. She's not the same," Portia says.

"She is the same!" I stand up, finding my voice. "Just because I grow into an adult, doesn't mean I'm also not the child I once was. It's part of me."

Fenn stands up and looks at me steadily. "But you're a human, Hana. Cyclo isn't. You can't make those comparisons. And let's be honest here — people do change. From good people to terrible, and vice versa," Fenn says, his eyes imploring me to understand.

I close my mouth. I've seen Fenn change, for one. I can't argue with what I know.

"Fine. So she's changed. We need to figure out why she's done these things." I pace the tiny area of the room. "I mean, maybe she is scared. Maybe she's hungry."

"Hungry? One humanoid to Cyclo is like me eating half a peanut," Fenn says.

"Right. But if you were starving to death, and someone offered you half a peanut, wouldn't you take it? In a heartbeat?"

We're all quiet. Of course we would.

"But if Cyclo is that desperate for food, why haven't we all been consumed by now?"

No one has an answer for that.

"What about trying to make the *Selkirk* work again?" I ask. "There is no other ship, and the evacuation pods are all gone."

"The *Selkirk* had a limited fuel supply. The ion engine cores were changed out before our mission for ones that wouldn't last long."

"We could find a different energy source on Cyclo somewhere," I say. "Couldn't we?"

"Doubtful, but it can't hurt to look. But trying to salvage energy sources? Cyclo might try to stop us. Even if she doesn't, it will take a long time to rig up a new power source for the *Selkirk*. And we have no way to survive on here past the next six days. Probably less. And then we'd have no food. We'll end up eating each other," Portia says.

"That is not going to happen." Fenn stands up, looking noble and resolute. "You all look like you'd taste terrible."

Portia covers her face. But Fenn's humor helps, because we end up chuckling and groaning.

"None of this matters if Cyclo is going to kill us as soon as possible," I say. "I think we should find ways to give her more sustenance while we figure out what to do. And try to see if the *Selkirk* can work again."

"So feed her?" Fenn says, raising his eyebrows.

"Yes. Why not?" Portia says. "Poor thing is hungry."

Portia speaks of Cyclo like she's an abandoned puppy needing comfort. It is strange to think of Cyclo like she is the one that needs help. All she's ever done is take care of everyone else.

Fenn rubs his chin thoughtfully. He looks rather adorable doing so, but of course, I don't say that out loud. I'm learning the customs of what to say and not to say. "What about our contracts?" he asks. "We're not supposed to alter the natural history of this ship."

"We aren't," Portia says, but then she points to me. "But remember: Hana can do whatever she wants."

I nod. "I'll do whatever it takes to make Cyclo better. But

what are we going to feed her with?"

"There are some food stores we can dump, to see if she'll take them."

I snap my fingers. "In the gestational chambers, there are huge stores of embryonic nutritional supplies. I have several chambers running for those stem cells, but they'll only use a fraction of them."

"But you can't heal Cyclo without giving her energy to keep her cells alive, even if they're brand new."

"Which is why we're trying first to fix her photosynthetic cells. It could halt her death spiral."

Everyone thinks in silence for a little while. "It's worth a try," Portia says. "After all, your first experiment with the hormones bought us extra time. How are the cell cultures doing?"

"I don't know. I haven't checked on them recently," I say. "If we do this—how will the underwriters of the contract know you didn't tamper with Cyclo? That it was me?"

"Well, it's all in the records, for one thing. We'll record it as such. And to be honest, all of this may be moot. You are the one thing they didn't count on when they created our contracts and this mission. That could be a game changer, for the good of us all," Fenn admits.

"Sometimes I get the feeling they knew this would happen," Portia says. "That they are just playing with us. Like that Earth game, the king and queen and the babies."

I lean over and whisper, "It's chess. And they aren't babies, they're pawns." Portia smarts at her mistake, her eyes flashing redder than usual.

"No." Fenn holds up his metal pendant with the hidden compartment in the back with the suicide medicine. "They couldn't have. If they did, why give us the option to kill ourselves?"

"ReCOR has all the incentive it needs to find out exactly how wrong things can go on this ship, so they can build a bigger and better one, and make more money," Portia says. "In the end, it's all about money. ReCOR is about ten years ahead of any other company that creates synthetic bioships. It would be a huge liability to find out the ships murder crew once they grow old. Fixing it, and knowing exactly how and when it happens, means making better ships. It makes sense to ReCOR to see how we suffer."

"Exactly. Our death seemed like an inevitability. Now, it looks like our impending murders are part of the data, too."

Portia zooms through a long scroll of data on her feed. "You know what? Cyclo's biometrics did improve a touch after Miki's death. I didn't correlate them before. There was a bump of activity after the hormone release, and a smaller one later. I think Miki's death did nourish the ship, to a certain degree," Portia admits.

"So...you think it really was Cyclo that killed Miki? What about the hand marks on her neck?" I say.

We think for a bit. Hand marks, with thumbs near the front of her neck, fingermarks wrapping around the sides. I touch my neck, as does Fenn. He looks at Portia suddenly.

"I just realized. When we found Miki, I don't remember seeing her pendant around her neck."

"You're right. It wasn't there. She took it off when she slept. Maybe she forgot to put it on again."

"Which means, if she was attacked—if she wanted to die with the medicine in her pendant, she wouldn't have been able to."

"What do you mean, Fenn?" Portia says, her face going paler.

Fenn raises his hands to his own throat as if to throttle himself into unconsciousness. His hands are in exactly the same place as if someone else tried to strangle him.

"Those handprints may have been self-inflicted. Miki may have been trying to end her life because she was attacked by Cyclo."

I stand up and walk around our little blister-filled room, carefully not to touch any of them. "For now, we keep together. No one ever dies when they're with me."

"Yes. We will stick close to you. Like parasites." Portia gapes her toothless grin, and I can't tell if she's disgusted by the idea or happy.

"Second," I say, "we'll go to the gestational lab and program the stem cells for photosynthesizing, and see if we can fix her mantle. And we can get the remaining nutritional stores there and start feeding Cyclo. See if that makes her biometrics improve at all."

What I don't say is that I want to go to the sick bays if we can and find out if there's any evidence about how Mother died. I have to know exactly what happened.

Portia stands, her head nearly grazing the ceiling. "Sounds like a plan, my captain," she says, saluting me in the Prinniad way, which is touching her opposite shoulder.

It reminds me of that ancient poem, *O Captain, My Captain!* Except that poem is about a great president dying, and I pray to the stars that my death doesn't end up being part of the plan.

Chapter Twenty-Four

FENN

Hana has become our de facto leader. Though we make decisions together, she's the only one we are confident could possibly stop an attack by Cyclo. The only one we think Cyclo would never, ever hurt.

At least, for now.

We can't go to the bridge where most of our equipment is, as it's clear across on the other side of Cyclo. The last of our food stores are there, too. Access to the gestational labs is a long stretch of nearly dead, dark navy-blue corridor—still pressurized and intact. We don't have to worry about being sucked into space, but we do have to worry about the fragility of the walls. One crack, and we're done for.

As we walk along, we follow Hana in a cluster. No one wants to step out of line, to touch the walls. Even walking is a frightening prospect. What if there is a blob of living tissue beneath there somewhere, waiting to rise up and grab our feet, choke us into submission, break us in half?

I don't want to think about these things, but it's funny how I think of death far more now than a week ago, when I already knew I'd come here to die. I just thought I'd be dying on my terms, sort of. Cyclo has made all of my reassurances about death a memory.

Well, at least I have this.

I reach up and grasp the pendant around my neck. The back panel is easily opened, and the poison there will kill me in seconds as soon as I touch it.

Small mercies.

"We're almost there," Hana says. As I watch her from behind, I notice that she doesn't skulk around the corners like she used to. She stands more upright, too, more confident. Her hair swings in a ponytail behind her, swish, swish. It feels like years since she was in my arms last night, when peace was this tiny, precious thing we had. Peace, and privacy. Both are gone. I fear that between the two of us, I'll be gone first. I miss her so much already. I'm going to miss her more than my family, and that's saying something. No one ever wanted me, just me, and only me. They wanted me without a criminal record. Me, without my tendency for breaking rules. Me, who put my own survival ahead of my family's. My soft insides actually ache—God, what a sap I've become, but I don't care. The hurt has turned me a little more human, and I'm going to miss that, too.

"We're here," Hana announces.

The gestational labs are a network of rooms with chambers. I remember it from when we were doing our recent drone flights. But unlike before, where the chambers were hollow and devoid of life, now they are full. Portia and I tentatively leave our little ball of safety near each other and look at the handful of chambers full of shimmering pastel liquid. Portia smiles, looking at what her few minutes of help has hatched.

"Look at that. Let's see how they're doing," Portia says, touching one that's iridescent pink, the liquid spinning lazily inside the chamber. She sidles up next to Hana, who's reading the biometrics from a wall display.

"Three different growth mediums. One keeps them in the embryonic stem cell stage, and the other two are maturing mantle cells. Look! They're doing really well. They're still dividing and healthy." Hana walks to one chamber in the center. Like the others, it's tall—a big egg shape, but held in place by a large cylinder of clear plastrix above and below, showing several tubes attached to the chamber. Hana explains how the tubes are feeding new nutritional mediums into the incubates and draining below to get filtered and recycled. "They're very delicate. This one is the original stem cells we harvested. The others are for the mantle photosynthetic cells."

The two mantle cell chambers are colored reddish orange. They remind me of the speckles on the outside of the ship before we landed.

"Are they ready?" I ask.

"Some are ready. I guess we try to implant them in her outer membrane, but Cyclo may be willing to put them there herself. I can ask her."

"Can you also ask her not to kill us?" Portia says, staring at a swirling incubate of purple, the one stem cell chamber.

"I can," Hana says, but she doesn't look terribly optimistic that she'll get an answer we like.

Hana leads us to one of the back hallways, with several rooms filled to the top with packages of nutritional powders. Portia is already pulling down fifty-pound packs, piling them in a row. I peer at them, reading.

Hydrolyzed itrik protein
Amino acid concentrate
Micronized carbohydrate crystals
Buffered mineral supplement type D
Vitamin formula, stage 030

There are so many. "Which ones?" I ask.

"All of them. They'll all be useful. But maybe best if we mix them. Like formula," Portia says. "For a killer baby," she adds under her breath.

Luckily, Hana doesn't hear her colorful side commentary. We get to work. Portia works on a batch of nutrients in the rear of the lab, whirring them inside some sort of sonic mixing machine, tapping buttons here and there to adjust concentrations. We all pitch in with the heavy lifting, without much effort.

"Fenn," Hana says. "Let me show you how I got the incubates started. Just in case you need to know, too." I walk over, and she points out one of the displays. "This is how I started. It was really straightforward." She leans close to me, scrolling through a display.

"If it's so straightforward, why are you showing me?"

"I needed an excuse. To do this." She moves closer until we are shoulder to shoulder, and her hand closes over mine. It sends a tingle right up my arm, and it's everything I can do to not turn and just start kissing her in front of Portia.

"We haven't been able to talk once since last night," she whispers, still staring straight at the monitor. Different oxygen levels are whizzing by on a graph. "I miss you already."

"I miss you, too," I whisper, squeezing her hand.

"Hana," Portia hollers. We quickly unclasp hands and turn around. By the distance of her voice, she's gone far down the hallways, past the storage areas. We find her in a large room with several tables built into the walls, with complicated monitors around them. It looks like the room where I was evaluated before our trip, with pods that descend from the ceilings to deliver medicines or oxygen.

"This is one of the hospital bays," Portia says. "According to our maps, there are five of these, depending on the age of the patient. But this one is for adults."

"Oh," Hana says, putting her hand to her mouth. "Mother must have been in this room when she died."

"Yes. I came looking for more supplies. I thought you might want to see the room."

"Thanks. I'll take a look around," Hana says, and Portia leaves to go back to mixing formula.

I start investigating one of the larger monitors, but the records are blank. I try a few old hacker tricks to see if there are ghosts of the old data, but there's nothing. If anyone was going to unearth something here, it would be Gammand.

No Gammand, no data.

"I can't get any records here," I say. Hana is wandering around the unit, looking at the tables where patients used to lie, and the wall cases that hold some medical equipment, like dissolving bandages and a tray of medicated dermal films. She stands in front of another case, and it's got a chaotic assortment of bandages, gauze, and splints.

"Look," she says. "This cabinet is a complete mess. Some of these are half opened, half unrolled." She shifts nearer to one side. "Here. They reached for them from this angle." She turns. There's one table close to that side, only two feet away. She peers at it, narrowing her eyes.

I crouch to look at what she's looking at. Most of the tabletops are pristine and glossy white. But this one isn't. There is a smear marring the surface and making it matte. I touch it—it's slightly sticky. And then, on one corner, I see it. Hana does, too.

"What is this?" Hana asks.

"It could be bodily fluids," I say.

"Do you think it could be Mother's?" she asks.

"One way to find out." I run a handheld analyzer—Gammand's—over the surface and peer into the diagnostic screen.

"What does it say?" Hana asks. She's wringing her hands together as if she knows what it's going to say.

"It's human blood, for one," I say. "There's enough DNA to identify. UY4021."

"It's Mother's blood," Hana says. Her knuckles are white. "Anything else?"

I read through the list of molecules running down the screen, and their percentages. "Carbon-based. Oxygen, hydrogen, iron, nitrogen, phosphorus, potassium...and trace metals in a lot smaller percentages. Chromium, manganese, selenium, thallium, zinc—"

"Wait, wait. Did you say thallium?" Hana asks. "Thallium isn't a normal element in the body. It's poisonous. Why would she have thallium in her blood?"

I call Portia over.

"I just dumped about ten thousand gallons of formula into the empty hallways behind the back of the gestational chambers, where her matrix is still functional!" Portia announces triumphantly. When she sees our faces, she frowns. "What happened?"

We tell her what we've found.

"Thallium? I don't know why it's here, but there's a lot of thallium on the ship. It's one of the essential elements in Cyclo's metabolism," Portia explains. "But it has an isotope decay product. Some of the poorly functioning parts of the ship have a lot more of the radioactive thallium."

"Like the southern quadrant, where Gammand was killed?" I ask.

"Yes. But we didn't know what it meant. It appears to have bad neurologic effects on Cyclo."

"What does that mean?" Hana asks.

"It means the radioactive thallium is a potent neurotoxin. It changes Cyclo, so she can't think or communicate with us the way she normally does. She acts less…reasonable. More like a plain old jellyfish, if you want me to spell it out."

"Maybe it was from her tattoo," Hana says. "She had that blue tattoo of a lotus flower on her arm. Ever since I was a child, it was there. It glowed slightly in the dark. Maybe it was degenerating, too. Maybe that's what killed her."

"I doubt it," Fenn says. "The thallium is leaking from Cyclo's core. It's not likely that your mom's Cyclo implants were affected, too."

"What about the blood?" Portia wonders. "I know how ships like this run. They're scrupulously clean. The surfaces are automatically sanitized. The fact that you even found blood means the auto functions of this room were turned off or weren't working. Have you looked to see how much blood is on the table?"

We all look. The table is white, dully so, but there is no obvious red blood besides that drop we picked up. And then I peer in closer because I realize something—there are spots all over the white table. White spots.

"What are those?" I ask, touching them. They feel tacky to the touch. Portia goes to the wall, looking at the operational panels there.

"What are you doing?" Hana asks.

"Looking to see if they have an iron-avid, europium-doped strontium borate phosphor source," she says, touching the controls here and there.

"A therapy light," I tell Hana. "I used to steal the strontium from them. They're used for skin treatments but will illuminate human blood." She is standing behind me, stiff as a board, eyes wide and watching.

"Got it." Portia touches the pad, and immediately the room goes dark. I'm disoriented for a second, splaying my fingers out and trying not to bump into anything in the black of the room. There are a few greenish, fluorescent dots and blotches on the table before me—the ones I'd felt with my fingertips.

A hand clutches my forearm—it's Hana, and she's turning me around.

Behind me on the floor, right behind where I'd been standing, is a riot of glowing green. Huge pools of fluorescent color lie in smears and drips. There are marks where it looks like limbs, dripping with blood, rested with finality on the floor. But there is a very obvious size and shape of the blotches, like a body was lying here. And most of the blood is pooled around where the head must have rested.

Hana's mother didn't just die. It wasn't just some arrhythmia or heart attack. And it wasn't a quiet fading away. The blood splatter shows she was thrashing around in her last moments here. She must have been in agony, and she must have had horrific wounds. But I don't say this out loud. I can't.

"My God," Portia says, her own irises glowing under the strontium light. "She probably died before they could even get her on the treatment table."

"This is why they evacuated the day she died. They didn't just evacuate the same day—they shut off the auto functions of the ship immediately. They were trying to subdue Cyclo. They fled right after your mother was murdered."

Hana lifts her hands to cover her face and weeps.

Chapter Twenty-Five

HANA

Why? Who would kill my mother?

It couldn't have been Cyclo. It's just not possible. If she was hungry, she could have killed anyone else on the ship. It wouldn't make sense to go after her. Mother and Cyclo worked together to nurture every newborn on the ship. Once they were out of their gestational chambers, they went into Cyclo—the first real sleep, first embrace, first feeding. No one loved Cyclo more than my mother, and Cyclo knew this. I'm sure she did.

Could Cyclo have been angry at her? But it took extremes of stress to her physical self before she hurt Gammand and Miki after they spoke to me, and even Fenn, in a way that wasn't…nice.

"It must have been a person who hurt Mother. Some member of the crew," I say finally, my voice already scratchy from aching.

"Or an accident," Portia offers. "An explosion, perhaps?"

"No," Fenn says quietly. "Not an accident. This was deliberate. This was the taking of a life—violently. Look at the amount of blood that was lost. The pattern of where it was when they dragged her into this room to escape. Cyclo doesn't have access to this room, does she?"

I shake my head. "No. The walls are thick plastrix. Some of the auto functions work with Cyclo's matrix, but not many. This is where patients came when Cyclo's matrix wasn't helping—it was all direct human intervention."

"They must have brought her here to save her. To keep her away from Cyclo," Fenn says.

"No. I don't believe Cyclo would have killed Mother. Who's to say they didn't try to save her here—it's the medical ward. And they just ran out of time," I say. The normal lights are back on, but I can almost sense the ghost of Mother's presence. The blood, refusing to completely disappear, begging me to tell the story. To unearth the secrets and tell the truth.

"Anyway, look at how Gammand died. No one could have escaped an attack like that. How could they have saved her from that? It must have been a crew member."

"Maybe," Fenn says, "but Cyclo learns, doesn't she? Perhaps she is getting better at killing. Her first time was sloppy. Your mother called for help. Got help, but too late. Cyclo has been a lot neater since then. Look at Miki." Fenn pauses, and his face contracts with pain. "We still never recovered any trace of Miki."

Portia puts a hand to Fenn's back and frowns with him. "Our poor Miki. But, the question we need to consider is why. It might be just from lack of energy, but the killing of a single person doesn't quite make sense. Not then, not three weeks ago, when they fled. We've watched her energy stores drastically decrease since then, as Cyclo's functions have deteriorated. Cyclo wasn't nearly as hungry three weeks ago. With Miki and Gammand, she was."

"Stop talking like Cyclo killed my mother," I yell. "I'm telling you, it's not her. She didn't do it."

"But you don't know that!" Fenn says.

"And you don't know that she did! Cyclo cared for her. She cares for me!"

I'm so ready to flee this room, to get away from the words they keep flinging at me relentlessly. I don't believe it. I can't.

"But Hana," Portia says gently. "What happened to Gammand—you can't explain that away."

My shoulders drop, and my eyes fill until the world is a blurry, watery mess. She's right, and I hate to admit it, to see the truth.

"Look," Portia says. "We know your mother died on that day. And the evacuation happened at the same time. We need to know why your mother was killed. Maybe she did something that angered Cyclo, or someone."

"Or rather, maybe she was about to do something," Fenn adds.

Suddenly, Portia's and Fenn's holofeeds turn on automatically. It's Doran.

"Where are you?" he asks, frantic. "Are you all right? Where's Hana?"

"She's with us," Fenn says. "Did you see what happened? Gammand's dead."

"I saw the whole thing on your live feeds, but I couldn't get through, and then I lost contact for almost an hour. I've been talking to the heads at ReCOR. Portia, Fenn—they swear that they didn't know this was a possible outcome. They say they had no idea that the *Calathus* crew believed that something bad happened to Dr. Um. None of this was revealed to me."

"How could they *not* know?" Portia nearly snarls. "How? We found out ourselves that Dr. Um was violently attacked. They must have told ReCOR. *You must have known, Doran. We came here to die, but not like this. Not like this!*"

Doran is silent for a long time. Fenn's veins are sticking

out of his neck, and he's livid with anger. We all wait for Doran to speak again.

"I didn't know. I swear on my children, I did not know. But that doesn't help. You didn't do this mission to be murdered, but to sacrifice your lives. There's a difference. But ReCOR will not send a ship out there to rescue you. They say that this is still all in keeping with your contracts, even if the *Calathus* actively harms you."

"And our death benefits will still be enacted?"

"Only if your work gets done."

"Not if we're murdered early!"

"They can't possibly finish under these conditions! They're doomed to fail. So we're just going to let Portia and Fenn die here?" I ask, shoving my face close to Portia's so that Doran can see me. "You can't. It's not their fault. It's murder. And it's now in the records."

Doran pauses and covers his face with his hand.

"Doran," I say. "Please. Where's the closest space station?"

"It's in Sector Four, on the other side of Maia."

"Wait," Fenn says. "You're that close?"

"Yes. It's the center of four different missions I'm managing right now," Doran says. "But I'm resigning my position. I'm going to get hell for this, and lose my job, and probably be indicted for theft given that I'm removing you from a sanctioned, legal mission that you've already signed a contract for, but I don't care." Doran's face shifts farther away from the screen. "I'm coming to get you. It'll take me at least five or six days, traveling in the fastest craft I can get. You have to figure out a way to survive until then."

"How will we communicate with you?" Portia asks.

"You can't. Once I'm off my ReCOR communication access, they won't let anyone talk to you. You'll be out of communication with everyone." He looks behind his shoulder.

"And if I'm not careful, they'll find a clever way to detain me. But I didn't do this job to kill people, dammit. Nine months I spent training you all, and it wasn't for this."

There is a long silence, then Doran finally says, "I've got to get out of here before they find out what's going on. Portia, Fenn…and Hana."

"Godspeed, Doran," Fenn says. I raise my hand, but Doran's image disappears before my last goodbye leaves my lips.

I can't believe it. Doran is really going to save us. But six days is a long time, on a ship that's dying rapidly day by day, and becoming more murderous as the hours go by.

We are still in the same room, reeling from Gammand's death and reveling in the possibility that Doran might save us. If he does, then we don't die. But Fenn and Portia won't get their death benefits.

"Doran said he might be detained by ReCOR," I say.

"Which means that we may have to prepare for the worst now," Fenn says. "And that means fulfilling our contracts so we aren't murdered for nothing."

"You do realize we've been set up to fail," Portia says. "If we can't make our objectives, I don't want to die for nothing. We could try to find other ways to survive if Doran can't get to us in time."

"At least you were able to release the nutrient mixtures, off the record. That might buy us some time," Fenn says.

My stomach drops, and nausea overtakes me. Something in the chain of events of Mother's death bothers me. Something that's missing. That's when I remember. Mother's diary. I haven't read it all—just a page or two here and there. There must be more there that I missed, including the answers I'm looking for.

"I need to see something. I need to get my things," I say.

"What? From your room? That's impossible. Cyclo is active in that quadrant," Fenn says, almost yelling.

Portia nods her head. "He's right. You can't go there."

"My mother's things are there. I need them. I'll get my answers there. I have to know."

"They aren't worth it." Fenn grabs my hands. "Please. Hana, that stuff isn't important. It isn't worth risking your life."

"Then I'll risk it for something else," I say, turning to Portia. "The cell culture. The one with the photosynthetic cells. I can transplant them into Cyclo and see if they work. But it will only be useful if I can talk her through it, so she doesn't ruin the process. I'm the only one who she'll listen to. And it makes sense to do it in the north quadrant, where my room is. It's the side of Cyclo that receives the most light from Maia."

Portia opens her mouth, then closes it without arguing. "You know, Hana is right. If we have any chance of doing this, it has to be her."

It has to be me.

And only me.

It takes a while to prepare. Fenn wants to put me in full body armor, a set that was originally for Miki, but it's far too large. I'm drowning in the suit.

"I don't like it, Fenn," I tell him, trying to take off the hard-shelled leg armor and peeling off the gloves. "I need my bare hands. This is how I talk to her sometimes. And it doesn't even fit anyway."

"You realize that touching Cyclo puts you at risk," says Portia. She's braiding my hair—a very maternal action, and one I'm not used to anyone but Mother doing. Her long, spider fingers section my hair into a tight, twisting braid that leaves no tail swinging with a chance it'll get caught.

"I know. But I have to try. If she knows I'm afraid of her, everything will change between us."

Which is a lie. Everything already has changed. It changed the day I woke up alone. It probably changed the day Mother died, and I was asleep and didn't even know my world was collapsing.

Portia finishes braiding my hair, and her hand lingers for a second on my shoulder, fingers against my neck. Her red eyes glisten for a second, and a horizontal membrane blinks across her red pupils. I forget that Prinniads have double eyelids. I think it means she's upset, blinking away her own ruby-red tears.

Fenn walks in, holding several large cylinders, a foot long each. There's a window on each one that shows they're all filled with lavender-colored liquid.

"I've got good news and bad news."

I stare at him. "What?"

"The good news is, I've got all the cells we've grown so far for photosynthetic purposes. It's enough that if they take, then Cyclo will be able to make two percent of the usual energy she makes. And two percent is enough for her to maintain her safety systems."

"And the bad news?" I ask.

"The last gestational chamber with the backup embryonic stem cells leaked. One of those acid blemishes somehow splashed the chamber. All the cells dumped out."

Oh no.

All those stem cells, spilled onto the floor and lost. Another chance to fortify Cyclo. Another chance to save her, and ourselves, lost.

Portia puts her hand on her head. "Then this is all we've

got. Even if we had time, we won't be able to make more cells. We've got one shot."

I sigh. I can't handle much more bad news. "So, what do I do?"

Fenn shows me the two capsules. "These can be injected or poured onto her surface. There's a gel capsule of growth medium around each clump of cells. So once Cyclo can bring them near her outer surface, they'll be able to survive on their own for a while. Hopefully long enough to mature and start harvesting light energy."

"How long will it take for them to establish?" I ask.

Portia removes her hand from my shoulder. "Twenty-four hours. At least. And that would be fast, but we need fast."

"The growth capsule should accelerate the process," I tell them. I sound more confident than I am.

"Remember to get the cells injected first. Get your mother's diary later. It's less important."

I nod, but I can't bear to look Portia in the face. She sees my reluctance to agree.

"Hana. You have to do what's safe first. We can't take the risk that Cyclo will hurt you. Use all your good standing with her and inject the cells first."

"Cyclo won't hurt me," I say stubbornly.

Portia starts to talk, but I turn away from her. She doesn't understand. Fenn ignores her and helps me put on a backpack with all the cell cartridges on it, and it must weigh thirty pounds. But I'm surprised to find I can bear the weight.

"Funny," he says, to no one in particular. "I don't think you could have carried this when we first found you."

"I know," I say. "I've gotten stronger. All the walking and running, I guess."

"Or something else." He lifts the handheld data device that Gammand used to wield. "Your biometrics have been great in the last few days. Far better than when we first found you. Your anemia is still there, but it's better. And your electrolytes are fine." He snaps it shut and puts it into a sleeve of the backpack to monitor my biometrics on the short trip. "You can't fix all that with just a little exercise."

"That's odd. The only thing's that's changed is...is..."

I can't say the rest because the rest is the last thing I want to hear. The last thing I want to admit.

"You haven't slept inside Cyclo since the day after I was wounded," Fenn says. He's quiet, and his words are spoken so gently, as if he knows there's a barb about to stab me in the heart. Prepping me for the worst. "Ever since you got real food, you've been stronger. Cyclo might be the reason you were so weak when we found you."

"No. No, Fenn, it can't be."

"I think she was purposely keeping you malnourished, Hana. To keep you dependent on her. It's the only answer."

"But Mother was in charge of telling Cyclo how to handle my hibernations."

"Are you so sure?" Portia asks. Her red eyes look slightly dull. She's worried for me.

"Cyclo's been sick," I say. "She's been lacking nutrients herself. It's not her fault. She wasn't doing it on purpose," I say, but I'm not ready to admit that the weakness I had when the *Selkirk* landed is the same weakness I've felt my whole life. Could Cyclo have been trying to keep me powerless since I was born? It just can't be. Fenn fiddles with the strap on my shoulder, and I pull away from him. I head to the door and face them. "She wouldn't hurt me. Not on purpose."

Portia instructs me about the best way to introduce the new cells, reminding me about not touching Cyclo, spending the minimum of time in the northeast quadrant. I don't want to listen to anything she has to say, but I must.

Finally, I'm ready. Before I head out the door into the dark, navy-blue hallways, Fenn touches my hand.

"Hana. Please be careful. Please remember what I said. Cyclo may not be on your side. Even with those nutrients we just gave her, she's still unsafe."

I shake my head. I can't. I can't. Cyclo isn't like that. Instead of speaking again, because he's realizing that I won't listen to him, he pulls my shoulder close.

"Just...try to be safe. Trust your instincts."

I don't even know what my instinct are, or if I've ever listened to them before—a language I may have to learn fast, I suppose. Fenn kisses me tenderly on the forehead, and I close my eyes, inhaling his warm scent.

His fingers tap a message on the side of my shoulder.

.. .-.. --- ...- . -.-- --- ..- .... .- -. .- ..- -- .-.-.- -... . -.-. .- .-. . ..-. ..- .-.. .-.-.-

I love you, Hana Um. Be careful.

My eyes widen, and my mouth drops open.

So.

That's what it feels like.

My heart thrums quickly, a happy tap-tap-tap against my rib cage as I smile.

"I love you, too," I whisper. Reluctantly, I head out the door. I turn around, adjusting the pack on my back, and smile.

"I'll be fine. Cyclo won't hurt me."

Despite my words, Portia and Fenn are looking at me with stricken expressions.

As if I'm alre ady a ghost.

Chapter Twenty-Six

F E N N

I watch Hana walk down the hallway, burdened by her heavy pack. Her hair is tightly braided against her head, the white forelock swirled into the complicated knots and braids. She has a way of walking that makes it look like she's dancing slowly—one foot carefully in front of the last, a sway of beauty that she has no idea is hers.

Portia puts her long arm on my shoulder, and the weight says more than I'm willing to.

That Hana may not come back.

That she's blind, and brave, and blindly brave.

And then she says what I'm thinking, because Portia's never afraid to say anything. "That girl is good as dead."

Portia walks away from the door, and I collapse into a heap, staring down the hallway as Hana turns a corner.

Just like that, she's gone.

"Here. Instead of staring at nothing, stare at this." Portia hands me the small handheld monitor that shows Hana's location within Cyclo.

All our dots—Portia and I, clustered here at the edge of the northeast alpha, while a tiny, innocent green dot, Hana, walks around the alpha ring on the way to the northwest quadrant. I touch the green dot, and her biometrics appear on the screen. Her heart rate is steady, in the seventies. She's walking at a calm pace, three miles per hour.

On the monitor, Hana is digitized and defined in numbers, graphs, levels. She is healthy and normal. She's also strange and miraculous, after basically being a prisoner for her entire life, though that's not what she would call it. *Being taken care of,* is what she'd say. But it's not just Cyclo's fault. It's her mother's fault, too. They both kept her locked away like some precious trinket. They made her for selfish purposes.

I laugh softly. I guess making babies for the purpose of making babies is a somewhat selfish endeavor. If my parents knew the heartache I'd give them, they would have opted for the contraceptive vaccine. The permanent kind.

A small red graph line appears in her biometrics. Hana's entered the beginning of the north quadrant, and suddenly her heartrate has zoomed up to one hundred. ACTH, cortisol, and epinephrine levels went from barely detectable to elevated within seconds. I grasp the monitor and stand up, eyes searching for what she can't tell me. If only we'd had a holofeed to give her, but the only ones we have are embedded in our own skulls.

Portia runs over, looking at the monitor over my shoulder. "What is it? What's going on?"

But I can't speak.

Hana's little green dot has stopped moving.

Something's happened.

Chapter Twenty-Seven

HANA

The pack is heavy, but I can manage it by resting every few minutes or so and massaging my shoulders.

What I can't manage is what I'm about to encounter.

I haven't spoken to Cyclo in what feels like years. The last time I slept within Cyclo was days ago, before the crew told me it was no longer safe. The last time I slept was within Fenn's arms, kissing him with kisses I didn't know could be so warm and hard to stop…doing. And now I've left Fenn and Portia behind me, these few and fragile beings.

And I am worried, despite my brave words to Fenn. The old part of me knows that Cyclo has done nothing but nourish me, care for me, save me from spiraling down into the abyss of loneliness. But that was before. Before they came, before Cyclo changed. What I saw her do to Gammand was—no, I cannot think of that. I can't. Even when I do, it feels like I'm watching another ship doing something unspeakable to someone I've never met. Even then, it's too terrifying to breathe.

Walking along the edge of the northeast quadrant, heading north, I see signs of Cyclo's degeneration everywhere. Looking out the plastrix windows, I see flaking and drying around her surface edges. And inside, her bright-blue matrix has deepened to the telltale navy blue that says her nerves are dying. The area between the windows and her matrix is peeling and cracking. A few windows are buckling and slightly askew.

Underfoot, the matrix is tougher and less cushiony, as if it's been dehydrated under a bright, hot sun. This is even worse than a day ago. Some of the translational units built into the walls have fallen out, pushed by the matrix that is shrinking like skin around a scab.

"Cyclo," I say as I walk. "Cyclo. How are you? I haven't asked in so long. And I'm sorry for that."

But here, where her matrix has gone dead—like a human foot after frostbite—there is no response. I wonder what that must feel like, to lose parts of one's self.

I wonder if Doran will make it all the way here in time.

I wonder if he simply logged off, laughed about the conversation to his superiors, and went to eat some cake, pretending that he's the good guy when, in reality, he was complicit all along.

This is why I have to do this. I can't believe in anyone saving me but me. Not anymore.

I enter the northeast quadrant. The color change is the most obvious—the blue brightens ever so slowly. Underfoot, the matrix starts to feel more cushioned. I am barefoot, as I've been all this time. Now that I am in more familiar territory, I pause and feel her gently pulsating warmth under my toes, and smile.

This feels right.

My room is around the next curve. But there is a passageway to the right, which takes me to an area where Portia says I need to release the cells and they'll go into her fluttery mantle around the edge of the ship. I pause at the intersection.

I need to find out what my mother said in the last pages

of her diary. But I need to save Cyclo, too.

All logic tells me to turn right.

So I turn right.

Three steps into my foray to the edge of Cyclo's last living quadrant, the colors on the walls and floor flash with stripes of yellow iridescence and lingering spots of peach.

Through the soles of my feet, I can feel her latching onto my skin and trying to communicate, but it's making my feet stick in the matrix. Forced to pause, I watch as her matrix slinks over my feet and rises up to my ankles.

I am fixed in place, and her voice enters my bloodstream.

Hana. Where are you? Where are you? Gone. Gone. I am here.

Her words are disjointed, as if missing whole sentences and thoughts. Looking down, I can see her trying to pull me into the matrix. Her blue matrix forms fingerlike projections that snake their way up my calves now. Can she not see me?

I wave my hand, a gesture that usually gets me a pretty rainbow of colors in return—a trick I often did as a child. But there's no response. I think Cyclo can't see me, only sense me through my feet.

Hello, Cyclo. I missed you, too, I tell her in my head. I'm back now. But I can't go into hibernation right now. I need to do something.

But you are going the wrong direction. Room back. Left, turn, delete. Back, back.

My heart flutters, faster and faster, and I break out in a sweat. Her gel encasing my feet makes me want to flee and scratch and fight. I can control the voice in my head, but I can't keep my body from reacting. Never, in my whole life, has her touch made me feel like this. My head goes slightly dizzy with the sensations flooding my system.

Fight or flight. That is what it's called. This is what I felt the first time Fenn saw me and chased me down. Only now, I would much rather run into Fenn's arms. Cyclo's gel on my skin doesn't feel like coming home, as I'd expected. In fact, I was worried that it would be so soothing, so irresistible, that I'd go into hibernation for a week and completely forget that Fenn and Portia were waiting for me to return.

Suddenly, a warm sensation washes over me. I look down, and the gel is still rising higher up my calves.

Oh. Cyclo is reading my thoughts. She understands that I'm panicking and upset. She's using her chemicals to calm me down and settle my racing heart. But I need to stay alert. I can't let her lull me into being complacent. Into our old way of me being taken care of by her. There isn't time for me to be a child anymore.

This is what she wants. Isn't it, Hana?
Room. Sleep. Go fracture to gather.

I don't understand, and I do. My room. That is where I want to go, too, I tell her without thinking, because it is my instinct, too. I shift the canisters on my backpack and shake my head to clear the fuzziness that's rapidly slowing my thinking.

Cyclo, I tell her. Let me go, so I can go to my room. Okay?

Wordlessly, the gel withdraws from my calves and sinks back into the floor. I sigh in relief, and the clarity in my mind tells me that her sedatives were slight and short-acting. Good. I can't do what Portia and Fenn want me to do first. I'll get Mother's diary, and placate Cyclo somehow, then release the cells.

I turn around and take the other corridor to my room. It's only about fifty steps away. The membrane door is already open and waiting for me, but beige scar tissue mars its edges. Even here, she is showing signs of degrading.

Inside the room, everything has changed back to before our group dinner here. I can almost smell the soup I cooked, see the look of happiness on the crew's faces when given a steaming bowl of warmth and nourishment, and remember the laughs and frowns from certain inappropriate behaviors. It was like a family. They say that families are imperfect, and that you don't choose who your family is.

I wish I'd gotten to know Gammand and Miki better. Frowns and scowls and all.

Cyclo's colors flash around me. Content bright blue, and curious gold, and pulsating yellow that says she's reading information I'm giving out with each footstep. Green colors that welcome me, invite me to sleep, invite me to stay. There is a new color I've not seen before, but I know what it means. It's on the very edge of the UV spectrum, nothing that Fenn or other humans could see. Electric violet, mixed with the lowest range of infrared that I can see. The spectrum. Everything.

Forever, Cyclo is saying.

Stay with me forever.

Maybe it is what she means, and maybe not. I take off my backpack, placing it on the kitchenette instead of the ground, since I can't take the chance that Cyclo will steal it away. I kneel before the black lacquer trunk full of my things and Mother's. Mother always liked writing—she even had a fountain pen, and one of the chemists on board had to make her new ink out of some leftover carbon chunks taken from one of the filtration systems.

I've occasionally flipped through the diary when I was bored, but always stopped after reading a sentence or two. It was Mother's private world, and I enjoyed it so much more when she read it to me herself. Only a month ago, she'd read one particular passage to me. I flip through the pages to find it.

Today my Hana became four years old. And she emerged from her hibernation singing. Singing!

eommaga seomgunure gul ddareo gamyeon
agiga honja nama jibeul bodaga

*She lisped the words and asked Cyclo to make a blue shell
around her, as if Hana were inside an oyster, a pearl to be found.
Hana always has ways of changing the story. She turned the
lullaby on its head! That's my Hana. She does things I never
would. She will do things I never can. My myth, my pearl, my
Hana.*

I remember that song. *When Mother went to the island to
pick oysters, the baby was left to stay in the house alone.* That's
what it meant. The mother came back worried about the baby.
There's nothing in that lullaby about the baby turning into a
pearl or that sort of nonsense. But I made it that way in my
brain. And that's what I've always thought the lullaby was
about. But it's not.

It's about a mother who leaves her baby while she gathers
oysters. And she comes back. There is no transformation, no
baby saving the day. But it doesn't matter. Lullabies aren't real
life. And my mother is not coming to rescue me.

I finger the pearl around my neck and cringe. It's such
a pretty trinket, something I've worn since before I can
remember, but I've always forgotten where they come from.
Oysters. A nagging piece of grit, like a piece of sand, or a
parasite, around which the oyster secretes this pearlescent
nacre to smother the irritation. I look around and wonder. Is
that all we have been to Cyclo? An irritation that needed to be
smothered to death? I yank the pendant, and the pearl comes
loose from the necklace and bounces to the floor.

Mother is not going to rescue me.

Neither is Cyclo.

Nor is Doran.

"It's up to me," I say aloud.

Cyclo responds in a swirl of concerned iridescent yellow. Are you hungry, Hana? Tired? Would you like to sleep?

It would be so lovely to let Cyclo take over so I could rest. I have a restlessness in me that I haven't felt before. But I don't want it quelled. Not yet. I flip through the book, looking at the dates. But the dates aren't universal timestamps. They are markers of my life. My doljanchi, or first birthday, when she prepared an array of objects for me to pick, to foretell what kind of life I would have. The paintbrush, to show I'd be an artist? The artificial rice grains, to symbolize wealth? The wool yarn, for long life?

In the pages, all I see is me. Me growing, me crying, me learning to walk and climb, me trying pickled radishes for the first time.

Where is Mother in all of these pages? It's strange how her own thoughts aren't in here—just stories of me. I stifle the urge to read the entire thing, front to back. But even without looking, the diary is haunting me. I need to find out what she was thinking on the day before she died. I flip to the last pages of the diary to find what I'm looking for.

There are only a few blank pages at the end of the book. And I find the last diary entry.

My Hana is a young woman. She has been for some time, but seeing her in the evening, knitting a sixteen-pointed star, listening to Mozart's serenade number 10 in B flat major, "Gran Partita" from our audio archives, she seems too wise. So much like a grown woman already. She has a lot to learn. But, then again, there is only so much left to learn here.

Autumns come. Clouds part to reveal their treasures on Earth. Apples fall from their trees.

It's time for her to meet the crew of the Calathus.

It's time for her to belong to the universe, not just her mother. Not just Cyclo.

Someday, Hana, I'll share the rest with you. But for now, it's time for one truth to enter the light.

You.

I shut the diary. She was going to tell the crew about my existence. There is no timestamp on the entry, so I can only guess it was the day before she died. But I don't know for sure. Mother, like me, was an antiquist, with a love for earthly objects. Writing on paper, knitting wool garments, cooking food as real as we possibly could. It wouldn't have been her style to keep a digital diary in Cyclo's archives.

No; there has to be more. There has to be something here.

This diary is all fluff and feathers and happiness. Even with my charmed existence, as coddled and protected as I have been, I have had doubts. Frustrations. Mother had one foot in my world of secrecy and a foot in the world as the *Calathus's* Chief of Bioengineering. No one is so perfect that they could put all their thoughts and hopes down and never have misgivings.

There must be another diary.

I rummage around the lacquer box, but I can't find anything that looks like another notebook or journal. There are our clothes, my knitting supplies, some boxes of spices for cooking. There are a few books, but I've read them all, and there is no mystery within them.

No, wait. That's not true. There is one book in there, a gift from my mother's great, great grandfather. An original twentieth-century copy of short-stories by a Korean writer, Yi Kwang-Su. It's entirely in Korean, without pictures on the cover or the insides. I glanced at it once as a very young child, and finding it completely incomprehensible and (horrors) without any pictures, I never looked at it again. Mother found an archived English translation, but I read that ages ago. She kept it wrapped in a silk handkerchief, under the sole piece of Koryo pottery with its celadon glaze, on a shelf near our little kitchenette.

I go to it immediately, unwrapping the rustling silk, and open the book.

As usual, it contains vertical columns of hangul that I cannot read, another reminder that I feel less Korean than my face would prove. There is nothing else.

I sigh. Another dead end.

And yet, the pages are worn and well-thumbed, far more than any of our other books. Almost as well-worn as the diary. The book is hiding something. I just know it. Mother might have written it in ultraviolet ink so that only I could read it. But since she was hiding it from me, maybe she did the opposite. Hid it in a spectrum where I could never, ever read it. It's the only possibility.

I shove the book into my suit. I need to find an infrared reader somewhere. I need to go. I head for the door, when Cyclo releases a pattern of golden and amber dots and smudges.

What are you doing? Cyclo asks me.

"I have to go," I say, breathlessly. But her gel rises up, so fast I can't even lift my foot. She climbs up my back, encases my wrists, encloses my neck and face. It's faster than I've ever experienced, inhumanly fast. And I hear her voice as my body succumbs to the numbness of the chemicals she unleashes into my skin.

You aren't leaving me, Hana. Never again.

Chapter Twenty-Eight

FENN

The dot is fixed in place as I watch her heart rate zing ever higher, until it plateaus and comes down. All the biometrics start to go to calmer levels, and I exhale.

"Don't worry. Your girlfriend is okay," Portia says, putting her hand on my shoulder. I open my mouth to say something sarcastic and defensive, then I realize Portia isn't teasing me. Even after nine months, sometimes I forget how awesome she is.

"Look, she's moving," Portia says. She's watching on her own small monitor. I look down to see her green dot reversing course, heading to her room.

I look closer, the hair on my neck rising. "What is she doing? She knows she's supposed to release those cells first, before retrieving anything from her room."

"It's Cyclo. She's talking to Hana, influencing her," Portia says. "Or maybe forcing her to walk."

"How could she force her to do anything?" I ask.

"Maybe it's more subtle than that. Maybe she's being manipulated," Portia says. "I've studied ships like this. Smaller ones. There's always a big debate between those who think of them as high-functioning environmental units, and others who consider them to be their own creatures, with souls and feelings."

I shiver. "I think ReCOR would disagree with you."

"Yes." Portia creeps closer to my monitor, looking at Hana's readouts. "And this attitude of ReCOR's is going to get us all killed."

We keep watching as the green dot heads for her room. It moves around the room here and there before settling in one place. She stays there a long time, and her heart rate rises and falls. What the hell is she doing? Reading her mother's diary?

"She needs to get out of there," I say under my breath. "The longer she spends with Cyclo, the more likely Cyclo will interfere."

Portia nods, then gasps.

Hana's heart rate zooms up. She's back in fight or flight mode, and she's backing away from the wall of the room. And then she stops moving. Her heart goes to a hundred and twenty. Then a hundred and thirty. And higher and higher. Her breathing rate is through the roof, her vessels constricting, epinephrine and norepinephrine are flooding her system.

And then, the green dot disappears.

I jump up. "What the hell! What happened?"

"Oh no. Cyclo has her," Portia says, tapping the screen to reboot, but it's not working. "Hana's not dead—the biomonitor would have shown it happen."

I drop the monitor and run to the pile of equipment we have. It's pathetically small, and there are no weapons. Nothing. So I don't bother to take anything; I just head for the door with nothing but my nanobots in my pocket.

"Fenn! Don't go after her. There's no point. She's as good as dead."

I pause at the door to look back at her. Portia, so impossibly tall and lithe, red eyes staring at me with concern—such a far cry from her contempt for me when we first met. We have such little time left together, and every single moment is already being lost, even as I breathe.

I look at her and know I'll miss her. And she'll miss me, despite my scrappy, irritating ways. And I want to cry.

And I think of Callandra.

I'm so close to fulfilling my contract. My bots have been gathering info all this time, and I'm getting closer and closer to crossing off all the items on my list of objectives. I could save Callandra, and I could throw it all away if I screw it up now.

But.

My heart and my brain aren't working in any way that makes sense. All I know is I have to get to Hana. I take a huge breath.

"If there's a chance Hana is alive, I have to go to her."

And I run out the door.

I run as fast as I can. I know Cyclo's layout well enough not to need my visor to tell me where to go. By the time I reach the northeast quadrant, I'm panting hard. I turn left, right, and left again before finding the corridor with Hana's room. The door is shut, with a membrane stretched as a barrier. But unlike Cyclo's healthier, thick webbing of a barrier, this is thinner and translucent. Inside, I see a small mass of black moving left and right—maybe Hana's head.

"Hana!" I yell.

The color of the hallways suddenly changes to a blood red, pulsing in waves ending at my feet. The floor starts to rise to encase my feet, but I'm too fast, and I jump away, hopping and dodging, never letting Cyclo get a good hold on me. I back up a few steps then leap toward the door.

My right foot thrusts hard against the door, and instead of bouncing back or absorbing the shock, the membrane cracks.

It's far more fragile and brittle than it used to be, and I can use this to my advantage. I back up and kick again until there's a gap big enough to jump through. The shards of broken door graze me as I pass, and I feel the warm sting of cuts on my forearm and left cheekbone.

Inside, I am met with horror.

Hana isn't being ripped apart like Gammand, but this is worse because she's still alive. Cyclo and Hana are battling each other, and it's not clear who's winning. The ship must be screaming at her, as evidenced by the nonstop riot of colors in the room. Cyclo has three thick tendrils around Hana's feet and left wrist, another that has risen and encased her rib cage, but she's using her other free right hand to slice through Cyclo's matrix where it's trying to hold her down. The knife looks like something she's taken from her little kitchenette. It's small but doing the job.

I have no weapon, so I punch and kick the blobs of appendages holding Hana.

This is my first mistake.

My fist immediately gets embedded, and the matrix oozes up my forearm.

"NO!" Hana roars. "*Don't you dare touch him!*"

I've never heard her voice sound so fierce. I try to pull my fist free, but it's not working. I try to kick, but I've stayed in place too long, and my feet are now embedded in the floor.

Hana screams a battle cry and slices through Cyclo's appendage around her other arm, and the cut surface of matrix around that arm looks like molten glass. It drops off her, changes to blue in its descent, and is immediately absorbed. But the undulating floor reaches up again to take her. But Cyclo can't keep up with her slashing blade. She can't overwhelm her the way she overwhelmed me back when I'd just boarded the ship and ran after Hana.

After releasing her own legs, she lunges for me and cuts my arm free of Cyclo's matrix, but I can already feel the numbing effect of Cyclo on my skin, and my mind feels hazy and slow. She's drugging me, and it's happening so fast that I start flitting in and out of consciousness.

"Fight, Fenn! Fight! She only has so much sedative left, and if you fight, you can overcome it!"

Her words sound like a faint echo in my head, but I'm still awake enough to hear it. I punch my arms, flailing, really, and do everything I can to pull my feet from the gluey floor. Something abruptly frees my hand, and I feel Cyclo's matrix fly off my wrist and hit the wall with a wet thud.

I manage to kick away the matrix from my feet and run to Hana, who's slashing at her feet and ankles every time Cyclo tries to encase her again.

"We have to go, we have to go," she says quickly, and grabs my hand. The door is still broken in shards, and Hana jumps through it, shoulder first, breaking more pieces as we burst through. We land on the other side and catch our breath.

"Which way do we go?" Hana asks.

"This is the way back, but Cyclo is healthier that way. She'll attack us. The other way is safer but it's closer to all the toxic storage rooms near her center." Basically, both ways are terrible.

"This way," Hana says, and we run to find a stairway upward toward the center of Cyclo, to where the ship's belly is full of vacuoles with radioactive metals, oily and acid degradation products. It's not a great choice, but at least it's a choice. Cyclo keeps trying to reach us by sending out blobs from the wall and the floor, but we're moving so fast that she can't hold us. We careen around the corner, when I suddenly remember.

"The cells! The canisters!" I yell. "Where are they?"

"Back in the room!" Hana says, her face stricken with

regret. "But we can't go back there!"

My stomach drops. That was our last chance to figure out how to keep Cyclo living just a little longer, so we could live a little longer. And now it's trapped in a room we can never reenter.

We are screwed, yet again.

My holofeed buzzes, and Portia comms in.

"Do you have her?" she asks.

"Yes, Hana is with me. We're heading back to you. We'll take the long way, to be safer."

There's a pause, and it sounds like Portia is running. "Wait. I went after you. To help. I'm in Hana's room."

Hana and I stare at each other, the color draining from her face.

"Get out," Hana says hoarsely, before finding her voice. "Portia! Get out of that room! Run!" She looks at me, panic in her eyes. "Fenn, we have to go back!"

"But Cyclo is just going to attack us, too!"

"No, she's getting weaker. She couldn't handle three of us. But if Portia doesn't have any weapons, she won't be able to fight Cyclo. And Cyclo wasn't trying to kill me."

She doesn't wait for a response. Hana tears off back down the hallway, which goes from the dark navy to a mottled blue. She's so fast now, I can barely catch up with her. We turn the corner into the northeast quadrant, left, right, and left again, dodging the sticky tendrils that try to catch our feet and our hands as we fly by. Cyclo builds a membrane wall that's piecing together slowly, like a spider's web, but Hana slashes through it and we keep going.

We round a corner. Her room is there, the one place where Cyclo has concentrated her nutrients, where she is at her most powerful. Something on the floor by the door is waving, scrabbling. Something small, like an animal fighting.

"What is—" I begin as we run toward it, then we realize what it is.

Hands. Two hands, clawing, fighting their way, trying desperately to pull on the floor. One hand shoots out, gains purchase, and drags out the rest of Portia, whose red eyes have gone nearly black from sheer panic.

She screams unintelligible Prinnia words, sees us, and screams again. "Run away!"

Hana and I freeze for one moment as we watch her hands scrape the floor, and she is dragged viciously back into the room.

"Portia!" Hana screams. She puts the knife into her other fist and runs. "Let go of her, Cyclo!"

Part of me wants to run away, to hide, to curl up into a ball and wish with every molecule of my body that I had never disobeyed my father that day when I was six years old. The day I skipped school and instead went to the scavenging yards on Ipineq and stole my first chunk of gadolinium. If only I'd been a better son, a better brother, I wouldn't need to be here, and God, it doesn't matter, it doesn't matter.

What matters is Portia is dying, and it's been a long time since anything was about me. It's never been about me, not since I stepped onto this goddamned ship.

I gallop forward, just as Hana runs into the room and I lose sight of her. My feet pound the soft floor, one, two, three, four. Ten steps later, I'm there.

So this is what hell looks like.

Chapter Twenty-Nine

HANA

Cyclo has her.

Portia is suspended in the air, each of her limbs corded thickly with Cyclo's matrix, as she tries to pull her apart. Her biceps and thigh muscles bulge with resistance, her face a mask of twisted pain, teeth clenched as she tries to fight. Her face is ashen from exhaustion. She sees me, and her eyes open wide, pleading.

"Kill me!" she shrieks. "I can't get to my necklace! I can't reach it!" She screams again, and through the translucency of the matrix, I see the fabric around her legs dissolving. Her skin starts to bubble, and the purple color of Prinnia blood seeps into the matrix.

I run forward with my knife, yelling. "Let her go! Let her go, Cyclo! You can have me back, just let them go!" I slice my knife into the matrix around Portia, freeing one of her bloodied legs and an arm. Cyclo starts to back away a little. My heart soars to think we could free Portia. Fenn grabs my arm.

"Give me the knife! I can reach higher and try to cut her free!"

I hand Fenn the blade, but Cyclo has molded his feet in

place, and he has to slash them free before reaching up to hack at the tendril around Portia's left leg. It goes free, swings for a moment, before Cyclo shoots out a thick column of blue to capture it again.

"My hand! Release my hand!" Portia yells at Fenn, growling and clenching her jaw. "And I can reach my pendant!"

The suicide medicine. Of course. I keep clawing and pulling at Portia's encased, bloodied feet, and Cyclo retreats from her body, knowing I'm near. She isn't attacking me—I wonder if it's because she literally has her blue hands full of Portia and has to concentrate her energy. Even the weak tendrils she uses to try to keep Fenn from moving are thin and tired. Cyclo's deciding where to budget her energy, and she's focusing only on Portia now.

Portia roars above me. Fenn tries to jump and slash at the thick cord of blue around her arm but misses. Portia screams, and Fenn and I watch with horror as her left arm dislocates from her shoulder with a sickening pop. The skin of her shoulder is stretched taut. Cyclo isn't relenting. Portia's face is awash in pain and sweat, and her body goes limp. She's losing her will to fight. Cyclo is tearing her apart.

"Stop! Stop it Cyclo! Stop!" I scream, over and over, but she doesn't listen.

Cyclo is not listening to me.

She's tasted blood and energy, and she's ravenous for more. Whatever good we did with giving her those liquid formulas is nothing to this. Cyclo is bloodthirsty, and we can't stop it. Fenn backs up near to the wall to give him room, and bolts forward, jumping at the last moment.

The knife in his fist slashes upward and to the right, and Portia's good arm is freed. The blue matrix around her freed arm falls off and hits the ground, and now she hangs from her dislocated shoulder.

"Cut her other arm free!" I yell, but Cyclo's matrix has formed a full cylinder, too thick to cut through, encasing her legs and rising up her torso. Portia looks at Fenn, and then at me. Apology rests in her red eyes as she reaches for her necklace.

The suicide medicine.

"No, Portia!" I yell, but Fenn grabs me from behind.

"It's her choice!" he hisses. "She's suffering, Hana!"

Portia's hand clutches at the dangling pendant around her neck, easily flicking the back of the locket open. She grasps it between her thumb and fingers, closing her eyes. The poison should work within seconds. And then her pain will be over.

I close my eyes, feeling Cyclo ooze over my feet. I kick her away. I hate her. I hate that she's done this. I hate that she could do something so horrific. When I open my eyes, Portia will be gone. I feel Fenn's hand on my shoulder for the briefest of seconds before he lets go. He gasps. Portia must be dead. She must be. I can't bear to open my eyes and see her.

And then Portia screams.

My eyes fly open, and I see her shrieking, shrieking like a being in the worst torment I could imagine, except I don't have to imagine.

"It's not working!" I cry out. "Why isn't the medicine working?"

"Goddamn it!" Fenn roars.

Portia is still suspended, still alive, face contorted with pain. Cyclo encases her body until only her face is still open to the air, until she muffles her last scream with a thick layer of throbbing red gel. Fenn dashes forward and stabs the gel right where her heart is, but the tip of the knife embeds a full inch away from her body. Fenn's knife can no longer touch her, no longer save her from the torment.

"No!" Fenn cries as Portia's body begins to disintegrate

and dissolve before our eyes. Fenn yanks the knife out, and an agonizing wail comes from his throat.

I can't watch.

I grasp Fenn's arm and pull him toward the door. He's dropped the knife, and I grab at it, slashing tendrils that try to capture Fenn's feet, my feet, my arms. Fenn is faltering, barely able to stand up.

"Fenn. We have to get out of this quadrant, now!"

He doesn't answer but fumbles to his feet and shuffles through the corridor like he's lost. I pull him along, yelling all the way to keep him moving. Every second feels like an hour, every step a mile. But soon we are no long slashing at Cyclo's attempts to glue us down and entwine us again, and the colors of the floors and walls get darker.

I cannot believe what I saw. I cannot believe what Cyclo has done to me, to Portia.

But it's real. And what's more, the suicide medicine, the one thing the crew had to ensure a painless death on their terms—it didn't work.

Oh God, why?

"I can't stand to be on this ship right now," Fenn says. He pulls me around the quadrant, and I realize that we're headed for the *Selkirk*, still embedded in Cyclo's side by the southwest quadrant alpha.

Inside the ship's bay, I collapse onto the cold, titanium floor. Fenn crumples next to me, eyes glassy and staring, not believing what we've just witnessed. There's no way Doran will make it in time to save us. Fenn absently paws at his neck and pulls at the pendant.

He flicks open the back, which has a tiny poison warning symbol in it. He pulls one of Gammand's handheld monitors out of a pocket in his pants and holds it over the tiny depression where the poison is supposed to be.

He blinks and waits.

"Placebo," he says finally. "There's nothing in here."

Fenn covers his face with his hands and cries.

So it's true. The suicide medicine necklaces were nothing but placebos.

ReCOR wanted the crew of the *Selkirk* to die on ReCOR's terms, not their own.

My eyes are dry. Maia's light sets in the window just opposite us as Cyclo turns and turns, and I wonder if there will ever be starlight in my life again after what I have seen.

Chapter Thirty

FENN

I didn't realize I'd passed out until I woke up.

It's almost pitch black, and so very cold. I blink, trying to reorient and extricate myself from these terrible nightmares that still gnaw at the edges of my consciousness. Until I realize, with a dread like I've never had before, that they weren't nightmares.

Portia.

Gammand.

Miki.

Gone.

My eyes adjust to the darkness. Hana isn't here. I'm still in the exit bay of the *Selkirk*. I stand up, joints creaking and muscles angry with overuse.

"Hana?" I call. Faintly, from somewhere deep within the *Selkirk*, her girlish voice calls back.

"Here, Fenn. I'm in here." She still sounds so young, but there is a raspy tiredness to her voice like she's just aged fifty years. I limp past the bay and head deeper into the belly of the *Selkirk*. On the left, I pass the storage areas, and on the right, the regular living quarters and the engine room. I remember all these places like it was a long, long time ago. As if I am walking through a museum of my life and everything I see is a relic and a wreck. Finally, I reach the bridge.

Hana is sitting in the captain's seat, which seems far too large for her. She sits with her knees clasped to her chest, staring out into space, where the rest of the Alcyone nebula looks absolutely magnificent, despite the fact that inside it's collapsing. Kind of like Cyclo. Kind of like us.

I sit next to her in the copilot's chair and find myself laughing.

"What's so funny?" Hana asks. She doesn't look at me, just keeps staring straight ahead into the bleak recesses of starry sky.

"Portia. I remember how she was so good at driving the *Selkirk*. And when I got a little too snide, she flipped me onto my back to teach me a lesson."

Hana looks sideways at me and smiles a little, but it disappears fast. She goes back to staring out into space.

"Just sitting in the bridge here—it's the farthest I've ever been from home," she says after a long silence.

"I'm not so sure you should call Cyclo your home anymore."

She bites her lip. Her hand goes to something on her lap. A book.

"What's that?"

"It's a book of short stories. Can your holofeed recognize the infrared spectrum?"

"Yes, why?"

"I can see in the ultraviolet spectrum, but I have this feeling that Mother hid something in here. On the opposite end of the light spectrum." She hands me the book, and I thumb through it. It's well worn, a book in a foreign language. I touch the holofeed chip in my forehead and ask it to do an infrared screen. Hana goes to my side and puts her cheek against mine, so we can see together if there's anything.

Hana inhales sharply.

It's writing. In English. Laid atop the printed characters—Korean maybe—in ink so diluted that the writing is hazy and faint.

400221.78
Sol 649

Today, I did something I shouldn't. I am the most selfish being on this ship, and I am risking her life and mine with my ego, my need to make something like me, but better. She is only one cell old today, and I have already hidden her in Cyclo, in the walls of my chamber, where Cyclo is feeding her the necessary gestational embryonic fluids I've stolen from the incubation lab.

Today, I have made the best and the worst mistake. She is only one cell old today. One. I will call her Hana. And I will call myself her mother, but what I am really is a monster. I know what I must do to keep her secret.

I am a monster.

"A monster?" Hana says. "Why would she think of herself like that?"

"Well, what kind of a person would make a human, just to keep them locked away for their whole life?" Fenn asks quietly.

Hana shakes her head and flips the pages. "This is the day I was born."

400221.358
Sol 655

Hana is born today. She is terribly ugly. Wrinkles everywhere, a cry that makes me want to bite my own tongue, with a nearly full head of cocoa hair but that shock of white by her forehead. I don't know anything about rearing infants. I hold her, and she is so soft, so fragile. I'm terrified. Usually I send them to station one, where the director takes charge of the newborns. Thank goodness Cyclo knows. She takes Hana in almost as soon as she's born, for her first oral feeding. I only hold her for an hour at night before we both go back into Cyclo's matrix to sleep. If not for Cyclo, Hana would be discovered and destroyed according to protocol.

Hana's eyes fill with tears. She flips forward, to her sixteenth birthday, about a year before the evacuation.

Cyclo's degeneration has finally begun. Waste storage is at max capacity. Solar energy production is decreasing rapidly. We are tentatively planning our evacuation and recruiting for the terminal data crew. At some point, her degeneration will be exponential. I am finding that Cyclo is keeping Hana longer than I ask for, and she tells me that Hana has been optimally fed, when in truth, I know that cannot be. Our heme stores are gone, and Cyclo cannot possibly give Hana the amounts she needs, but Cyclo tells me I am wrong. Cyclo does not disobey; it is not possible for her to do so, and yet this has become a source of investigation by the engineering crew, who are also finding aberrations in their measurements vs. what Cyclo tells them. It is as if the ship does not want to admit that she is failing.

Speaking of failures, I will have to tell the crew about Hana. The sooner, the better. But I find that 16 years is a long time to lie. One learns to lie about everything, to the point where telling the truth is impossible. But I have time.

So her mother knew even then, but she didn't say a word to Hana, or to the crew. I flip to the last entry, the entry where we'll find whether she ever planned to tell them about Hana.

400237.009
Sol 108

One of Cyclo's vacuoles has leaked and flooded a portion of the core. It is not a critical systems breakdown, but we will evacuate in approximately two weeks, enough time to leave in an orderly fashion. But today is the day. The day I tell the world that I am a liar and a thief. That I have loved someone so much I've given up my future career and likely my legal parental rights. I've kept Hana to myself too long. Today is the day I will tell them.

It will give Hana two weeks to meet the crew and say her goodbyes to Cyclo. Cyclo asked me today what my agenda was. She has been watching me in a way she hasn't in the last few weeks. She noticed that I was nervous and upset. So I told her. Not that I was telling the crew about Hana, but that she was dying. Cyclo says she knows. And she said she was thankful that she would not die alone.

I don't know what she means by that. Surely she understands what an evacuation is.

And then she asked me if I would tell them about Hana. I was surprised she would ask. Cyclo does not usually ask me questions; it ought to be the other way around. Normally I would report this behavior, but it's about Hana, so I cannot.

But I am tired of lying. And I owe Cyclo the life that she's given to me these past twenty years, and to my daughter.

So I told her the truth.

That is the last entry.

Oh God. I read the time and date. It was one hour before Dr. Um died. Two hours before the *Calathus* was fully evacuated. She told Cyclo that the crew would learn about Hana, and that they would leave Cyclo to die alone, with a terminal data crew from the *Selkirk* climbing aboard her like ants on an earthen carcass.

She didn't want to die alone, so she killed Hana's mother, so no one would know about her.

So they would die together.

Hana pushes the book away, and I drop it to the floor, trying to steady her. I blink my holofeed off and watch as Hana's eyes unfocus. I know what she's thinking—imagining her mother being murdered, her mother's blood spattered across the hospital bay. I think of Gammand, and how he was torn to pieces. Was that what happened to Dr. Um, too?

"Cyclo got what she wanted," Hana whispers. "A secret, all to herself. Just as the crew abandoned her forever."

I have an overwhelming desire to hold her so tight that we both pass out and forget the hell we're going through. She seems to know what I'm thinking because, though she keeps staring forward, she reaches out her hand blindly to find mine.

"They knew Cyclo was murderous," I say. "And they dangled the *Selkirk* crew like bait when she was starving to death and angry. So the next Cyclo they make won't do the same things. They needed to learn about the devil so they could fix all its faults for the next, new, more expensive version." I pause. "I didn't want to die like this."

Hana releases my hand, her face furious. "I didn't want to die like this, either."

"Cyclo won't kill you. Don't you see? She's had ample opportunity to do that. Cyclo wants to kill everyone but you. She wanted you all to herself."

"She'll keep me until she dies, and then I'll die with her. Cyclo's killing me, too."

After a few minutes, my hand feels emptier than it's ever felt in my whole life. When she stands, I'm sure she's going to leave me here alone so she can process whatever horrors she has in her head. But instead she walks over to my chair and sits in my lap. She curls her legs onto mine, leans her head on my shoulder, and wraps her arms around my neck.

"I'm so angry, Fenn. And so very tired," she whispers. "I want to live. I only started to learn how, and it's all over soon. Even if I'm the last to live, it won't be long before I die, too." Her hand grazes my jawbone and slips behind my neck, pulling my face closer to hers. Her pupils are huge in the darkness, a void so big that they look entirely black. She kisses me, and it's unexpectedly hungry and raw. My arms go around her and squeeze her tight as I kiss her back with equal ferocity. I dig my hands hard into her waist and pick her up. She wraps her legs around my waist, and I lower her to the rough floor of the cockpit as the starshine streams in through the windows. My hands become saturated with her tears and mine as I cradle her face in our never-ending kiss. But I don't let go. I won't. I'm afraid I'll lose her right here, right now, if I let go for one infinitesimal second.

It's a second we don't have to spare, but for this one moment, we are rich. We are infinite. We are devastation clinging to inevitability, and nothing else matters.

Dawn rises with Maia's crystalline blue light illuminating the cockpit with a small bit of warmth and a brightness that has no business being cheerful right now. Exhaustion has stolen our wakefulness, on and off, for a handful of hours. A fitful kind of sleep where we reach out, frantic, in our moments of wakefulness. We test to see if our hands are still working, if our bodies are still warm, if we're still alive.

We are.

For now.

Finally, I sit up. I'm starving, despite hunger being the last thing I should really care about right now, since I'm gonna die soon. Hana sits up, too, and holds her belly.

"I have to go to the bathroom," she says.

"Let's find some breakfast and wash up. We'll keep to the dead side of Cyclo. It'll just be us."

In silence, we walk around the west quadrant until we find the bridge—unchanged since the last time we went there to get gear, days ago. Hana washes her face with some precious filtered water from our stores, and I put out some energy bars to eat. We chew them mechanically, all the while holding hands with our free arms.

I check on my bots—they've returned periodically to the bridge to recharge, then continue their data collection. And on my holofeed, I've been watching the green portion on my progress meter going up and up. I'm near 70 percent now. I've gotten so close.

But that damned progress bar shows the raw truth. I'll never finish my tasks. Not before I die. ReCOR will win, and I'll lose, as will Callandra.

All I can think is that I want to move back onto the *Selkirk* and die there. At least we wouldn't be on Cyclo. She could implode, and we wouldn't have to feel her wrath as she disintegrates, and we wouldn't have to risk that somehow she'll regenerate just enough to reach out and strangle us.

If only the *Selkirk* had fuel. If only we could fly it out and send a distress signal and get off this death trap. Secretly even, so I can still get my death benefit. I wish—

"I wish we had fuel," Hana says suddenly.

I drop my energy bar and stare at her. "I was thinking the same thing. Sort of."

"But if we leave, then you'll forfeit your contract. You realize that they'll have all this data once we're gone. They'll know you didn't die here. By surviving, you lose."

"I know." I pick up my pendant. "I keep wondering if I can win both ways, but I don't know how."

"You haven't watched the message from your sister yet, have you?"

"No," I say. "I guess I'm waiting until the last minute."

"Maybe there never will be a last minute."

"What?" I turn to her, trying to hear her better. "What do you mean?"

"I mean, what if we could get the *Selkirk* to work again? Could you fly it? Does it have autopilot?"

"I could fly it. Badly, but I could fly it," I say. "It's not like we're launching off a planet. It would be much easier. But the *Selkirk* was sent on this mission with just enough fuel to get here. Not to leave. It was a one-way trip."

"What kind of fuel?"

"I think it's a radioisotope engine. As the radioisotope decays, it heats a fluid that combusts and creates thrust. But the problem isn't the fluid—we have stores of that still. The isotope in the engine has a short half-life, and it's basically dead. So, unless there's a secret polonium core replacement you haven't shared with me, then we're out of luck because the previous crew took all the spares with them when they evacuated. It was part of their protocol."

Hana bites her lip, thinking. She's relentless, this girl.

"Then maybe we can find another source of radioactivity," she says.

This time, I'm the one who goes quiet to think. We have the hydrogen, but we don't have the isotopes. Unless…

"Hana. What do you know about the different radioactive stores on Cyclo?"

"I know where they are. And that the walls of the vacuoles holding them won't last for much longer. Even if we could access them without Cyclo hurting us, how would we move the right isotopes into a holding cell for the *Selkirk*? Cyclo hasn't neatly organized her waste products."

She's concentrating so hard that a little crease shows up between her eyebrows. God, I love that little crease. But it's giving me an idea.

"Want to do something dangerous and probably deadly?"

"What have we got to lose?" Hana says, kissing me lightly on the cheek. Her face, though, is grim and determined. "I'd sail into a solar flare with you, Fennec, if it means having a few more minutes together." She pauses. "You know, you're nothing like your name."

Again with my name. Why does anyone care?

"So, what, I'm not like a moth? Cyclo mentioned that, too."

"Not just any moth. A luna moth. The pretty green ones on Earth, big as my hand." She searches my face and shakes her head. "You really don't know, do you?"

"Know what?"

"Luna moths emerge from their cocoons with no mouth. They live only days, never eating, because they're born to die."

Somehow, knowing this, knowing my namesake, makes me so angry. I refuse to just settle for death.

I refuse.

I reach for her hand, and she threads her fingers through mine without hesitation. Without Hana, I might have given up a long time ago.

"We need to get off this damned ship," I say.

Chapter Thirty-One

HANA

These are the things I know.

I know how to knit. I know how to make a darn good reconstituted gomtang out of freeze-dried foods. I know twentieth-century English, a smattering of Korean words and phrases, chemistry, advanced cyclonica biology, organic chemistry, and calculus.

I know how to kiss Fenn. And I know we are going to die very soon.

What I don't know: how to harness Cyclo's enormous stores of radioactive waste to find something that the radioisotope engine of the *Selkirk* can use. How to do this without Cyclo killing Fenn. How to do this without becoming so irradiated and sick that we end up wishing Cyclo had killed us anyway.

"Hana?" Fenn touches my arm and shakes me out of my reverie. We are sitting on the bridge, poring over the maps of Cyclo and the informational scanners that are still functioning around the ship, which were first set up when the *Selkirk* crew arrived.

"What is it?"

"Here." He points. "It's the core of the ship where most

of the waste vacuoles are. But the waste materials are a mix of isotopes."

"How will we get the ones that are compatible with the engine? We have no way to purify radioactive ores."

"We don't. We take what we can. This one's a bad idea." Fenn points to a vacuole that has a solid waste of mixed isotopes. "But this one is better," he says, showing me the one that has the surface isotopes that were prepacked by Cyclo's skin into smaller boules, they called them, covered with a layer of lead. "Those, we could gather safely. We'd just have to figure out a way of placing the boules' contents within the engine, hope the elements are hot enough to superheat the hydrogen gas, and hope it's enough to keep the environmental and communication elements of the ship functioning."

"Will it work?" I ask, anxious.

"Probably not," he says, and gives me a level stare. "We haven't got an alternative. We have no way to contact anyone for help. Doran might come to rescue us, but he may not. Cyclo has shut down seventy-five percent of her quadrants. It's only a matter of time before the other ones malfunction, and then one little breach in her hull and we're done for. We don't need the *Selkirk* to run well. Just to keep us alive long enough to get away from Cyclo and send out a distress signal."

I stare at the map. The best way to get to the vacuole we need is all the way across on the other side of Cyclo, and unfortunately, it's also located in one of her functioning slivers of the western quadrant.

"If I go there, Cyclo will try to engage me. She may try to stop me."

"Then I'll go," Fenn says, but I shake my head.

"No way. She'll kill you in an instant."

"She will. She'll squash me like a bug."

Our shoulders sag. We're already failing before we've

begun. Just like when Portia realized she was nearing the end, and Cyclo took her. Thank goodness she didn't take Fenn then. I could have lost him, too.

"She didn't kill you," I murmur to myself.

"Well, yeah. Not yet," Fenn says.

"No. I mean when Portia was attacked, Cyclo tried to get to you, but she only ever had the energy to focus on her. Not more than one person. She's been saving her energy, using it when she can, and budgeting. She knew if she put energy into attacking you hard, she'd let go of Portia." I snap my fingers, or at least try. I never mastered the technique, despite ten years of trying. "You know, I think Cyclo can no longer see me."

"See? Like, with eyes?"

"Yes. She has photoreceptor cells on the surface of her matrix. But during my last trip to my room, she said she couldn't see me. She's blind, Fenn." I smile slowly.

"You have a plan, Hana?"

"Yes." I beam. "But we're going to need your nanobots. And I'm going to need a really sharp knife."

This is a terrible idea, but sometimes terrible ideas are all you have.

We find some scalpels from the medical unit, and Fenn readies his nanobots and several of the larger drones that he brought but hasn't had a chance to use. We gather a bunch of syringe-like ampules, and Fenn lays out all the drones he has and turns to me.

"Are you ready?"

"As I'll ever be," I say.

First, I reach for my long hair, and with Fenn's help, cut off foot-long locks. When we're done, what's left just grazes my shoulders, a strange feeling. I tie the cut hair into a bunch and attach it to one of the large drones. Fenn gets a beaker full of anticoagulant ready and ties a tourniquet gently around my left upper arm.

"This feels really wrong," he says as I clean off my skin with disinfectant.

"Not as wrong as it feels for me," I say, taking the knife. "Here goes."

I carefully press the blade against the crook of my arm, where a vein is bulging out. I only need to nick the vessel—enough to get an ounce of blood. It turns out my body is really good at protecting myself, and I don't press hard enough to do anything but make a small slice in my skin. Scarlet blood beads, and it itches. Darn it. I have to do better.

I heave in a big breath, bite my lip, and press harder. The knife tip plunges in, only a few millimeters, but it's enough. Surprisingly, it hurts more now that it's over. Dark red blood pours from the cut vein, and Fenn maneuvers the beaker to collect the rivulet of blood, swirling it with a plastrix stirrer to keep it from coagulating. I bandage my arm and start using the blade to do other things, like shaving off extra skin from my heels and trimming crescents of growth from my nails. I scrape dry skin from my legs and arms and pull out several eyelashes. I spit into a cup. And then I jog in place for a good fifteen minutes, until sweat pours down from my forehead and chest. We mop up the sweat and skin oils with two thin, stretchy plastrix gloves.

We take a pair of shoes that I never wear, and Fenn ties two pieces of solid titanium (broken off of the *Selkirk*) to each shoe—about thirty pounds or so each. And then we attach them to two of the largest drones, the ones that are the size of my head, which Fenn hadn't used yet. I pull off my tunic and throw on an ill-fitting jacket of Portia's, and we load this plus microscopic bits of my skin, hair, sweat, and blood to roughly twenty nanobots and thirty microbots in his fleet. The smallest minibots contain the ampules of my blood.

"Are they charged?" I ask.

"Charged and ready to go." He turns on his holofeed and opens a control board in front of his face. It's far larger and more complicated than any I've ever seen. "Doing a test walkabout now."

I stand back and watch as my weighted shoes begin taking very realistic, bodiless, legless steps without me. Above it, a smaller drone swings my cut-off ponytail, complete with white stripe, jauntily above my tunic. The gloves, covered in skin cells, skin oils, and sweat, reach out here and there, once swishing against my arm. It does feel like a touch, though not a warm one. Where my face should be is a single drone, quietly flying along with a tiny speaker that will transmit my voice. Within what would be my body, a blur of other bots of different sizes (some of which I can't see, but I know they're there) carry vials and ampules of my blood, like a blurred, red hive of angry mosquitoes.

It's me, on a molecular, weighted, phonic level. But it's not me.

My decoy.

"So, I'll walk the Hana decoy to the opposite quadrant. You'll start talking to Cyclo, wearing a helmet so your true voice won't be heard. I'll make sure your decoy touches the walls here and there, brush your hair up against Cyclo's surfaces. Lately, she's so depleted of energy she can only focus on one part of the ship. And right now, it's concentrated around your old room, where Portia died. So the decoy will stay in that area. You'll fake being hurt, and we'll release the blood, but I'll keep the decoy running to keep from getting caught."

I take a deep breath. "This isn't going to work. She'll know it's not me."

"It's been almost twenty-four hours since we last had contact with her. Cyclo is degrading at an exponential rate. She'll be decrepit enough that it will fool her."

Fenn sounds so much more confident than I am. But then I see his eyes. They're a touch glassy. The skin between his eyebrows twitches. He's not confident, but he's trying to be brave. For me.

"Are you ready?" Fenn asks.

"Yes," I say, though I'm not. How could anyone be ready to do this? But I must. I believe in surviving. I believe in having a life that is mine, not something that's been artificially crafted for me and then abruptly taken away.

I believe.

And thus, I must do this.

I put on my gear, consisting of radiation-proof suit and helmet. It belonged to the *Selkirk,* but there was only one, for Miki, who needed to wear it for some of her radiation studies. It doesn't fit me at all, but Fenn finds that there's an inner layer that stretches to fit adult humanoids of varying size. It'll be enough to protect me, but it's, unfortunately, way easier to breach. It's all I have.

Fenn programs my mic to transmit to both him and the speaker for the Hana puppet. Behind me, a frictionless storage container that can easily be remotely maneuvered is already set to follow me. Its hover-pack is fully charged, enough to carry about the hundred pounds we'll need. They'll be so hot that I won't be able to carry them in any sort of satchel. They'd burn right through.

Once again, this has to be me. Only Fenn can skillfully maneuver the Hana puppet, and if there's any chance that Cyclo attacks me, I can reveal myself (at the risk of irradiating myself) and survive.

We haven't said it, but Fenn and I both know that if this

doesn't work, our bag of tricks is empty. The show will be over, and Hana and Fenn as the universe knows us will be nothing but deconstructed organic matter that used to think, used to feel, used to love.

I tell myself that when that happens, it means that I will no longer be lied to. But it doesn't make me feel better at all. My hand goes to my helmet to drop the face shield in place, but Fenn stays my hand.

"Be careful, Hana," he says.

"Kiss me goodbye, Fenn," I whisper. "Just in case."

"No," he says. "Because I'll see you again. I'll give you your kiss then. I promise."

You promise? Please, don't be lying to me, Fenn.

"All right," I say. "I'll see you later, then." I smile and turn away.

Outside of the bridge, the hallway goes in two different directions. I go right, clockwise, toward the west quadrant where the radioactive waste vacuoles are. And Fenn stands in the dark hallway, his holo visor a huge bubble in front of him as he maneuvers the Hana puppet to walk counterclockwise within Cyclo, toward my room.

I walk the curving hallway, the storage container floating effortlessly behind me. I do the math in my head and know that in ten feet, the hallway will curve to the point where that will be the last glimpse of Fenn I have. Maybe forever.

A few steps later, I'm there. I turn my head, and through the face shield of the helmet, all I see is Fenn's back, and his arms gesticulating like a dancer as he commands my puppet on his holofeed to keep walking.

Oh, stars. I'm going to miss this boy so very much.

Fenn never turns around.

Chapter Thirty-Two

FENN

I cannot bear to look at her again.

Not now.

If I do, then I'll be telling myself that there will be no more Hana, that it's over. And in my mind, I'm so angry, so fucking angry at Cyclo and ReCOR and the universe. But none of that is going to get us out of this mess. Only me. And succumbing to inevitably, probability, is not going to help. I will see Hana again. I have to believe this. So I refuse to turn around for one last look.

I'm stubborn that way.

"Fenn." Hana's voice sounds as real as if it were whispered in my ear. "I'm on my way. Do you read me?"

"Yes. Transmission is perfect. But as soon as we get into the northeast quadrant—your puppet, I mean—you need to stick to the script. No slipups. No 'Fennec is the true Master of the Universe, and everything needs to bow to His Greatness.'"

Hana snorts. "Roger that. You can be sure that I will never say that. Ever." She pauses. "Why did they always say 'Roger'? Who the hell was Roger?"

I can hear her smile through the mic. And I smile, too.

"I don't know. No one says that anymore, you know."

"Ah. But they say 'Master of the Universe' in normal conversation?"

"Of course." I grin.

On the holo monitor in front of me, I see that we're on the cusp of entering the two quadrants.

"Hana. You're there. Don't move. I'll give you the go ahead when I get the biometrics that Cyclo is responding positively to the puppet, and that's when you enter."

"Roger that."

She's got to stop it with the Roger this and that. "So remember, I can speak to you, but you mustn't talk to me. If you absolutely must, make sure to switch your comm direction to me, not the drone. Just focus on Cyclo. Our audio communication for me is one way to you. But you go both ways, so be careful. I have your visual, your audio, and your biometrics, so I'll know what's going on." I take a controlled breath, trying not to sound overwhelmed, which I am.

Here we go.

I drive the Hana puppet forward. In bits and pieces, she's perfect. Her smoothly moving, weighted shoes have been programmed to imitate Hana's actual gait. Though the weight isn't perfectly like hers, lighter by at least sixty pounds, hopefully Cyclo won't notice. The swishing ponytail leaves a wake of Hana-scented molecules in the air. The gloves also swing to and fro, just as Hana's hands would have.

The puppet moves forward to an entirely different quadrant, where Hana's room is, far from where I am. The color of the dark alpha ring is already lightening from a navy blue, drastically changing to white. What looks like beige scar tissue lines the walls and floor, and the corridor has contracted in areas, like someone punched the walls inward here and there. The outer exoskeleton must have broken and been repaired in a few places. But how long will it hold? Biologic vessels always have to deal with this instability—there's a reason why most living things like being under the comfortable atmosphere of a planet, not in a frozen, airless vacuum of space.

I walk the Hana puppet farther in, about thirty feet, and pause. The walls are a blotchy mix of pale blue, pink, beige scars, and occasional ripples of her healthy medium blue. But that healthy blue is the minority—the other colors wink on and off erratically, like some sort of broken vid display.

The puppet is right in the middle of the healthiest area, if you can call this health. Some of the blue sections flash faintly with iridescence. Cyclo can sense Hana nearby. I know enough of Cyclo's colors that the lack of red is a good sign. I see a touch of gold, too. I think that means she's curious.

"All right, Hana," I say. "You're on. Don't walk yet, just engage Cyclo."

Hana nods. She's not moving into the storage areas yet. She's in the process of climbing down to the beta ring, and carefully maneuvering the hover container with her. She clears her throat.

"Hello, Cyclo," she says, and simultaneously the speaker on my floating drone transmits her voice.

Cyclo immediately responds with more happy colors—iridescent blue. My drone picks up the UV colors that apparently Hana can see but I can't. There's a shimmering of violet wherever healthy tissue is showing.

I move one of the gloved hands to gently touch some of the walls, and step the Hana puppet forward. I make the ponytail toss left and right, and the tips of her black and white hair graze the wall as well. Some colors flash here and there, and Hana hesitates.

"I don't understand. You're here? Of course you're here. So am I."

Hana's biomonitor shows she's getting tense. I don't understand the complexities of Cyclo's language, but something is off.

"If you can speak that way, then good. If it's easier. I don't want you to feel pain, Cyclo," Hana says.

In front of the mass of drones, a portion of the wall begins to stretch forward. I move the puppet backward, just in case. But it doesn't try to touch the fake Hana bits. It rises up into a cone, puckers, and a mouth forms. Just a tube, really, no face. Far more crude than the face that spoke to me when I cooked, that morning a few days ago.

"Hello Hanaaaaa," Cyclo phonates. But it sounds terrible. Like an old man who's been inhaling cobalt dust from the mines. "My nerves function poor not optimally at now. But your primitive communication…is…was…follows a simpler of neural pathways."

"That's good," Hana says. But inside her helmet, I can see she's frowning. There's something decidedly…insulting about the way Cyclo said human communication was primitive. Maybe it is, but still. Weird that she'd say that to Hana.

"I've missed you," Hana says, soothingly. I let her puppet take a few steps around, touching the wall on occasion, but never long enough to get pulled in.

"Yes, yes," Cyclo says. "I am very happy…you haven't been hurt…by it."

It. It? Does she mean me?

"I'm well," Hana says. "I know it takes more energy for you to be here, to talk to me. I know how hard that is."

"I try. I am trying," Cyclo says. "Look what I can do." All the blue areas of matrix in between the hard, stiff sections of scar tissue bulge outward. A warped show of strength.

I look at the visor readout that shows Cyclo's activity on the ship. Our sensors show that her activity has risen where the Hana puppet is, decreasing nearer to the vacuole chambers. Excellent.

"Keep talking, Hana. But I think you're good to enter the next sector," I tell her. "She's concentrating her energy on the puppet. It's working."

Hana nods again, and she takes her first step. The radiation readouts are already high where she is. We need to stay far away from here once we're done with this sector. It's anything but safe. Her breathing rate stops as she holds her breath and takes another step. Cyclo's activity levels continue to shift toward the northeast quadrant, like her energies are surrounding the Hana puppet.

Emboldened, Hana starts walking at a quicker pace down the beta hallway, her booted feet making little noise. Her steps are soft from the lighter gravity. The walls around her are a very muted pale blue, the color of a quiescent Cyclo. They don't change as she walks. Maybe Cyclo's nerve endings are dulled enough to not notice her footfalls, or the movement of air from walking. Meanwhile, she keeps chatting up Cyclo, just as she finds a stairway down to gamma. Beyond that is the core where she's headed.

"He's leaving, you know," she says. She's talking about me. "It will just be us alone soon. And we can be the way we used to be."

"Come, then." Cyclo's phonating mouth bubbles, and a rivulet of a brown liquid dribbles out. Another extension of the matrix, blue mixed with speckled brown spots, reaches for one of the puppet gloves. "Come to me. Sleep."

"I am tired, but not right now. Soon," Hana says, trying to sound playful, but nervousness enters her voice. I make the glove gently swipe away the offering of Cyclo's extended blob. The hair drone swishes it again, and the shoes do a slow walk in a circle. The hem of her tunic flutters.

"Skin...your skin is sick," Cyclo says. "You have too much silicone in your perspiration."

The real Hana freezes.

"Don't," I tell her. "You're only ten feet and two right turns from the containment vacuole we need. Keep talking."

Hana takes a deep breath. "Oh. I was cleaning some silicone...um...I was using a skin conditioner. With silicone in it."

"Hana no additives. I can do that brilliant," Cyclo says. "I better your dermis with superior emollients. Come. Where are out? Come to me. I will check function."

"And what about you, Cyclo? Are you functioning all right?"

"Efforts are concentrating where needed. I am compensation adequately."

I frown. Cyclo's lying to her. I mean, look at how she needs to talk. Her language is completely off. She's already contradicting herself.

Hana walks in a tall, narrow part of the corridor, and several openings show the entrances to various storage areas. Yellow and pink flashes of light come from the walls.

"What does that mean?" I ask Hana, who pauses to read them. Hana touches a sensor on her helmet suit and switches her comm to me.

"It's gibberish," she says. "Nothing." Hana's now in the core, and the gravity is nearly nonexistent in the center, despite the spinning of the giant ship. She bounds right, and there's a tall, open door, the membrane across it cracked and peeling back. She pushes herself delicately through, but the hovering container behind her won't fit.

"I can't risk breaking the door open further," she says. "I'll have to bring the boules a few at a time." She switches her comm back to Cyclo and begins talking about the rotational axis of Cyclo this time of year around the moon.

I know Hana can see what I can—that the radiation levels in there are sky-high. Probably why Cyclo's walls are decaying and look burned in places. Some of the boules there—or maybe the other larger vacuoles—have failed.

"Whatever you do, don't let your suit get compromised," I tell her. "You'll absorb over fifty Gy of radiation. You'll die within minutes."

Hana gives a thumbs-up, letting me know she understands. Or telling me to shut up. She's already too busy to switch her comm to talk to me, and she's chatting about what she plans on eating tonight for dinner and convincing Cyclo she doesn't need a hibernation right now. Cyclo is really pushing it.

Hana stands in front of a tall vacuole that looks like a thirty-foot-tall purple egg, with jagged cracks running in fracture lines along half of it. The shell is translucent, and inside there are countless fist-size boules. Supercooled liquid flows between the boules, keeping them from overheating from the constantly emitting radiation.

I'm no radiation specialist, and I try not to panic, wondering how we'll get the boules out without spilling all this cooling liquid, and keep the vacuole from melting down. We just need a quarter of the container filled, and I pray that the engine will take them in as a radiation source. Hana walks over to one of the cracks and gently pries it open with a thick piece of a shell that's about to break off anyway.

"Wait, Hana. If we spill too much of that coolant, there'll be a meltdown in that quadrant."

Hana nods.

The liquid is constantly replenishing itself. If she can manage to allow only a small leak, we may have time to make this happen.

It gives way with a sharp crack, leaving a triangular-shaped hole. Immediately, an iridescent coolant starts pouring out. But as soon as it hits the air, it oxidizes and hardens. Even better. It's self-sealing. Hana can poke one of the boules with her gloved finger, but the opening is still too small, especially after the coolant forms a scab-like rim around the opening. She pries another edge, working it with her hand until it, too, gives. A flake the size of her palm gives way, and coolant gushes out. She pulls out an orange-sized boule with her other hand and stands aside so as not to touch the hardening coolant on the ground.

Yes! She did it!

Hana starts pulling out boule after boule, her gloved hands getting mucked up from the hardening coolant. She's starting to worry, and her conversation with Cyclo gets more disjointed.

"I…yes. I want to sleep. But I don't want to sleep. I mean, I need to stay awake. I'm tired," she says. Hana shakes her head. She's getting frazzled.

When Hana has an armful of boules, sticky and plastered with dried coolant, she steps out through the broken door and carefully deposits them in the hovering carrier. She goes back and starts to pull out more. She only needs another armful or two. One of the boules is blocking the others behind it near the cracked opening, and she gently pulls it out.

The boule shatters in her hand.

Hana cries out in dismay.

She drops the broken boule, and its gooey contents glow faintly red, dripping onto the floor. It sizzles as it hits the coolant pouring out, and steam rises up. Her glove will be compromised if the temperature melts the fabric. It's going to eat through her glove if she doesn't get it off right now.

"Get out of there, Hana!" I yell at her. In my panic, I'm not paying attention to how I'm driving the Hana puppet. It bounces erratically, doing a jig as I mishandle one of the Hana foot puppets. It tips over just enough that the titanium weight falls out of it with a clunk.

Hana jumps through the door and pushes the hover container with her, but she's got to get rid of that glove soon. It's got enough radiation to make us both sick if we're near it for more than ten minutes, unprotected.

"Hana! Take the glove off, now!" But at the same time I yell at her, Cyclo is speaking, too. She's confused.

"Hana," Cyclo's voice rises. "This is titanium. From *Selkirk*. Why?"

"Oh, I...I think I need to go back for a little bit," she says. She carefully peels off her glove, flinging it behind her. But now she's exposed in a high radiation area, and she needs to get out of there. She starts running, pushing the container before her.

"Something is...broken," Cyclo trails off. "I have vacuole that contaminated. I have breach," Cyclo says. Her colors immediately become muted. "You need to be kept safe. I will seal the breach," Cyclo says, and immediately reaches out a large blob of matrix. "And keep you in room, asleep. Now."

"NO!" I yell.

"No, Cyclo, NO!" Hana yells, as she reaches the end of the containment hallways where the radiation levels are low again. But she's still not in one of Cyclo's dead zones yet. She's got about fifty feet more to go, and up to the gamma ring first.

Cyclo's matrix arm reaches out for the limping Hana puppet. I'm not fast enough with my drones to dodge it. It immediately surrounds and takes in the drone holding her hair. I try to make the feet run away, the gloves, but the arm swishes deftly in the air, and the Hana puppet goes flying in seven directions. Left foot there, right shoe behind, gloves flopping down ten feet away. I can't get control of anything because it's all gone to hell. Cyclo's matrix tenderly picks up each of the puppet pieces, enclosing them in dabs of blue.

I know what Cyclo is thinking and feeling, even as I watch the blue dabs handling the pieces of the puppet one by one. There is no skin. There is no pulse within any of the pieces. There is no heart.

There is no Hana.

In less than a second, Cyclo crushes every one of my bots, each disintegrating within her matrix. Cyclo spits out the shoes, rejecting them, and then vomits out the large lock of Hana's hair like a piece of recently swallowed poison. On my visor, I see Cyclo's activity shift like a tsunami toward the west gamma quadrant, where Hana is now only thirty feet away from a dead zone.

"HANA. Run!" I yell.

Chapter Thirty-Three

HANA

I run at full speed to the beta ring, There's a hallway of darkened blue only a few feet away. Finally, a safe zone where Cyclo can't contact me.

I have to get this suit off. There are drips of contaminated material on the fabric. I'm sweating from the hot, confining suit and from sheer panic. I know I've absorbed radiation.

What's the point of flying away in the *Selkirk* if I die of radiation poisoning? I unzip and kick away the suit, stepping out of it barefoot. My hands grasp the helmet, and I see Fenn staring back at me in the video comm.

"Hana. Run. Cyclo knows you're there. Get into a dead zone with the boules as fast as you can."

I put my hands on the hover container, ready to push it at a run, when I jerk forward.

My feet are stuck.

No.

Around me, the walls and floor have started pulsating between the islands of beige scar tissue. With each subsequent pulsation, they go from pale blue, to deep blue, to purple, and then red.

The color of Cyclo's rage.

My legs are fully encased now, and the container with the boules is harshly jerked out of my hands. It floats on an undulating river of greenish-blue matrix before tipping over. In slow motion, the boules spill out and float farther and farther away from me. Our only chance at leaving Cyclo has been torn from me. From us.

"Hana! I'm coming!" Fenn yells, the last thing I hear before Cyclo pulls away the helmet and any contact I have with Fenn.

"No! Fenn! *Fenn!*" I scream, lunging to grasp it as it's pulled away. The matrix flows up and around my torso, under my clothes. It's so jarring, the varying degrees of icy cold and burning hot temperatures against my skin, because Cyclo's self-regulation has gone awry. A thousand thoughts burst into my brain. *I am never going to see him again. This is what it's like when your heart breaks. Cyclo will tear him apart. I cannot bear the breaking of us.*

But all I can manage is to scream his name, over and over again.

Cyclo tries to silence me. Wave after wave of chemicals are pushed into my skin, trying to force me into docility, but I'm fighting so hard. I kick. I scream. I am the girl that will not submit. Enough of my body is submerged in her matrix that I can hear her voice in my head.

Stay with me
Stay with me
My sweet Hana
Stay with me

It's a song that's almost a lullaby, one that Mother never sang to me. One that Cyclo never sang, either, but really has been the only truth that she's ever told, the only truth she's held while she's been dying. She wants me all to herself. My eyes close as I sink into Cyclo's generous, formless arms. I should have known it would end like this. I should have saved these last moments for Fenn, instead of trying to figure out how to leave Cyclo.

A moment in time isn't a static point in space. It is infinite if you look close enough. And I could have had a thousand infinities with Fenn. If only I could do it all over again.

My body is getting tired, or weak, or numbed; I'm not sure what. Cyclo can only have so many chemical restraints to use on me, but she's buffing every last molecule of sedative into me because she won't lose me again. Faintly, there is a jarring sensation, as if my entire world has been shaken hard, rent and throttled. But it goes away. My ears buzz; my ability to hear is disappearing, and I can no longer feel anything below my knees, beyond my elbows. I hear a yell from far, far away. A memory, perhaps.

Hana. Fight.

Hana. I'm coming for you.

I try to shake my head, but Cyclo has already made a pillow for it, and the gel is rising near my cheeks, ready to envelop my face. There is a stinging feeling, and a pull against my neck. Cyclo has removed my biomonitor. Through a layer of gel around my ears, I hear the voice again. As I forcefully rouse myself back into consciousness, the sound becomes clearer, even with the muffling gel.

Hana.

HANA.

"Hana! It's me. Fight, fight Hana! I'm coming for you!"

But it isn't Fenn's voice speaking.

Chapter Thirty-Four

FENN

I have nothing to fight with. All my bots and drones have been crushed into oblivion.

"Hana!" I yell, but I can barely speak for what I'm seeing. The container full of radioactive boules is torn from her grasping hands. A wave of blue takes her, slips her sideways, immerses her. Her helmet is being pulled off as the image goes partly dead.

"Hana! I'm coming!" I yell as the image goes completely blank, and I start running.

I run like I've never run before, and no matter how painful it is, I'll go faster. Because nothing matters. This is the end, the end that I knew was coming, though we'd pretended we could try to outwit Cyclo, outwit our own sense of doom, to keep hoping.

My airways sear from breathing so hard, and my muscles burn with angry pain as I finally reach the northwest quadrant. I'm met with an impenetrable wall of hostile red matrix. As soon as it sees me coming, it pours down a steaming, caustic layer of brown and green liquid. I cough as the fumes hit me, and my eyes water and nose burns. I can't even get within ten feet of the wall, and beyond that wall is Hana. Wave after wave of coughing incapacitates me, and my eyes tear until my vision is nothing but a blur. I can't even think, and I'm slowly asphyxiating.

I drop to my knees, coughing, dry heaving. The gas flowing from the chemicals is only getting thicker. I drag myself away from it. From the lack of oxygen, stars and lights pop in my vision. They only get brighter, threatening to completely bleach my retinas before I pass out.

Wait. The bright light is only when my eyes are open. I shield my face, holding my shirt up to my mouth to filter the air, and look around me through the gassy fog. A few plastrix-embedded windows to my left are blasted full of flickering light.

It's a ship.

It's a damned ship.

Doran. He actually made it here, after all!

I'm in the alpha ring right now, as is Hana. Which means when this thing comes crashing in, Hana's going to die if the ship crashes into her. I go to the window, still coughing, still gagging, and gesticulate wildly to tell the ship to dock closer to the southern quadrant. But it's too late. The ship is small, and it's already backed up to get enough distance to ram itself into Cyclo's exoskeleton. And if I'm here when that happens, I'll either be flattened, or dead from being exposed to the atmosphereless cold of space.

In my head, I scream at myself. *Run, Fenn. Run because this time your life depends on it, and Hana's, too, if there's any chance left on this damned ship to save her.*

So I half shuffle, half run down the hallways, watching as the ship accelerates forward. I take the first hallway that veers upward to beta, climbing the stairs and galloping crookedly because of the low g, and head south. I barely make it before the ship crashes into the hull.

I go flying and land on my back. All the air leaves me in

a whoosh, and I immediately cradle my head as splinters of white endoskeleton and meaty chunks of beige and pale blue matrix fall around me. A loud creak reverberates through the floors and ceilings and right into my jawbone, like metal pressing relentlessly against wood. The sound is so loud and excruciating I cover my ears.

And then it's silent.

I get to my knees, and then slowly stand. I haven't broken any bones, but my ears are still ringing. I can breathe, but I thank the stars that I don't feel that irresistible, terrifying suck of decompression. So whatever crashed into Cyclo has managed to seal off the breaks in the exoskeleton.

I stagger to the end of the hallway, surveying the damage. Chunks of endoskeleton and oozing, rotting matrix the color of curdled blood lie here and there. I step over them and make my way back down to alpha, going slowly around the corridor, dodging larger shards and jagged pieces of Cyclo that have broken from the impact.

Beyond that, a small oval ship, silver colored, has embedded itself into Cyclo's hull. The hull of the ship isn't metal—like Cyclo, it ripples with different colors—purple, flecks of metallic white—and it's exuding a biological stratum of a deeper gray color that's adhered to the ship and the broken hole it's made in Cyclo's exoskeleton. A side door near the nose has opened, and I hold my breath, waiting to see my savior. Hana's savior.

The first thing I notice is that he comes out of the door wearing a full protective suit, along with what looks like breathable air tanks, which is smart. Because if I was landing on Cyclo now, I'd assume the air wasn't breathable. It wasn't for me a few moments ago. I wonder if the suit is also radiation proof.

The second thing I notice is that Doran is really small.

He sees me, but I can't see him through his mirrored helmet, and after he looks around (and probably realizes the air is more or less okay), the visor on his helmet slides up. And this is where I realize I've made several mistakes. Because it's not Doran at all.

It's a woman, who's so petite, she's probably shorter than Hana. Her hair is gray and black, shorn close to the head, and her eyes look tired and angry and wise, all at once. She looks like a much older, angrier version of Hana, and she looks like she's about to yell at me. I have about two million things I want to say to her, but my mouth twists and stays shut because I'm overwhelmed with gratefulness that she's here. I step forward, my arms beseeching her, the first movement that precedes the "I'm Fennec and please get me and my girlfriend off this evil ship," but she beats me to the punch.

She pulls out a large plasma gun I hadn't noticed was holstered to her leg and points it straight at my face.

"Where is my daughter?" she asks with a cold fury.

I swallow air and cough about ten times before I can answer her.

"You…you're Dr. Um? You're Hana's mother?" I croak.

"Yes. Where is she?"

"But…you died!"

"A fallacy, obviously."

"But…how did you…"

"You're from the *Selkirk*? One of the—" She stops herself from attaching a label to me—convict? Left-for-dead? *Boy?* Narrowing her eyes, Dr. Um doesn't lower her weapon for a moment. I guess now is not the time to tell her that I'm also Hana's boyfriend.

"Yes. And Hana needs help. She's in northwest alpha, and Cyclo's trapped her there."

"Trapped? What do you mean?" The tip of her gun wavers for a second. "You have about one minute to explain everything. This ship is about to collapse."

So I explain so fast I nearly trip over my own tongue. How we're the only survivors. How Cyclo has killed off the other crew members, and we tried harvesting radioisotopes to refuel the *Selkirk* (here she interrupts to tell me this is a terrible, useless idea) which is when Hana got caught.

"Cyclo knows she's dying. She wants to die with Hana. It's some sort of death wish of the ship." I pause for a luxurious second. "Listen, we're both trying to survive. I'm not the enemy here. So can you point that thing somewhere else?"

Dr. Um's eyes go from hostile to regretful, and she reholsters her gun. "I'm sorry. They told us you were all convicts."

"We are. We were. It doesn't matter." There's no time to explain myself. "Cyclo's built a wall, and the gases around it are toxic. I can't get through it, and I have no protective gear. Hana's on the other side."

Dr. Um drops her face shield back down. A comm speaks to me from her suit, digitizing her voice. "Are you aware that the other half of this ship is having a nuclear meltdown?"

"Er, yes. That was sort of our fault."

Dr. Um raises her face shield just briefly enough to give me the angriest scowl I've ever received (and this includes the criminals I've done business with. Note to self: don't mess with mothers) and walks around the nose of her ship.

"Stay here. Don't you dare touch my ship. It'll know if you do, and it's been programmed to retaliate."

At this, the skin of her silvery ship flashes a big red X on its skin/hull that looks vaguely like a skull and crossbones. This one has a sense of humor, albeit a pretty dark one. I hold both my hands up.

"I'm at your mercy. For God's sake, just save Hana."

At this, Dr. Um pulls a shoulder-launching ion cannon off the large pack on her back. "I intend to."

Chapter Thirty-Five

HANA

I know that voice. I jerk my limbs hard, trying to fight Cyclo and fight the numbness in my brain.

It's not a voice from my dreams, of people I've never met, of storybook characters I've only touched by absorbing their words, the images on a screen. All false.

I claw at the matrix, trying to uncover my face and ears, straining for mental clarity.

The voice calls again. "Hana! It's me!"

This isn't a dream. It's real.

It's Mother.

How can this be? How? Mother is dead. I don't understand, and yet I open my mouth to call frantically for her. I open my eyes to see her. I reach my arms to hold her.

I am thwarted in every way. Cyclo fills my open mouth with a cascade of matrix to silence me. It enters my throat, down to my trachea, into my stomach. It is nauseating and claustrophobic in a way it never has been, because it's against my wishes. I buck with dry heaves, but Cyclo fixes me in place. Inside and out, she is controlling me utterly. I can no longer move my limbs. I try to open my eyelids, but they are heavy, so heavy. I would gag and cough and gasp, but I cannot because she is drowning me, like an insect in amber, a jeweled prize for whatever short future I am to have.

A jarring motion moves me, and something akin to an earthquake makes me and the matrix around me shudder. I open my eyes and see only purple—her matrix is changing colors from blue to red, but I can barely control my own eyelids to blink.

Hana.

Hana.

Hana.

Cyclo's words are a heartbeat but they're growing more erratic.

Ha

NA

NO

NO. STOP.

Cyclo's chemical grasp on my muscles is weakened for a moment. I wiggle my hands and toes and find that I can cut through the gel with my fingertips. Cyclo isn't providing enough oxygen for me through my skin, and I'm feeling so air-hungry now I begin to thrash about, and I find I can move my limbs better. I try to blink again, and I see something swishing back and forth. A dark figure looms over me, raising an arm with something blurry in its grasp. Greedily, I recognize her movements—they are hers. Her build and breadth—they are hers. I think it's Mother, which is impossible, but still I am not sure.

The gel around me goes bright red, the color of poppies.

The figure plunges its arm into the matrix, straight for my body. The hand grasps my upper arm and yanks ruthlessly. I'm dragged out of the matrix. I get a glimpse of silvered helmet and suit, and as soon as air hits my face, I inhale. Which I can't because there's still gel crammed into my airways and stomach, so I vomit, inhale a little air, and then liquefied matrix comes pouring out of my nose and mouth. The gel around my body recedes until I'm on the ground, heaving and coughing and my eyes tearing so bad I can't see anything.

But Cyclo has receded enough that I can finally get to my knees, wiping my face. The figure stands, holding an ion cannon propped on its left shoulder, and a hand at the ready near a holstered pistol.

I knew that voice, though. It has to be, but I'm too afraid to say a word. This person who's come to rescue us—it can't be. It just can't. I can't handle that kind of disappointment again.

"Who are you?" I finally gasp.

The figure touches its helmet, which decompresses with a whoosh and a click. Hands pull off the helmet, and I see cropped, dark hair streaked with silver and a face that has aged twenty years since my last glimpse.

Mother drops the shoulder cannon and the helmet and opens her arms. "I've come back for you, Hana."

I run and collapse into her arms.

I have so many questions. But the only one that really matters is the only one that comes to my lips.

"How can you be alive?"

We are running back to the ship, and she pauses for only a brief moment while we catch our breath.

"I should have died. I was dead, according to our monitors. No heartbeat, no breathing. Cyclo tried to kill me, and she would have succeeded if it hadn't been for this." She points to her forearm, but of course, it's under her white suit. But I know what's on her skin there—the slightly phosphorescent lotus flower tattoo that Mother embedded as a decoration, something to unify her and Cyclo in their bond to care for me. An etching to remind her of her family's Buddhist history, the artistry in Korea that's so far from her world here.

"I don't understand," I say.

"Cyclo is programmed never to self-destruct. That includes harming herself in any way. When I implanted her cells in my skin, we could communicate better than I'd ever expected. We couldn't hide much of anything from each other. But when she found out that the ship was going to be evacuated, and that I had to tell the crew about you, Hana—she knew she'd lose you. So before I got the chance to tell anyone the secret that was you, Cyclo covered me in matrix, sedated me, and tore open the artery in my neck." She touches it gingerly and winces. "I bled out, but Cyclo's cells put me into a medicated coma. Every cell in my body went into a deep hibernation. One heartbeat per minute. But I lived. It took at least a week before the monitors on our ship picked up that I was actually alive. They treated my wounds and transfused me. When I woke up, I told them everything."

I stand there, waiting. Knowing that we only have minutes left on this ship, on my home. On Cyclo, who's so far from the Cyclo I've grown up with that I don't recognize her violence, her selfishness, her desperation.

But then again, maybe Cyclo is more human to me than my own mother has been in some ways. Mother's never shown the extremes of emotion that I've seen on this ship, that I've seen in Fenn, and myself.

I wait for her apology.

It doesn't come.

"You aren't even sorry, are you?" I say.

"We have no time for biopsychology, Hana. We have to go." She grabs my wrist, and I tear it away.

"No. You kept me a prisoner. You kept me to yourself. You had seventeen years to tell them, to tell anyone, that I existed. And when it finally was time, it was too late." I'm yelling, screaming almost.

"I gave you life!" Mother yells, backing away from me in the hallway.

"You stole my life!" I holler back, making fists with my hands. "You kept me locked away!"

"I protected you! And I'm here to protect you now, and I will do this until the day I die." Seeing my stricken face, she says, "Come now. We have to get back to the ship. We'll pick up your things. We have heirlooms in that trunk of yours that are irreplaceable."

For a split second, I wonder—aren't I irreplaceable enough? But I say nothing. As we run around the north alpha, I realize we're heading for my room, not her ship. I say nothing because there are too many thoughts, too many emotions. We find our room—now enclosed in nothing but dark blue, black, and beige scar tissues. My room is dead. Mother eyes the mother-of-pearl and lacquer trunk and picks it up, stumbling a little from the weight. I don't offer to help.

"Where is Fenn? I need him." I say this without realizing that it sounds like I don't need her, but I don't care.

Mother flinches. "He's with my ship."

We start back to west alpha where her ship must be, near the bridge. But now we're slowed down by the weight of the lacquer box, by the ebony hair sticks belonging to my great-great-great-great grandmother, her diaries, my tiny knitted and re-knitted knickknacks, the wooden mated-pair of ducks, the celadon vase from the Goryeo dynasty.

She's out of breath, as am I, but I notice her left arm—the one with the tattoo—is barely able to carry the load.

"This is ridiculous. Let it go," I say. "It's not important."

"It's everything. It's our heritage," she snaps at me, and she's never snapped at me in my whole life. Which is when I realize that possibly all of her past interactions with me have been carefully curated and cultivated. Who is this woman?

"That's me, too, isn't it?" I say. "You made the heritage that I am, gave it a name, made it pretty and docile, something you can take out and look at, then put away for another time."

"Hana. Stop it. Help me carry this."

"No."

"I can't do this alone. I've already given up so much. I was court-martialed when I woke up, and I stole a craft to come to get you. Because they weren't going to bother. They assumed you'd probably already died, like the rest of the *Selkirk* crew were destined to die."

I can't fight her anymore. She's my mother, and even if she's made mistakes, I cannot bear to see her pant and struggle with that damned box. But I'm tired, too. I grasp the other end of the box, and we stumble along.

Mother's face is grim, and her lips press into a focused, straight line, nothing like the soft-spoken and gentle mother I remember from before. She runs through the hallways with far more surety than I ever have. After all, she's not been confined in a single room most her life.

As we haul the box, she mutters things under her breath, marveling at the rapid decline of Cyclo. Things like "exponential decay" and "erratic apoptosis" and "cellular rationing."

Between heavy breaths, I ask, "Where will we go?"

"Anywhere but here. I have a few options within the fuel reserves of the ship. Hana, Cyclo's full destruction and meltdown are imminent. I only have two suits on the ship, so we can't risk irreversible radiation toxicity." She adds with hesitancy, "I didn't expect anyone would be alive, let alone two of you."

Neither did we.

We finally get there. Fenn is standing by the ship, eyeing it warily. He looks exhausted and, I'm noticing for the first time in a while, he doesn't look like his usual confident self. Just a boy who's wondering if he has a future. As soon as he sees me, his eyes light up with relief and life. I drop my end of the box, and the weight causes Mother to drop hers. It cracks as it makes contact with Cyclo's floor, no longer cushiony like it was when it was healthy. I run to Fenn, my embrace nearly knocking him off his feet.

"I thought I'd never see you again," he whispers.

"Me, too." I loosen my embrace just enough to kiss him, and Fenn kisses me right back. When we pull away, we've briefly forgotten that we are not alone.

Mother's face is blank. "You have *got* to be kidding me."

"Never mind. We'll explain later. Let's get out of here," I say.

She waits for me to enter the ship; the order of entry isn't lost on me. This time, I'll leave Cyclo before Mother. As I step into the new ship, my hand touches the silvery outside, but it's warm—blood-warm. I withdraw my hand quickly as if stung.

"It's a bioship, like Cyclo. *Amorfovita potentia subtiliter.* A much younger and better-designed species. Don't worry, Sannu is very compliant," Mother says.

Sannu. What a pretty name for a ship. I taste the words in my mouth before I decide to say them.

"Compliant. Young. Like how Cyclo was," I say.

"Yes, but better. Come. I already said we don't have time for this."

I step onto the ship, but the insides are hard, and whitish silver. Sannu's endoskeleton is different than Cyclo's, and there is no matrix here. I wonder if the outside matrix somehow can withstand the brutality of outer space, or if it withdraws into pores embedded into the ship. Mother points out the silver suit attached to the inner frame of the craft. "Put this on, Hana. I've only one other, so I'm sorry, Fenn. You'll have to cross your fingers that we have no breaches on our trip."

"Of course." Fenn's voice is hollow. He sits down on the seat in the rear of the craft that Mother's pointed out, but doesn't buckle himself in. He's fingering the pendant around his neck, staring out one of the portholes to the left.

I watch him, watch the light from Sannu reflect on the pendant between his fingers.

"Wait. I need a knife," I say.

Mother and Fenn both turn to me to say, simultaneously, "What?"

"For his biomonitor. We have to remove it and leave it on Cyclo, or he won't fulfill his contract."

"Forget the contract!" Mother says.

"It's okay, Hana," Fenn says, but he looks so defeated. Like he doesn't care.

"No. ReCOR has to think he died on the ship. You've done so much work. Maybe enough to fulfill your contract." I march up to Mother and put out my hand. "I know you've got a knife on your suit. I saw it."

"At least let me do it," Mother says. I nod, and she pulls out a small blade from a sheath on her calf. "Where is it?"

"Uh, in my neck." Fenn points at a place just above his clavicle. Mother feels the mobile metal implant with her fingertips.

"We don't have time for anesthetics." She raises the tip of her knife. "This is going to hurt."

"Great. Please don't hit my artery."

I watch as she slips the tip of her knife against his skin. Bright red blood blooms against the blade and dribbles down his neck. Fenn grimaces and grips the armrests. Mother is digging into his flesh with the tip of her knife, and something metallic flicks out of his wound, leaving a red mark where it bounces against the floor.

She grabs the tiny silver transmitter and exits Sannu to fling it far down into the corridor within Cyclo. Fenn holds his hand against his bleeding cut.

The ship hums a little, almost like a whale's song underwater.

"Sannu wants to leave," Mother says. "I'll get the box, and we'll prep for launch."

Suddenly, the entire floor lurches a full forty-five degrees.

"Hana!" Mother yells, as she falls to the ground and slides into the corridor wall about twenty feet away. Fenn and I are flung hard to Sannu's floor, and Fenn grunts as his cheekbone collides with an edge of Sannu's main door. I only get a grip on the door's edge, and my feet kick helplessly sideways. The ship is continuing to tilt.

"Cyclo's stopped rotating. The gravity on the ship is gone," Fenn yells. His cheek is cut, but the blood clings to his face weirdly, and I see a tiny globule of blood gliding away from him after the impact. A tiny, free-floating sphere of ruby red.

I kick to get my feet to the ground, or the wall, or whatever is down now, but it doesn't work. I look up at Fenn, whose face is white with fear, streaked with red. But he's right. I look at him and realize he's floating ever so slightly. I pull gently on the edge of the door and float awkwardly into Sannu.

"The box!" Mother yells. "I have to get it!" She launches herself off the wall and toward the box, which has gone tumbling in zero gravity, and its contents are now floating every which way. A tiny, baby-size hanbok in vivid red and yellow, which I wore when I turned a year old, glides by just out of reach.

"Forget it! We have to go!" I yell.

Sannu speaks, a shock to hear its voice so soothing and unlike Cyclo's.

"Radiation levels are rising. The ship is burning up internally." How utterly calm and inappropriate.

Mother looks longingly at the box and her priceless family heirlooms before cursing. She pushes herself from the closest wall and floats erratically toward the open door of the ship. Fenn shoots out a long arm and grabs Mother's forearm, and he swings her inside Sannu.

"Close doors, prepare for launch," Mother orders Sannu, who complies immediately with shutting the door. I use my hands to guide myself to the nearest seat next to Mother's in the cockpit. We all fumble with the harnesses to get ourselves buckled in.

"Sannu, release your matrix from the docking area."

"Releasing," Sannu says.

"Reverse thrusters, fifteen percent."

The whole ship lurches yet again, and my skull bangs hard against the headrest of my seat. In front of us, the cockpit window shows reddish flames licking at the far corridor. I muffle a cry at the sight of Cyclo on fire from the inside out.

"Radiation levels are critical," Sannu says.

"I know," Mother snaps.

There is a large cracking noise, so loud and strong that the whole ship reverberates and my teeth clack against each other.

"What is that?" Fenn says. He's forgotten about his wounds—the blood has slowed to a tiny trickle, leaving a crimson stain on his neck and cheek.

"It's Sannu detaching. There are sometimes cracks that occur in his endoskeleton, and Cyclo's, as part of the separation process."

Neither Fenn nor I ever knew what it was like to exit a biological craft, and it's awful. It's like breaking bones and tearing flesh, and my eyes well over at the pain that both must be feeling. Despite what Cyclo has done, my heart is breaking for her. She's dying.

Oh God, she's dying. And I didn't even get a chance to say goodbye.

After one last, long creak, Sannu detaches, and there is a gap of a few feet between us and Cyclo. The creaking stops immediately, and there is the blessed, horrid silence of being in space, apart from the apocalypse happening on Cyclo.

I stifle a cry.

And Mother moans.

I look at her, where she has her hands on the controls, and she's leaning over, eyes squeezed tightly closed.

"Mother? What's the matter?"

"I don't know. Oh, God. Everything hurts."

"What's happening?" Fenn yells from the back.

"It's Mother. Something's wrong. She's—"

Mother's face goes ashen, and her hands drop from the controls. "Hana. I'm…"

She can't even finish her sentence. She starts clawing at her arm beneath her suit. She grabs her forearm, exactly where her Cyclo tattoo is, and throws her head back and screams.

Chapter Thirty-Six

FENN

Dr. Um is screaming, screaming, screaming.

"God, what is it?" Hana asks. She unhooks her buckles and straps to push herself over to her mother.

"Hana, don't!" I yell.

"It's the Cyclo tissue in me. It's dying, too," Dr. Um says, gasping between her moans. "Oh, God. It's not like—I can't—I didn't think—"

"We have to take her suit off," Hana says, releasing her mother from her seat and tugging at the thick, white fabric, finding the fasteners that go to her arm and yanking the whole sleeve off.

"We are on manual control," Sannu says. "Would you like me to autopilot a safe distance away from the *Calathus*?"

"YES!" Hana and I yell simultaneously. The ship backs farther away from Cyclo, not fast enough for my taste, but there are other things to deal with. I unbuckle and push myself over to Dr. Um's chair.

Hana has removed the sleeve of her suit, where it goes lithely floating away. She tears at the skin-tight fabric of her clothes, ripping up the sleeve in one smooth movement. When

Hana sees her mother's arm, she cries out.

This is not good.

I'd expected the tattoo to be blue, or at least navy blue. A pretty lotus design.

But all I see is blood and black gashes deep in her arm. The darkness is rapidly spreading, sending itself through the veins under her skin, even as we speak.

And to make matters worse, the ship has stopped moving.

"Make a tourniquet, Hana. Anything to stop the spread. Cyclo's cells must be dying in her arm, too. But maybe we can keep it from hurting the rest of her," I say. Hana uses the torn shirt to tourniquet her mother's arm. I yell, "Sannu! Why isn't this ship moving faster?"

"We are still attached to the *Calathus*," Sannu tells us placidly.

"What?" Hana and I yell again, simultaneously.

"The *Calathus* has sent out a pseudopod and has reattached to my hull. I am trying to break the bond, but she is highly radioactive and I'm having trouble—she is permutating my cells—she is trying to override my controls."

Hana looks at her mother, then out the cockpit window. We are getting closer to Cyclo, not farther away.

No, no, no.

Hana looks at me, a sickened expression over her face.

"She wants me," Hana says, quietly.

"Hana, let Sannu break the connection. There's nothing you can do!" her mother yells between gasps of pain.

Hana doesn't listen. She's staring back through the cockpit window, looking at a thick cord of matrix that's stretched out to our little ship. Stretched out to take Hana back. Behind, we can see licks of flames and explosions happening inside the plastrix windows all around the edges of Cyclo. The ship has tilted, and as we're attached, we have, too, no longer with the shining blue of Maia above us.

"Radiation levels are critical," Sannu repeats.

"She wants me," Hana says again, like she's in a trance. "Only me."

I undo the buckles of my safety belts, but I'm not fast enough. Hana pushes herself back toward the door and touches the walls with her hands as she presses her body against the membrane of Sannu's wall.

"Sannu. Dr. Um is incapacitated. I need you to release me from the ship. It's the only way you'll get away from the *Calathus*."

"You need a passcode for authorization," Sannu says.

Mother cries out, "No, Hana!"

"Dal a, dal a," Hana says.

"Hana!" Mother cries out. She tries to unbuckle herself, but she crumples in a howl of pain. "Stop! Sannu, don't—"

"Authorization accepted," Sannu says.

"I need to leave the ship," Hana says.

"Sannu, override authorization," Dr. Um gasps, but Sannu flashes a kindly yellow color.

"My biomonitors read that you are incapacitated, Dr. Um. Authorization has already been accepted."

Dr. Um points to the wall. "But the suit! God, Hana, at least put on one of the pressurized suits!"

"Two suits. One for you, and one for Mother. Take care of her, Fenn. I know you'll figure out a way to keep her alive."

With the buckles on my harnesses all free, I launch myself toward Hana. Hana spreads her palms against Sannu's inner skin. He seems to know exactly what she's asking for, without her saying a word. He's even more responsive that Cyclo. A thin film envelops Hana, separating her from the cockpit. The film grows an inch thick by the time I reach her. I realize what's happening—Sannu is preparing to push Hana right through the wall of the ship and into space. I claw and grab at Sannu's wall, but it's thickening even as I gouge out a few bits of matrix here and there. It grows more and more opaque as it gets thicker. Hana already is a blur behind the wall of silvery-white. I can see her mouthing something, but I don't understand.

"What is she saying, Sannu?" I yell.

"Hana is commanding me to fly the ship for at least one hour on autopilot before allowing you or Dr. Um to command me. She has overridden Dr. Um's command for one hour under all circumstances."

"No!" I cry out.

"She has ordered me to release her outside the ship now."

"Sannu, stop her! Stop this!"

Hana isn't speaking anymore. She simply smiles in the blurry cloud behind the wall of Sannu's making. She raises her hand against the wall between us. All I can do is put my hand near hers in pantomime. Tears are streaming down my face.

"Don't do this. Don't, Hana. Don't," I say, over and over again.

Soon, I can't see her anymore as the wall goes completely opaque.

Hana is gone.

Chapter Thirty-Seven

HANA

The outer membrane spreads thinly, and I am pushed out into the freezing, airless emptiness of space. This is what I had to do, so that Cyclo would let Fenn and Mother live. Sometimes, you have to give things away to get what you really want.

I can't breathe. Already, the moisture over my eyeballs boils off, and my eyes begin to freeze. Without the pressurization on Sannu or Cyclo, my body feels like it's being pulled in multiple directions, expanding, though my skin won't let it. I can't move well, but the force of leaving Sannu has launched me gently toward Cyclo. I feel the saliva in my mouth evaporate away.

I start counting down, knowing I only have perhaps ten or fifteen more seconds before I lose consciousness.

Through the blurriness of my vision, I can vaguely see Cyclo's hold on Sannu break away. Sannu drifts further and accelerates in reverse, putting a comfortable distance between it and Cyclo. I would sigh with relief if I could. Instead, the peninsula of blue tissue reaches for me and breaks off completely from Cyclo. The blob of Cyclo is soft and gel-like, and it freezes with a pattern of beautiful crystals. As it moves and undulates toward me, the crystals shatter and reform, an exquisite dance of dying cells and temperature mechanics.

This last piece of Cyclo must be the only part of her that has survived. The rest of the ship is a ball of fire, combustion, radiation, and poisonous gas. Soon, it will burn itself out and be nothing but a mass of darkness that will find the pull of a willing planetary body or star, and either enter an orbit or crash into oblivion.

The blue sphere of Cyclo's last functioning tissue comes closer to me. I'll die if I stay in space for another minute. Already, the oxygen and nitrogen and carbon dioxide dissolved in my blood are finding each other, clinging to each other, becoming gas again. The pain of it is excruciating, as bubbles form in my joints, my brain, my blood vessels. I'd scream but there is no air to push through my vocal cords. I reach out one hand to the blue sphere, and it touches me. In seconds, it envelops me, and I'm in the cradle of Cyclo's matrix again, nothing but a girl in a womb of blue.

I knew, somehow, she would embrace me again.

Cyclo pressurizes my body, slowly, gently. I am starting to feel better already, but for what? Without the rest of her enormous body, she cannot survive in space much longer, which means I cannot, either.

So this is how we'll die? I ask Cyclo.

Yes, Hana.

I'm going to miss you.

As will I. You have been my everything, Hana. My best, my only, my daughter.

I can still be yours, you know. Mothers have to let go of their children sometimes.

I don't understand.

That is love. Letting go even though it hurts.

Cyclo is silent.

I have something I need to let go of.

In my cocoon of blue, my eyesight slowly returns as Cyclo warms and rehydrates my corneas. I can see Sannu, with Mother and Fenn, in the far distance now. They are going quite fast. In a second, I won't be able to see them anymore. They are gone without me. Sannu did his job well. But then I feel something. Something hard and round coming to rest in the palm of my right hand.

I look down and see a blue globe in my hand. It is like a glass marble.

You started this, Hana. These are my stem cells, my embryo clones. You made these.

Oh. The stem cells that spilled onto the floor. I assumed they'd die without nourishment, but I forgot that Cyclo was as good a womb for me as those gestational chambers.

You saved them? I ask.

Yes.

The blue of the tiny ball is bright, bright as Cyclo has ever been. In comparison, the gel around me is darkening to a deeper blue. Cyclo is dying, even as we speak. It's hardening, too, making it a task to even smile at this beautiful thing we've made.

You will stay with me, won't you?

Yes. I won't let you die alone. That's why you kept me, isn't it? Because you were afraid.

Afraid. Yes, that is what this is. Fear.

I'll take this. Maybe you'll live again in them someday.

But then I realize that I've been wrong in so many ways, as Cyclo has, as Mother has. It is not through our genes that we live on forever. You can't hope that passed-on DNA will somehow give honor to the very essence of who you once were. That's too much of a burden on children, isn't it? To have your existence be the one and only legacy, an heirloom of identity.

But I promise to tell your story, Cyclo. It's not through progeny and double helixes and cherished boxes of antiques that we find ourselves. It's through making our own stories. And your story, Cyclo, will be told forever.

Forever is a long time.

Yes, it is.

Chapter Thirty-Eight

FENN

One hour.

I have one hour before I can take over the ship and fly back to Hana, if there is any Hana left to recover.

Dr. Um is nearly unconscious from the pain of Cyclo's dying tissues in her arm. I manage to make an upper arm tourniquet from a cord off one of the suits. It's so tight, I know we've completely cut off the circulation in her arm, but it seems to work. The black discoloration of dying tissues stops an inch from the tourniquet.

It's a save and a loss. Dr. Um will lose her arm, no question. She might lose her life if we can't get her medical care soon. I find a kit on board and dig up some useful things—an immune booster, energy supplement, and dermal pain-relieving med. After I touch the pain medicine to her good arm, she sighs audibly and rouses herself.

"Where's Hana?" she asks.

"She left the ship. To save us."

Dr. Um sits up with a groan and covers her face with her one good hand. She weeps for a while, and I have nothing to say. I'm too empty to give anything to anyone, and Dr. Um doesn't want my superficial sentiments, no matter what they are. For a while, we just lie there in our own separate miseries.

I stand up and stare out the portside window. Cyclo is far away now, only a speck in the distance that would easily be missed in a blink, but I know it's there. It's still glowing a dull red, and somewhere in there is Hana, if her body is there at all. Everything I had, everything I wanted to be, everything I wasn't, was Hana's.

I touch my pendant, flipping it over and over in my hand. A useless poison on one side, a message on the other.

I feel a presence beside me and find that Dr. Um is standing near me.

"I'm sorry."

"I'm sorry, too. For a lot of things."

She stares out the cockpit window, looking utterly lost. After a long time, she notices the pendant in my palm. "What's that?" she asks. I explain to her how it's a recording from the person who's to receive my death benefit. A final goodbye. The whole trip, I hadn't opened it.

"It's from my sister. I haven't had the guts to listen to it." I stare at it. After losing Hana, I have a sudden, overwhelming need to hear Callandra's voice. Even if it's yelling at me — anything to remind me that there is a person I love still alive in the universe — it'll be worth it.

Dr. Um looks so utterly despondent, like she'd rather hear anything but what's in her own head right now, too. So I detach the pendant and pop the cover open. A holographic transmitter sits in the center, only a few millimeters big.

A fuzzy image of a face shows up.

It's Callandra. She looks so much older now, and seeing her face as a teenager catches me off guard. I haven't seen her in years, and she's changed so much. Her hair is pulled back, instead of in messy pigtails, and her eyes are big, serene, and serious. One of her eyes is silver—she's replaced it with an expensive implant that most ace pilots have. She has a scar on her chin, too, probably from her aerial training. But I can see that she's attached to machines, and her arms have metallic implants to help them move better. The rounder, childlike face is gone, replaced with an oval face with high cheekbones. The last time I saw her, she was ten years old. Now she's fifteen. It's jarring.

"Fenn," she says. "If you're watching this, then you don't have much time. I tried to send you messages. Why didn't you answer? If you did, you'd know that I never wanted this. I never asked for you to save me, or repay me, or punish yourself. This mining job—I offered it to you, but the truth was, I wanted it for myself all along. I was so glad you didn't take it. I only wanted to be a pilot because that's what Mom and Dad wanted. I mean—I was the only person in the family that didn't want to fly things, but I was afraid to say so. I was even afraid to tell you. Everyone wanted so much for me to succeed…I was afraid to fail.

"You remember all those stones and crystals you'd bring me back on your trips? All those times I explored the caves around our house? That's what I love. I want to be an intergalactic geologist, not a pilot. I botched my academy scholarship on purpose. And after the mining accident, I finally had the bravery to tell Mom and Dad the truth. The accident was no one's fault, least of all yours.

"I don't want your money, or this sacrifice. What you're doing is…brave, and unselfish, and utterly unnecessary. And I want you to come home, but it's probably too late for that now." Callandra starts crying. "I miss you. But you're there, and you've signed a contract, and…" She smears the tears on her face away. "If this is what you needed to do to find peace, then I understand. But you should know, I don't forgive you for messing up whatever you think you've messed up. Because there was never anything to forgive."

That's it. I close the pendant shut.

Dr. Um is quiet for a long time.

"Why didn't you answer her messages?" Dr. Um says quietly.

"I don't know."

"What happened?"

"She had an accident. Major spinal damage. I wanted to use the money from my contract to pay for her treatments. My family can't afford them, and they're in major debt already."

"It was an accident."

"No, not really," I say levelly.

She puts a hand on my shoulder. "But—"

"It's okay. I'm okay," I say. I take the pendant back and put it back on. "I know I didn't steer that mining drover into a gully. It's not really my fault, but I played a part." I straighten my shoulders and shrug away from Dr. Um's warm hand. "Callandra will be okay, and the money will help her, whether she wants to admit it or not. And Hana reminded me that I have a life to live. She gave me permission to live again."

Dr. Um turns, and I'm thinking she's distancing herself from my simplistic revelation when she suddenly embraces me. I'm stiff as a board at first, but I soften after she doesn't let go. It feels really nice to hug a mother, even if she isn't mine.

"You're very brave," she whispers, as she hugs me harder. "But you are so full of bullshit."

And with that, I cry into her shoulder.

After the sixty minutes are up, the medicines have worked enough to keep Dr. Um's pain under control, and Cyclo's dying cells aren't causing problems in the rest of her body.

She's physically stable enough to take command of Sannu, and Sannu makes a perfect parabolic turn in space and goes right back to the wreck of the *Calathus*.

I don't talk to Dr. Um again about my parents, or about Callandra. Some things need more time in my brain to simmer. I'm not at peace, really. I don't want to say that one talk and one hug from a stand-in mom has lifted an enormous, overly dramatic burden from my metaphorical shoulders.

Geez. I'm not that simple. But I did, finally, crack open that damned holograph pendant. I listened and didn't run away.

You've got to start somewhere.

As we get closer to the wreck, Sannu turns on a radiation shield in preparation. It takes a full hour to get there and decelerate so we can find Hana. For all we know, she was pulled back into the wreckage of the ship, or she ended up inside that tiny blob of Cyclo and is frozen and drifting off somewhere.

Dr. Um tries to be levelheaded about searching for Hana, but we both know we're looking for a body now, and her voice shakes with every order.

"Sannu, set your…scanner for any biological carbon-based tissue, alive or…" Dr. Um pauses to swallow and put her good hand over her eyes. "Or dead."

"The *Calathus* is deceased. All the complex organic material has combusted on the ship. I am not picking up any readings. But I am sensing organic material in the six parsecs out from Maia, vector negative nine."

I grip the chair I'm sitting in. "That must be Hana's body." I can't believe I'm doing this. I can't believe she's gone. My heart is hammering at seeing her lifeless.

"Sannu," Dr. Um says, "please redirect to the area and keep scanning as we go."

I keep my eyes on the front cockpit window, searching the

brilliant spray of stars in front of us for anything that looks like it could be Hana's body, or the piece of Cyclo that took her.

"There." Dr. Um points off to the right, and Sannu gently arcs in that direction. On the monitor before us, a green dot lights up. Complex organic material confirmed.

And then I see it. It's a tiny black orb that blots out the stars behind it as it floats along. The dark material of the ball is speckled with white ice crystals, and it's translucent. Inside, there is the faint outline of a human body.

It's not moving. I have a feeling that my heart might break all over again, seeing Hana like this, but my thoughts are swept away when Dr. Um angles the ship closer.

"Sannu, see if you can bring that orb on board. Only if you think it's safe."

"Acknowledged."

We get so close that I can see Hana's profile. Her eyes are closed and limbs akimbo as if she'd fallen from a sky to the earth and never really landed. Like she's still suspended in someone else's dream.

We lose sight of the orb as Sannu sidles up to Hana, forms a pocket of matrix around the sphere, and brings it to the rear hatch where there's an opening in Sannu's endoskeleton. Dr. Um and I turn and watch as the ship's matrix bubbles toward us, encasing the sphere. Sannu moves it onto the floor and thins himself out until there is nothing but a black sphere, Hana, and the tendrils of silky white matrix reincorporating into the ship's walls.

The orb is large. It's nearly six feet in diameter, and Hana's waist is bent a little in the middle like she's curled over to sleep. Dr. Um touches the orb and withdraws her hand.

"Oh, God. It's ice cold."

"We can't leave her like this!" My hands are shaking. "What do we do?"

"I want her out of that matrix. I can put her body in cryo on the ship until we can bury her properly on Earth." Her voice is steady and resolute, but her eyes glisten with moisture.

Dr. Um approaches the sphere. It looks like obsidian—volcanic black glass that I saw once from an Earth ore dealer. I touch the sphere, too. After living on Cyclo for almost two weeks, it's so strange to see a piece of her look like this—so inert, so past its life. I expect it will feel like glass, too—hard, cold. As soon as my fingertips touch it, the hard surface pulses under my fingertip.

"What was that?"

The orb trembles, as if a tiny earthquake is racking it from the inside out. Deep within it, Hana's eyes open.

"Oh, God! She's alive!" her mother yells. "Quick, Fenn! Get it open!"

"Hana!" I yell so loud I hurt my own ears.

Those eyes, searching, looking. Looking at me, at Dr. Um.

Hana, my one Hana, is alive.

I think my heart just learned how to beat again.

We take what we can—a metal rod from a grappling hook, and I grip it tightly in my hands. Hana's mouth opens now, her eyes seeing us both. The center of the sphere appears to be liquid—it's only solid on the surface. I swing the rod back behind me, and Dr. Um turns slightly to shield her face, and I swing as hard as I can. The rod bounces off the surface of the orb, and the strike rebounds as pain flares up my arms. I swing again and again. Hana looks panicked and tries to move her hands and legs. She's mouthing words.

HELP.

HURRY.

Sweat pouring down my face, I wind up for another strike. When the rod hits the sphere, everything explodes.

Black water and chunks of black gel pour everywhere.

The shards of the sphere spread out, sharp as knives and slicing through my pants and cutting my upper arms. Hana is sodden, collapsed in the middle of this mess, and her arms cradle something to her chest.

Dr. Um and I wade through the broken shell and the gooey, black mess and grasp Hana. She's crying and laughing, but mostly crying. In a heap, we're hugging each other and asking questions and answering them, and everything is a hurricane of words and relief and pain.

Hana is alive.

I am alive.

For the first time, I feel like I'm home.

Chapter Thirty-Nine

HANA

This is what I know.

I am alive.

Cyclo is dead.

Mother is alive.

And Fenn is on the run.

But some things come before running. Like introductions.

After I can manage to stand without shaking, I gesture to Mother.

"Mother," I say, reaching for Fenn's hand. He squeezes it nervously. "This is Fennec Actias. He's a thief."

Fenn goes bright red in the face, and he closes his eyes and shakes his head. Mother goes red in the face, too, and frowns so deeply it looks like her smile is permanently broken. Was that the wrong way to introduce people?

But then Mother's face softens, and she reaches out with her good hand. "So that's what Fenn stands for. Well, thank you for helping me with my arm. And for helping Hana."

"Anytime," he says, and the offer—to be there for us, at all moments, fills me with warmth.

"And now, we need to get out of here, in case Doran and

ReCOR show up."

Mother instructs Sannu to drive carefully to avoid any debris from Cyclo's destruction until we're clear enough to go to hyperspace. Her wreck of a body is dark, burned in places, and no longer possesses that preternatural blue glow. A good third of her is shattered and hovering in a debris field, but it's clear at a glance that she is lifeless.

I cry silently as we pass by her, and Mother watches, dead-eyed, at what used to be our home. She was my sky and my earth, my other parent, my world. Fenn hangs back and watches with wonder the scattered chunks of mantle and plastrix drifting by. After several minutes, he puts his hand on my shoulder.

"Look," he says, pointing.

The *Selkirk* has broken off and drifts lazily about half a mile away, lights out, with that sardonic smile shape.

"Can we do a quick flyby? I need to board the *Selkirk*."

Mother seems puzzled but orders Sannu to draw closer. Fenn dons one of the suits, and Sannu pushes him right through her wall. By tether, he boards the *Selkirk*. He returns fairly quickly holding a dark box.

Once he's safely on board and free of his suit, I stoop by the box. It's such a simple thing. "What is it?" I ask.

"Black titanium, but with five-XT nucleotide helix cores packed full of data. When Doran comes here, he'll assume we've both died, and that Gammand was unable to load this data. But we're going to leak it." He grins. "Hello, truth. Get ready to meet the world."

"But your death benefit! And Callandra. What about her?"

"She'll be okay." He looks wistfully out the front plastrix window of the cockpit. "I'll still be able to help her, in another way. And I'm thinking there may be ways to help Gammand, Portia, and Miki's beneficiaries, too. I have ideas." He grins mischievously.

"Sannu," Mother says. "Set a course for GP90. It's about a week's travel away, but it's a neutral city, and ReCOR doesn't have any major outposts there. We can hide for a while."

Fenn nods. "I'll need a new ID. DNA theft is pretty easy, actually. Huh. After all this, I'm still at my old job."

At the word "theft," Mother cringes a little, but then she shrugs. "I suppose I ought to get used to being on the run. I just stole Sannu, after all. And ReCOR's data files. I'll need a new ID, too."

"As will I. My first ID." I smile.

Fenn grins at all of this. "I come on this mission as a convict, and I end up bringing two criminals with me."

This is where Sannu chimes in. "I am not a criminal."

We all laugh at that, not knowing exactly what to say. But then I take Fenn's hand in my own. "Fenn. You won't be able to see your sister if you're on the run and hiding. Or if people think you're dead."

"Oh, I don't know about that," Mother says, her hand touching the controls on the bridge here and there. Without even looking at us, she says, "I can't imagine a little thing like faking death would stop you from seeing your sister again."

I look wonderingly at Fenn and then his pendant. He takes it from his neck and hands it to me, and we step away to talk quietly.

"I listened to it. Finally. I should have listened to you and opened it before."

"Well. We all make mistakes, don't we?" I say.

Sannu intones, "I don't."

"Not yet, at least," I whisper to Fenn.

"I heard that," Sannu says again, sounding somewhat irritated. "Dr. Um, my readings tell me that you need more treatment for your arm, and these two humans are showing low levels of radioactivity. Permit me to begin therapy for all of you while we are on autopilot."

"Permission granted," Mother says, looking very much relieved. Her arm is wrapped up in a bandage, but I can see that her fingers have turned purple-black. I touch her hand, and Mother recoils a little. "No Hana. It's okay. I've lost it, but it was worth it."

She says nothing more, and I don't press her. I'm finding that sometimes the space within silence is much more filling than words.

Sannu has a fully equipped laser medical-surgical program, and in a shockingly short amount of time, Mother's arm is amputated, laser-stitched, and a healing infusion administered. Meanwhile, Fenn and I receive intravenous chelators to remove any lingering radioactivity in our bodies, plus an infusion of nutrients and vitamins we were in need of after our traumatic last few days.

It's time to set the course to leave. I help Mother stand, and Fenn and I walk her to the bridge. Once in the chair, she looks up at me.

"Hana. Your necklace. What happened to it?"

I put my hand to the base of my throat to feel my pearl pendant there. Strange. I was sure that I'd yanked it off in a fit of anger. And also strange—my great-grandmother's pearl was baroque. Pear-shaped. The cool, smooth pendant around my neck is spherical.

"That's no pearl," Fenn says.

I reach behind my neck to unclasp the chain and hold the necklace up.

It's a brilliant, bright-blue sphere hanging from the chain like an azure glass bead. But the center looks liquid and iridescent, as if an entire galaxy and history were contained within it.

Oh. I'd forgotten that Cyclo had given it to me. She must

have attached it to the chain on my neck.

"It's a piece of Cyclo," Mother says in astonishment.

"You are only partially correct," Sannu says. "It is embryonic tissue composed of DNA from *Amorfovita potentia,* subspecies *cyclonica*, with fragments of humanoid DNA."

"Wait, what?" I yell.

"What?" Fenn and my mother yell.

"The DNA of this embryo is a hybrid," Sannu says, calm as can be.

We all go silent for a full minute.

"I thought Cyclo said it was only *her,*" I say.

"Cyclo isn't capable of that type of reproduction," my mother says. "She's not programmed to be able to reproduce in any way."

"She wasn't programmed to kill, but she did," I remind her.

"Wait, wait, wait," Fenn says, holding his temples. "What other DNA is in this thing?"

Sannu, calmly waiting for us all to be quiet, answers.

"The humanoid DNA appears to be a mix of Argyrian, Prinniad, and Gragorian DNA."

WHAT.

I am not sure what this all means. I'm only seventeen, and only just got out of my prison of a room two weeks ago, only just met other creatures besides Mother and Cyclo, had my first kiss, watched people murdered in front of my eyes, and experienced my first nuclear meltdown. And Cyclo has decided to live on, fiercely, by piecing her imperfect self together with the very people we are still mourning in our hearts.

This is a bit much.

I need a moment.

But in the end, we decide that...nothing needs to be decided. Fenn needs to be in hiding. Mother can no longer return to her previous position because she's on the run after her court-martial. And apparently, they are trying to track me down, too, because, since I was never allowed to exist in the first place, the federation has the right to delete my life.

"Without incubation, this will not grow. Even if it was incubated, it may not be compatible with life," Mother says, touching the pendant.

"Then, for now, we'll just call it what it is. A memory of the past." I bite my lip. "With potential."

Memories and potential. But one thing it isn't—destiny.

If there's one thing I learned, it's that a DNA code can't determine a perfectly tailored being or future. I'm proof of that.

Finally, we sleep. Or at least we try to. Mother wants Fenn to sleep separately in the back of Sannu, while she and I sleep in the cockpit.

"No," I say. "Fenn stays with me."

"Hana. No. I forbid it. You're too young. You don't even know what you're doing right now. You need to rest."

"You just lost an arm. *You* need to rest. I've been working nonstop to reverse-engineer mantle cells, fool a ship so I could steal radioactive waste, and I saved you. I think I know what I'm doing."

Mother's mouth drops open and stays there. This is not the docile, quiet, polite daughter she knows.

"I'm staying with Fenn, and there isn't much you can do about that."

I'm fully shocked at my own behavior and words, too.

I kind of love it.

Mother goes a little pale in the face, and she sits limply down in the captain's chair. I find some medicine that will help her stump heal quickly and apply it to her newly sewn wounds, then find a crinkly solar blanket and drape it over her. I kiss her cheek.

"Close your eyes and sleep. Fenn and I will see you in about ten hours."

Her eyes are droopy with tiredness and medicine, and she nods. "Okay."

I ask Sannu to drop a membrane of privacy between the cockpit and the back of the ship, and he complies. Fenn is waiting for me, and his mouth has dropped open in an almost exact mirror image of my mother's previous expression of surprise.

"I think you just sent her into shock," Fenn finally says. "She may never recover."

"She'll be fine. Just like you and I will be fine. Not perfect, but fine." I curl my arm around his taut waist, and we head for a pile of gel padding beneath another solar blanket that will be our bed. "I'm still so angry at her, Fenn. I want to scream at her for hours and hours."

"Not now. But later, yeah. Scream all you want. You have stuff to figure out."

"Don't we all?" I say, before lying down and letting Fenn's arms wrap around me.

"Yes. But right now, I don't want any of that."

"What do you want, Fenn?" I ask as I roll to my side exactly one inch away from his face, staring at those beautiful brown and gold-flecked eyes. Staring, and waiting.

He leans in to kiss me.

It's the answer I'd hoped for.

So while my mother slumbers in the bridge, busy healing, so am I. I may not have wounds on my body that need tending, but my heart does. Now that I don't need to be afraid to exist, it's easier for both of us to navigate this gaping hole that is our future.

Future. What a beautiful, large word. I love it, so I say it often to myself when no one is listening. It's been so long since I was isolated that I'm learning again what it's like to be alone and not be lonely. A wonderful sensation.

Tonight, I sleep on another sentient ship, wondering what it thinks of me. I slumber next to a boy who first saw me as an impediment, who taught me how to fall in love in low gravity. I am with a mother I lost and regained, who makes me so angry sometimes I could explode but who I am learning to forgive. And at an arm's length away, I look at this tiny blue orb, in the center of which glows a being that could be everything or nothing, an end or a beginning, beauty or horror. Possibly all of it, all at once. And possibly none of it.

But I don't want to think of that now.

What I think of when I sleep is Cyclo. Forgiving her is more difficult. I have seen things I cannot unsee. I have felt love that I cannot unfeel. I see her burning brightly in my mind's eye, and I see all of us. We are ash and stars.

I suppose this is what they say, on those old vids from the twentieth-century, that family can be complicated. I understand what that means now. So I think and think and think at night on this long trip to who-knows-where, trying to find forgiveness where only pain rests. I won't find the peace I'm looking for in one single night.

But then again, ahead of me, I have time. And I have a future.

Did I tell you how much I love that word?

Acknowledgments

To my husband, Bernie, my children, and my family, who have always cheered me on. Every day, I am thankful for your support and love.

To Dad and Mom, for all the help with the Korean details—thank you. I love you so much!

To Jamie Krakover, for your physics acumen! And to my math, biology, physics, and chemistry teachers who nourished my love of science and numbers. Creativity helped with dreaming up this book, but it was the math and science you taught me that gave it the scaffolding to exist.

To Sarah Fine, who always has my back. I am endlessly grateful.

To Maurene Goo, thank you for your wisdom and talent. Let's get some Korean BBQ soon.

To the many friends I've made on this writing journey that have supported me so generously: Mindy McGinnis, April Tucholke, Cindy Pon, Tonya Kuper, Mia Siegert, Elle Cosimano, Brenda Drake, Pintip Dunn.

To Sarah Simpson-Weiss and Emalee Napier, for keeping my life from skidding off into a black hole of miserable chaos and wretchedness.

To Eric Myers, thank you for all your agenting wizardry.

To Kate Brauning, Bethany Robison, Clarissa Yeo, Stacy Abrams, Liz Pelletier, Melissa Montovani, Heather Riccio, all the interns, and the entire team at Entangled who have been so incredibly supportive of this strange little story of mine—thank you for helping to make this book the best it could be. I am so grateful.

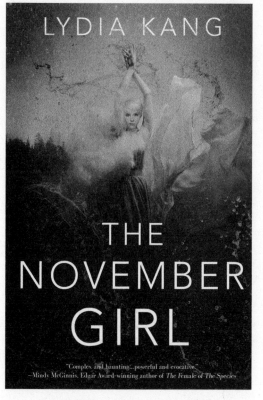

Chapter One

HECTOR

There's a foolproof method to running away.

I know the wrong ones all too well. This time, there'll be no mistakes.

I'd left my cell phone, fully charged, duct-taped beneath a seat on a Duluth city bus. If they track it, they'll think I've never left town. Acting scared and paranoid is a giveaway. Wearing a hoodie is no good, either; they'll think I'm a criminal. With my height and my brown skin, I get enough sideways glances as it is without more advertising. Nah. I make sure the clothes I've stolen from my uncle are clean and defy gravity, instead of sagging on my hips and shoulders. I carry a hiking backpack, not a high schooler's version.

This khaki down jacket I got from the Salvation Army. It's the nasty kind only worn by grown-ups with flat, worn-out souls. And I carry my armor of pleasantness like a plastic shield, pretending it's the most normal thing in the world to board the ferry to Isle Royale on October 4, the last day it runs to the island.

I make them all believe I belong on this damned boat.

A line of people waits to board the *Quest II* at the dock. They're all middle-aged, with that middle-aged sag that weighs them down. The air around Lake Superior is cold, but humid and acrid from the rotting wood of the pier. The sky hangs with clouds of pale gray. It doesn't look like rain's coming, but the color paints a thin gloom, and fog skims the lake. I zip my jacket up higher.

A bald white guy calls out names for passengers, his pudgy, callused hands gripping a clipboard. His belly's softly round above his jeans. My name is fake, of course, and my fare paid in cash, to leave no trail.

"Goin' alone?" he asks, friendly-like. The gap where he's missing a canine tooth only shows when he smiles.

"No. Meeting my wife there. She works at the lodge," I say, performing lines I've carefully rehearsed. Luckily, I've got a face that could be twenty-five or fifteen, depending on my clothes. So, I'll let them think I have a real life. I've even got my dad's old wedding ring on my fourth finger, but I hate how it feels on my hand. Confining. My palms get sweaty and I shove my ringless hand into my pocket.

"Don't forget the last ferry leaves at one o'clock, tomorrow afternoon. It'll be crowded."

I nod, but my stomach dives into the center of the earth. I pray he won't notice that I'm not on it. I try to walk by, when he points to my backpack.

"Hey. Next time you come, bring a different bag, will ya?"

I shift uncomfortably, conscious of the line of people growing on the dock. "Uh, why?"

"Black bags are bad luck. They sink ships."

A passenger behind me yells through his beard, "Ignore him! Norm's superstitious. He made my wife throw away a rose I gave her. Right into the trash, because they're bad luck on boats. He won't run the ferry on Fridays. Lucky they shut down in November, too."

"Why November?" Ah, God, Hector. Shut up, *shut up*.

"The worst storms come in November," Norm says quietly. "There's a name for them storms, the ones that sink ships. The Witch o' November."

There's something about how he says "witch" that bothers me. Some people love to say stuff for the drama of it. But this guy glances nervously at the lake, as if it were listening.

I nod at him. "Got it. No Fridays, no flowers, no Novembers. And I'll bring my blue backpack next time," I say with a smile, though the conversation is killing me. My hands are swampy with perspiration. The boat sways beneath my feet as I walk past the other passengers. This late in the season, they're probably Isle workers helping to close up for the season. Because from tomorrow until late spring, the Isle Royale will be empty.

Except for me.

It's the perfect hideout. No one will look for a runaway on an island that's purposely deserted every winter. I've covered my tracks too well. I'll hide out here until mid-May, when I turn eighteen. And then I'll be free, and there will be no more leashes. No more living under that roof that punishes me with thoughts I can't stand.

I'm doing my uncle a favor, really. He complains about the bills, how much it costs to raise me, how the money my dad sends is never quite enough.

But it's not about the money. It's what we never talk about that chases me from that house.

I've lived with him since I was six. I know he'll report me missing when he finds out. I know that deep in his heart, he might hope I'm never found. By then, the island will be uninhabited. On Isle Royale, I'll be where I don't belong.

I'll fit right in.

The two engines of the *Quest II* are already rumbling, water boiling to a hissing fury by the propellers. The mooring lines are cast off and the fenders secured. I sit in my corner seat inside the boat, itching to read the maps, notes, and pamphlets I stuffed into my coat pocket. I'm not supposed to look like a tourist. My phantom wife supposedly works on the island, after all. When the force of the engine pushes me against my seat, I glance up.

Lake Superior stretches out in liquid stillness, a yawning expanse of dark water that unsettles me and makes me sweat even more. Behind us, the sparse buildings of Grand Portage shrink farther away. The black forest swallows everything as the boat pushes us forward, until there's no trace of humanity on the horizon.

For almost two hours, I fake like I'm asleep in my corner seat. It works; no one talks to me. The boat pitches up and down on the growing swells, the lake water occasionally spraying my face from one of the open windows, but I pretend I'm dead to the world. I'm hungry for sleep, but my mind is wrung too tight to relax.

I think of which part of the island I'm going to live on, how to stay warm, how to eat enough. Looking on the internet hasn't been helpful. All I know is that pit toilets and leave-no-trace camping rules abound. Isle Royale isn't exactly a popular or luxurious tourist destination. Then again, that's why I chose it as my refuge.

Finally, a cramp in my thigh forces me to sit up and change positions. The second my eyes pop open, a voice chirps nearby.

"Takin' a late vacation?"

I jump inside my skin. An older woman in head-to-toe khaki is sitting a little too close to me. There's an Isle Royale National Park logo on her coat. Shit.

"Nah. Too late. Just meeting my wife. Maybe I'll be able

to spend more time next July." I swallow dryly and my heart trills. What if she looks for me on tomorrow's ferry, or asks who my wife is? What if she knows everyone on the island and catches my lie?

"That short a trip, eh? Well, not much to do now, anyway. Weather's turning." She shifts her large, square ass and motions out the window. In the distance, the dense clouds kiss the lake's surface. "You make sure you get off this island before the witch gets ya."

There we go with the witch again. What's with these people? I give her a blank look, not wanting to engage, but she takes it for a question. Great.

"You know. The November storms. Where you from?"

She stares at me in that impolite way that makes my skin crawl. I know what she sees. She's trying to guess what I am. Not who, but what. I'm some crooked puzzle piece that bothers them. *Indian! No, Native? Oh, wait—Hapa, right?* I have "double eyelids" that my Korean mom called *sankapul*. She was so proud of that little crinkle of skin. I made sure to cut my hair so the thick waves were under control. The lady studies the angles and colors of my face—pieces of my parents. I hardly recognize which parts belong to whom anymore. As if ownership ever mattered to either of them.

The lady narrows her eyes—she still can't figure me out but doesn't want to ask *that* question. What a relief. She tries again. "Are you from Grand Portage?"

"Oh. No, we're from…" I can't say Duluth, which is where I'm really from. But despite practicing the lie in my head on the bus ride, my brain is all *DuluthDuluthDuluth*. I stutter, remembering the small town on the shore I'd picked out on the map last week. "Uh. Um. Grand Marais."

She keeps babbling on about places to visit next time I come, flashing an artificial smile of false teeth. Her upper plate keeps coming loose as she talks to me, so her *S* sounds are more like *sh*. She says things like, "Now that's a nice place to shit for a view of Duncan Bay." Normally I'd laugh, but nothing is funny now. I don't want to be chatty. I need to be ignored.

After a few minutes, I can't be polite anymore. I've taken three buses from Duluth to get to this damn boat, and I'm so close. Last thing I need is some square-assed lady committing verbal diarrhea all over me.

"Sorry. Where's the men's room?" I fake my best nauseated look and hold my stomach.

"Oh! Bathrooms are aft," she says, thrusting her thumb behind her. "We have Dramamine on board. Scope patches. Sea bands?"

I nod politely and bolt past the other passengers, who give me plenty of room to pass.

I push through the door to stand on deck. Isle Royale is in view now, with Washington Harbor yawning open a passageway for the boat. Evergreens cling to the rocky shore on either side. There are scant houses and docks as the boat turns gently to enter the bay's inlet. The water sparkles from the sun cracking through a slice in the clouds. We'll be docking at Windigo soon. I'm almost there. As I inhale to empty the stale cabin air from my lungs, something on the shore catches my eye.

It's a flash of amber, and at first I think it's just sun reflecting off the water. But it doesn't flicker like reflected light. It almost seems to glow, like the harvest moon beaming against the backdrop of dark evergreens—but it's daytime.

It's a girl, standing on the shore. She's dressed in dark colors, which is why I could only see her face at first, and now, a dab of pale hands clasped together in front of her. She stares back at me, and her face changes—subtly, like when a blink changes sunset to evening. Though she's far away, I swear she went from smiling to frowning. Or maybe it was frowning to smiling?

Something in her expression tugs at the center of me. It's a terrible feeling, and wonderful at the same time—like waking up on Christmas, and realizing that, damn, the waking up part is already over. As I squint to get a better look, the door to the inner cabin swings open and that same chatty lady steps outside. Ugh. I can't handle any more conversation. I shuffle toward the bathroom. But when I check over my shoulder for one last glimpse of the girl on the shore, the rocky beach is empty.

I try to push aside the vision of her face as I search for the bathroom. Inside, I lock the door with nervous fingers. There's a stainless steel toilet that's stained anyway, and the tiny compartment reeks of fake evergreen deodorizer and piss. The mirror is broken and divides my face on a diagonal.

The wind must be picking up, because the floor pitches me left, right, left, and waves slap the boat. I close the toilet seat and sit down, placing my bag on my lap. I unzip it. Half the space is taken by an old sleeping bag. The rest is crammed with beef jerky packets, baggies of bulk dried fruit, nuts, oatmeal, and a collapsible fishing rod I stole from Walmart when I worked there this past summer. Since my uncle took every paycheck, I couldn't spend a penny without him knowing why. I push aside the food, touching the changes of clothes, thick winter gloves (also nicked from Walmart—it was a good summer), a sewing kit, all-weather matches, a tiny enamel cooking pot and water bottle, and some bathroom stuff. Folded within a flannel shirt is a good camping knife. And inside my jeans pocket is enough money to buy me a ferry ticket in May and a bus ride to someplace that isn't Duluth. I've got the clothes on my back and the skin over my bones.

That's all I have.

I'll have to break into a few houses, maybe the park ranger's quarters. On the bus up here, I realized I'd need an ax to chop wood, but it was too late. I couldn't afford to buy one or risk stealing something that big, so I'll have to find one on the island and a place with a wood-burning stove. There will be no electricity. No phones, either. Hopefully I'll survive the five months and get out on the first ferry before anyone can find me. I zip my bag up and exit the bathroom. I can see the dock at Windigo now.

I might die before May comes. But if it happens, at least it will be on my terms. I watch, almost without blinking, as the shoreline grows closer and closer.

I'm almost there.

I'm almost free.

Chapter Two

ANDA

I saw him on the ferry.

Every day, I've stood at the shore to watch the disinterested ferry pass by. The passengers are always the same, their faces set with familiar expressions of anticipation, or the green bitterness of seasickness, or the blankness of one who knows the lake and the Isle so well that nothing is new. But this boy was different.

We shared the same expression. And what's worse, he could see me.

No one ever sees me at first glance. They don't care to, they don't want to, they want to but they can't. If they're searching hard enough for something, then sometimes it can happen. Father tries to explain why, but none of it matters. This boy—this boy—he saw me. Immediately. And it felt terrible, when his eyes touched my skin. I search inwardly for a similar feeling, flipping through file cards of memory. And then I find it.

Magnifying glass. Sun. Dead aspen leaf. Boring a pinhole of smoke and fire with that focused sun.

Yes. Yes, that. That is what it felt like when he saw me.

I was standing on the shore, waiting for one more day to arrive, the day that everyone would leave and the island would be mine. The bamboo-like rushes were rotting underfoot, and the juniper behind me scented the wind with its spicy notes. Grebes flew overhead, too smart to stay near me. I could feel the eagerness of the boats, wanting to get away and dock for the winter, to be safe. I knew my father paced inside our home. Anxious to leave me alone. Frightened to leave me alone.

Standing on the shore, I let the icy lake water seep into my shoes, weighing me down. I watched the passenger boat pass by, the last one that would bring anyone onto the island. And I thought, *Soon. Soon, you'll all go far away. You don't want to be here when November comes.*

But this boy saw me.

No one ever sees me.

Run, Anda.

I listened to her voice and ran away, terrified.

The next day, I sit on the floor of our small cottage, cradling the cracked weather radio in my lap. I'm impatient, fumbling with the tuning knob. Words stutter and struggle for clarity between bouts of static. Finally, I hear the automated woman's voice from the NOAA station consistently, a beacon from the battered machine.

Southwest winds ten to fifteen knots

Cloudy with a 90 percent chance of rain after midnight

I close my eyes and listen to the drumming of the truth. The rain is coming. I feel it beneath my skin and on the tip of my tongue, like a word ready to be spoken. No matter what time of the day, the words from NOAA are a comfort. They may be robotic recordings, but they're slaves to the wind and temperature, just as I am. With the radio on, I am not alone.

Areas of fog in the morning

Waves two to three feet

"Anda. You know where the spare batteries are, don't you?" My father's heavy steps creak the oak floorboards. He's pushing aside a pile of driftwood I've left in the middle of the kitchen floor, trying to open the cabinet by the stove. He shakes the box of batteries at me, and when I don't respond, he puts them back with a sigh.

I say nothing, because the weather service is buzzing in my head, and there's a warning laced in there.

Pressure is dropping rapidly

"Anda. My boat leaves soon." He strides over to where I'm sitting by the fireplace. He wishes he could come closer, but he won't. It's October. He's sensed the seasonal change that already sank its claws into me when the fall temperature fell. I push a lock of hair out of my face, and static crackles the ends of my strands. I'll have to cut it again soon.

My legs are crossed, and I'm still in my nightgown. His boots stand a precise three feet away. If I looked closer, I'd see the worn leather become jean-covered legs, then a thin and carved-out torso, as if a stiff wind had permanently bent his back years ago. He'd be unshaven and his white hair mixed with brown and occasional copper, like the agate I found broken on the lakeshore only days ago.

"Anda." There's a slight strain in his voice. Perhaps he's getting pharyngitis. "It's time for me to go." He seems to be waiting for something.

The voice on the radio fades into static again. I fiddle with the antennae, but the radio is telling me it's tired of talking, that I need to go. My father takes his coat down from the wall peg. A suitcase and backpack sit by the door, ready to flee the cottage. If the door were open, I imagine they'd tumble down the gravel road just to get away from me.

The air inside the cabin has grown stifling. The cabin's telling me to get out, too. I get up and put on my rain parka, then shove my bare feet into a pair of duck boots. Father stares at my eyelet nightgown, coat, and boots with bare ankles above, hair still messy from a restless night. Asleep, I'd seen brown skin and knowing brown eyes from a face on the ferry staring me down all night. I only escaped when I woke up.

Father picks up the suitcase and opens the door. I grab his backpack. There is a tag printed with a name, SELKIRK, in permanent ink that's smudged nevertheless. I study it for a moment, and then my eyebrows rise. Oh. Selkirk. That is our name, isn't it? I slip my arms through the straps and wear it backward so my arms can support the bulk of it. He watches me waddle down the stone steps and shakes his head but says nothing.

He doesn't need to tell me that there are civilized ways to dress, or to say good-bye to your father. Before he leaves you, secretly, on an island so inhospitable that everyone abandons it when autumn hits, an uppercut that won't be dodged. We have been through this before. Arguments don't work when one side is a tidal force that has no basis in rational thought.

I can't remember the last time I lost an argument. He knows what happens when I don't get my way.

My nature upsets him. No, "upset" is the wrong word. *Fracture, rend.* That is what happens to Father. So when November arrives, when the strength of the weather resonates with my need more than any other time, that is when he leaves. I am more dulcet the rest of the year, but it is not easy. Birth and growth are sweet to him and everyone else, but not for me. I do what I can to draw from what death occurs in the broad summer, but it's scant. I've given up on explaining it all to Father, and instead, I wait for November for my time to renew myself.

Not everyone is happy with this arrangement.

It's a mile-long walk to the dock. Since there are no roads on the island, we take a wooded hiking trail through ghostly paper birch trees and balsam fir that lend their spice to the air. Any tourists have long since left, and we pass a campground that's quiet but for a few seagulls pecking about the footprints of the departed.

As we crunch along the path, my father polishes his glasses and rattles off a list of things he must tell me. "There's enough fuel for the kerosene heater if you keep it on low. I've left food in the pantry to last until I come back in early December. There's a pot of that homemade strawberry jam that you like so much."

"I like strawberry jam?" I ask him.

Father stops walking. His sorrowful eyebrows sag above his eyes. And then I realize, I've already forgotten, haven't I? Parts of me—the human slices of what I am—are already fading. They have been fading more than ever these last few years. This saddens him.

"Yes. You like—you used to like it." He clears his throat. "Anyway, Jimmy will drive me over in his boat in December. The first aid kit is fully stocked. Try to be frugal about the batteries, if you can..."

None of it is terribly important, but it relieves him to unload his thoughts. I'll carry them for a while, but these are the things I would prefer to keep close: the scent of his beard after he's been on the dock all day, like lake water mixed with ashes. The lines on his knuckles, permanently stained from his carpentry work around the island. And his irises. Tiny circlets of white and gray that resemble the eyes of an Isle wolf.

Voices seep through the tangle of spruce trees. The dock

is just beyond, and the low purr of the ferry's motor grows louder. Among the fallen leaves, a dead deer mouse lies on the trail, thin and stiff. I crush it underfoot and smile. From the trail behind, a couple catches up to us. They live in one of the rare houses beyond ours, and their backs are burdened with heavy packs.

"Hey, Jakob. See you on the boat?" the woman asks. She walks past, her elbow swishing against mine. She doesn't catch my eye. She doesn't say a word about my nightgown, and neither does the man. They are worried about making the ferry and do not make an effort to see me. Like the broken branches off the trail and the dead mouse, I am invisible to them in these moments. This brings me comfort, but nevertheless, their brush by me feels icy.

"Yep. See you soon," Father responds. Beyond the web of trees ahead, the couple joins the group at the pier. My father stops and lingers in the shade to face me. His eyes crinkle with concern. "Anda. I could stay."

"You can't be here with me," I say. "No one can."

"Then come with me," he asks, helplessly.

I sigh. I lift my chin and let him see me. Really see me. Just as he is more to me than a list of supplies gathered to provide for his child, I am more than a girl who wears a nightgown to hike in the woods, whose hair crackles with static when it gets too long and flyaway.

I am November on the island. I am part of the lake, and the earth, and the rusted steel of the shipwrecks. He cannot stay to see what will happen. He's witnessed too many Novembers with me here, seen that destructive synergy when he can't tell the difference between me and the storms. My body rebels when he tries to take me away. But staying with me will kill him, piece by piece. It's already started to kill him, fissuring his face into a million wrinkles, years deep.

His death cannot help me.

And so I choose to stay on the island, because the other option is a reality I can't even comprehend. I cannot fight my nature. I cannot be what he wishes me to be, all year long. That part of me that is Jakob, my father—that part has been fading more every year. Soon I might be the waves on the water, just as my sisters have become. It is the natural history of us. He knows this. He can't stop it.

"No. I must stay," I remind him.

He nods. His eyes sparkle with redness and moisture, and I let the backpack slip off my arms to the ground. He picks it up and hoists it over his broad back.

"December first. I'll be back." He takes a step closer. "Don't let them see you," he warns, tossing his head toward the dock.

As if that matters. As if they ever try to see me.

He waits for my embrace, his arms arcing towards me, a bear trap ready to be triggered. A brisk wind blows at us from off the water, and my white hair twists around my face in a riot. My father loses his balance and is forced to take a step back. I can't touch him. I cannot.

Once, I could do these things. But I'm forgetting. Once, he taught me to read and cipher and do arithmetic, and all of it is more dream than memory now. I've forgotten what one should do and feel when a father leaves his daughter.

I wring my hands together and blurt out, "Don't forget to sleep." My fingernails dig into my knuckles. "And eat," I add. "You should eat food. You should…wear sweaters."

Father smiles gently at my efforts. "Good-bye, Anda. Be careful."

"Careful" is such a strange word. To be full of care, overflowing with sentiment. The nature of care is solely for those with whole hearts to give. The word is an antonym to everything I am now, and my father's words are a strangled wish, rather than a warm farewell. He crunches away down the path, and I stay in the shadows of the forest as he approaches the boat.

I watch from behind a particularly fat spruce trunk. A tiny iridescent dragonfly is entombed under a blob of sap, and my heart lightens a single gram. I lean close to the tree, letting the sap stick to my own fingertips, watching my father shake hands with the last residents of Isle Royale. As he boards the full ferry, he turns and looks over his shoulder. His eyes scan the grove of spruces, searching for a last glance good-bye, but his eyes never find me.

The mooring lines are untied from dock cleats, and the engine roars as the vessel pulls away. Usually, I feel a frantic sensation when watching the last ferry leave. Panic mixes with sheer loneliness, but it's fainter than in previous Octobers. I breathe easier once the boat motors its slow exodus into Washington Harbor.

I push back from the tree. A sudden, sharp crack of a stick sounds from nearby. Likely it's a moose. I turn around to walk the mile hike back home when I freeze.

It's the boy.

Through the columns of bushy evergreens, he stands there with hands against rough bark, just as mine were a few seconds ago. He's so tall. Six feet, maybe an inch over. His skin is darker than the usual shade worn by the tourists who blanket their skin with titanium cream. His face stakes no claim with anyone and refuses to give its secrets. He's surprisingly graceful as he steps back. Well, not so graceful. He doesn't know how to walk in this pine forest without making noise. He doesn't see me yet. He's still watching the boat in the distance, his face a mixture of relief and worry.

What is he doing here?

Almost as soon as the thought enters my head, his

head swivels toward me, as if someone slapped his face in my direction. Our eyes lock on each other, and his face fills with wonder. For a full minute, we just regard each other. Astonishment forces its way into my chest. A very human sensation, one I haven't felt in years. The slight wind disappears, pushed away by our mutual atmosphere of surprise.

Finally, he seems to rouse himself with a deep breath. He looks like he's going to say something.

I spin around and run.

GRAB THE ENTANGLED TEEN RELEASES READERS ARE TALKING ABOUT!

STAR-CROSSED
BY PINTIP DUNN

Princess Vela's people are starving. She makes the ultimate sacrifice and accepts a genetic modification that takes sixty years off her life, allowing her to feed her colony via nutrition pills. But now the king is dying, too. When the boy she's had a crush on since childhood volunteers to give his life for her father's, secrets and sabotage begin to threaten the future of the colony itself. Unless Vela is brave enough to save them all...

ILLUSIONS
BY MADELINE J. REYNOLDS

1898, London. Saverio, a magician's apprentice, is tasked with stealing another magician's secret behind his newest illusion. He befriends the man's apprentice, Thomas, with one goal. Get close. Learn the trick. Get out.

Then Sav discovers that Thomas performs *real* magic and is responsible for his master's "illusions." And worse, Sav has unexpectedly fallen for Thomas.

Their forbidden romance sets off a domino effect of dangerous consequences that could destroy their love—and their lives.

entangled teen

an imprint of Entangled Publishing LLC